AMERICAN CANNIBAL

Edited by
Rebecca Rowland

For the two of Murderers' Row.

Twice.

CONTENTS

FOREWORD

Over the centuries, horror authors have invented myriad monsters to frighten and entertain us: dragons, minotaurs, sea monsters, gargoyles, griffins, golems, zombies, and werewolves, all manner of terrifying creatures. That primal fear of being hunted and consumed by a larger, stronger, faster predator has shaped our nightmares since we huddled in caves. We imagined these mythical monsters gnashing their terrible teeth and flexing their terrible claws as they waited for us in the shadows to rend the flesh from our bones. But there is nothing more violent, more destructive, more vicious, than the human animal.

We sit atop the food chain above all other predators, above lions, tigers, bears, and wolves; alligators, crocodiles, snakes, and sharks. We hunt these creatures for sport. Hang their heads on our walls as trophies. Wear their skins for clothing. Make tools, jewelry, art, and trinkets of their teeth, claws, and bones. We consume their meat. Our survival depends upon their death. We are the reaper of their flesh. When the deer or the ram lay down to sleep at night, we are the monsters that haunt their dreams. There is no more terrifying a creature than mankind, the apex predator.

As a child, I once asked my mother why animals killed each other. She explained to me that if predators did not kill off the old, the weak, and the sick, animal populations would grow out of control and there would not be enough resources to support them all. They would suffer, starve, and die slowly. Culling the herd was a mercy that assured the strong would survive and flourish. We need predators, she explained. I asked her who *our* predators were. Who culled the herds of humanity? Who killed off the weak and the sick to make sure our numbers did not get out of control so that *we* would not suffer, starve, and die slowly as our resources were depleted by an ever-increasing tidal wave of human beings? She explained to me that humans are our own predators. We kill our own.

And, sometimes, we eat our own.

The eating of the flesh of one person by another person—cannibalism, or anthropophagy—is one of our greatest and oldest taboos. But that wasn't always so. Cannibalism was once a widespread practice among ancient humans. It occurred on nearly every continent dating back to the dawn of mankind. Consuming the flesh of fallen enemies to absorb their spirit or power was practiced by many tribes and nations, as was ritual cannibalism in witchcraft, sorcery, and religious sacrifices. Christianity's communion service has its roots in pagan cannibalistic rituals, devouring the body of a god in effigy:*"This is my body. This is my blood."*

The eating of the flesh of a deceased loved one was even seen as a show of respect in some cultures. But most often, the act of cannibalism was just a biological function to satisfy our most primal urges and instinct: to survive, to eat. Our fellow humans were simply a convenient source of food. Prey for the apex predators among us. When it comes down to pure survival, there is no creature on earth safe from human beings, not even ourselves. Everything is on the menu. Then, there are those who derive an erotic thrill from breaking that taboo.

Many serial killers—Jeffery Dahmer, Andrei Chikatilo, even Ted Bundy—engaged in some form of cannibalism to fuel their psychopathic sexual appetite for sadism, murder, and domination. Eating the flesh of their victims was a way to own and control them even post-mortem. In my novel *Succulent Prey*, the antagonist Joseph Miles suffered from a compulsion to eat other human beings and achieved sexual release when he indulged this compulsion. This was a rather extreme imagining of what cannibal serial killers might experience. But taboos can often become fetishes. And I know a thing or two about fetishes. Yet mankind is not the only beast that engages in cannibalism.

More than fifteen hundred other species have been documented eating the flesh of animals of the same species, though humans are perhaps the only animals who do so out of pure cruelty and sexual perversion. I wonder what is the greater horror: to eat another person because one is compelled to by a pathological urge, or to do so because there is nothing else around to eat. The latter suggests we are all just a few missed meals away from devouring each other, a tummy rumble or two away from murder. Better to imagine it as a deviancy than as a normal innate survival instinct.

It is the nature of speculative fiction to ponder the fantastic, the tragic, the hilarious, the disturbing, the thought-provoking, the romantic, and in this case, the utterly horrific. In horror, we explore the darkest aspects of humanity, the grim underbelly of existence, the violence and depravity nestled within the human heart. We ask, "What if?"

What if there was a reason to fear that dark alley, that creaky old cabin or house, those primordial woods, the shadows under the bed, that creepy guy who stares at you a little too long and whose smile is just a little wrong? What if the very worst thing, the thing we fear the most, happened? What if we did that terrible thing we feel so guilty for fantasizing about? What if there was a reason for the taboos humanity has held for so long? What if breaking those taboos would unleash something terrible within us? What if key moments in history—the Gold Rush, the Civil War, the suffrage movement, prohibition, the AIDs crisis, Y2K—were much, much more terrifying than we ever imagined?

In *American Cannibal*, twenty of horror's most daring and creative authors turn an eye toward that dark terrible thing within us all and ask, "What if?" What if the very worst happened? What would it take to unleash the ravenous remorseless beasts within us? How close to the surface is it? How far beneath the thin facade of civilization lies that monster that would kill and eat other people to satisfy its appetites? What if that rare occurrence, that odd set of circumstances that would turn an average man or woman into a murderer and a cannibal had already occurred several times throughout history, right under our noses? What if they were buried in our history books, waiting for the right imaginations to uncover them? What if these twenty authors did just that?

At our core, we are still the wild animals we were hundreds of years ago. This is why most of the monsters in my own stories are humans, mass-murderers, serial killers, and yes, cannibals. There is no need for devils and demons. They could never compare to the evil of humanity. The monster under the bed has a human face, and human history is the most terrifying horror story of all.

Wrath James White
September 11th, 2022
Somewhere in Texas

THE LOST DIARY
BY CANDACE NOLA

Roanoke, November 20, 1587

In August of 1587, an expedition of English colonists arrived on Roanoke Island with hopes of settling in the New World. Governor John White departed within several months for a supply trip with a promise to return in three months' time. When he finally returned, three years had passed, and the entire colony of one hundred and fifteen souls had vanished, leaving behind two clues carved into the trees. The colonists were never found, but a single diary was discovered, hidden in a chest of John White's own possessions, which had been buried and left behind on the island.

From the diary of Roger Prat:

December 12, 1587

Five months have passed since our most revered Governor John White departed in haste for England. In that time, our supplies have dwindled to naught but a scant few cups of grain which has given way to mold and rot in their sacks. Manteo, the Secotan savage, has gone forth to his people thrice on our behalf for fresh grain and dried venison. Each time, his entreaties for sustenance have produced less and less for our hungry mouths. Many of our numbers are wasting away, skeletons in swallowed skin, sick with cold and disease, bundled into every clothing piece they own.

Winter has set in, and we were not prepared for such conditions. The bitter wind blows across the isle even now as I sit shivering by a fire in this small cabin, listening to the waves crash upon the rocky shoals. We were meant to go inland after the governor had set his course for England, to seek shelter among the Secotan tribe. Manteo was to secure safe passage for us to travel to their village and dwell among them as we readied our own houses. We have not yet gone, and every day brings us closer to death.

There is talk of violent battles between the savage tribes and many of them are openly hostile when they encounter our hunters in the forests. Several of our men have died, wounded by errant arrows as they seek to drive us from their lands. We forage and hunt in small groups to appease them and remain very near to the shores but there is not much game to be found in the area. The drought has driven the animals deeper inland in search of food and water, much like we are driven to do now.

I, along with the others, eagerly await what news may be had when our native friend returns. Tonight, I shall seek my slumber with an empty stomach as my hope and my strength wanes. I pray for the expedient return of Governor White, although even as I write these words, I fear that it is already too late. May God bless us and hasten a swift return to our governor.

December 15, 1587:

The isle is burdened with a frenzied snowfall and blustering winds. The entire day has been spent huddled indoors, trying to stay as warm as possible, a thin gruel barely filling my bowl. The dining hall in the fort boils a constant stew for the people, and the women and the children huddle around the hearth there, bundled in wool and furs. Those that are able add what they can to the weak broth, but it is not enough to go around. A small roast of an old rabbit had been added and left to boil down to the marrow, a handful of almost moldy grain to thicken it and the rest of the wild onion that Manteo had brought with the last offering from his tribe. Even still, the smell is maddening. Food, even if scant, is food.

My mouth salivates once more at the mere thought as I huddle by my own hearth, with the nub of my quill and this stump of candle. I long for home, for warm bread, meat pies, fresh ale.

I struggle to quiet the rumblings of my stomach with another mug of weak gruel as Manteo has not yet appeared. The men grow anxious, desperate for word, for movement, for any plan to be made and carried out but none hold such sway over the others, not anymore, not since John White has departed and left us here alone.

Discord and discontent can be heard most days, the moment any one of us tries to converse with another. Today was one such day. Fear is taking over the colony, what is left of it, fear and desperation. There is a story of something foul that was spoken of by a savage the hunters met in the wilds, a Mandoag, a vile act which no human can comprehend. Even hearing the suggestion of it repulsed my nature so violently that I immediately turned and left the discussion, despite the calls to return. They are turning delirious in their ills; sickness and starvation burrow into their very souls. My own tears seek bitter release as I write these words.

I fear God has abandoned us here in this savage land. We were not meant to be here, far from society and civilization. What fools we were to come here. God does not suffer the fool: this much has been made clear as we suffer here, dying slowly from disease and desperation. We are lost! The women, the babes, the men we once were; we are all lost. As my slumber comes, I, once more, shall pray to not see the morning light, seeking my quiet peace in the eternal night.

December 17, 1587

Three of our people have gone missing in the night. Manteo arrived at first light with a scant offering of corn, ramps, and stale bread made by savage hands. He carried a small ration of venison with him and some root vegetables. It has already gone into the kettle at the fort along with a hearty portion of fresh meat the hunters brought in today. It had a rather peculiar taste, but the starving mouths found no quarrel with it, not as the hot broth ran down their chins and they sucked every stringy piece from the bones.

When I asked Cutbert what kind of animal they had brought back, he simply shrugged and said, "wild boar," then walked away with a most peculiar look upon his face. I noticed he did not eat from the kettle but rather sat by the hearth with a torn piece of bread clutched in shaking hands. Ambrose had been with the hunters as well, and he, also, sat alone in a quiet corner, a mug of weak brew in front of him, an empty stare on his face. The trousers of both men were heavily stained with a brick brown color, and splatters of the same coated their sleeves and dotted their faces.

The children ate heartily as meat was handed out, freshly roasted over the fire, grease sopped up by crusts of bread. The women ate their fill as Manteo looked on. His meager rations had been well-received. We were grateful for any form of ration in our weakened state. As the people filed in for warmth, food, or fire, the men huddled at one end of the great table, eager for any news from Manteo.

"What say your people?" Thomas asked as Manteo stood before us.

"The elders talk; they have not made a decision. Weather is bad and supplies are low. They fear that there are too many mouths and not enough corn for all."

"Tell them we will hunt. We will forage every day for our people. We are dying here on this blasted island. The winds and the cold push us closer to a grave state with every gust." John spoke, his chin glistening with warm broth that he still drank.

"I have spoken of your perils and your distress. The women and the children all have been noted." Manteo said softly, his sincerity genuine in his warm voice.

"There are more animal skins in my pack for warmth. I will return to my people tomorrow and await their answer." The native lifted his pack and set the skins in a pile on the table, and they were handed out to the women as Manteo left for his own room within the fort.

I sat with the others, dejected, as he left. The more impassioned among them began to talk amongst themselves once more about moving inland, with or without the savage tribes to help. The discussion that had been had with Governor White was raised as were his instructions if we were to move the colony or were in distress.

"I say we pack up and leave, we dismantle everything we can, and take it as far inland as we can. Then, we rebuild. At least we will be far from this forsaken isle and its constant gales, the pounding of the waves, and the icy cold from the sea," Henry Payne burst out. "At least inland, we would have a chance to survive. God only knows when the governor will return. They could be lost at sea, ravaged by the storms, famine on the ships; there is no way for us to know if anyone will ever return."

"God will provide for us as he does for those that dwell here. We only need to learn the land, learn their ways, not frown upon it." Richard Berrye spoke then, his booming voice loud in the drafty room. "We can survive, by the grace of God and our own strength and goodwill. It may take days, but we can move and rebuild. Some of us are still strong, still hearty. The meat from today's hunt will restore the others and there is enough for seven days yet." He spoke from the head of the table, where he sat with a bone still half-eaten on his platter, a fur over his broad shoulders.

"How far did you travel for the hunt?" I inquired. "The meat had a flavor that I did not know."

Richard looked at me for a long moment as the men fell silent, waiting for his response.

"Dog," he finally said in a low voice. "We killed their dogs. A far-off tribe."

"Dog?!" I said, aghast. "But Cutbert…" I trailed off, not sure if I was accusing or just confused.

"Yes. We told them to say boar, in case the women inquired. We do not wish to upset their delicate sensibilities." He shrugged as he watched my reaction. I found the idea barbaric, but I knew stories of soldiers that had eaten dog and rat to survive. The harsh conditions left no beast protected from death. I chose not to pursue my questions but pushed away my almost empty bowl, a sick feeling in my stomach.

"Now, then…" Richard said simply, then continued his planning.

"Who here is in agreement?" He called for a show of hands, but it was not enough, not for that night. The men were too weak, robbed of their courage and their strength.

We filed out to our small cottages as night fell over the isle and the heavy gusts of frigid sea air whipped through our clothes and torn boots. Sleep would not find me for many hours that night as the freezing cold snuck between the slats of my walls and chilled me to my bones.

December 21, 1587

Days have passed with no word from Manteo. Two more villagers have died, a child and a woman. Both were half-starved and had been delirious for the last several days, in spite of the fresh rations that we had been given from the hunters and from Manteo's tribe. It had not been enough to save them. Words were spoken over them in the main hall and the hunters departed to bury them.

Hours later, they returned triumphant but somber. A wild pig had been found this time, purely by chance as they returned from the burial. A small sack, full of edible roots, had been emptied into the pot, a scant offering of dried herbs from the various kitchens, and another handful of moldy grains all went into the pot as the lean pink meat boiled and steamed. The scent filled the hall, mixed with the frigid ocean air, and wafted outside as the colonists braved the cold to gather wood and water to boil on their small fires for tea or broth for those too weak for the stew.

The mood was pallid and sickly over all in the community as the storms ravaged the sea around us. The waves crashed on shore and the waters crept further and further ashore. The hunters began to dismantle the small dwellings of those that had perished, handing out the scraps for firewood and bundling the lumber to be moved inland. Richard and his men were determined to move as soon as he could get enough of the people to agree.

The governor's own daughter, Elyoner Dare and her husband, had agreed to join Richard in his endeavors to get the colony moved. The new mother was desperate to keep her small daughter, Virginia, safe and alive, until her father returned from England. Even now, the babe was swaddled on Elyoner's back, native-style like Manteo had shown her, swathed in furs in a snug pack.

I watched as the villagers ate their fill of the stew that evening, my own stomach rumbling in protest as I only took a mug of broth with a few herbs and thin slices of meat in it. The odds of our small band of hunters finding more meat so quickly again were not in our favor. Not in winter on this dreadful island, not with so many savages in the wooded areas inland doing hunting of their own. I was grateful for the food but found myself more logical and rational than many here, who were once more eating their fill.

I was sickened by the sight of the men ripping the steaming flesh from long bones with their teeth, repulsed by the juices dripping down their chins and into scraggly beards, quaking with ill feeling in my stomach as a rare piece of meat gushed blood as it was bit into, blood that looked too red, too bright, in the amber glow of the fires.

Richard was not bothered by the raw flesh that he chewed, grinning from a full mouth and reddened lips. I left the hall, sickened in my soul. The story about the Mandoag filled my slumber with dreams black as pitch that night, and the next. The Mandoag were the most violent tribe near the area, a tribe that even the Secotan were loath to cross. They called them snakes and serpents, creatures that consorted in all kinds of vile indulgences.

I woke from my dreams numerous times, screaming and feverish.

Dec. 25, 1587

Tis Christmas day and there is no joy to be found. Not in this place where the frigid air rakes my bones and makes my teeth chatter. The cold is bone-deep, seated in a place where the fire will never reach. The shallow shoals between the mainland and the isle are frozen solid, causing many treacherous calamities as we begin transporting dismantled houses to the mainland. Bundles of wood and supplies lie atop canvas and animal skins as we drag them across the sand. Richard has gotten most of the men to comply, ordering the sickly and frail into the fort to wait with the women and children until new houses are built.

For now, we work in small groups. Fifteen or twenty of us at a time dismantle the small cabins, drag bundles across to the other groups to drag inland, and repeat the process. Two more groups are hunting for game or for edible plants and roots. The stronger of the women sit inside and try to fashion cloaks and gloves from the furs and bits of string that Manteo had brought. Some of the women have spools of thread with them and a small measure of success had been had when we joined them for the evening meal.

Four pairs of thick mittens had been fashioned and three cloaks for the men. Weary smiles were shared, and thanks given, even as we noted our numbers were smaller still. Three more had died, these from the second hunting party: as we labored all day on moving the village, three of our own had been pierced through with arrows from the natives. Manteo had declared the arrows to be those of the Mandoag and I felt a chill travel down my spine as Richard and the others just looked on, faces void of surprise or sorrow.

"We will bury them on the morrow," Richard declared. "This evening, let us mourn them and say our farewells. May God grant them peace and eternal rest."

Those gathered hung their heads as he recited several fitting scriptures and declared the funeral to be done. While many eyes were red, most were too weary to cry, too sorrowful in their own minds to shed tears for another. And a few, secretly, were grateful for three less mouths to feed. I hung my head in shame as I realized one of them was me.

The evening meal was quiet but filling as more strange meat had been roasted and added to the pot. The salty broth added what little flavor it could. I ate my fill that night, having worked my fingers raw that day with picking out nails, tearing down slats, and dragging twine-tied bundles across the sands to the mainland. Dog, pig, horse, rat: at this point, did it even matter?

I knew not what I ate, but I ate it, that night, and every night. We all ate, we all went to our abodes and tried to find peace in the bone-chilling night.

The Mandoag were hunting us. I could feel it. Something dreadful was coming or was already here to devour us, one by one. I knew Richard and his men were hiding something. This had to be it. The Mandoag must be coming into the village at night and murdering us where we lay or sneaking among the sick while the hunters were gone. I was sure this was the case. Fear gripped me as I finally understood the urgency in Richard's insistent plans.

Jan. 1, 1588

Work has begun on dismantling the inner rooms of the fort, leaving only the dining hall and a few sleeping rooms intact for the women and children. Most of the cottages have been removed and pillaged for anything of value. Every scrap of wood, brick, or nail has been collected and carried to the mainland. I was given the harsh task of carving what was to be our new location into the trees: one on the island, one near the shore. I engraved "CRO" into the first, and "CROATOAN" into the other as the governor had requested. Barrye insisted that he would know to seek us near the Croatoan village. I nearly severed my own fingers as I carved the icy bark.

Manteo was engaged once more in talks with his people as our people dwindled ever faster. We number less than 70 now, shallow husks of the proud and dignified people we once were. Filth covered our clothing, hair, and skin. The icy winds chafed our lips and burned our fair skin as much as the bright sun overhead.

A new year, in the New World, and things were more dismal than they had ever been. The new babe, Virginia Dare, and her mother, Elyoner, had been stolen away in the night while Elyoner's husband, Ananias, lay slain in his bed. His throat had been cut with a ragged blade. There were no more tears to shed, not anymore. Barely anyone blinked an eye as his body was covered and removed for burial. Richard led a small group of the hunters on a search party, but their efforts were futile. No tracks going on and off the island had been found save our own, and with so many prints, it was impossible to tell our own from native ones. They returned to bury Ananias and we resumed transporting what materials we could.

Arrows had been found near the far end of the fort, arrows identified as Mandoag and Secotan by Hugh and Clement, both men who often went on hunts with Manteo. We believed them to be correct, but I remained bewildered as to why Secotan arrows would be close to the fort. Richard supposed that it was possible that Manteo had engaged a Mandoag scout on our behalf. He also suspected they were responsible for our rapidly declining numbers.

God was showing him the truth of these lands, he confessed to us at dinner that night. God would provide and protect us. God alone was showing him what the savages knew, showing him how to lead us. Richard claimed he was being called to save us all. His booming voice preached to us all by the fires as the women wept, inconsolable from the loss of Elyonor and the babe. Elyonor was beloved among the women and carried the most wealth among us. Her father, the governor, had left all his possessions with her when he departed for England. It was her kindness, and his extensive chest of herbs and teas, which had been providing the most comfort in his absence.

I no longer knew what to believe. I only wanted to survive. I worked. I transported materials and I followed the others to the fort each night to lay by the fire and to eat meat from the bone of whatever animal lay roasting on the ever-turning spit. My body, my mind, and my spirit were broken, as were we all.

As darkness falls, on this our New Year's Day, I know many more than myself wish to die upon closing their eyes. You can smell the wretchedness and desperation in the air, mixed with the scent of the endlessly boiling meat-laden stew inside the fort.

Jan. 10, 1588

It is night once more, and I fear for my life now more than I have in these recent months. I no longer trust Richard and his men. Manteo has drawn distant, watching us from dark corners. He only speaks with Richard and will approach no one else, even when beckoned. His village has denied us safety among them, fearing war with the other savages. There was another paleface, an Englishman by the name of Lane, a treacherous fool, who had landed here three years hence, and the tribes had been forced to war with each other and with his men. A king had been killed; a slaughter had ensued, causing much bloodshed for all.

The paleface shall not be trusted, and that included us all. In spite of our friendly dealings with them and Manteo, we could not be trusted. I laugh bitterly at the very idea, a savage refusing to put their trust in a civilized man, a man of knowledge and of society, of enlightenment and of God! A God they know nothing about, claiming instead to worship the earth, the trees, and animals. Utter rubbish! There is only one God, the God of us all. These savages are ignorant of the world and refuse to see the true order of things.

Tonight, I pray once more for the return of our governor, for ships and supplies. I shall beg for passage back to London. I will work upon the ship, I will swab the decks, if that is the price. I long for London, for my home, for my church. There is nothing here for me, not in this cold, savage desolation. This is not the New World of wonder and riches that we were promised. There is only death.

Jan. 15, 1588

More men have gone missing this past fortnight: lost to the sea, or savage arrows, or sickness. Richard and his men discover, remove, and bury the body, if there is a body. Several of the lesser hunters have been ordered to keep watch during the day while we work, but it is the nighttime that needs to be watched. I suspect the savages have gotten closer, while all but the hunters grow sicker.

Hunting seems to have gotten more dangerous, but each trip brings forth more of the strange meat, dripping deep scarlet fresh from the carcass. Flesh that does not taste like meat of which I know but have now grown accustomed, as have we all. The children eat heartily of the soup in their bowls, tiny fingers scoop bits of gristle and meat into their mouths as fast as possible while more boils in the constant stew of ramps, herbs, bark, and berries, and a scant handful of grain.

We eat the thick sludge as it simmers. Stomachs rumble as the fresh bone on the spit drips fat into the fire, splattering and hissing as it steams amongst the embers.

The hunters are celebrated when they return with more meat in the folds of the canvas bags they use, but none have questioned as to why they do not drag the beast back to the fort to skin and butcher in the kitchen. None have asked where the hide is, or the fur to make cloaks, gloves. They only hold out their hands, eager for cuts of fresh meat to add to the fires. Blood drips from each roast and stains their aprons as the women add long strips of the stringy tissue to the pot, watching with salivating mouths as it turns a gruesome gray color in the stew.

My curiosity has battled my better senses long enough. I suspect that

Richard and his men are roasting the better parts for themselves out in the trees, eating their fill before they return to us, greed filling their gullets, and leaving us the castoffs. We all deserve whatever meat there is, however, much there is to be had. What other food might they be withholding from the rest of us? Does Manteo know what they do on their hunts, or is he part of it, too?

Richard has us toiling all day, dismantling the remaining houses and the unnecessary parts of the fort, while they hunt. Tomorrow, I shall insist on joining the hunters. I will seek the truth of this matter for myself, if only to discern the truth of Richard and what he hides. I will prove him to be a thief, uncloak him for the scoundrel that he is!

May God guide me and keep me while I seek justice for our people, for the women and children that are wasting away by a pitiful fire in an empty fort beside the sea. If God is truly providing, then it is meant for all, not only for Richard Barrye and his ilk!

Jan. 22, 1588

My mind grows ever wary as Richard Barrye and his men stalk the island, vanishing into the mainland as they bury our dead and hunt for any animal they can seek out. The ground remains covered with a constant blanket of white. Snow, finer than the sand under it, blows across the shore, gusts, and whirls into the air, blinding us as we trudge and toil across the frozen lands. There has been no meat for three days and more have perished, lost to sickness. Two children and a woman taken from their beds. The fear is tangible. The remaining women and children are kept under constant watch in the fort, but I no longer believe that to be enough.

Barrye has become a tyrant and his men follow his lead, blindly praising his commands as he calls them out, ordered by God. His God, he says, as if the man himself converses with the Almighty in the flesh.

We grow ever weaker, but I continue to join the hunters daily, keeping watch with the second group as I spy on Barrye and the other men, anxiously seeking out their trail to the mainland the best I can. He does not yet trust me, not fully, though he is polite when we are together. I cast my praises with the others, falsely so, as he watches all with a keen eye. It hurts my spirit as I rave over his skill, over his wisdom, and new leadership of the village.

He eyes the few women like animals in a pen, the children are never more than a passing glance, but I catch looks of significance betwixt his trusted mates and himself. A nod, a glance, a casual nod at this woman or that child. Something does not sit well within my spirit about this situation. The Mandoag must be behind it. The savages must have struck a bargain with Barrye, food for the women and children, grain, or furs. Something was afoot. Manteo has not been seen in a long while, I fear he is lost to us as well.

We are only told of our dead now, never witness to the death ourselves, only told of the missing, but none among us has discovered them gone from their beds.

Only Richard or Ambrose, sometimes Cutbert, never the others. The three of them are the fattest and the strongest among a company that was once seventeen and one hundred strong but has since declined to less than fifty men and ten women and children.

Tonight, I will pray once more to our God for guidance, for deliverance from this treachery that has befallen us. I pray for the return of John White, the true governor of our small group, even as I pray for comfort for the grief that will surely set upon him when he arrives. Tomorrow, I will feign illness, and then I will track Barrye to the mainland. I must know what bargain he has struck with the savages that control this land.

Jan. 25, 1588

Aghast, I sit here in the dreary corner, scribbling my last of this ill-fated journey. Tonight, I will steal away into the night. I will save myself from its sickness! Madness has taken them all! Barrye and his men, every one of them murderers! A depraved lunacy has twisted them into wretched corruptions of themselves, warped satires of civilized men. My God, I beseech thee, bring forth the governor from the bosom of the sea, bring him forth this night! All is lost. My God, why hast thou forsaken us so desperately? Why is this our fate?

I must calm my trembling hand even as my gut roils and spews forth from my gullet once more! I am damned! Barrye's corruption has damned us all to Hell!

Three days past, I followed the hunters to the mainland. I watched from the shadows as they took another deceased villager to be buried, but to the small burial plot they did not go. They carried the body far into the wood, into a small grove, where a large boulder stood, darkly stained. A fetid odor clung to the brisk air as the company commenced to undress the young woman that had passed. But deceased, she had not been! Oh my God! What have we done?

I saw her limbs move. I saw her head turn and her lips move to speak. I saw the blade Barrye carried rise before her throat and swing down upon her. I saw it all and collapsed to my knees as her blood spurted from the ragged wound in her neck. Butchers! Savage murderers, corrupted by the savage rituals of those that live here!

God help me! I stood by and watched as they cut her from her garments. They burned every stitch over a small fire. They stood by as Barrye cut her open from neck to belly. I retched through my hands, trying to muffle my sounds of repulsion as he removed her organs. The others began to carve thick slices of meat from her arms, from her sides, and from her bosom as Barrye sank his teeth into her heart, chewing the scarlet muscle as steaming blood spilled from his lips.

The others cut as much meat as they could from the half-starved girl, then severed her legs, flayed them, and wrapped them in heavy canvas to bring back to the isle. They hung the strips of skin over the fire and threaded the heartiest organs onto a spit to cook. They took the head and cracked the skull, scooping out the gray matter within it like barbarians. They ate of her flesh, raw and bloody, and crimson ran down the boulder as they skinned the parts meant for the colony.

I retched once more and began to stumble through the misty trees as my vision began to blur. Panic gripped me, and I clutched my chest as I struggled to breathe. Several times, I had to stop and spew forth the contents of my own stomach as my body and mind rejected the sustenance I had learned to crave.

They had fed them to us! Barrye and his men had killed half our number and fed them to us! How many did not die from sickness? How many were stolen in the night? How many children had been fed to their own mothers while Barrye preached from the head of the table? The horror of it all shattered all rational thought as I ran. The vilest sin imaginable, forced upon us all!

I wept as I ran, as I weep now. Hell and damnation have been brought upon us all. We have all sinned in our ignorance. We all consumed the flesh of the murdered, of the innocent! We ate it and fed it to the children! We begged for it! Our hunger has damned us all to the fires.

I cannot bear this burden any longer. God forgive me, forgive us all. This is my last entry, my last confession. Tonight, I will hide this diary in the governor's chest and take myself into the sea. I would rather death by the sea than one consumed by my brethren.

Roanoke has become the doom of us all.

Candace Nola is an award-winning Pittsburgh horror author. Four novels currently available including *Breach*, *Beyond the Breach* (2021 novel of the year from the Horror Authors Guild), *Hank Flynn*, and *Bishop*. She curated and edited the Splatterpunk Award-winning extreme horror anthology *The Baker's Dozen* and has various poems and short stories published in several magazines and anthologies with more set to release in the next year. She is currently the V.P. for the *House of Stitched* magazine and Stitched Smile Publications. She operates the horror website UncomfortablyDark.com, which showcases her work and functions as a large supporter for the indie horror community. The website features weekly author interviews, book reviews, new release features and more. Her mission to her readers is to bring them "*the best in horror, one uncomfortably dark page at a time.*"

CARNIVORE
BY JEREMY MEGARGEE

The little girl runs into thistle, lost under the shadow of towering pines, and Violet walks slowly behind, letting the wanderlust light up in her daughter's heart. The young mother looks back over her shoulder, seeing the carriages, cookfires, and travelers all socializing and hunkering down together after a long day of weary trudging. Oxen grunt, horses whinny, and other children around Daisy's age shout and chase each other in playful circles. Evening has arrived, the sky a purple vista with twists of sunlight soon to die, and Violet breathes in deep of the night still to come. The fireflies dart lazily around Daisy as she runs on her little girl legs, living lamps to guide her, and there's a break in the treeline, a clearing rich with the floral scent of wildflowers.

The trip from Missouri has been slow and exhausting, and soon Violet and Daisy will split off from the Oregon Trail and continue along the California Trail until they reach the coast where the trees grow larger than one could ever dream. Violet's husband William is there already, a year into establishing a homestead for his family, and the letter finally came, calling his kin to his side. Violet has missed him terribly, and it's been a struggle to raise willful little Daisy on her own these past few months. She often questions if she's doing the right thing as a mother, for there was no pamphlet given to teach her the way. It is trial and error, a strange covenant with a tiny human that relies on her for continued survival. She worries more than she'd like, and she gets nervous. When she gets too nervous, she picks at the skin around her fingernails until it is in tatters, and then come the white silk gloves to hide the shame of it all.

But it'll be better in California. William has always grounded her when her mind grows too thick with thorns. He wrote in his letter that it's always warm out there, the sea is like a salty dream, and Violet looks forward to taking her daughter's small hand and wading into it. The wagon trains keep rolling into the West because the West is a place where there is potential to flourish. She wants that for herself and her daughter.

It's too late now for the bees, so they buzz off into their hives, and as the hour dims, the birds stop singing. Violet sits on a stump and thoughts run off in scattered directions, time slipping along in increments. Soon the sunlight is all gone, and there is only starlight painting her daughter. Daisy dances among the wildflowers, picking herself a colorful bouquet, and she whispers and giggles to her imaginary friends.

Violet daydreams about what the bark of those coastal trees will feel like under her fingertips, and as she sits and stares into nothing, the night grows deeper and closer, enveloping with new sounds, new smells, and new beasts.

"It's dark, Mommy. There's no moon."

Violet comes back to reality, and she realizes they've been out here for far longer than she had intended. She rises, stretching out stiff legs, and she glances around. She can't hear people. She can't see fires or smell smoke. The camping spot can't be far, but she's not sure which direction they walked in to reach this clearing. There are just black branches and insects chittering at her from the brush. Those insects seem to mock, and Violet doesn't like that.

"Come along."

She takes the warmth of her daughter's hand into her own, and she confidently leads her through the vines, ivy catching at her hair and leaves grazing her cheeks. She is the adult, the mother, the big one, and it is her responsibility to bring her child to safety. But everything looks different after dark. The wilderness is less friendly. The people they've come so far with along the Oregon Trail seemed close, but now there's no sign of them. It's like they weren't people at all, just shadows masquerading, and now they've bled into the cracks in the earth.

The forest has to open up somewhere ahead, but it doesn't feel that way. It feels like the forest is swallowing them, grinding wooden teeth, eating them up. The deeper into the gullet they go, the tighter it gets. Violet wishes for a guiding light, but Daisy's words come back to haunt her in a singsong tone. *No moon, no moon, no moon…*

Why can't there be a moon? Doesn't she deserve a moon?

Violet is the mother, and the mother will make it all okay. She keeps telling herself that. She can't panic like she did last year when Daisy fell in the garden and bonked her head on the rock. She gripped that small body in her arms and she wailed like a desperate animal until she got herself under control. Daisy woke up just fine with nothing but a lumpy bruise on her forehead, but in the heat of the moment, maternal instinct burned through Violet and she slipped into a well of madness. She wasn't there long, only moments, but it felt like a lifetime before she surfaced again.

They'll find the wagon train in no time, and they'll get to California, and Violet will hug her husband tight and tell him how hard it has been. No journey is without peril.

She bats away the branches, and leans down and scoops Daisy up into her arms, holding her close to her own chest. Violet doesn't want this deep dark dirty woodland to touch her daughter too much.

"Mommy, are we lost?"

"Everything is okay, baby."

The foliage is tearing at her dress, and Violet wrenches it free, moving forward quicker as the adrenaline surges into her petite form.

"Everything is always okay."

They walk for hours that first night. Rain comes, and mud with it. Violet feels the soil trying to suck her down with each step, her trembling hand clutching Daisy's head closer to her bosom. She never finds the trail, the camp, or the wagon train. She finds only the unforgiving wild, and it beckons. Exhaustion grips both mother and daughter, and before dawn can break, she seeks refuge in a dead, hollowed out hemlock. They spend those bleak black hours shivering together, and when daylight returns, hope doesn't come with it.

They're lost in uncharted wilderness, and the only point of reference Violet has are mountain peaks far above the treeline. She spent most of her life in the eastern country, and the mountains there were familiar to her. Soft, green, and like big rolling hills. These are not her mountains. They are stark, jagged, and shaped of harder things. Teeth on the horizon. Teeth all around her. The Rockies on all sides, and she finds no comfort in the valleys beneath.

Hours turn to days, days to weeks, and weeks to months. Violet is scared all the time, but she does her best. She builds them up a ramshackle shelter of spruce boughs. She cups handfuls of creek water and brings it up still cold to Daisy's lips. She tears strips from her dress and forages, thankful that her grandmother taught her about edible mushrooms, nuts, and berries. She brings back the bundles, feeds Daisy, and eats what is left to keep up her own strength. Sometimes she brings insects, fat ones full of protein, and she instructs her daughter to close her eyes before placing them into her mouth. Foul to the taste, but when lost in the forest, food is food.

She tries many times to make a fire, but her efforts always fail. It goes on like this for some time. Violet will walk in the day and try to reach something like civilization. A town, a military fort, anything with humans, but these searches prove fruitless each time.

As she is competing with the local wildlife, the nuts become harder to come by. The berries shrivel up and rot on the bush. The mushrooms vanish. Violet has no tools or weapons at her disposal, and no knowledge of hunting, so obtaining wild game isn't an option.

She doesn't know what to do. She finds herself staring at her daughter long into the night, seeing the skin tightening on her bones and the color fading from her cheeks. It will only get worse.

Summer fades into autumn.

And when all is dead and dry in the forest except for Violet and Daisy, winter comes last.

Violet finds the cave just as the bitter winds start howling and cutting into skin, and it couldn't have come at a better time. She and Daisy have spent several nights huddled together in the flimsy shelter, and with the temperature steadily dropping, Violet was worried that frostbite would creep in on them.

The cave isn't much to look at, just an aperture set into a wall of granite about ten feet deep, but it's spacious enough to allow them to crawl in and find shelter from the elements. But after nestling Daisy into a corner and rubbing at her arms to warm her up, Violet notices that they're not the first people to have sought refuge here.

She almost gets choked up with gratitude to see it, but there's dust-coated flint and steel in the corner, and an archaic hunting knife in a leather sheath that's been here so long that it's falling apart at the seams. It's clearly been many years since a person has passed through this area, but the trapper that once sheltered here has given them an everlasting gift. She can now make a fire to warm their bones, and perhaps she'll find use for the knife if any small animals come close enough to attack.

There's a circle of soot near the center of the cave floor where old fires once burned, and Violet builds up her own hearth in the same spot. It doesn't take her long to gather wood and feed the embers, and soon flames dance in their new dwelling, painting Daisy's sunken cheeks in shades of dark orange.

There isn't much talk between mother and daughter. There hasn't been for awhile, because bellies are empty and morale is low. Violet absently moves over to the knife, and when she removes the sheath it crumbles into dust between her feet. The handle is fashioned from an antler, and the blade itself is flecked in rust but still keen when she tests it with her fingertips. A bead of red appears, and she sucks it from her finger while gazing at Daisy.

The knife casts long shadows on the cave walls, and Daisy watches it from the other side of the fire. The little girl's eyes shine bright in the gloom.

Violet keeps the blade close to her, cradled against her bosom, and they get close to the fire and do their best to rest. The dark comes quick, and with it, a single snowflake falls.

It is the first of many to come.

The snow comes and it never stops. It's often a whiteout mere feet from the cave entrance, swirling frigid air and drifts that pile up. A blizzard to start, and brief periodic storms that come after. Violet has forgotten what the world looks like when it's not blanketed in alabaster.

She watched Daisy clutch at her abdomen and curl into herself during that first week snowed in, and something clicked in Violet's head. It came as a dark revelation, and once born in thought, she could not shake it.

And so, one morning, she trudges out of the cave while Daisy sleeps huddled by the flames, she pulls up the tattered bell of her dress, and she uses the knife to cut shallow strips from her thighs. They're so numb from the cold that it doesn't even hurt, just superficial grooves in her flesh, almost bloodless. She bandages them to the best of her ability with ripped cloth from her dress, and she brings the strips in and dries them atop the fire while Daisy still dozes. The smell in the cave is heavenly, and once done, the strips have the consistency of jerky.

"Daisy, wake up, baby. Eat some squirrel."

Her daughter's eyes roll wide, and a droplet of saliva slips down her chin. Violet watches as the famished little girl gnaws into the jerky, relishing each bite, and she realizes that they have a chance. She doesn't have to be a useless mother that cannot provide. She has the means to feed her daughter.

After that, it gets easier.

"Little Daisy, come get supper. I've caught a rabbit."

There's a pallor in Violet's cheeks that wasn't there before. The shallow cuts didn't provide much, so she's been digging deeper, taking whole chunks from her thighs and calves, digging the tip of the blade past veins and plucking the meat free. The pain gets more intense each time, but beyond the pain is a deeper emotion. Maternal instinct. The desire to sacrifice for her daughter so that she may live.

Her dress is a great billowing thing, as is the fashion for the time, and it conceals the lacerations well. There's a tinge of pink at the rim where the blood has stained from within, but it's barely visibly in the shadows of the cave, and it looks like nothing but an accumulation of dirt and grime.

Daisy is looking better. There's a glow in her cheeks and a twinkle in her eyes, and she isn't the emaciated little creature that can barely gather the energy to move anymore. Violet brushes her daughter's hair with her fingers as she eats. Her tiny mouth is smeared in red, and it looks like she's been glutting herself on raspberries. The meat is sustaining her. The meat is making her all better.

"Do you like it, Daisy?"

The little girl smiles up at her mother with gristle caught in her teeth. Her breathing is quick and erratic, almost like a bird.

"It's juicy."

Violet flutters around the candlelit kitchen, humming to herself and wiping her hands against her apron. She plucks the feathers from the turkey and reaches into the cabinet for proper seasoning, taking her time with the basting and the preparation. There are beets, cucumbers, and even pumpkin pie for dessert. William sits at the head of the table, but he won't speak. He's wispy and he fades in and out, but at least he's there.

She feels dizzy, like the whole universe is spinning, but it's strangely nice. Her entire little family at the dinner table, an intimate affair, and that soft California sunlight is drifting in through the window.

"It's wild turkey tonight. We're lucky. Should we say a prayer?"

William doesn't respond, and Daisy's head hangs low, dirty locks of hair obscuring her face.

The vision of the kitchen shifts and blurs, and reality oozes back. Violet is leaning over the fire, and she's roasting two round hunks of meat on a long stick. Infection burns through her, and the delirium comes and goes. The rich smell of fat and connective tissue cooking creates a miasma in the cave, and Violet can't help but notice that her daughter is drooling. There's a pool on the cave floor between her filthy little feet.

It was very hard to carve her own breasts off, but it was worth it. There are just ragged wet holes on her chest now, and her upper torso feels lighter. An agonizing pulse comes from both open wounds, and blood roses paint the bosom of her dress, but Violet strains to smile reassuringly at her daughter. She mumbles out words that she can barely even make sense of.

"It's almost ready. Turkey to fill you up."

"It's okay, mommy. You don't have to lie."

A small hand coated in soot reaches out, and it wrenches one of the roasted breasts from the spit. The dripping flesh is brought to a mouth of blackened teeth, and the chewing starts. It's a primitive sound, full of vigor, and Daisy licks every scrap from her palms and her fingers.

"Squirrel, rabbit, wild turkey: I wondered why it all tasted the same. But I saw, and I know where the meat comes from."

Daisy greedily snatches the second breast from the spit, and she crawls over to cuddle up in the fetal position on her mother's ruined dress. She munches slowly, appreciating the flavor of each bite.

"The meat comes from you. Thank you for feeding me."

Violet can't think of a single thing to say, so she quietly sobs instead, tears burning down her cheeks. Her fingers shake from shock and blood loss, but she manages to reach down and pat her daughter's head as best she can. She pats her like she's a dog.

Bacteria bubbles up in odd places, and Violet's starved and mutilated body twitches occasionally on the cave floor. Her mind has gone rotten like a bad piece of fruit, and she's so hungry that she can't help but pick the breeding maggots out of the gaping wounds where her breasts used to be. She pops the little white worms into her mouth and sucks on them, pretending that they're sweets from the bakery.

The infection will kill her soon, so she's been at work on a last meal for her daughter. It has been horrible and strenuous labor to use the knife on her ankle, cutting at tendon, severing muscle, and smashing at bone with the heavier part of the antler handle, but the work is finally done. She pulls with what might she has left, and a few flesh webs snap as her left foot is brutally amputated. She bites down against her own ragged lips to keep from screaming. The blood pours out onto the cave floor like slow molasses, and Daisy kneels and laps at it, taking that warmth into her fragile chest.

Those howls are coming again, mournful and closer than before. Violet thought it was just another hallucination brought on from the infection, but no, the noises are real. There are wolves in the area, and the scent coming from the cave has called to them.

Violet beckons to her daughter, crooning from blood-speckled lips, and Daisy scrambles over to her. The child is barely recognizable as a human now. Tangled hair, dress dark with soot and soil, skin the color of smoke. Even the eyes are different, not the eyes Violet remembers. They're just glittering animal shine, vaguely feral. Her daughter is changing, and for what is to come, maybe that is good.

"I've always loved you, Daisy. I'll do anything for you."

She reaches up, and she runs a trembling thumb across her daughter's cheek, leaving a smeared crimson imprint there. There are sounds of paws at the entrance of the cave, and deep rumbling breathing. Violet lifts up her head, and she can just make out the crouched musculature of wolves at the door, dark lethal shapes silhouetted in falling snow.

There's a she-wolf in front, much larger than the others in the pack, all shaggy gray fur and yellow lamp eyes that stare without feeling. The wolves do not cross the threshold. They simply stand and watch, curious about the scene unfolding in front of them.

Violet lifts up her severed foot, her fingers slipping on the mutilated meat of the stump, and she thrusts it into her daughter's hands.

"I can't cook it, baby. I don't have the strength."

Tears shine in Daisy's eyes, something human still there behind the awakening animal. A spark of what once was. She weeps, and the last of her humanity washes through the grime on her apple-bud cheeks.

"I'll eat it raw, and you'll be inside me forever, mommy. Please don't go."

Violet begins to cough, her ravaged body quickly losing steam, but she hangs on just a little longer.

"See them out there? They're your new family, Daisy. They'll take you in. They'll smell the blood on you, and they'll know what you are. You're like them now. I want you to live, baby, and you must now live as they live. Hunt, kill, and eat meat. I wish I could give you a better life. But promise me you'll live. Even if you must tear with teeth and scream at the moon when your heart hurts, promise me you'll live."

Violet inhales deeply, eyelids fluttering.

"Be a carnivore."

Daisy struggles to convey emotion, but she finds it harder and harder to cry. When she tries, it is like words have abandoned her, and all that comes out is a sorrowful snarl. She settles for leaning down and running her warm tongue across her mother's brow, lovingly licking up the blood and offering what comfort she can.

Violet watches as her daughter clamps her teeth tightly on the severed foot, the final offering from mother to child, and the little girl moves away from her, heading for the threshold of the cave. She starts out on two legs, but the closer to the wolves she gets, the further she falls down to all four limbs, and Violet watches as her daughter begins to clamber up out of the dark chasm.

The wolves don't attack the girl. They sniff at her, exploring her, and the she-wolf pauses long before nuzzling Daisy with a wet snout before pushing her with a shaggy head deeper into their ranks. Accepted into the pack. Daisy is gone now, lost among fur and fang, just another pair of glittering eyes in a clan of carnivores.

Violet watches the snowflakes fall on gray shoulders as the wolves depart. She closes her eyes, and she dreams.

She dreams of an infant in her arms in a hospital bed. She dreams of how she felt those first few moments after the birth. She dreams of bringing that hungry little baby intimately close and feeding her for the very first time.

Jeremy Megargee has always loved dark fiction. He cut his teeth on R.L Stine's *Goosebumps* series as a child and a fascination with Stephen King, Jack London, Algernon Blackwood, and many others followed later in life. Jeremy weaves his tales of personal horror from Martinsburg, West Virginia with his cat Lazarus acting as his muse/familiar. He is an active member of the West Virginia chapter of the Horror Writer's Association and you can often find him peddling his dark words in various mountain hollers deep within the Appalachians.

GOLD RUSH
BY V. CASTRO

1850, California

Arthur sharpened his blade every morning just as the sun rose above the indigo sky across the mountains that protruded across the landscape like buried bodies rising from the ground. He loved the freshness of the air on his bare chest and the stillness at this time of day. His gray hair fell across his slightly pink forehead; it hung in front of one eye as he looked down in deep concentration through thin spectacles. It was the same way he looked at her when he gazed into her eyes as he rocked in and out of her body. The sounds of the piano and drunken carousing or occasional fights didn't break his mood or desire to give her the deepest of orgasms, even when the night was devoid of moonlight and all they had was the sensation of each other's skin and breath. His touch was the first real act of love she experienced in an effortless sensation of feeling full beyond the contents of her belly.

And Maria Violetta knew so much emptiness in her life.

Yes, there were the pangs of hunger when famine hit after she ran away from an arranged marriage at thirteen. But there was the other hunger, the need to fill a soul full of pits of pecked out flesh from life's vultures of heartache and anger. The many ways people disappointed left a bitter taste on her tongue. However, she wouldn't bite off her own tongue and digest it to avoid the acrid. No, she must wait for it to fade into memory.

Arthur's fluids were honey and manna down her throat when she swallowed him night after night. His groans as deep as her own when his stubble scraped her thighs. His nibbles always the perfect amount of pressure. He made a meal of her body every time, stretching her flesh with lips and teeth to the point she thought he might eat her alive. He never did. He could if he asked, and he would allow her to do the same if she wanted to.

After, they slept heavy.

Maria Violetta watched him from the top window of The Bellows Inn. He knew it excited her to watch him sharpening their instruments of life and death and would turn to wave to her as she stood with just a thin serape covering her naked body. Sometimes the window would be open if they had made love just before. This was most mornings.

He was so different from the others, so she let him live. His existence back east was a world away from this dusty, arid patch of land that saw people come and go. From this place, some never left. He had to be made of tough leather to survive the journey from one coast of water to the other.

He could handle a knife because in his life before this, he made his money as a doctor and surgeon. His services, only for those who could pay. The west was a lure of adventure, respite from mid-life malaise, something he could not ignore as the career that had brought him the treasure of security had become something that lost its shine year after year.

Arthur walked through the doors of the inn all those years ago, looking out of place with his hair damp against his sunburned face. The clothing he wore and cases in hand told her he was not the usual, down on their luck with fool's gold glinting in their eyes and scratching their palms. His eyes searched for a spot away from the crowd, the lines between his forehead and the corner of his mouth prominent with a hint of worry. The man didn't want trouble after making it this far. Maria Violetta sat on a table she used for telling the fortunes of clients and drunks with maize. His eyes moved from her black hair, as straight and fine as corn silk, to the top of her exposed brown breasts.

As he passed, she grabbed hold of his hand. Rarely did she want to take hold of someone. Many tried, few allowed in, but they always left or revealed themselves to be as hollow as a cleaned carcass. No one stuck to her ribs. It was all too easy to shit them out.

"Sit down. Have a drink. I can tell you if you will find fortune or not."

His eyes met hers. "Or will you just put a spell on me?"

Maria Violetta rose from her seat. "Are you hungry or thirsty?"

He licked his lips as he looked at the sparse but diverse crowd of half-clothed women, Native men and women trading or eating, and white prospectors who were surprisingly docile here, drinking while they ate.

"Both. Starving. Not much on the way out here."

Maria Violetta's lips curved with the softness of a petal. "That is why business is so good. And as you can see, we cater to everyone. If you have a problem with my relationship with the Native people, then you can go. I probably don't have to tell you this, but bad behavior is not tolerated and dealt with swiftly."

He looked down at her skirt, a large leather sheathed machete hanging from a leather belt. "I am not looking for a fight. Not sure what I am…" His eyes and voice trailed off like a tumbleweed.

Maria Violetta turned to the bar. "Anci, bring me pulque and the special for my new friend."

Arthur's entire body relaxed, with all eyes previously on him returning to whatever they were doing before. "I guess I must have my fortune read now."

"I am just a guide. The rest is up to you."

As Arthur sat down, a bowl of meat smothered in a rich mole sauce with one corn tortilla was placed in front of him.

"Wow, this smells incredible. I didn't see many animals around here."

Arthur wasted no time taking large forkfuls. His lips smacked with every tear into the mole-drenched tortilla. The dark brown sauce splashed his chin.

"All the recipes and sauces are traditional. I come from Mexico. The meat is sourced from a secret location. Many thieves wander here, so we must be careful. No one who walks through those doors goes hungry. Most pay but if they can't, then we come up with an arrangement."

Maria Violetta couldn't take her eyes off him for a reason she could not completely explain. Then her eyes shifted to his baggage he placed on the floor.

"What is in that black case?"

He wiped his mouth and fingers with the rough cotton cloth next to the bowl. "Oh, I was trained as a doctor. It was good for a while but then…I don't know, I felt something was missing. It wasn't the money."

"A type of spiritual hunger perhaps?"

He looked up from his bowl that was nearly empty. "Yes. No matter how much I acquired or how good things were. It just seemed…I don't know. That's why I'm here."

There was a vulnerability in his pale skin sprinkled with dirt that made her think of the moment she stood inside this place for the first time. It wasn't gold he searched for, it was his destiny, or at least if the concept even existed.

Maria Violetta believed in destiny. She lived it. It had to be destiny that she met Nicolas Haas before she unfortunately became a widow. He taught her to read, and she inherited the inn her former husband purposely built away from the nearest town. It would be the first place in a long journey people travelling west would find. An intruder entered the inn three years previously and caught them both off guard as they slept—at least, as *he* slept. Maria Violetta only dozed. And that is what saved her. It was unlucky her machete sliced the guts from the thief after he slit the throat of her not so beloved husband. She stood next to Anci in the light from the oil lamp to watch both men die. The blood from both men's bodies as dark as a wet chili paste. *Mole,* she thought to herself.

Maria Violetta and her maid Anci had no choice but to bury both and mourn Nicolas in the good Christian way. It was a small price to pay because the business was hers. Instead of it being an inn for soldiers and prospectors, it became a sort of haven.

As the wave of greed went from a crawl to a stomp, the Native people suffered immensely. There were no words to describe or explain why the land had become an abattoir for the innocent. But it happened in her own land, too. Maria Violetta hated hearing Nicolas speak about the Native people on "their" land. Maria was herself of the Native people of Mexico. Nicolas saw her through the eyes of lust and service. She may have escaped marriage at thirteen; however, even in a new land, she could not escape it. Death, not her own, was the only solution, and it graced her life when she became a widow.

When Arthur finished his food, he removed a wallet from the inside of the light cotton vest he wore and left Maria Violetta more than what the meal or room was worth.

"Would you like to sleep now? I will leave you with a basin so you can also wash."

"Thank you. That would be wonderful."

She rose from her seat and to the bar again. Anci leaned in to hear what she was saying.

Maria returned to the table. "Give her a few minutes. Then she will guide you up. But I want to see what you use as a doctor."

"Of course. You may find it boring."

He placed the small leather case on the table then removed a rectangular wooden box. He unlatched it. Maria's eyes went large seeing the contents. There was a thick saw with small jagged teeth, blades of various lengths, a small hose, and other instruments she didn't recognize. She ran her fingertips across the cold metal. "I find this anything but boring. Maybe we will become very good friends."

Beyond the sunburn, his cheeks flushed as he looked away.

"I'm glad you find it…interesting. If you need anything, then I guess I am your man."

Anci approached the table and placed a hand on Arthur's shoulder. Maria Violetta closed the wooden box. "Your room is ready. It is a pleasure to host you as long as you would like. I promise good food and a comfortable bed."

His eyes met hers. "Thank you and good night."

The entire inn was asleep when Maria Violetta took soft steps toward Arthur's room. This was one chance that could go either way. She knocked on his door slower than the pace of her heartbeat.

"It is just me," she said with her lips and breasts almost pressed to the door.

Was he sound asleep—weary from travel, awake but pretending to be asleep, or would he answer?

Then she heard footsteps followed by the unlocking of the door. He opened it wide enough to see her. "Everything alright?"

"I am fine. Do you want to come with me?" She lifted the oil lamp for him to see she only wore a nearly translucent white nightgown.

He swallowed hard and brushed his hair away from his forehead as he opened the door wider. "Yes," he answered.

Maria Violetta turned with Arthur following behind until they entered her room at the very top of the inn.

She placed the oil lamp next to the bed that gave them enough light to see each other. There was little in decoration except a large tomahawk on the wall.

Without words, she removed her gossamer white cotton gown. Arthur dropped the blanket around his nude body. The hair on his chest and trail leading to his cock was salt and pepper. Yes, he was older than she, but still irresistible. The memory of her fingertips on his blades made her wet. She stepped closer to stroke his cock before she would take it into her mouth for a taste.

"How is any of this real or happening?" he said between moans.

"Maybe this is the lifetime that we get everything we want. Let us enjoy our flesh before we must surrender to the hunger of the ground."

Arthur took her by the waist and kissed her hard.

The sun broke through the window early. She blinked, realizing she slept the entire night without moving. She turned to Arthur snoring. He was a man who needed to rest before the second half of his journey. Her eyes caught the tomahawk on the wall. It was the gift that shifted her from one life to another, when the other half of her destiny became clear. She hoped maybe Arthur would understand who she was and not be afraid. The truth could cleave like a sharpened bloody tomahawk.

Maria Violetta didn't intend on consuming human flesh. Like many things, including her marriage to Nicolas, it just happened.

After Nicolas' death, a local Chief knew of her inn as a safe place. The band of women from every imaginable location living with her were as fierce and ruthless as any of the men wandering in those lawless lands. Like the mountains, lakes, and gorges, they were shaped by the harsh elements of life.

The Chief's daughter had to translate for her father and the four other men with him. She was beautiful and most of all, innocent. She could not become a spoil of war or purchased to become a wife to barter deals for her husband. Maria Violetta agreed to hide her until their tribe decided where to go next so that his daughter might avoid a fate undeserving of any human. The white tide was as relentless as sea foam on a shore.

When he returned weeks later, he had tears in his eyes. He handed Maria Violetta a tomahawk as a gift. She accepted it.

But his daughter soon began to argue.

"What more can I do?" asked Maria Violetta.

"I told my father he must get rid of those men he has taken. Others will look for them and our people will be in danger."

The four warriors with the Chief had two white men barely alive on horseback.

"Give them to me. I will dispose of them. Take them back to the shed."

She looked back at Maria Violetta then translated. Her father nodded his head and rode toward the shed.

Anci followed him.

Maria Violetta and Anci stared at the groaning men writhing on the ground. There had been so little meat lately. Supplies fluctuated greatly with so many people flooding in. And the journey to town and back took time. Maria Violetta hated turning people away. How many infants had been left on her doorstep and didn't make it through the night with no one to nurse them? When she did keep goats and chickens, they were often stolen. No one dared fuck with her and the women, but it was known there was no man around, so only a grain of respect was given.

Maria Violetta unsheathed her machete. "Anci, build two fires. One to spit roast and the other to boil. We will also dry slices in here."

Anci left the shed and Maria Violetta raised the machete above her head to divide the men into parts by their joints. Her dress would be ruined after this, but at least she and her patrons would not go hungry. No one who walked through her doors would feel that pain, not with so many out there inflicting it.

Arthur brought his skill of working with bodies and Maria Violetta, the skill in doing the rest. Together, their bellies remained full. Their bed warm. The extra given in charity or sold. What was one less missing gold prospector? The softer meats and organs were roasted on a fire while the tougher cuts were boiled. It was a good life.

To her surprise, Arthur fell into her life with ease.

For two weeks, he shared her bed and looked after patrons and their ailments. He didn't question when she would leave early in the morning. She would tell him, "Sleep, *mi amor*. It is just a delivery of meat and preparation of our sauces."

He simply kissed her and nestled into the warm spot where she was moments before. Then, one morning, he pulled her back into bed. "Let me come with you. I want to learn. Show me. Maybe I can help. I am good with my hands. Bodies or animals, it isn't too far off."

"You are amazing with your hands and every part of your body, but I…"

He brushed the hair from her face. "Please. I want to know everything about you. I'm starting to crave you."

Maria Violetta's heart ached when he looked at her, through her. She didn't just crave his body next to her and his taste. She felt like an equal with him. He asked nothing of her but to be by her side. The truth could be the tomahawk to end it all.

"I will show you. But if it all ends, then you must walk away and tell no one. Leave in peace."

He had a confused expression on his face. "Why would you say that? I am not easily shaken by blood or flesh. I have performed surgery."

Maria Violetta rose from the bed. "Then put your trousers on but no shirt."

Arthur jumped from the bed and followed her to the shed.

Her hand hesitated on the lock before opening the door. Inside were two wooden tables dyed red and dripping with fresh water splashed across the top. Along the wall hung human appendages drying. In the corner, on the ground, were their belongings. Anci held a knife as she tore skin from muscle on one of the tables. There were also dried chilis plumped back to life in a large basin.

"This is what we do and this is who I am," said Maria Violetta.

Arthur's eyes scanned the small room of human flesh and basins of drained blood.

He lifted the back of his hand to his nose.

"What you fed me the first night was this? Human flesh? What we have eaten every night was this?"

Maria Violetta had one hand on her machete. "Yes, I sell flesh in the bedrooms of the inn and on the table. The hungry come here because there is always something to fill their belly. The ones who end up on the slab are people brought to me because they need to disappear or they cause trouble."

"Are you okay with this?"

"Are you okay with what you have seen on your journey? Make your choice, Arthur. I have made mine and am at peace with it. You stay or you go."

Arthur looked at Anci at the table, peeling skin from muscle.

"The blade you are using is all wrong for that. Let me grab my bag and I will show you a more efficient way of doing it."

Before walking out the shed door, he took hold of Maria Violetta's hand. "You feed me day after day. And I think I do the same for you. I have no loyalty but to you."

"I will kill for you, Arthur. That is how deep I love."

Arthur returned to the shed with his fancy doctor's kit and stripped the body of muscle and organ with precision. Maria Violetta stood by his side, absorbing the movement so she could learn, too.

The couple walked in with bibles in hand. Maria Violetta knew their type. Missionaries. They were making their way out west, too. Lots of them. This could be bad as there were no crosses on the walls of the inn nor did she express faith in the same way they did. Her beliefs were more aligned with the Native men and women in this land.

"We are here to rest our weary bones and tell anyone who is interested about the healing power of Christ. Real riches await in heaven."

The woman, wearing a dress made from faded blue fabric and stained with sweat, approached Maria Violetta, who was in the middle of a reading.

The woman's eyes narrowed. "Divination? It is the devil's game. Are you one of them? A godless savage?"

Maria Violetta stood to face her. "I am the owner of this inn, and no one talks to me like that. I can only turn the other cheek so many times."

Maria Violetta tapped her finger on the machete hanging on her waist.

"How did you even get this place? Witchcraft?" There was a hint of jealousy in her tone.

"I eat the ones I know spread their filth and greed, then I take what is theirs before I give it away as I see fit."

The woman huffed before bringing her bible closer to her chest. "Let's go, Joseph. There is no God here. And don't forget, witches burn."

Joseph looked around to see the patrons standing in defiance. "We will be on our way to spread the good word to the many souls in this godless place, Sarah."

"Yes, you do that. Maybe there will be less slaughter, but I doubt that."

Arthur was by her side with his hand on her waist. He leaned in and whispered, "I pray to God they don't ever come back."

She turned to him. "If they do, I will eat their hearts raw so that ours may continue to beat."

Anci shook Maria Violetta and Arthur hard. "There is a fire. It's spreading fast."

Arthur ignored his nudity and jumped to dress, grabbing only his doctor's bag. Maria Violetta did the same, taking only her leather belt and the tomahawk on the wall. The rest of the patrons ran through the inn to escape the flames licking the property as the fire spread.

Maria Violetta knew nothing would be left, including the evidence of her hunger. She tried to listen for anyone trapped, but it seemed most of them made it out. Once outside, she watched the inn burn to the ground with Arthur next to her. Was it a total loss? Some might say so, but maybe she had to start again, an old life with its memories ablaze because this place was only temporary. She and Arthur had a different path to follow together.

"What happens now?" Arthur said with his arm wrapped around her shoulders.

She took hold of Arthur's hand. "Everything we need to start again we already have."

"I know. But where?"

"Texas. We ready the wagons and leave. I heard travelers pass through and never return or are never heard from again."

His lips tasted delicious on hers as he kissed her gently. But he was not for consuming. They had devoured each other's souls long ago.

V.Castro is a Mexican American writer from San Antonio, Texas now residing in the UK. As a full-time mother, she dedicates her time to her family and writing Latinx narratives in horror, erotic horror, and science fiction. Her most recent releases include *Mestiza Blood* and *The Queen of the Cicadas* from Flame Tree Press and *Goddess of Filth* from Creature Publishing.

Her forthcoming novels are *Alien: Vasquez from Titan* and *The Haunting of Alejandra from Del Rey*. Connect with Violet via Instagram and Twitter @vlatinalondon or www.vcastrostories.com. She can also be found on Goodreads and Amazon.

OZARK DEVIL CULT BLUES
BY JON STEFFENS

Wind started to blow at Captain John McCoy's back as he rode into Buffalo River Valley. His sandy-colored hair, worn at shoulder length, rustled in the cool breeze. Nestled in the northern Arkansas Ozarks, the endless green, mild temperatures and abundant wildlife let it be known unequivocally this was God's country. Spring was something to be experienced here. A well-fed white-tailed doe leaped from the trees ahead, quickly crossed the path, and entered the forest to the Captain's left. In the soft wind drifted the sweet smell of honeysuckle.

As beautiful as it was, John's wrinkled brow let it be known he was troubled, though there was likely no one for miles to see the unease etched on his weathered face. It had been four years since the end of the Civil War. Four years, yet memories of that accursed time haunted him still. He imagined some of them always would.

The road was getting smoother, less rocky, and the trees a bit sparser. Grey smoke rising into the distance let him know he was getting closer to his destination. Couldn't be further than a few hours ride. Though he once called this beautiful part of the Ozarks home—in fact, he'd been born and raised less than twenty miles from this spot—he couldn't bear to be here once the war ended.

It wasn't merely the terrors of war that ensured John wished to be as far from his Ozark home as possible for a time. John had lost his beloved Emma to consumption at the end of that damned war. He watched her waste away in body and mind, his heart rending in two as she eventually was unable to recognize the man she once loved. Shortly after, God mercifully took her from him.

In the last four years, he'd traveled far and wide. He had visited New York City and seen the sprawling marvel that part of the nation was quickly becoming. John had spent considerable time in New Orleans and sharpened his gambling skills. In Far West Texas, he had experienced a sky so vast that at night, the multitudinous stars seemed to have no end. The man had even gone as far north as the frozen wastelands of Canada to hunt caribou and grizzly. There he'd learned a bit of French, though he paid for it with a bit of his mobility, as he now sported a slight limp after one massive swipe of a paw from a protective mother bear.

The Ozarks were not a fun place to be during the war or the years leading up to it. John figured that even after all the blood had been shed, the slaves freed and the wild Confederates beaten into submission, it would be no different. This part of the nation had been split in sympathies during the war. About half the folks were pro-Union, while the other half believed the Confederacy was the way of the future.

Up ahead was a wooden sign reading "Welcome to Hotspur." His mount held steady as John urged him to pick up speed. He'd arrived. Hotspur was the hometown of his lifelong friend, George Bellflower. George *was* his lifelong friend, at least, until the war and patriotism and the rage of proud men had made things a mess this beautiful country was still recovering from. George was intelligent, kind, and fair. During the war he was also a captain, like John, only for the opposing side. John took George's loyalty to the Confederate cause as a personal affront. When John's Company C, 1st Regiment Arkansas Infantry Volunteers, met George and the 2nd Arkansas Infantry Regiment on the fields of war, John made it his mission to punish his friend. John's regiment slaughtered George's unit, down to the very last man. All but George. John had him left alive to carry the weight of his choices.

The memories of his own fury sickened him. The recollection of the despair etched into his friend's face haunted John to a worse degree. He was determined to make amends if George would see him. If he still lived here, or lived at all, that is.

Before long, John arrived at a large red brick building with dark brown wood trim in the center of the tiny town. It appeared to be a hotel, and a busy one at that. He tied his horse's reins near the water trough, his mount but one of many. The sounds of merriment and lively piano music drifted outside through the door. The sign was painted a pale green. It was originally a much deeper shade, but it had been weathered by the summer sun. It read "The Captain's House." John was hungry, and after reading the sign, was hopeful he'd find his old confidante as well as a hot meal inside.

The interior light was a dim glow provided by sputtering oil lamps, dampened with cigar smoke. On a far wall was a piano player, pounding out a heartfelt rendition of "Dixie." Several patrons sang along. John despised the tune, though he refused to let his expression reveal his distaste. The tables seemed to stretch on forever, each filled with men, and at least one or two women. Up on the balcony were more tables, with a row of rooms behind. Painted girls in tight dresses brought piping-hot cuts of meat garnished with bread and potatoes. The saloon served as brothel, chophouse, and likely, hotel.

While making his way to the bar, John saw him. At a large table tucked into a back corner sat George Bellflower. Aside from his well-coiffed hair and goatee streaked with silver, George looked to be in fine shape. He was dressed well, and looked as happy the man as he'd been before the war. Three men sat with him, hanging on his every word as he undoubtedly spun some yarn of his adventures. On each side of George sat a woman, each breathtaking in her beauty, one with walnut-brown skin and dark eyes, the other a redhead with an ample bosom and flesh as pale as moonlight.

John approached, clearing his throat as he reached the table. George looked up, the surprise on his face quickly changing into delight. George hurriedly stood to greet his old friend.

"Captain John McCoy! Aren't you a sight!" George looked back at the men sitting at his table. "Gentlemen, allow me to introduce you to a dear friend I haven't seen in over six years. This is Captain John McCoy. He commanded Company C, 1st Regiment Arkansas Infantry Volunteers. For the Union, unfortunately, but don't hold that against him." George chuckled. "He and I go back to childhood." His compatriots nodded, doing as best they could to mask their disgust.

"Gentlemen," John nodded back, refusing to break eye contact.

George motioned to the two men to get up. "If you'll excuse us, I really must catch up with the Captain. Go have you some fun, on the house." His silent female companions remained seated while a pair of new girls met the men near the table, and up the stairs the foursome went, smiles spread across the men's once-gruff faces.

"John! Please sit! We have much to catch up on," George said merrily. The childhood friends sat. A comely woman with blonde locks curled about her face brought ale, and one of the women sitting with George inched toward John.

"George, old friend, I have to say I'm terribly sorry. My actions during the war were horrendous and would be unforgivable if committed against any man, let alone a friend. I came to find you to make peace, but I am quite understanding if you're unable to accept my apology. I could apologize for an eternity, and it wouldn't make right the pain I've caused you."

The former Confederate captain sat for a moment, then smiled. "John McCoy, pay no mind to that dark part of our past. All is forgiven. Water under the bridge. A friend such as yourself comes once in a lifetime." John felt a massive weight lift from his very being. For the first time in nearly a decade, the world felt right again.

The two companions sat and spoke for quite some time. John told George of his adventures across the plains and frozen wastes, and George informed McCoy of his rise to prominence in Hotspur.

"Now, as you remember, this place was nothing more than a church, a few hill folk, and some wilderness when we were children. Look at what it's become!" George smiled.

John thought it a bit odd, as aside from this saloon, there were only a few ramshackle buildings that made up the rest of Hotspur. "There are certainly more folk in this building than what resided in four of the settlements from our childhood. Do they live here? Has Hotspur grown so much?"

"John, my boy, as you can see," George gripped the shoulder of the girl sitting at his left, "our atmosphere and sights are second-to-none 'round these parts, but what keeps the tables full is the food and drink!"

As if on cue, a twinge of hunger growled inside of the captain. He was halfway through his third ale and could not recall the last time he had eaten. "Say, George, could I get one of those steaks? Every time one passes the table, the smell is magnificent!"

"Why of course! Lillian—" George raised his hand and snapped his fingers at a wide-hipped brunette girl, no older than nineteen. "Could you please bring my companion here one of our finest cuts of meat?"

"Yes, Daddy George. Right away!" Her hazel eyes met John's. "How would you like it cooked?"

"Medium, please."

"Yes sir!"

"Isn't she a peach? A bit of a dunce, though." George clapped his hands once, the smile never leaving his lips.

Just when John's hunger pangs were becoming nearly unbearable, a large plate was set down before him. A slice of dark bread, beans, and stewed okra with tomatoes formed a half-moon around the glorious centerpiece: a massive round steak, thicker than any he'd ever seen, the edges blackened and seared, a valley of melted butter poured at the center. John was impressed: cattle were scarce in these parts, never mind beasts of this robust size. The scent emanating from the piece of flesh caused his mouth to water.

As he sliced into the steak, the knife slid through the meat as if it were hasty pudding. It was cooked a perfect medium, pink juice spreading across his plate. Its chew was nice and tender—easy on his teeth—and the meat was well-seasoned. The only time John had experienced a steak this fine was when he visited a New York chophouse a year after the war ended. In all honesty, that slab of beef couldn't hold a candle the exquisite taste he was currently experiencing.

George looked on eagerly. "Well, how is it?"

"Incredible. Quite possibly the best slice of meat I've ever eaten." Spirited piano music and laughter drifted through the room while John quickly finished the steak and beans. He sopped the juices from his plate with a slice of bread and devoured the okra. Afterward, he downed the remainder of his ale. "George, old friend, you've got a wonderful establishment here. I hadn't realized I was so famished until I bit into that cut of beef."

"John, your words flatter me! I'm pleased as punch you decided to drop in. Let me let you in on a little secret."

John leaned in. "I'm all ears." He could feel the effects of the ale beginning to take hold.

"Well sir, that wasn't beef you were dining on. I haven't had cattle, not any worth eating, anyhow, since the drought. It wasn't until this season the rain returned, praise the Lord!"

"Come on, now! There's no way that was pork or mutton!"

"No, no, nothing like that! Say, let's go show you the kitchen. You can meet our chef, and he can fill you in on the secret of our delectable steaks and chops."

"Sounds like a plan, George." The two gentlemen stood and pushed in their chairs. John was swaying a bit, and standing had become more difficult than he thought it should be, but he thought nothing of it. After all, the ale had tasted quite strong, and he'd had three sizable flagons of the stuff. The two women who had been quietly sitting with the pair had left the table some time ago.

George led John past tables of happy brothel patrons. All were deep in celebration of one fashion or another. One group of men played cards while another table was filled with rough farmhands loudly telling crude jokes. Every man had a pretty girl caressing his arm or sitting in his lap, hanging on his every word. As he walked, John thought to himself that George had built a man's heaven in brick-and-mortar form. The music was deftly played, the liquor strong and plentiful, the food rich and palatable, and the girls—all of them—far too pretty for this remote Arkansas locale. They seemed to exist in every size, look, and build a man could desire: each a treat for the eye in the way those steaks were for the stomach.

John made his way through a heavy double door into a hallway illuminated by sparse, flickering candlelight. George was just behind his old friend. The overwhelming metallic smell—unmistakably of blood—flooded John's nostrils the moment the heavy doors closed behind him. Still, he thought nothing of it until his old friend and rival gently pushed him through a second heavy double door.

The grisly scene laid out before him far surpassed any horrors the former Union captain had witnessed on the battlefield. John and George stood in a massive earthen chamber with oil lamps hanging from the ceiling. At the far end of the room was a large metal cell holding more women than John could count. Some were standing, though most sat, pressed against the bars. From what John could see, all were nude, minus the iron shackles and collars each woman wore and the brown leather cords that had been used to crudely sew their mouths shut. Two of the girls made soft whimpering sounds. Most seemed resigned to their fates.

"Mother of God…" John was whispering, hardly able to bring himself to believe his eyes. His knees buckled, and he fell, landing hard on his backside. One girl reached toward him through the bars. Her eyes were wide and pleading, the flesh of her ample bosom pressing through the bars, her skin caked with mud and grime.

"No, none of that here." George chuckled, looking down at John. "We pray to something far more powerful than God, old friend." He gestured toward the butcher's table and cooktop. "Now, meet our masters of the culinary arts!"

Two hulking figures, creatures that appeared like men crossed with feral hogs, were preparing the food. They each had wild, bushy hair covering their bodies and yellow tusks protruding from their faces. One was stirring a vast pot with a great fire below it while the other was gutting what was once a young girl. Her headless carcass hung from its feet, and the way the beast cut the remains was not unlike how a man might field dress a deer.

Blood covered everything—the floor, the cooking utensils, the saws and knives, and the pile of bones and offal next to the butcher's table, near-black and sticky. John tried to scream. His world went dark.

John awoke with a pounding headache, his mouth dry as the Texas plains in August. He tried to lick his lips and winced in pain. His mouth had been sewn shut. Blood began to run from the holes in his lips into his mouth. He couldn't feel his legs. As his eyes adjusted to the low light, John saw he was in a great room with a stonework ceiling lit by torches along two walls. George stepped from the dark to stand by John's side. He was adorned in a red robe covered in symbols John couldn't recognize.

"Glad to see you're awake, old friend." George said, his words dripping in sarcasm. "You dumb son of a bitch." The second sentence was soaked in pure venom.

The two pig creatures lumbered into view, each holding a chain. Attached to the chains were the two women who sat at the table with George and John. Both were equipped with an iron collar and bit. Their faces were blank and expressionless.

"John McCoy! I, George Bellflower, steward of His dominion, find you guilty of crimes against me, the men I lead into battle, and by extension, the Lord I serve." George went on. "You had my men slaughtered like pigs! We were tired, hungry, many of us ill. I'll never get over what you did to me that day, and for what? Your wretched regiment burned our crops, slaughtered our livestock, and a few of you dogs even raped our women. Union filth." John moaned in protest. George laughed. "To think I could forgive such wrongdoing—regardless of our previous friendship—is pure narcissism.

"After the war, I went up to the peak of Red Wolf Mountain to pray. It was there I met these two gentlemen." He motioned to the hog beasts. "They are priests of the God 'round these parts, and they opened my eyes to the true Lord in darkness." One of the creatures started pulling a chain hoist, and the large wooden "X" to which John was strapped tilted forward, hauling him to a vertical position. "All here have tasted your flesh tonight, and soon, so will He. I hope you're conscious enough to meet him when he arrives."

John looked down. His legs and pelvis were completely stripped of skin, meat, and sinew, leaving only crimson-bathed bone. He nodded out for a length of time he couldn't determine. John awoke to a deep rumble vibrating through the chamber, followed by a roar akin to a bull's bellow. Out of the darkness stepped George, stark naked and drenched in blood, his pupils milky white. He held two sawtooth butcher's knives and charged toward his old friend, laughing like a madman.

John screamed through his sutures. He saw the meadow behind his childhood home, green grass wet with dew, a sweet smell on the wind, then his world went black.

Jon Steffens is the author of the Splatterpunk Award-nominated novelette *The God in the Hills* and his short story "The Bone Mother" was nominated for a Horror Authors Guild Award. He lives on the outskirts of Fort Worth, Texas with his wife and three sons. Though his writing tends to lean toward the extreme, the books that made him fall in love with horror fiction are the kid-friendly spookfests of Bruce Coville and James Howe. He's currently working on a follow up to *The God in the Hills* and a Texas-centric crime novella that may or may not be based on true events.

WENDIGO DREAMS
BY OWL GOINGBACK

February 10, 1879

She came in his nocturnal dreams, calling to him, luring, whispering deadly promises in his ears, filling him with unclean thoughts and desires, cravings for flesh and blood, sweetbreads, carnal desires best not to think about. The images that crept nightly into his mind were a curse, sick and depraved nightmares, making him feel less than human, unclean, pushing him to the brink of eternal damnation.

Only cheap firewater kept the images at bay, pushed back the dreams and kept his body from trembling in fear. White man's whiskey, and lots of it, was his only earthly salvation, the one thing keeping him from going stark raving mad.

Swift Runner opened his eyes and looked around. A boreal forest surrounded him, a vast wilderness, frozen in the midst of a brutal winter, silent and cruel as the grave, not a single bird or animal to be seen. He had been standing there for several minutes, eyes closed, carefully listening to his surroundings, hoping to hear sounds alerting him to the presence of game. But all was silent; the blanket of snow laying heavy on the ground, and in the branches of the pine trees, muffling all noises and making it seem like he had stuffed cotton deep into his ears.

Winter in the Canadian territories could be terrible, even deadly. Endless days of freezing cold, blizzard conditions, hunger, and possible starvation. Those who dared venture into remote areas faced isolation, loneliness, and hardships unimaginable. The icy cold cut like a knife; frigid winds howling like hungry wolves as they rushed down from the mountains, seeking passage beneath protective garments of leather and fur, burning the skin and turning toes black as rotted teeth.

A full-blooded Cree Indian, known to his people as Ka-Ki-Si-Kutchin, he had learned at an early age how to survive in the wilderness, even during the terrible winter months, mastering the art of hunting and trapping, providing meat for his people, and trading furs for needed supplies at Fort Saskatchewan, bartering with the white men for tools, blankets, dried goods, and other necessities.

Trading for whiskey.

He leaned his Sharps rifle against the trunk of a pine tree and removed his heavy leather gloves, blowing into his cupped hands in a feeble attempt to warm them. His feet were also cold inside his moose-hide moccasins, but there was nothing he could do for them at the moment. Not without a campfire to warm his flesh, and there was no time for such luxuries. Luckily, the rest of his body was protected by a bright-red hooded capote, made from a warm Hudson Bay blanket, and a pair of leather leggings.

He had been following the tracks of a small heard of elk for days, and could not afford to lose their trail before making a kill. Failing to gather meat could mean his wife and six children, even his in-laws, would starve. He had left his family at the hunting camp, crowded inside the simple wooden cabin he built with his own two hands. Crowded, but not cold; but soon the dried rations would run out and their bellies would be empty. The little ones, too young to understand the reason behind their gnawing hunger, would set to crying, their pitiful wails drawing wolves and other dangerous predators into the camp.

Drawing her.

"Stop it. They are just dreams."

Swift Runner's words fell erroneous at his feet. He knew they were more than just dreams, far worse than nightmares. The hideous images and whispered voice entering his mind every night was a curse from a cannibal spirit, known to the Cree people as the Wendigo.

Reaching into the front-pocket of his capote, he pulled out a half-full bottle of whiskey. Removing the cork, he put the bottle to his lips and took a long drink. The liquid burned his throat and warmed his belly, pushing back the chill and allowing feelings to return to his fingers and toes. He took a second drink, then recorked the bottle.

He wanted to drink more, desired to find a sheltered spot and finish the whole damn bottle, but dared not. People depended on him. If he consumed too much, his mind would get cloudy; he might even get sleepy. Taking a nap in such harsh conditions could mean never waking up.

Swift Runner was once one of the best hunters and trackers on the frontier. He had provided meat for the Hudson Bay Company, and the people of Fort Saskatchewan, and served as a guide for the North-West Mounted Police. But that was before being introduced to the white man's alcohol.

He had developed a strong taste for firewater, a craving that often overtook him and pushed all other thoughts aside. Even his family took second place in his life when there was a bottle in his hand.

Well-liked by his tribe and the people at the fort when sober; the tall, muscular Indian was terrifying when drinking. He was a nasty drunk, who loved to fight, beating down many a man with his fists and feet. Things had gotten so bad they kicked him out of the fort, and he had been forced to move his family back to the Cree village. But even his own people didn't want to put up with his drinking, and the violence that came with it, and he had to relocate to his hunting camp twenty miles north of the fort.

Swift Runner wiped his bare hand across his face, removing the ice crystals clinging to his eyelashes and nostrils. He wiped a few drops of whiskey from the corners of his mouth, licking the drops from the tips of his fingers.

Blinking several times, he studied his surroundings. It was a little before noon, but the forest was draped in layers of shadows making tracking difficult. Not that it would be much brighter out in the open, because the winter sun remained hidden behind thick, gray clouds heavy with snow.

Blizzard is coming.

If it snowed, he would have to call off the hunt rather than risk wandering aimlessly in the forest. The light powdering of snow that fell the previous evening already partially filled in the elk tracks, adding to the difficulty of his hunt.

Grabbing his rifle, he half-cocked the hammer and worked the lever to make sure the metal had not frozen in place. His Sharps model 1874 fired a 45-70 government cartridge. It was deadly up to one thousand yards, but he had taken game at three times the distance. The gun was powerful enough to stop the charge of a bull moose, or put a grizzly in its place.

Reaching under his coat and shirt, he pulled out the leather medicine pouch hanging around his neck on a leather thong, kissing the pouch and whispering a quick prayer to the spirits for luck in his hunt. He also whispered a prayer to the elk god, apologizing for the life he would soon be taking and asking for forgiveness.

Every Cree hunter knew to pray to the animal spirits before taking the life of a furred brother. Failure to do so could result in sickness, or crippling rheumatism, payback for killing without offering the proper words.

Tucking the rifle under his arm, he slipped the medicine pouch back beneath his clothing and pulled on his gloves. Holding his rifle in both hands across his chest, he continued on, following the tracks, his snowshoes allowing him to move easily along the game trail.

He had just reached a clearing when the tracks became very confusing. Here, the ground was heavily trampled and it looked like the elk herd had darted this way and that, possibly in panic, doubling back on itself and running around in a tight circle. In the end, it looked like the animals had separated and run off in different directions.

Swift Runner frowned, studying the impressions. Mixed in with the hoofprints were fecal dropping, proving something had scared the herd causing them to separate.

But what could have caused such fear? He knew from the tracks there had been two bucks and several does in the herd. Had they encountered a big cat, or a pack of wolves? Not a bear; the grizzlies were all hibernating, and would not emerge from their dens until the spring thaw.

But even if they had encountered such predators, the herd would not have run off in different directions. The bucks would have protected the does, positioning themselves at the front and rear of the pack.

As the Indian stood there, trying to decipher the puzzle at his feet, he heard a strange cry coming from the forest on the other side of the clearing.

He looked up and listened carefully, feeling a tingle of fear march down his spine. At first, he thought it was the calling of a wounded deer, or a rabbit, because he knew they could both scream like a woman when in pain. But this sounded like the wailing of a human infant.

He heard it again, a wavering sound, coming from the shadows beneath the towering pine trees. He squinted his eyes, trying to see better, but his gaze could not penetrate the darkness of the forest.

Swift Runner stepped into the clearing, walking cautiously in the direction of the sound. Perhaps a family had gotten into trouble and needed help, and what he heard was their baby crying. If so, he had to act quickly. If another blizzard hit, they would all be trapped and have to shelter in place.

The unhappy weeping came again, the noise floating on the chill air. Only this time, it did not sound like an infant. Instead, it resembled a much older child. And it came from off to his left.

It is moving.

"Hello," Swift Runner called out, his voice sounding muffled by the surrounding forest.

He heard it again, his stomach knotting in fear for the cry sounded like his youngest daughter.

But that was impossible; his daughter was at the cabin with her mother and siblings. He had kissed the sleeping child on the forehead before leaving on the hunt.

"Hello," came the reply of a little girl's voice, speaking in the Algonquian dialect of his people.

It sounded exactly like his daughter.

"Papa," the voice said.

He knew it was not his daughter, but something that mimicked a little girl's voice. No bird or animal of the north woods had the talent to imitate human speech. Only one thing he knew of had the gift of mimicry, using it to lure victims deeper into the forest, leading them to their doom.

Wendigo.

The child's voice faded out, replaced by a strained silence. It seemed the forest waited and watched with hushed anticipation.

Swift Runner slowly opened the breech of his Sharps rifle, slipping a cartridge into the chamber.

"Hello," he said again. "Is someone there?"

No reply; only the still quiet of a winter forest.

The sharp snapping of a branch suddenly echoed across the clearing, the sound coming from in front of him but high in the trees, at least twenty feet off the ground.

Swift Runner raised his rifle, aiming in the direction of the sound. The crack had been loud, the branch obviously large. It had not snapped from the weight of snow. Someone, or something, had broken it.

"Help me."

The voice came from the same spot as the snapping branch. A woman's voice, soft, but not afraid. The voice lacked any emotion; definitely not the voice of a woman in trouble, or someone with small children needing protection.

The skin at Swift Runner's temples pulled tight, goosebumps breaking out along his arms. He breathed out, a cloud of steamy mist momentarily obscuring his vision. A drop of fearful sweat trickled down the side of his face.

He suddenly wanted another drink, needed it to block out the voice. He thought about the bottle in his coat pocket, but he dared not lower his rifle to reach for it, or take his gaze off the forest in front of him.

Something moved in the dark shadows beneath the trees, barely visible but much taller than a man. He saw the branches of the big pines sway as it brushed against them, pure white snow showering down. Impossibly tall and very thin, standing much higher than a grizzly on two legs, easily twelve to fifteen feet in height.

Every fiber in Swift Runner's body told him to turn around and run, forget about the hunt and flee for his life. But his feet refused to listen, and continued to compel him forward. He took a step, then two, moving as if in a dream.

My dreams.

"Please, help me."

Again, a woman's voice called out from the shade of the tree line, stopping him dead in his tracks.

He raised his rifle and sighted carefully, aiming at the shadows where he had seen movement moments before.

Swift Runner took a deep breath, let out a little air, willing his body to be as still as a stone, concentrating with all his might on seeing what hid in the darkness.

He pulled the rifle's set trigger, placing his finger lightly on the front trigger. Only four pounds of pressure was now needed to fire the rifle, a touch light as a feather.

And then he saw something standing very still, using the pine trees to hide, watching him; perhaps toying with him like a cat does with a mouse before a kill.

"I see you," he said aloud.

It smiled then. A hideous grin appeared in the shadows, twelve feet off the ground, revealing yellowed teeth, long and sharp. Above that demonic smile, a pair of glowing red eyes.

He pulled the trigger and the Sharps roared like a cannon, a loud boom echoing off the surrounding trees, flame and black powder smoke erupting from the end of the barrel.

Swift Runner saw the smile disappear, the towering shadow collapsing down upon itself, shrinking but not falling, changing but not dying. Shape-shifting into another form.

He hurried to open the breach of his rifle, ejecting the smoking, empty cartridge and replacing it with a new one. He closed the rifle, raising it to his shoulder, ready to shoot again.

But it was not a towering beast that suddenly emerged from the forest.

Instead, it was an Indian woman, dressed only in a thin buckskin dress and moccasins, her tangled, black hair cascading over her shoulders.

She was terribly thin, probably to the point of starvation, emaciated like a corpse fresh from the grave, her skin stretched tight against her bones. So thin, her footsteps barely sank into the snow.

Swift Runner lowered his rifle, shocked by what he saw.

The woman walked straight toward him, weak and staggering. As she got closer, he saw her flesh was yellowed and decayed, marred with ulcers and signs of decomposition.

Her lips were almost completely gone, just thin strips of tattered skin hanging down, exposing the teeth and gums beneath. Frozen blood covered her chin and the front of her neck, so dark in color it appeared black.

The flesh from the tips of several fingers on her right hand was also missing, fingers bones protruding like sun-bleached driftwood. The pain must have been unbearable.

He thought at first her injuries were due to frostbite; but the remaining flesh was not discolored, nor had it turned black.

Maybe she had been attacked by a wild animal. Perhaps she had attempted to free something caught in a trap and suffered the consequences. A lynx, or a wolverine.

But as these thoughts passed through his mind, she raised her left hand to her mouth and bit down on her index finger. Bit down hard, the sound of her teeth rending flesh and crunching into the bone. Blood spurted, running down her chin.

Oh, my god.

Staring at Swift Runner, she pulled her hand away while still biting down, stripping the flesh from her fingertip as easily as one would remove a pair of gloves.

She stopped before him, blood dripping bright red on the terribly white snow. But she did not look down at her hand, paid no attention to the bleeding. Staring at Swift Runner, she chewed slowly, methodically, grinding the morsel of human flesh between powerful molars, chewing, savoring.

As she chewed, the woman continued to stare at him, unblinking, her face showing no emotion or pain.

"What are you doing?" he asked, finally finding his voice. "Stop it."

She did not reply, offered no spoken word of explanation. Instead, she swallowed the morsel of finger, running her tongue over the place where lips had once existed, licking the tiny dangling shreds of skin and tissue.

"Hungry," she said, placing her right hand on her stomach.

Swift Runner's grip on his rifle went slack, the Sharps hitting the ground and sinking into the snow. He did not bother to look down, for he knew the rifle could not help him, or save his soul; realized he was helpless to even try to pick it up, for the voice of the woman standing before him was the same voice that whispered to him in his nightmares.

"Wendigo."

She looked at Swift Runner, studying his face. Perhaps she smiled at him, knowing he recognized her. He could not tell if she smiled for she had no lips, all of her teeth fully visible like the death grin of a skull.

"Feed me," she said, stepping closer to him. Her breath reeked of flesh and blood, the front of her dress stained and littered with bits of gore from previous meals, remnants of the men, women, and children she had feasted upon.

She reached down and took his left hand, raising it and slipping off the heavy leather glove. There was no warmth in the touch of her hand, her flesh as cold as the grave.

Raising his hand to her face, she closed her eyes and made a soft, almost sexual, moan in her throat as she licked his fingers and palm.

Swift Runner felt the Wendigo's spirit enter his mind, filling him with whispered words and horrible images. He saw children being slowly roasted over a fire, or consumed raw; saw men and women devoured until there was nothing left but bones, and then saw those bones cracked open and the juicy marrow sucked out. The images sickened him, but also filled him with a strange desire.

But those images shattered in an instant, replaced by a pain exploding through his brain. Swift Runner screamed in agony.

The woman no longer closed her eyes, or made soft moaning sounds. Her eyes were wide open, gaze focused on him, her teeth clamped tight around the first two fingers of his left hand.

She bit down harder and jerked her head like a hungry wolf, tearing flesh and cracking bone, severing his two fingers at the second knuckle, and swallowing the digits whole.

He screamed again, trying to pull away. But she grabbed his wrist with both hands, shoving his fingers and hand deeper into her mouth.

She bit down again. He saw blood spurt bright red and run down his arm, dripping from his elbow to the ground.

Dizziness overcame him. Swift Runner sank to his knees. She sank with him, kneeling before him, continuing to feed.

The Wendigo removed his hand from her mouth, what was left of it. All that remained was the little finger, thumb, and the base of his hand. Everything else had been chewed and swallowed. Blood spurted from the mangled flesh.

Swift Runner knew he would bleed out and die. Dizziness rushed over him; darkness would soon follow. He tried to lie back in the snow, but she held his arm, keeping him from falling backward.

She pulled him forward, sniffing his neck and breathing in his scent. Grabbing the front of his capote and shirt in her left hand, she pulled aside the fabric, exposing his bare chest.

Swift Runner screamed again as she bit into his chest, just below his left collar bone, tearing away skin, muscle, and tendons.

The Wendigo chewed the mouthful of bloody flesh, then threw her head back to swallow it down. She lowered her head and studied him, perhaps deciding what part to eat next.

He tried to retrieve the bottle in his left pocket, knowing the whiskey would help dull the pain, but couldn't reach it with his right hand.

"Please," he said, his voice barely a whisper. "Mercy."

Swift Runner thought about his wife and children, tears forming and quickly freezing at the corners of his eyes.

"I have a family. Children."

The Wendigo paused and looked at him.

"Children? Babies?" she asked, licking the tatters of her lips.

He nodded.

She released his hand, reaching out to pluck one of the frozen tears from his face. She studied the tear, rolling it between bloody fingertips and thumb.

Some legends say the Wendigo's heart is made of ice, and the only way to kill it is to cut out that frozen heart and toss it into a fire. But Swift Runner didn't believe that legend. The Wendigo was not a monster, or some unknown creature with a head full of antlers, but a human possessed by a cannibal spirit, someone cursed for eternity with an unstoppable appetite for human flesh.

Maybe the sight of his frozen tear, or his begging for mercy, had reached something deep down inside the woman, touching a part of her that existed before the curse.

She opened her hand, allowing the frozen tear to fall to the ground.

Swift Runner watched it fall.

And then she put the middle finger of her left hand into her mouth, biting through her flesh. Removing the injured finger from her mouth, she quickly stripped the skin and muscles from the tip.

"Mercy," she said, shoving the morsel of her flesh into Swift Runner's mouth. He coughed and tried to spit it out, but she covered his mouth with the bloody palm of her hand.

He struggled and tried to pull away, but she grabbed the back of his head with her other hand and held on tight.

"I give you mercy," she whispered into his ear. "Eat."

Swift Runner felt the cold blackness of death slip over him, welcoming the darkness as he chewed the ghastly tidbit in his mouth, praying silently to the Great Spirit that he would go quickly to the spirit world and rejoin his ancestors, asking forgiveness for past sins. He also prayed his family would not starve as he swallowed the tiny piece of meat, amazed it was so tasty. Very, very, tasty.

He wanted more.

Swift Runner no longer had his warm capote, presented to him by the North-West Mounted Police for his service as an excellent guide. But that was okay because he no longer felt the cold, certain that his heart was now made of ice. She had also taken his snowshoes, but he did not need them. He had lost so much weight, his feet barely sank into the snow.

She had spared his life, leaving him alone in the forest. But he would never be truly alone, for the Wendigo was now a part of him, the cannibal spirit deep inside his mind, controlling him.

He was terribly thin, and hungry. But there was food waiting for him at his cabin, and he would soon get to eat. His wife was there, and her flesh was tasty.

So very delicious.

And his children, young and still tender.

He began to drool at the thought of the wonderful meat waiting for him at the cabin, flesh to appease his insatiable appetite. Tender, juicy meat he could cook in his wife's large black kettle until the fat floated to the surface, or eat raw; arm and leg bones that could be cracked and the marrow sucked.

He would have licked his lips at such thoughts, had he not already chewed and eaten them.

Hungry, so very hungry.

And where the fingertips of his right hand once existed, only bone remained.

But there would be food soon. Very soon. Tender thighs and fatty cheeks; the bellies of infants, and his wife's luscious breasts.

His mind filling with images of flesh and blood, Swift Runner started to run.

He was almost home. Wouldn't his family be happy to see him?

Wouldn't they be delicious?

Owl Goingback has been writing professionally for over thirty years, and is the author of numerous novels, children's book, screenplays, magazine articles, short stories, and comics. He is a HWA Lifetime Achievement Award Recipient, a two-time Bram Stoker Award Winner, and a Nebula Award Nominee. His books include *Crota*, *Darker Than Night*, *Evil Whispers*, *Breed*, *Shaman Moon*, *Coyote Rage*, *Eagle Feathers*, *The Gift*, and *Tribal Screams*. In addition to writing under his own name, Owl has ghostwritten several books for Hollywood celebrities.

MASTICATION STATION
BY CLINT SMITH

An hour of flood, a night of flame,
A week of woe without a name—
A week when sleep, with hope, had fled,
While misery hunted for its dead;
A week of corpses by the mile,
One long, long week, without one smile,
A week whose tale no tongue can tell,
A week without a parallel!

All the horrors that hell could wish,
Such was the price that was paid for—fish!

-Isaac G. Reed

My appetite is not what it once was: I haven't eaten a proper meal in months, and I fear my lack of nourishment may be, in some way, galvanizing this narrative. I wake in the dead hours most nights, the sensation identical to that pre-dawn darkness nearly forty years ago; yet, no longer do I dwell within that lingering inhalation of being born, but rather the sense of having been deprived the peaceful exhalation of oblivion.

So yes: for the (complicated) intent and purpose of this account, I'll cleave to that simile: the twilight into which I'd been on June 1, 1889 was a panoramic pandemonium of flames and water and contorted horror. To be clear, I'd not gained lucidity on my own but had been mercifully retrieved from the wreckage by other survivors, tugging at my limbs, confirming whether or not I was a corpse.

With the aid of bystanders, I was able to hobble my way up the forested hillside, one of those anonymous saints propping me against a tree. Though my vision listed, the world before me, a new world I'd once known as Johnstown, was a sprawling archipelago of infernos. I would later learn that the flood-tide—what would be colloquially called "the black wave" and the "death mist"—was near forty-feet deep at its center when it descended on the town at 4:07 p.m. the day prior. I remember nothing about the collision that sent me into unconsciousness.

The stone railway bridge, though a stout testament to engineering, served as an obstruction, an ersatz dam itself, collecting acres of splintered forestry, broken houses, dead animals and people alike. The wireworks, not far from my place of employ, was destroyed and supplied the hideous floodwaters with miles and miles of barbed wire, which only aided to the baroque carnage.

I'm recording this account with a remove of over three decades, and though the images perpetually play within the morbid theater of my mind, I, to this day, struggle to accurately articulate those appalling sights.

The valley had been transformed: tree trunks high on the hillside imitating columns in an abominable amphitheater, the musical arrangement set to a chorus of hoarse shouts and sonorous pleas. Figures were praying in German as I fought against a demanding drowsiness, sagged sideways, and was again smothered by an afghan of blackness.

Rain continued to scalpel the air throughout the morning and into the afternoon. After shivering awake, I got moving, doing what I could to repay the benefactors that salvaged my life.

Though a sad chapter of my juvenility, my military training amid the *sturm und drang* of Pittsburgh's Great Railroad Strike served to preserve my instincts over the forthcoming days.

I staggered to where townsfolk were beginning to organize rescue efforts. As I assisted to lift a makeshift stretcher, I succumbed to a vicious twinge in my wrist, indeed a fracture from the night before. A stranger noticed my injury and led me to sit down; she searched for a moment among the wreckage, discovering a railroad spike which she quickly fashioned into a provisional splint, expertly affixing it with a length of filthy cloth. With blood-and-mud-caked fingers she tilted my chin, appraised me, and simply said, "You may be concussed, son." Nothing more was said as she returned to work, receding into the rush of nameless saviors. I murmured my *thank you* too late. I merely rested long enough to build my resolve, stood, and rejoined the struggle.

I'm submitting this document for potential publication in the fall of 1927, quite close to four decades following the events of that weekend in 1889. That said, as it's certainly a cliché in my time, it will no doubt ring as a trite metaphor to eyes and ears in the future; nevertheless, it serves my purpose. It is no exaggeration that Johnstown had become a heaving, pulsing Bosch painting, made manifest in sodden reality.

By Sunday, the bridge fire was exhausted by fire engineers from Pittsburgh, and that same day would mark the merciful arrival of medical corps and military surgeons. But for now we contended with the horror before us. The water itself bore myriads of despicable sights: limbless human trunks bobbing along the surface, fleshless skeletons—all this fortified by the sickening stench of burned bedding and roasted flesh.

Word had come that the upper floors of Alma Hall, Union Street School, as well as the Morrell Institute had been used as safe harbor for people fleeing the tide. By the afternoon, flimsy infirmaries had been assembled, rafts erected to float to survivors, and from the hillsides, people were arriving with food, water, clothing. A pair of local gents, Tom Johnson and Charles Zimmerman, were placed in charge of removing general wreckage and animal carcasses, while Reverends Beale and Chapman had saddled themselves with establishing morgues.

Nature possesses a signature creativity when devising her demises, with how she crafts her cataclysms. But what had occurred at Johnstown had purely been an exhibition in the artistic incompetence of man.

I've thought about this at length: the manifold spectrum of mankind's malevolence. At one end lies the isolated depravity of, say, that fellow in Chicago by the name of H. H. Holmes who, it was reported, murdered a number of women who'd attended the World's Fair in 1893. It's reputed that Holmes (who was hanged twenty-nine years ago in Philadelphia) concocted what some have called a "Murder Castle" in his residence. On the other end of this terrifying tether is something more opulent: the stolid voracity of war; and though the carnage in Europe concluded ten years ago, I fear our political machinery's insatiable appetite and its capacity to consume so much more.

On that weekend in 1889, I'd begun to yield to the creeping claws of exhaustion, and for the first time in hours I took a seat on the outskirts of one of the infirmaries. No sooner had I settled down that I heard a shout, *"Leroy Temple!"*

I reacted too quickly and had to steady my teetering vision, but clarity took hold and I recognized Bill Kegg, a cohort from Haws Cement Works where we were mutually employed, though the Bill Kegg who strode toward me was of appalling appearance, having adopted a sunken, cadaverous quality since I'd last seen him the week prior.

Anticipating a fellow-survivor's embrace (though many among us would have traded this prolonged torment for the peace of the grave), Kegg instead seized my upper arms. "Have you seen her?"

I inspected his features: eyes sunken in sooty sockets, sallow skin tinged with fish-belly paleness. Gently, I pried his fingers away. "Kegg," I said, "Tell me who you're talking about—have I seen *who*?"

"Maggie," he replied, "my sister *Maggie*, damn it."

My mouth opened and closed. "I, um." It occurred to me that while I was coping with a concussion, Kegg was dealing with some sort of emotional unmooring. His aspect, I wagered, was simply a manifestation of how most survivors felt internally. Perhaps he was in some state of shock. Perhaps we both were. "Bill," I said, "let's talk—"

He shoved me, hard enough to cause me to falter. "Can't you *see?* They have her."

Not unkindly, I gripped him by the shirt-collar. "Kegg," I said in a low voice, "get a hold of yourself, man."

His obsessive smolder began to abate, replaced by a stricken expression. I lowered him to a crouch and settled him against a sycamore. From one of the pocket infirmaries, I retrieved a small allotment of rum. When I returned, Kegg was looking at something in his hand—a locket on a chain. I handed him the spirit, which he consumed in a gulp.

After a time, I indicated the locket. "This is her?"

Kegg nodded, weakly handing me the silver trinket. Even in the picture's diminutiveness, Maggie Kegg radiated an arresting beauty, the black-and-white photo—though abridged to mere head and shoulders— produced the illusion of warmth.

"My mother," Kegg murmured, "wore that locket until last year, when she passed. I promised her I'd take care of my little sister." A short silence transpired before he said, "She's still up there."

I cleared my throat and handed the locket back to Kegg. Though I suspected he may have been referring to the folly of heaven itself, I asked: "Up where, Kegg?"

He shook his head, eyes slimy with sorrow. "That bloody club, Leroy," and then he sprang to his feet—through clenched teeth he said, "The South Fork Fishing and Hunting Club," he gestured at Johnstown's devastation, "the fucking cause of all this."

Of course, there had been snippets of this, that the flood's culprit was indeed the private club, that the massive, mountaintop lake had ruptured, hemorrhaging its contents into the Conemaugh Valley. In my years in Johnstown, I'd heard repeated variations of this warning, that the dam would eventually disintegrate. Parents used the lake's instability as a sort of bogey-tale—*The dam'll give way if you don't behave*—but the cautionary adages were so commonplace that they'd lost their potency.

I said, "Why would she even be there?"

Kegg, jittering, looked away, now almost reluctant to speak. "She's been...*seeing* someone up there—the lake's engineer." He wagged his head. "Maggie's been visiting the property at his...his *invitation* for some months now. Talks all the time about some Queen Anne where she's"—Kegg looked away—"slept."

"Well," I tried, "maybe she's safe and—"

Kegg's demeanor once again grew preoccupied—he stabbed a finger to the northeast. "Don't you see? They're all going to flee and take everything they can with them, including Maggie." I raised my hands, but he stifled my attempt at reason. "There's already a group of men agreed to it—going up there and demanding recompense for what they've done." And it was then that he produced the revolver, rattling it with emphasis. "They'll hang for this."

It was inopportune to remind him of the caliber of 'those men' up there at South Fork, club members with surnames such as Rockefeller, Vanderbilt, Gould, Carnegie—capitalistic luminaries. Powerful men of industry, of influence.

Kegg began pacing, the revolver dangling by his side, his sights set on a hillside horse barn in the distance. Though many were bustling about, we were in an isolated area, and I wagered he had designs on the equine. I trailed behind. "What do you intend to do?"

"Rescue my sister, blast it," he said, speeding into a trot, "and no one can stop me."

I shuffled to a halt, watched Kegg as he cut through a stand of evergreens, rounded the back of the barn, propped open the gate, then emerged atop a horse. He tore out across a narrow path, the rumble of hooves drawing no attention.

Reluctantly, I turned back toward the valley, gazing at the devastation. I had a sense, as a man whose years had not long before eclipsed thirty, that the scenes of gruesomeness and grief would remain with me forever. I'm penning this narrative now as a man in his late sixties, and these morbid *mise en scenes* remain supernaturally crystalline.

Kegg was, of course, on a fool's errand—perhaps even, depending on the demeanor of those he'd encounter on the mountain, a suicide mission—but as the gray day withered into evening, I began to wonder if, as an antidote to the lavish carnage in town, I might allay further, and senseless, violence.

I felt myself accelerating up the hill, rounding the barn as Kegg had done and discovered several horses. As I mounted the animal, the acknowledgment of crime occurred to me, but in the face of voluptuous atrocity, I dismissed it for a potential greater good.

In the days and months ahead, tales would emerge of shadowy marauders: trophy-hunters scavenging the Johnstown dead…ghouls creeping about to violate cadavers, to outrage female corpses. Most all these anecdotes, in some sensationalized fashion, were falsehoods aimed to gain press. Though false, I'd witnessed enough in my time to understand that these embellishments were sutured to some basis in fact. No, my own horrors were yet to come, and certainly worse, because they were not fabricated fictions of the mind, but rather the flesh-and-bone whimsy of men.

The journey, I estimated, was near fourteen miles, but the horse I'd commandeered was strong and maintained resolute speed. This would put me within striking distance of the property several notches over an hour. And aside from obvious tracks on the muddy trail, there'd been no sign of Kegg, so I suspected we'd adopted a similar pace.

While my ambition remained intact for stemming further violence, I must confess that the vision which floated in my mind was that of Maggie Kegg, a disembodied beauty framed in that ovule locket. The past three years in Johnstown had been lonely ones, and of all the days that could use a dose of heroism, this would be the one.

Near as I was, I thought to supply the horse a well-deserved respite; I slowed at the crest of a forested bluff, near to which a narrow, wooden bridge spanned a drop to a churning, debris-drowned creek. The bridge overlooked a swath of the scarred valley where 20 million tons of water (a number calculated in subsequent years) and accumulated detritus fell upon Johnstown.

Sunlight had not once punctured the clouds that day, and darkness was swelling on the horizon. I finally pushed away from the bridge's rail, remounted the horse, and resumed my undertaking.

I began to see the well-manicured makings of the club's private property; I also noticed a rickety gate which let on to a poorly-kempt thoroughfare: a rutted service entrance.

Woods cloaked my approach, but I was able to glimpse the eviscerated cavity of the man-made lake, the centerpiece of the South Fork Fishing and Hunting Club. There had been tales of sailboats gliding on the mountain, eliciting no small amount of wonder and envy from simple Johnstonians (myself not immune). We would later learn that it was a five-mile trek around the snaky circumference of the lake. There remained now only ragged remnants of the faulty earthen dam from which a bile-colored stream still oozed.

I often think of something I'd read several years back, penned by that curmudgeon Bierce, that his definition of a corporation was an ingenious device for obtaining individual profit without individual responsibility.

I proceeded deeper along the trail. In a quiet covey insulted by cypresses, I tethered the horse and opted for a stealthy course on foot.

Now, where the lake-road converged on a scattering of extravagant cottages, I detected some commotion near what I presumed to be the clubhouse. Carriages and wagons were being hastily loaded with crates, trunks, luxuries intended for a summer retreat. Yet on the other side of the massive house, over the invectives of the exodus, I caught the intonation of an argument—Kegg's voice. Cowering, I crept out of the woods and wove between several outbuildings; soon, I was gliding along the far side of the clubhouse. At the corner of the porch, I peeked.

"Tell me where she is!" Kegg was in the courtyard, facing a tall man who

I recognized as Colonel E. J. Unger. I'd known of Unger from newspaper articles. A product of Dauphin County, he'd made his business bones in Pittsburgh (a practice from which he was now retired), but it was known among Johnstonians that Unger was now not only the club's president, but also its year-round caretaker. Several men bustled about, evidently paying no mind to this confrontation.

Unger had affected a temperate posture, showing Kegg his pale palms and speaking calmly. "Now, sir—as I'm certain you're aware, this is private property—"

"I know she's in there!" Kegg jutted his chin toward a two-story, navy blue cottage, a Queen Anne whose windows glowed behind a network of oaks.

"—and you are trespassing."

Then Kegg produced the revolver, not necessarily directing it at Unger, but calling attention to a weapon in play.

Now another individual emerged near Unger, a larger man who circled slowly—a footman, certainly.

Unger said, "Easy, easy. Nothing hasty, young man. It's clear you've endured much. Let's say we discuss this like civilized men in the clubhouse. Mr. Boyer," Unger cocked his head toward his meaty underling, "would you kindly escort our guest inside."

Kegg raised the revolver, aiming it at Unger.

"Wait!" I cried, rushing from the shadows. "Bill—stop!" Kegg whirled, now training the gun on me. "Bill—it's *me*, damn it."

Colonel Unger shifted his tone as he said, "Ah—well, two trespassers certainly solves our dilemma, does it not, Boyer?"

In the commotion, I'd lost track of the one Unger called Boyer, and I saw the henchman sweep up behind Kegg, knocking the gun free and catching the man's throat in the crook of his arm.

I looked over at Unger, who was smiling. Though I believed he was gazing at me, I realized his gaze was aligned with the figure looming behind me. As I turned, a wooden object connected with my heretofore-traumatized skull, ushering me back to a familiar darkness.

A sour irony as I write now: to be clubbed by one of the clubmen.

I was swaying, both bodily and optically—hanging upside down, no less.

I was being carried over someone's shoulder. Between weakly-slitted lids, I saw a cobblestone floor, sound echoed between narrow walls fixed with flickering lights. Paired with a stale, time-spoiled aroma, I surmised I was in some sort of cellar. Sneakily, I angled my capsized eyeline to see Bill Kegg in an identical position, slung over the shoulder of another man, the footman Unger had called Boyer. I thought all this too melodramatic a punishment for trespassing.

With the jangling of keys, we slowed at a door; Unger's voice: "...and we'll need to work quickly if we're to make the train to Altoona."

We entered a low-ceilinged cavern, generously lit by sconces of jumpy gas flames. Kegg was unceremoniously unloaded onto a long, wooden table, while I was dropped on a wall-mounted bench. Echoing throughout the space was the silvery babble of running water.

I lay still, slyly peering to appraise my situation: Unger gave instructions before one of the men exited—a lock grated on the heavy door. Boyer, with his back to me, hovered over a work bench. There came the clatter of metal. When the man turned, he had donned a long apron and was presently tying thick strings on the spatter-slick garment.

Unger, meanwhile, was occupied near a wide plate faced with a hinged, oven-like panel. Using a button-box along the brick wall, he entered a stuttery code. Though my ears perked at the emergence of Morse, I thought, perhaps, I'd misinterpreted the peculiar cipher. Seconds later came the grinding of gears and the hum of pulleys. Unger opened the panel's rectangular jaw, revealing the interior of a dumbwaiter-like contraption.

And then it came over me. For the better part of a day and a half in Johnstown, I'd been entrenched in death, so much so that I'd grown inured to the perfume of putrefaction. The cellar was rife with rot.

Unger was staring at me with a lopsided grin, a consequence of my inept squinting. "No need to play possum any longer, friend." I opened my eyes to a wince and attempted to lift myself into a more dignified position on the bench. "You are in no fighting position," said Unger, cordially offering a hand; with his help, I stood uneasily, the pain in my wrist resuming its electric melody. "And besides, you are, sadly, outnumbered. What's your name?"

I hesitated, deciding against instinct to concoct a lie. "Leroy," I wet my chapped lips, "Leroy Temple."

"Come," said Unger. "This is something most outsiders do not see." He paced to the half-wall of the circular structure, what I took to be a massive well. He beckoned me to follow which, limping, I did.

It was some type of holding pen for fish, a kind of vivarium.

I saw then the dark, unsettled surface of the water, discerning the slick shapes of amphibious creatures. Yes, they moved and slid like fish, but their aspect was like no fish I'd ever seen.

"This was originally what brought all of us to this place," said Unger, "what compelled us to create, oh, a community of like-minded businessmen." He flashed a smile at my lack of comprehension. "Fishing, my friend. Just plain-old fishing."

The backs of the fish frequently broke the water, and I saw a mottling of ocherous inks and lurid tangerines. They reminded me of the lampreys I'd occasionally caught in the river-arteries of the Great Lakes.

"Some of our associates have traveled to distant locations for sport: hunting, safari. The natives called these sacred animals something the translators could not accurately define. The nearest phrase they managed to convert from heathen tongue were things like *glutao de carne...fabricante de esqueletos*," he rested his forearm on the lip of the wall and glanced at me, "skeleton makers." He *humphed* something like a chuckle. "Anyway, they worshiped these creatures as gods, but like most barbaric intellects, they failed to understand the potential existing not only in the fish, their 'flesh-shedders,' but in *man* himself."

Unger continued, disclosing that the South Fork men on the expedition had witnessed the fish feeding—that several small animals were sacrificed, but Unger relayed that the number of bones along the shoreline implied larger mammals as well. The natives vehemently forbid consumption of the sacred fish. The men on the expedition, of course, disregarded this warning.

"It was that night," Unger continued, "After partaking in their exotic prizes that the men claimed to have gained an altered state of consciousness as they woke on the river banks. And, as we understand now, a heightened and amended appetite.

"The hunger—the new hunger—was so acute that the men were gifted with the sublime inspiration to liberate a great quantity of these *esfoladores*."

Though narratively unprompted thus far, Unger grew vague about the details of how, precisely, these men had stolen the fish, but I had the sense that some violence was exacted to extricate the creatures.

"There had been some obvious concern about habituating the freshwater fish from one environment to another, but," he spread his hands wide, "we have nurtured a bounty of these beautiful animals." Unger gestured at the compact water wheel, which appeared to be drawing in water from some unseen well, and circulating it through a system in the floor.

I narrowed my eyes. "To…eat them?"

"Ah—that's the key here," Unger continued. "When the men returned home, we dined on the prizes, had a feast; but the men confessed: the flesh produced a majestic sensation, and as we had fed the fish small carcasses, we soon realized and unified the vertices of this glorious trinity."

I looked at the surface of the water, at the mosaic of butchery on the floor, and comprehension stitched with nausea swept over me. "You feed the fish…*people*…and then you eat the *fish*?"

Unger spoke rapidly. "Certainly—but you see one of the unintended consequences of this appetite was the unconventional, though wholly refined and methodical, full-circle consumption of human flesh."

I blurted, "You fucking eat—*people*?"

Unger shrugged. "On occasion."

My thoughts slipped and slid. *Where had they obtained their mortal inventory over the years?* Yet more pertinent: "Why are you telling me this?"

Another dark chuckle. "A preamble, I suppose. Or just trying to untangle the voluble knot in my mind." Unger pressed fingers to brow, and for a moment I thought he might be in pain, but he proceeded. "But you must know that men who go in search of limitless opportunities do so in both commerce and corporeality. This was a place where men of industry could fish, hunt, and find some semblance of tranquility. What they discovered— what we *all* discovered—was transcendence."

"No," I said, flexing my lower lip at Unger's absurd assertion. I thought about the unfolding horrors I'd witnessed down in Johnstown, the four miles of devastation in the name of excess and negligence. It was not lost on me that the hubris to which I presently objected was precisely the same impulse that had led me here to this dead end. "No, Colonel. It's just the same old story. It's not transcendence—just garden-variety greed."

"Oh, my boy," he said, "but it is so much more than that." Unger opened his mouth, brought a thumb to his palate. There came a soft pop as the man removed a half-moon of ivory dentures. Unger smiled fully, revealing grisly, spade-shaped teeth. The triangular aberrations were irregular, filed to fangs.

"Despite your common-laborer's philosophies, we created something extraordinary here—or rather, something extraordinary was revealed to us here. But, how did our exalted Chaucer put it? At last, all good things must end." Unger turned and nodded at Boyer.

With a butcher's proficiency, the big man twisted Kegg's head, breaking his neck with a pulpy crack.

Having already resigned myself to a dark demise, I merely flinched, but the next part made me, I confess, quite weak.

Boyer produced a rust-freckled kukri, and with a practiced stroke brought the enormous weapon down on Kegg's kneecap—*thwack*—his shin and boot rattling off his body. Boyer then went to work on the other leg, eventually excising both thighs. Like stove lengths, Boyer collected the pieces and lifted them into the dumbwaiter; he then thumbed-in the same jittery Morse Code, and this time I followed more closely: *chef.* The wide dumbwaiter made its screeching ascent.

I continued suppressing my gorge, pressing the back of my hand against my mouth. It was Unger who redressed the lingering question. "Our club members prefer their provender as fresh as possible, while," Unger nodded to the pool, "the fish prefer living nourishment." My rejoinder, whatever it may have been, fell short as Unger continued: "We've noticed a certain elevation in the transmutation's influence. And as relocation is imminent, we must expedite—for lack of a better phrase—our last supper." Unger chortled, "And none of us, I surmise, is willing to remain here long enough to assume the role of Nero."

A pistol then appeared in Unger's hand. Kegg's pistol. With the weapon, Unger urged me to the pool.

All right: the preceding passages are a recitation of my and Unger's exchange, but truth told, a portion of my conscious mind was elsewhere, as in, how I could save my own skin. As Unger explained and praised the practices of his South Fork brethren, I was preoccupied by the ongoing ache in my wrist. Or more accurately, the makeshift brace that had been concocted the previous morning, along with its supporting, metallic component.

I had but seconds left to imaginatively rehearse this last-ditch, and unrealistic, figment.

"I can and will shoot you," said Unger, "but I encourage you to maximize your courage here: it will be a benefit to all of us."

I looked over Unger's shoulder to see Boyer—*thwack*—occupied with fabricating a portion of Kegg's forearm. I winced and gave another heave as though to vomit, and Unger, as it was my intent, registered something amiss, and he glanced, only a few inches, to eye Boyer's progress.

I slipped the rail spike from the bandage, palmed the head, and—just as Unger turned back toward me—I thrust the nail into the side of his throat.

Unger went rigid, but in doing so squeezed off an errant shot, the blast singing past my ear and undulated the air. Ricochet pinged off stone. Unger's free hand went to the dog spike, his fingers scrabbling at the device; he made the mistake of yanking it free, and in doing so bore thumping gouts of blood.

Unger wavered and fell, the pistol clattering on stone. Boyer, I believe, faltered as he assumed another victim had been claimed as fish fodder, but he strode toward me now, that kukri fixed for a blow. I merely had time to snatch the pistol and raise it. Boyer's long knife swung out, connecting with the gun and knocking it from my hand.

I staggered back as Boyer steadied himself, but as he advanced, he neglected his fallen boss who was writhing on the floor. Boyer's boot caught the man's hip, and Boyer staggered forward, crashing against the stone wall of the pool. My instinct was to go for the knife, but Boyer still clutched it firmly. Instead, I noticed the long, loose ties of his apron—I grabbed hold, tugging the garment until the neck-loop tightened on his throat, and then the burbling of running water asserted itself. I twisted the apron as hard as I could, wrenching the fabric over to the water wheel, quickly looping the ribbon's slack into its spinning, central gear. From there, it was just a matter of getting out of the way. He dropped the kukri in an attempt to free himself from what had become his winding sheet but was unable to slow his progression over the lip of the pool.

The creatures began feeding before Boyer was fully in the water, and his shrieks were nearly smothered amid the frantic splashing. The thick-scaled bodies converged, shiver-scouring his body, those voracious, razor-rimmed mouths scrubbing the flesh from his body. I pivoted, unable to watch.

The door, of course, was locked, and the key, as I'd seen, was in Boyer's pocket. I strode toward the pool, where the fish continued feeding violently, and picked up the kukri. In my out-of-mind state, I'd done my best not to peer at what remained of Bill Kegg there on that butcher's block. I gave a solemn glance at Kegg's remains and couldn't help but notice the gas light glint on something metallic at the terminus of Kegg's avulsed forearm. With reverence, I peeled back the clasped fingers. It was the locket, containing, I knew, the photo of his beloved sister. I slipped the piece of jewelry into my pocket, turned, and appraised the dumbwaiter.

On the black-buttoned panel, I thumbed-in Unger's code——-.-. ....-.—and in seconds, a yawn of machinery commenced. I lifted the panel, hesitating for only a moment on the blood-slick interior, before sliding in, feeding myself into the dumbwaiter's maw.

Clutching the kukri, I was elevated through that grim chimney. I was prepared for further fighting when the panel opened on an elderly, bespeckled man who, as it may go without saying, was confounded to be confronted with an ambulatory edible—in one piece, I might add. His spectacles were murky with a thin film of blood, but behind the glass his eyes went wide. I'd arrived in a preparatory kitchen of sorts, and the man, at a glance, appeared to be alone.

Having dispatched two men in as many minutes, I swept up one of the cast-iron pans from the stovetop and walloped the sinewy old goat, who accommodatingly collapsed.

I was prepared to resume my escape, but caught my reflection in the glass of an elaborate buffet cabinet: I was coated in gore from both the dumbwaiter and Unger's crimson suppuration. Thinking quickly, I located a livery in one of the corridors, cleaned myself as I could, and changed my shirt. I snatched a burlap satchel hanging from a nail and slung it over my shoulder. There were a number of pickling jars lining the shelves, their dark liquid and mysterious contents caused my stomach to wobble, rather compelling me to pilfer some apples and dried fruit, which I stowed in the bag along with the kukri.

The corridor led me to a rear-door of the house.

Outside, night's tint was softening to a pre-dawn dullness. I was making my way toward the cypress-stubbled hill where I'd stowed the horse when the locket in my trousers seemed to gain weight. I looked over my shoulder. Through the oaks I could see the hulking, navy blue Queen Anne. *I know she's in there*, Kegg had said.

Through gritted teeth I exhaled an expletive and began winding my way back. Once upon the house, I gave it a cursory appraisal. Candles flickered, but the peace and quiet impelled my progress. I vaulted the porch railing and slunk to a side door.

The knob twisted easily, and I slid into the house, moving through a dark parlor, weaving my way to the foyer. The ribs of an elaborate banister came into view, and just as I placed my hand on the bulky newel there came a feathery tread at the head of the stairs.

I froze, momentarily absorbing the presence of Maggie Kegg, her features an elevation of the lineaments captured in the locket. With hands clutched at her sternum, she imitated my paralysis. I got my mouth working. "Maggie? Maggie Kegg?" She gave the slightest affirmative. "It's not safe for you here," I said. Maggie made a mincing step back, glanced to either side, but I advanced onto the riser, removing the locket, clicking it open to show her her own face. "I'm a friend of your brother…William. You must come with me now."

"My brother?" Maggie's expression flickered between hope and fear. "Where is Bill?"

The question pierced me. I shook my head. "There's no time to explain, dear, we must leave."

Again Maggie looked left and right, bit her lower lip, then quickly descended the stairs and took my hand. I led her through the dark house, back to my point of entry, and then set out over the patch of grass; seconds later, we were wending through the woods. My horse still tethered in its hidden spot, I mounted the faithful animal before genteelly hauling Maggie to join me on the saddle.

At a keen canter, I steered the horse along the service trail, and when it opened up, we took off, bypassing the main clubhouse and giving a wide berth to the sprawling, swampy chasm that had once been the illustrious lake.

We'd gained a safe distance. With labored breath I began explaining what had happened in Johnstown two days before, of the chance meeting with her brother. I was careful about what I said next, mainly to temporarily spare her feelings, but I admitted that Bill had not made it off the South Fork property, that there had been significant trouble. I felt Maggie's carriage sag with emotion. I was assembling what I wagered would be words of comfort.

Up ahead was the wooden bridge spanning that short distance across the creek, and I decided it was an appropriate place to profess my part in her brother's demise.

"Maggie," I said, "it was Bill's intention to safely retrieve you…"

Near my ear, I heard a soft click, which I took for the commencement of tears. I glanced over my shoulder, and from the tail of my eye saw in Maggie's hand the crescent-shaped curve of false teeth—this a heartbeat before I felt the semi-circle-sting of cannibal fangs pierce the base of my neck.

I spasmed, twisted, and threw an elbow into Maggie's ribcage. She let go, but not without gouging a chunk of flesh as we both slid, ungainly crashing from the horse, the animal speeding off in the direction of town.

I lurched to one knee, brought my hand to my nape, confirming the wound.

Maggie, appropriating a hunched, predatory posture, rose from the carpet of fallen leaves, eyes fixed on me; her lips, which suddenly flexed to a ghastly smile, bore the crimson cosmetic of my own blood. With a giggly screech and fingers curled into claws, she bolted forward. I jittered back, colliding against the wooden rail.

I'd not necessarily forgotten about the kukri but had dismissed it, believing we'd achieved safe harbor. Reflex tugged at my gut: I slid the weapon from the satchel, and just as those self-fashioned fangs were upon me, swung the blade in haymaker fashion, catching the trunk of her throat, severing head from shoulders.

I spun, watching Maggie's body crumple while her head careened over the rail, her fair hair a comet's tail as it plunged into the roiling creek.

Chest heaving, I saw the head of Maggie Kegg momentarily bob along the surface before disappearing, commencing its murky trek to larger arteries, pulsing toward the cataclysmic confluence that was Johnstown.

I flung the kukri into the creek, my final penance. No horse, no home. Dawn emerged in gray, monochromatic glory, and that godforsaken vault of sky supplied no compass for me. I regarded the huddled smudge of the shadow-shafted forest, and started walking.

Clint Smith is the author of the short story collections *The Skeleton Melodies* (2020), *Ghouljaw and Other Stories* (2014), as well as the novella *When It's Time for Dead Things to Die* (2019). Of late, his work has appeared in *Looming Low, Vol. II, Nightscript,* and *Vastarien: A Literary Journal.* A chef, Clint lives in Indiana, along with his wife and children, just outside Deacon's Creek. Read more at clintsmithfiction.com.

AND THE WINDOW WAS BOARDED SHUT
BY ELIZABETH MASSIE

If she could pretend the window was the one in her bedroom at home, adorned with yellow cotton curtains and offering a view of the family's barn and the field beyond, Becky thought she might keep her sanity.

Remember the grass, Becky. Think of the lilac shrubs. Of Mama at the clothesline and your sweet pet goat, George, hopping in and out of the old wagon. Of the white fence and the cattle grazing in the field out near the trees.

She stood on tiptoes in her filthy, bare feet in a puddle caused by last night's rain, gazing out through the rusty bars, trying to envision what her soul begged her to see. The November air was cold but she didn't care.

See the farm, Becky. See Georgie, my best friend.

It didn't work.

I'm going mad.

Stop thinking that, Becky.

But I am!

The narrow, chin-high window looked out at the twin brick workhouse building across the cracked pavement of the access road. Instead of happy animals, she saw prison guards on break, smoking and stroking their mustaches, joking aloud about which inmates were the best-looking without their clothes and how difficult it was to get the feeding tube up the nose and down to the stomach of one particularly thin woman.

"Like threading a rope through a needle," said one guard as he tapped his cigarette on the side of his shoe. "Damn, but she didn't make a sound 'cept for a couple grunts. Just stared at us with those hate-filled eyes. We pulled the tube out, shoved it back in. Bloody mess, it was. Finally, we got it up the nose, down the throat to her stomach, and pumped in the raw eggs. Saw her stomach bloat up like a balloon. Had I a pin, I'd have tried to pop it. I had to laugh."

"Should just let those women starve," said another. "Too much effort with 'em and they ain' giving up their stance."

"I don't care. They deserve the pain and humiliation. Show 'em reality. Women voting? Can you imagine what that would do to our country? They can't control their emotions. Men are leaders. Women are followers. God's plan."

"Becky," came a voice from behind. Becky went down from her toes and turned in the cell to face Bonnie, her older sister. "Please don't look out. There's nothing you want to see. Here, come hold my hand. We're going to be fine."

"They're talking about the women in the other wing," said Becky as she shuffled to Bonnie's cot and sat. "The ladies on hunger strikes are being force-fed now, with tubes up their noses into their stomachs."

"We won't be here forever," Bonnie said, taking Becky's hand. The hand was cold. "Another few days, perhaps? We've done nothing wrong. There are people on the outside—men as well as women—who care. They will demand our freedom."

"But do they care enough?"

Bonnie didn't have an answer. She only said, "Not long, sweetheart. We'll be released and we'll continue to protest. Soon, our goal will be reached."

She's so much stronger than me, thought Becky. She bit the inside of her cheek. *I've always been weak.*

"Canton will bring our meal soon," said Bonnie. She pulled up one of the two blankets and wrapped it around Becky's thin shoulders. It helped very little, as the two women had been stripped of their clothing and left only with their undergarments. "Won't you sing with me until then?"

"Canton doesn't bring meals," said Becky, unintentionally biting the inside of her cheek and wincing. "We had meals at home. Here we get only foul bread filled with worms and meats gone rancid."

"We'll just keep picking out the worms," said Bonnie. "We'll be set free soon."

"It's so nasty, Bonnie."

"We can't not eat, Becky. We won't join the hunger strike. We can't. You know that."

Becky knew that. She had been frail since childhood. Measles had almost been her death at age seven. An infected lung had laid her up for months several years later. A hunger strike would kill her quickly.

"Come," said Bonnie, drawing her sister close and putting her chin on Becky's head.

"Sing with me?"

They sat, clinging to each other, staring out through the bars of the cell window, watching an occasional bird fly past, singing "Down by the Old Mill Stream" and "Let Me Call You Sweetheart." Becky's cheek hurt and her tongue felt stupid. But she sang because there was nothing else to do and she had to do something to pass the minutes that felt like hours that felt like days that felt like a lifetime.

They had been arrested outside the White House on October 22nd, protesting with other members of the National Women's Party and demanding women be given the right to vote. Their earlier protests and rallies had been viewed as curiosities—harmless voices raised in a worthless effort. Yet the NWP persistence began to enrage passersby, the police, and even President Wilson himself. On this day, officers demanded the women disperse, but they refused. A police sergeant ordered that the women in front of the gate be arrested, including the leader, Alice Paul. They were thrown into the back of a police wagon. Bonnie and Becky were grabbed at the last moment and tossed into the rear of a second wagon.

The women were taken before a judge and sentenced to imprisonment in the Occoquan Workhouse in Lorton, Virginia. Alice was given seven months. The others, thirty days. The judge told the policeman who'd arrested Becky and Bonnie to release them as they'd not blocked the gate. The officer agreed, but instead drove them to the workhouse and threw them into a cell on a vacant corridor far from the other women, and laughed as he did so.

Canton, the guard responsible for this corridor, stripped the sisters the first night and forced full-body searches. Bonnie struggled and kicked but several strikes with Canton's baton sent her down to the cot where he proceeded with his exploration. When he determined the women were virgins, he snorted and said, "So nobody wants you, do they?" Instead of workhouse uniforms, Canton allowed them to put their undergarments—bodice and bloomers—back on but confiscated their blouses, skirts, shoes. He had not molested them a second time but it was clear from his twitching eyes that he savored their circumstance and his power.

Becky and Bonnie continued to sing, first "Meet Me Tonight in Dreamland" and then "By the Beautiful Sea." Becky tried to imagine the scene offered in each song—the Coney Island amusement park, the rolling ocean waves—to take her away from the cell. It was impossible, but still she sang.

If George were here, I'd hug him. He always made me feel better when I was scared or sick. I love Georgie!

But, of course, George wasn't there. Just Becky. Just Bonnie.

As the afternoon sun began to withdraw its glow from the cell floor,

Becky fell into a troubled sleep on her cot. She dreamed of a dark, barred cell in which her pet George was being clubbed by police officers. One straddled the goat while the other thrust a tube up its nose and down to its belly. The goat made no sound but watched Becky with pity in his eyes. Becky flailed on the cot, waking herself. Bonnie was up, pacing and praying. Becky joined in. It was late afternoon.

The meal came with twilight, heralding another excruciatingly long night in the cell. Canton stood at the bars with a bowl and pitcher and stared at the two in their undergarments and blankets.

Bonnie stood up, put her fists on her hips, and glared at the guard.

"Look! I've brought quite a feast, young lady," said Canton with a wink. "Meat and potatoes and, why, here's a couple of sweets."

Becky drew her blanket more tightly around her shoulders. Canton picked his nose, wiped the mucus on his sleeve, and slid the bowl under the lowest bar. Becky could smell something burned. The food all appeared to be dark brown or black.

"Why aren't you on a hunger strike like those other whores?" asked Canton. "It's so much more fun for everyone."

Bonnie didn't answer. She collected the bowl and took it back to the cot where Becky sat.

"If you slip out of your bodice for a moment and lemme have a look, I'll bring you something truly tasty later tonight," said Canton. He cupped his crotch.

Bonnie didn't answer, only spit on the floor. Becky looked from Canton to the bowl on her cot. Burned bread. Burned meat of some sort. Some slimy, singed potato slices. All in a nasty jumble. No sweets, of course. The guard liked to lie.

"Bring your water cups, girls," said Canton. He whistled as if he were calling a dog.

Bonnie took both cups to the bars and stared past Canton as he poured water into each, making sure some of it splashed on Bonnie's chest. Then he winked again and left, strolling down the corridor with an exaggerated swagger.

Becky and Bonnie picked through the scorched foods and ate as much as they were able. Most was pure charcoal, a taste that wouldn't leave the tongue. Becky was sure she'd bitten into a large black spider but Bonnie checked and said there was none. Bonnie slid the bowl back into the hall where, at some point, Canton would come to take it away.

Full, dark night came. Keeping their eyes averted from each other at an attempt at privacy, the women relieved themselves in the corner slop bucket then dumped the contents through the window bars. Bonnie sat on her cot and recited Bible verses while Becky, on tiptoe once more, stared out the window at the pewter sky, the stars.

God help us. God save us.

Then, down at the north end of the access road, in the faint glow of the moon, was a goat. It bobbed and shook its head as goats will do, then turned and limped away.

"George!" Becky said. "Bonnie, there was Georgie out there!"

"Honey, you're so tired."

"No! I saw him!"

"If it were truly a goat then can't be George. It must be a goat that escaped from a nearby farm. Come to bed."

Becky looked at the space where the goat had been then returned to her cot and dropped down. She thought she slept but wasn't sure.

Dim morning came. Canton banged on the bars even though Becky and Bonnie were already awake, staring at the walls and thinking their own thoughts.

"You girls still refuse to hunger strike," said Canton. "Why?"

Bonnie glared at the guard. Becky covered her ears but it kept nothing out.

"Thought you women were all of a mind," said Canton. "They're sacrificing for your cause. Why aren't you? Don't care that much for the vote, eh?"

Bonnie spoke evenly, slowly. "You have no right to ask me anything. You know nothing about sacrifice. Women weren't created by God to be abused."

Becky studied Canton's concave face, thin lips, the scar across his nose. She hated him. She hated them all, everyone in this workhouse save for Bonnie. For a moment, she was filled with a rage so thick that she knew if she could reach him, she would dive into him, bite him, claw him, kill him, eat him and spit him out. But then the guard laughed loud and long and the rage inside her melted until there was nothing left but despair and dread.

Canton left. Bonnie made up stories about what life would be like when women had the right to vote, painting a glorious, sunny existence where women's voices were respected and carried as much weight as that of their husbands, their fathers, their brothers, their sons.

Day crawled on.

Dark night came. The sisters slept fitfully, tossing on their cots, rolled in their blankets.

Dim morning came. With it, clouds threatening rain. Becky looked out the window on tiptoes. She saw the guards on break, smoking, laughing. And there! George, the goat. He had a bloody streak at its neck as if he had been caught in barbed wire. He stumbled past the guards who took no notice, paused, and looked up at Becky and nodded his head. Becky lifted her hand in greeting. Then George moved on up the access road and out of view.

"Georgie!" said Becky. "He's back."

Bonnie sighed, shook her head, and didn't come to look. She sang softly and after a while, as afternoon gave way to evening, Canton brought the partially rancid meal. Bonnie gagged and tried not to cry. Becky cried.

Dark night came.

Dim morning came.

Around midday, Canton came to the cell. He unlocked the door and stormed in, carrying a wooden board slightly larger than the window and a small tool box. He placed the board against the wall, then used nails and a hammer to seal up the window as Bonnie decried this intrusion.

"What are you doing?"

Canton tested the plank to make sure it was secure, then went back into the corridor and locked the cell door.

"That's horribly cruel! Take that down, now!"

Canton left. Becky grabbed Bonnie's arm. It was trembling, which surprised Becky. "Why'd he board up the window, Becky?"

There was a long and terrifying moment when Bonnie looked horrified. Then she took a breath and said, "Because he could."

"The window was the only thing saving me!"

"I'm here, dear. I will save you no matter what." Bonnie went to the window and clawed at the board and the nails. Two of her fingernails were stripped back at the quick, leaving bloody streaks on her fingers. She whimpered but didn't cry aloud. The wood didn't give way.

At dinner time, Canton didn't return.

Bonnie paced. Becky wrung her hands. "Surely it's time for the meal?" said Becky.

"It's hard to tell now, with no view of the sky."

More time passed. Bonnie shouted through the bars, "Bring our meal, Canton! Now! We're hungry!" Her voice echoed down the corridor. The electric lights in the ceiling sputtered, causing yellow specters to dance off the floor.

"We will die!" said Becky.

"No, dear. I'm sure he'll bring a meal. He's playing with us, punishing us for being women. Hold on to me, Becky. We will survive."

Becky went to the window. Through the wooden board and down below, she heard the bleating of a goat. The goat knew Becky was there and wanted, somehow, to give her comfort.

"Bonnie! Surely you hear that! George is out there, calling to me!"

"I hear nothing, Sweet," said Bonnie.

Becky listened until the bleating stopped. The only thing she could hear now was the rattle of wind against the board. She went to her cot where Bonnie rocked her and retold a story of their childhood when the sisters let George and three other goats into the kitchen and their mother, angry at first, couldn't stop giggling at their silly antics.

"Our goats were wonderful," said Becky. "They brought joy and happiness. I always felt better when I was with them, especially Georgie."

"They still are wonderful," said Bonnie. "That hasn't changed."

It felt to be well after midnight when Canton brought a meal. Becky and Bonnie were dozing, but the banging on the bars woke them immediately. Canton was oddly cordial, smiling, carrying on the tray fried eggs—cold but tasty—as well as cheese and bread that had not a trace of mold or bugs. Canton said nothing offensive or harsh. He slid the tray beneath the bars, filled their cups with lukewarm tea water from his pitcher, and left.

"Truly? Tea?" said Becky, feeling the first twinge of hope since their arrest. "Eggs and cheese? Has he been instructed not to be so harsh with us?"

Bonnie looked doubtful but said a blessing over the food, and the two ate and drank. Becky felt a bit odd afterward and guessed it was due to having decent food for the first time in a while. Bonnie said she felt a bit strange, too. Soon after, they slept.

Becky dreamed of George, this time in a prison kitchen, laid out on a table, ready to be butchered. George watched Becky as she stood, unable to move, in the doorway. George looked worn out but at peace. He smiled at Becky as Canton slowly slit the sweet creature's throat, then bathed his own face in the blood. Canton laughed and threw a pillowcase over Becky's head. Becky struggled, unable to shout.

No air! God, no air!

Becky woke, gasping, clutching her chest. Her body ached as if she'd been run over by a wagon. Her head pounded. She could hear Bonnie turning restlessly in her sleep.

George! My sweet Georgie! Are you dead? Did they kill you?

Becky forced herself to stand.

No, that was a dream.

Or was it?

God!

She was sure it should be morning by now, but clearly night remained in place. There were lights in the corridor that should be shining into the cell.

But there was no light.

Still night?

Is this night eternal?

Becky felt her way to the door and touched a bar. She slid her hand through and encountered something rough, cold, and solid. She moved her hand to another bar, slid through, felt the same rough and solid surface.

What is this?

She continued reaching hand through different bars. Up, down, right, left. And through each one there was an obstruction. Becky stared at the bars until her eyes adjusted as best they could to what was before her. She sank to her knees and cried out.

The other side of the bars had been completely sealed with a stack of concrete blocks.

Bonnie rustled awake, coughed. "Becky! Where are you? What's the matter?"

"We're sealed in! Canton has put us in a coffin!"

Becky saw Bonnie's shadowy figure rise and move forward, arms outstretched. Becky caught her hand and drew her down.

"Bonnie! There are heavy blocks against the bars!"

"This can't be true. You must have had a bad dream."

"Can you see me?" asked Becky. "Oh, please, you have to see me!"

Bonnie touched Becky's face, "Not yet. But don't worry. I'm here."

"I wasn't dreaming, Bonnie! Feel!"

Bonnie reached forward through the bars, traced the blocks. She drew a sharp breath.

"Who? How—?"

"Canton!" said Becky. "Or some other hateful guard? The warden? I don't know. But we have to knock them away!"

"Yes!"

The sisters put their knuckles through the bars and pushed as hard as they could. The blocks didn't budge.

Bonnie began to pant. "I need air."

"I found a crack. Here." Becky guided Bonnie's hand to a small gap near the left side of the door."

Bonnie put her face to the gap. "This isn't real, this isn't real," she whispered. She was silent for a long moment, and then: "All right, Becky. We can breathe. We have air. We'll be all right. This is another cruel trick that won't last long."

"But how will Canton give us food?"

"We'll be all right."

"But how will we get our meals?"

The voice on the other side of the blocks was close, snide, hateful.

"I wondered how long it would be before you would discover what I did. I've been standing here since completion."

"How did we not hear you put those blocks up?" asked Bonnie.

"Oh, I'm quite witty and slipped a little something into your tea last night. You were out like dead ducks on a lake shore. Did you enjoy that meal? It's the last one I'll bring."

"Canton!" said Bonnie. Her voice had lost some of its power but the fury was clear. "I demand that you take these down right now!"

Canton made a wet, kissing sound.

"Who else is out there?" Bonnie shouted. "Someone must be out there! Hello! Hear me! See what Canton's done! Remove these blocks!"

"You know I'm the only guard on this corridor," said Canton.

"Remove them now!"

"No, indeed. I've put you on hunger strike. Such a gift, yes? You can be proud to be protesting like the other women now. So brave! So stoic!"

Bonnie banged on the bars. "Move these damnable blocks!"

Canton said nothing more. There was a faint shuffling as he walked away.

Bonnie clutched Becky so tightly it hurt. Pain was better than dread. *I cannot do this. I cannot face this.*
I want to hug George! I want to go home!

Dark night came.

George came to Becky, nuzzled her, licked her face. She could not see him clearly but knew his smell, his rough hair. She ran her hands down his neck and felt the gash where Canton had slit his throat.

George!

She wept into his shoulder and then he went away.

Dark morning came, heralded only by the faint sound of the guards outside on the cracked pavement, smoking and joking with each other about how drunk they'd gotten the night before. Becky stood on tiptoe at the boarded window, her cheek pressed to the plank, trying to imagine it was gone and the bars were gone and she was gone home to the farm and was in the barn rocking George back and forth.

In the deep shadows, Bonnie said, "I won't let anything happen to you." She'd never sounded so tired.

At some point, as she listened through the board, a thought came into Becky's mind.

It's your fault, Bonnie.

It startled her. She frowned. *Don't think that don't think that don't think that!*

Bonnie had talked Becky into joining the cause for women's vote. She'd said, "This is for your future, our future, and any daughters we might have. I'll be with you. We'll be fine."

It's your fault.

Bonnie called Becky to her cot. She put her arm around her sister's waist. "I'm so sorry for all this," she said. "But believe me, we'll be all right."

We'll starve! And it's your fault!

"I'm sorry, too," said Becky.

"Sorry? What for?"

For thinking bad thoughts, Bonnie, oh, my mind is twisting inside my skull! But she only said, "Everything."

Bonnie and Becky napped, woke, sang, paced, prayed in the grayness of the cell. Surely Canton would finally get rid of the blocks and bring a meal.

He didn't.

Dark night came.

Dark morning came. Bonnie tried again to pick the board from the window but could not move it. Becky's stomach growled, ached. She felt as if she were caving in on herself.

Dark night came. And George came to the cell and Becky, so very thirsty, drank the blood at his throat. She didn't feel sated but felt a bit comforted.

Dark morning came.

The women urinated in the bucket and defecated in the corner, though without food there was little more than wet, runny scat. Bonnie said it was all right to drink their urine for a while but, "They'll let us out soon. Don't worry, Sweetheart."

Dark night came.

Becky heard Bonnie crying on her cot. On her cot under her blanket, Becky held her stomach and squeezed against the agony of hunger. She closed her eyes and stars flew like fireworks.

I hurt! God, I hurt so badly!

George, with his slashed throat, came to her in the darkness. She held him in the darkness and thanked him for loving her.

Dark morning came.

Bonnie did not pace nor pray nor sing but lay on her cot, shaking, and squirming.

Becky stood at the door of the cell and screamed for Canton as best she could, though little sound came out. Her throat was so dry it was nearly closed off. Her body felt as if it were it beginning to eat itself. Sharp spears of hunger and thirst twisted through her gut.

Nobody came. No one heard.

Becky went back to her cot. She could hear Bonnie muttering incoherently, and her voice was like sand in a wind. Becky pressed her fists against her stomach and listened to it gurgle.

Dark night came. Becky writhed with the pain of starvation. George came. Becky held him. And he left.

Dark morning came.

Becky got up and found the bucket in the corner. She sipped the urine but there was very little. She pulled down her filthy bloomers and tried to relieve herself but it seemed there was nothing more to be hand.

Bonnie lay groaning.

Becky didn't bother pulling up her bloomers. She kicked out of them, leaving them rumpled, discarded. Her throat hurt so much she wanted to claw it open and air it out, like Canton had done to George.

"Bonnie," she managed.

Across the cell from her cot, Bonnie said, "Shh. I won't let anything happen to you." Or maybe Becky only thought she'd spoken. Only Bonnie's hand fluttered as if she were swimming in a dream.

"This is your fault, Bonnie!"

Becky went to the cot and sat beside her sister. She closed her eyes. When she opened them, Georgie was beside the cot, gazing up at her. Bonnie took Becky's hands and said, "Look at me." Becky did. Bonnie's face glowed like that of an angel. Even her voice was strangely ethereal. "I know it's my fault. I'm sorry. But I promised to keep you safe. I will do that."

How Bonnie? How can you? The words didn't come out.

Bonnie patted the cot, inviting George to hop up with them. He lay beside Bonnie and tipped his head back, exposing the wound of his neck. It gaped scarlet, rich with blood.

Rich with glistening meat.

Becky put her hand to the wound.

George sighed and said, "I'm here for you, Becky. Take what you need."
I can't, George!

"I'm here for you, Becky. Eat."
Georgie…

"Please."

Becky's lips lowered to his neck and she began to feed. Her teeth sank into the flesh of his throat, ripping away skin, veins. Her hands tightened around the goat's bony shoulders and she bit even deeper into the neck, tearing away a delicious chunk of muscle. And as she did, George began to writhe with joyous, sacrificial frenzy. He bucked and twisted beneath her, bleating happily.

Bite.

Chew.

Swallow.

The meat was delicious, hot, sweet. Becky's heart pounded. She panted between bites, taking deep and uncontrollable breaths as George thrashed ecstatically beneath her. His bony legs kicked out; his eyes rolling back as if in the most beautiful trance.

Becky continued to eat. George continued to buck and bleat. The pace of Becky's heart, the heat in her body grew, matching the thrill of George's glorious gift. The thrill swelled until it exploded with a rapture of release and satisfaction.

"Ah!" Becky wailed. She fell back on the cot then rolled onto the floor with a thud. She lay there with her eyes shut, chewing the remains of the meat in her mouth, holding her chest with trembling hands and wondering at the life there, at the renewal she was feeling.

Thank you, George. Thank you! Now share with Bonnie, please! Save my sister, too!

There was a crashing sound close by. Becky opened her eyes. Two men were angrily shouting at each other. Someone was pulling the blocks away from the cell door. Dim light began to filter through the bars.

"Damn you, Canton!" said one of the unseen men. "You had no right!"

More blocks fell away.

"You'd have done the same thing if you knew how haughty these bitches have been!" said Canton.

"All the other women were released two days ago! And here you've barricaded two up without any food."

"It was a hunger strike."

"One you devised, you idiot! I wouldn't care if they'd died, but they were supposed to be let go. I'm your supervisor. You and I will both be reprimanded severely at the very least."

More blocks came down. Becky could now see both Canton and the other man. They stared at her and then their eyes shifted to Bonnie's cot.

"Dear Heavenly Father!" cried Canton's supervisor.

Canton put one hand to his mouth.

Becky followed their gazes to the cot.

Bonnie lay there, her neck ripped open and eaten down to the spine. Her bodice was torn and some of her shoulder was consumed as was part of one breast. Her arms and legs were askew as if she had thrashed and fought mightily.

In pain.

Not ecstasy.

There was no George.

Bonnie?

"Bonnie!"

Canton and the supervisor removed the rest of the blocks and took

Becky from the cell. She was spirited away to the West Virginia Hospital for the Insane where the staff was sternly instructed to keep her away from other patients. Snippets of hushed and horrified commentary volleyed back and forth between the nurses and orderlies. Becky heard but none of it registered.

"…dangerous…"

"…suffrage…hunger…"

"…cannibal…"

And in her new solitary cell, apart from the other inmates, Becky patiently waited for George.

Elizabeth (Beth) Massie is a two-time Bram Stoker Award and Scribe Award-winning author of horror/suspense, historical fiction, media tie-ins, nonfiction, and short fiction for adults. Her horror fiction has appeared in a variety of magazines and anthologies, including *Best New Fantasy and Horror, Best New Horror, Splatterpunks, Inhuman Magazine, Grue, Hottest Blood, A Whisper of Blood*, and *Kolchak the Night Stalker: Casebook*. She also writes novels for teens and middle grade readers. Her series *Ameri-Scares* was optioned for television by Warner Horizon (Warner Brothers). She lives in the Shenandoah Valley with her husband, illustrator Cortney Skinner.

THE FLANNIGAN CURE
BY EV KNIGHT

Two in the morning, and the shakes were getting worse. He hadn't eaten since his release—whether due to the withdrawal or his nerves, Dr. Flannigan wasn't sure. But the sweats, shakes, and the loss of a lucrative business? Well, that could all be blamed on those temperance fools.

He limped around his townhouse and considered raiding the cabinets, closets, any possible hidey-hole once more, just in case he missed a bottle, but he knew better. It was gone, all of it. More importantly, he could not afford to get caught—not again. Michigan's "life for a pint" laws could put someone in the cooler for the rest of their lives on their third offense.

"If you're caught sipping from as little as sixteen ounces, you're through, Dr. Flannigan. Do you understand? This is your last chance."

He'd nodded and thanked the stupid judge for his leniency in the matter, promised to dry up and go straight.

A travesty, really. Locking up a skilled surgeon—a war veteran, no less—for indulging in a drink now and then. A herd of ignorant fools, being led around by a bunch of nosy, unattractive spinsters with nothing better to do with their time besides trying to ruin a good man's life. Do they really think sobering a man up will aid them in finding a husband?

He huffed. "My dears, your attractiveness increases ten-fold when I'm deep into my spirits and even then, a good look brings me close to purging myself sober."

What was that? Voices? A group of protestors outside his home in the wee hours of morning? He stood perfectly still, ignoring the ache in his bad leg, and held his breath. A thump against the kitchen wall, the one facing the courtyard, echoed in the empty house. How had they gotten past the fence? He was sure it was locked.

"Hallucinations. Forty-eight hours or so into alcohol withdrawal could, in fact, bring on either auditory or visual hallucinations. Go to bed, Joe. There's nothing out there." His voice sounded just as real as the noises he'd just heard, but the fact remained: he could no longer trust his own mind.

Best to rest, sleep it off. Even if folks were marching around outside, there was little he could do about it in his condition. His weak and trembling state would only further their campaign.

A glass of water, then to bed. The counter was cluttered with surgical instruments, files, a potted plant, and his prized collection of surgical specimens. The specimens once belonged to his grandfather, a celebrated civil war surgeon who inspired young Joseph's desire to follow in the man's footsteps as both a soldier and physician. The items had been delivered by his former employer, earlier the day before—with a note of termination from the medical staff.

He held the small glass in his hands, and his mouth began to water as he considered—only for a fleeting and foolish moment—the pure grain alcohol his grandfather used to preserve organs while on the battlefield. The liquid in the jars, had, over the last sixty-some years, turned a rusty red color from the leeching of blood and other bodily fluids out of the organs it kept preserved. In the past, he'd considered draining the alcohol and replacing it with formaldehyde but simply never gotten around to it. Now he wondered—really only due to his addled brain—if the fluid might ease some of the withdrawal symptoms and allow him to sleep.

Whether the glass he held shattered on the floor because of his tremors or from the shock of the back door splintering open, he'd never know. The two events seemed to happen simultaneously.

Eddie Axler held a young kid who was bleeding from a chest wound in the middle of the kitchen. Eddie never went anywhere without an entourage, so while Flannigan recognized several faces, he couldn't think of a single name for the others who pushed in behind him and crowded the small room.

"Doc, you gotta help my son. He got shot. Fucking broad. I told her to stay home. I *told* her not to bring him here."

As he spoke, the rest of his Purple Gang goons swiped the table clean. A vase of long dead flowers broke on impact while pages from anatomy atlases flapped like wounded doves on their way to the floor. Eddie laid his son down gently on the free space.

The kid couldn't have been more than ten. *What kind of stupid bird brings a child around dangerous gangsters?* Flannigan would like to have a little one on one with her. A nice close-up chat was what she needed.

The impact of the bullet was to the right of the sternum. Flannigan didn't think it hit the heart, but it was damn close. He started to reach out to undress the boy for a better look when he saw just how bad his hand shook. He stuffed it into the pocket of his robe.

"Eddie, come on. Take him to the hospital. I told you I can't do this anymore. I just got out of the clink. My second trip, you get me? I can't be associating with you guys anymore. I can't."

Eddie wasn't having it. He grabbed the doctor by the collar of his robe.

"You save my boy, or you ain't ever gonna have to worry about a life sentence. Catch my drift, Doc?"

"Look, Ed, even if I wanted to help you…" He thought better of his words when he saw all the guns surrounding him. "And I *do*—of course I do—but, I had to go clean. No more hooch. I'm not in any state to be doing surgery. Take him to the hospital. I don't think the bullet hit his heart. He'll be ok, they just need to get it out before it travels any deeper.

That's all. Easy as pie for a good surgeon. Eddie, please. I can't be your medical guy anymore. I can't risk it."

One of Eddie's main goons—Abe? Flannigan thought his name was Abe—dropped a handful of instruments onto the table beside the boy.

"You save my boy, right here, right now, Doc, and you'll never see the whites of my eyes again. Now, I'm through asking, you understand?"

Flannigan nodded. He understood. He also understood what would happen to him if he messed up.

The boy grunted when Flannigan lengthened the wound's opening with his scalpel, but put up no fight. He'd lost a lot of blood. Under different circumstances, it would have been simple. The bullet sat just above the right pulmonary artery. It nicked the edge of the sternum which slowed it significantly. A few bigger vessels were damaged, which explained the blood loss, but a hit to the pulmonary artery would have meant instant death. Keeping it from migrating and rupturing any of the larger vessels was all that needed to be done. His hands shook something fierce, and everything was blurry. Vessels undulated like snakes in the dim light of his kitchen. The hallucinations slithered about in the boy's chest, striking up at the pointed tweezers shaking precariously in Flannigan's hand. He squinted and steeled himself. *Just grab the bullet and lift it out, easy as that. Don't hit a vessel with anything and you're free.*

Pressure from the boy's beating heart sent blood shooting high into the space above the table, tearing the small puncture he'd inadvertently made in the artery. Dr. Flannigan watched helplessly as the tiny hole enlarged into first, a small tributary and then a river of gushing blood that flooded the boy's chest cavity, collapsing his right and then his left lung. His heart slowed to a weak, fluttering beat that resembled the tremors in the surgeon's hands that worsened the initial problem exponentially.

The boy was dead within seconds—maybe a minute, no more than that. The silence was cotton in his ears. Had there been noises before? Had Eddie been screaming something at him as they stood there, watching the boy's life force drain away in a sea of red? Everything had slowed. The drawing of guns, the uneasy shuffling of weight from one foot to the other as all eyes rolled to their leader who slowly and painstakingly stood up from his knees beside the boy and stepped toward Joseph Flannigan.

Flannigan put his hands up in a surrender. They were covered in blood and shaking in both fear and chemical need. "I…I said…I tried to tell you I was in no shape to—"

The impact of Eddie's fist on his jaw was much less painful than he'd expected, dulled by the shock.

"I ought to take that scalpel of yours and gut you like a fish. Stuff your balls down your throat and watch you choke on them, you worthless, piece of shit drunk," Eddie said.

Flannigan could only nod. *Sure, sure, you absolutely should. That makes perfect sense. Do what you gotta do, then leave me alone. Just leave me alone, so I can sleep this off.* He wanted to vomit. He wanted to collapse into a coma for the next year or so. His thoughts were no longer coherent—all a jumble of chemicals trying to organize into some semblance of order without the glue of alcohol to keep them all in line. How was he expected to function like this? He was an Irish Catholic, for Christ's sake. Alcohol was as important as blood in the proper functioning of his body.

"You want me to take him out, boss?" Abe asked.

Eddie, red faced, breathing hard, like a bull about to charge, shook his head. A sweat-soaked lock of hair fell across his forehead. "Nah, look at him. Let him suffer. Death is too good for this piece of shit." He turned his attention to Flannigan and hit him hard with a single finger in the center of the surgeon's own sternum. "I own you now, Doc. You get me? I fucking own you. Anything I need—drugs, scratch, some goon to bite it in the hospital—you're my guy. And you know how you're gonna do all that successfully? You're going clean, just like you wanted, Doc. Ain't nobody in this town gonna sell to you. Got that? Nobody. You're gonna get a respectable job, you're gonna keep yourself out of trouble, and you're gonna be at my beck and call for the rest of your miserable, stinkin' life."

Eddie didn't wait for a response. He didn't need to. Abe had already picked up the boy's body and slung it over his shoulder like a sack of trash. The rest filed out behind him.

Eddie stopped in the door and turned around. "Clean this place up. You're a fucking doctor. Act like one." And then, he was gone.

The kitchen looked like a war zone. His mind, already cyclonic with panicked and chaotic thought fragments, blew up in an explosion of memories. Bombs, shrapnel embedded deep into the bones of his right leg, blood mixing with the dust of the battlefield to form slick puddles of human gore. The floor buckled and sunk beneath his feet, so he grabbed the counter beside him to keep from falling. A polycystic kidney—three times its normal size—sloshed inside one of his grandfather's jars. The word "preservation" swam to the center of his mind. Without further thought, he opened the jar and drank.

Metallic and bitter, the drink sunk into the alcohol-starved mucosa of his mouth and made its way as fast as possible to his vessels before heading straight to his brain. All that was left for his throat was a fiery, almost acidic burn that spread through his gullet and belly like the caress of a beautiful woman.

He sunk to the floor, laying with his lover returned. The shaking eased. His thoughts settled, and slept.

"This will be your office. You'll have two clinical rooms, one for procedures and a small lab. We have hired a nurse for you, as well. She'll start tomorrow but is available to come meet with you today."

Dr. Flannigan nodded his approval. It was wonderful. The office, the new hospital, a new life. "I can't tell you how much I appreciate you putting in a good word for me, Bill. It means a lot."

The other doctor—a little shorter than Flannigan, with black hair and mustache in stark contrast to Flannigan's deep red hair and clean-shaven face—allowed a quick smile to cross his face before settling back to seriousness. "Listen, Joe, you saved my life once, and I'll always be grateful for that. I'm glad I can help you now. You seem like you're serious about turning yourself around, and from what I can see, have done a bang-up job getting sober. Still, I need you to understand I will not hesitate to turn you in if I even so much as think you might be drinking again. We take medicine seriously here at Henry Ford and we expect our physicians to do the same."

Well, that's a fine howdy-do for someone who took a blast to the leg while shielding a buddy from harm. But it was alright. It didn't matter. The daily "vitamin shot" he'd been taking from his grandfather's collection helped to keep the symptoms in check, all the while allowing him the appearance of clean and pious living.

By the end of his first week as a surgeon at Henry Ford Hospital, Dr. Joseph Flannigan knew three things. First, he did not like the way his nurse, Miss Anna Fletcher, looked at him. Second, that the stress of living a double life without a good supply of hooch was quickly catching up with him. Most importantly, if he continued at his current rate of usage, he would run out of his "vitamin" liquid before the end of the year.

He kept the jars in his lab and tried very hard to stick to the once-a-day-before-the-start-of-surgery dose. It was quite astonishing the way one could get used to such a foul thing in order to feed the beast of addiction. There were days, he hated to admit, when he craved the cloying stink of the bitter, tainted drink.

Thinking of his saving grace, he bee-lined past Anna's desk without acknowledging her presence. Her WCTU ribbon pin flashed a reflected bit of light at him as she turned to watch him pass.

Just as he reached the threshold of the lab, Anna cleared her throat. "Dr. Flannigan? I wanted to let you know that I think one of those specimen jars was leaking, so I went ahead and dumped it out and put it in a new container. I think from the odor, it had only alcohol as a preservative, so I thought you might prefer something a little more up to date. I filled it with formaldehyde. It already looks so much clearer, and the smell, while chemical, is less offensive. I took it upon myself to order more for the other jars and would be happy to switch them out as soon as it arrives if you'd like."

Flannigan's cheeks flamed with anger, warming as she spoke until he could no longer keep it in check.

"Nurse Fletcher, I will thank you to stay out of my office and lab. Those specimens were my grandfather's from his time as a war surgeon. You are never to touch them, nor are you to assume you have the privilege or even the intellect to make any changes to my possessions." He slammed the door of the lab behind him and frantically inspected the other jars for signs of tampering.

Did she know? Had she seen him drinking from them? Was this more elaborate nonsense from the Women's Christian Temperance Union? *How dare she? Stupid, stupid woman. I'd like to have a long chat with her—the hand to mouth sort of chat.*

Four jars left. Just four. He took a big pull from the one with a heart in it. The organ flowed with the fluid and bumped into his lips. Cool and rubbery but not unpleasant. It gave him an idea. Flannigan could not trust his nurse, and he couldn't trust that Bill had his back, if the bird decided to sing. She knew it was alcohol and Bill knew about Flannigan's addiction. He had to be smarter than both of them. If he tried to go clean, the symptoms would come back and they would be proof that he'd been imbibing. If Anna ran her mouth and Bill started watching the level of "preservative" in his jars… Well, it wouldn't take much to put it all together.

Flannigan fished the dusky purple organ out of its alcohol bath and laid it on the white enamel-covered instrument stand. He patted it dry with a surgical towel. It looked so dark and meaty against the bright white of the room. Like the heart of evil, torn from some confederate villain sixty-five years before, it dared him to do it.

"No different than a pickled egg," he mumbled. As he cut a small piece, about the size of a die, alcohol spilled out like juice from a fresh plum. "Well, it certainly can't be worse than that bathtub gin some of these rubes are selling," he announced. Without allowing himself to think too much about it, he dropped the cube of muscle into his mouth.

The texture was just as he expected. Firm, rubbery—like a giant piece of tapioca. The immediate sensation on his tongue tingled with a warm electricity that gave way to a metallic leathery base as he chewed. Flannigan swallowed the tiny squirts of liquid that were forced out through mastication. Ignoring the hint of soured beef, he worked the ropey muscle with his teeth and tongue smiling at his discovery. Chewing the alcohol-preserved pieces like gum would make his supplies last much longer.

Flannigan was about to cut another bite for later when a sharp knock on the lab's door made him jump, knocking the heart onto the floor where it thudded with a wet squelch.

"Doctor! They need you in the OR immediately. A terrible motor car accident—they need all available surgeons," Anna yelled. "Hurry!"

He shoved past her without a word and made his way to the operating room, chewing hard on the heart of a soldier, extracting liquid courage as he went.

Flannigan trudged back to his lab after far too many hours in the operating room. Too much blood, sweat, guts, and death. His bite of heart long since swallowed, he was pleased to note no shaking or hallucinations. This new plan, he had to admit, was genius.

As his eyes adjusted to the bright white of the room, he saw it. The heart sans a small chunk of meat off the apical tip floated in its jar. Flannigan eyed the fluid; did it look a little clearer? A little less rusty-yellow with age? Had Anna dared yet again to put the organ back in the preservative and add formaldehyde? He'd have her head.

"And maybe I'll eat it." He pounded his fist on the counter. It wasn't as if he could ask her if she'd done it. She'd deny it, make him think he'd taken the time to pick it up and put it back in the jar—*he hadn't though, he was almost sure of it.* And if she did admit to it, daring him to complain, what could he say? *Hey! I was going to eat that, you stupid cow.*

"Damn you, woman." He turned to look at the remaining two vessels. One contained a gangrenous hand. He'd have to be in complete delirium tremens without any sense left to consider tasting that one. The other had been the biggest mystery, one his grandfather refused to discuss, refused to explain how he came upon it on the battlefield. A fetus, about twenty-eight weeks along with anencephaly. It had always inspired a horrified fascination for him as a child. The thing's eyes bulging out of orbits supported by nothing, as the skull and brain never developed by some terrible defect of formation.

He was exhausted, and frankly, couldn't decide what to do. Dare he cut into the last piece of his grandfather's legacy? Should he try to go dry again? *Damn Purple Gang, Goddamned Nurse Anna, her WCTU spinsters, and the whole country can be damned to hell.* He grabbed the only jar safe for consumption, tore off the lid, closed his eyes to the pitiful creature inside, and drank right from the vessel itself.

"Come on, doc. Drink me up," the baby whispered from its watery grave.

And Flannigan obliged.

Joseph Flannigan dreamt the dreams of the drunk.

His hand was black, shriveled, and dripping as it reached for the jar. Floating within were eggs surrounded by strips of flesh. He pulled one out. It wriggled in his grasp, wily and rubbery. Tilting his head back, Flannigan opened his mouth like a baby bird and dropped the flesh noodle in. He chewed in satisfaction.

"It's good, isn't it?" the skulless baby asked.

"You know, it is," dream-Flannigan replied. "Like veal."

"Well, I won't last forever. You're going to have to get more. That won't be a problem though. You're a surgeon after all." The baby winked one of his bulging eyes.

"You're right, baby. I *am* a surgeon. I'll take my payment as a pound of flesh!"

They laughed like a couple of drunks enjoying their misbegotten gains in his own private speakeasy.

"Hey, baby, you should consider wearing a top hat." They laughed again. It was a real knee-slapper. Then the baby stopped and got serious.

"You know it's not really about the alcohol, right? You've conquered that little problem already." The baby scaled the jar and plucked out another strip of flesh. "The Flannigan Cure for Alcoholism—Pickled People!"

Flannigan chewed on the baby's offering, considering what it had just said. There was no alcohol in that jar—it was all just vinegar and pickling spices. The joy—nay, the relief—came from the chewing, the constant working of flesh with teeth and tongue. No mundane flesh would work for this cure. Just like the taboo of hooch, the transference of addiction had to go to something of equal ethical ambiguity.

Of course!

"Physician, heal thyself," he whispered through dry, parched lips. He opened his eyes, for only a split second. Long enough for the bright white light of the lab to jam an icepick into his brain. "Ugh," he grumbled, rubbing his head.

He pulled himself up, using the counter for balance. His body ached and muscles screamed as they were pulled from their resting positions.

The lab bench was a horror show. The anencephalic baby lay face down, it's back devoid of skin. The flesh had been cut into strips and dropped into the only jar he hadn't yet disturbed. The dusky, diseased hand was draped in ribbons of baby skin.

Curious more so than disgusted, he fished a piece out and tested it. The immediate taste was quite revolting. Bitter, musky, and he couldn't think of a better work than *thick*—thick with the taste of rot. He struggled past his initial reaction and kept working the soft piece of tissue. That was the reward, the joy…the cure.

The tiny baby had very little to offer, and frankly, it was wrong for him to ask any more of the poor thing. Hadn't it suffered enough?

"You deserve better. You saved my life, after all." He almost expected the thing to answer him, but that would be madness. Dr. Joseph Flannigan was not mad. He was, he decided, clear-headed for the first time in a long time. He had begun the Flannigan Cure and he knew what he had to do.

By the time he was finished cleaning up, the baby had its own jar again—residing in the terrible, nasty liquid that had once housed the diseased hand. He'd managed to fight past the disgust of its flavor to chew another strip of baby-back flesh sacrificed for the good of the cure. Four final strips of flesh remained. His little friend was safe from further molestation.

That left one single glass crock free. After his surgical cases, which would help to supply new contents, he'd go to town and pick up some preservatives. It was the perfect solution, The Flannigan Cure.

No one dared question the surgeon as he removed wide strips of skin from each incision and requested they be placed in biopsy containers. The nurses nodded as he explained without prompt how he was doing some research on burn victims. He was brilliant and they knew it.

At the end of the day, he had amassed a good amount of flesh, and even an ovary, which he had explained to his staff appeared cancerous. He almost couldn't wait to try the taste of it. A truly forbidden delicacy. But no, it had to be preserved first, otherwise he was nothing better than some primitive cannibal in the jungles of South America. Preserving the flesh, firming it, allowed one to chew on it, work it, masticate—that truly was the cure. It gave the mouth a distraction but kept the distraction on the taboo side of morality—something for the WCTU to gnash their teeth on. He chuckled at his cleverness. He'd never admit they were right, although he did realize how badly alcohol had muddied his thoughts, slowed his intellect. The Flannigan Cure allowed for the thrill of slight social depravity without the troublesome side effects.

Bill Levard waited for him in his office. Flannigan placed the last of his spoils for the day on his lab counter and joined his colleague.

"Bill! To what do I owe this unannounced but much-welcomed visit?"

"You look well, Joe. It's good to see you like this." Bill shifted in his seat, clearly uncomfortable with whatever he had come to discuss.

"Well, I'd offer you a cordial, but—"

Levard waved off the joke. "Enough. This isn't easy for me to say. There have been some complaints."

"Now, listen. I have not had a single drink—"

"Please, let me finish. No one has given any indication that they think you've been imbibing. No, the complaints have been about your breath. Words used to describe it include foul, spoiled ground beef, and I quote, 'like a dead and bloated sewer rat.' Is there a chance you have a tooth that's gone bad?"

It was all he could do to keep from laughing out loud at his friend. Flannigan had not considered the odor of his cure. Hadn't noticed it himself, but he supposed Anna gossiped about him to her fellow busy bodies. They were all just looking for reasons to despise him.

It didn't matter. He was working on the next phase of his treatment, one that did not require eating long-since-dead flesh. The worst they'd smell going forward would be the clean, acrid scent of spiced vinegar. He didn't have time to explain, though. Fresh specimens awaited preservation.

"Yes, I suppose it's possible. I'll see to making an appointment. I'm sorry to rush out, Bill, but I have some research to get to and need to make a trip for some supplies."

"Is that so? What are you working on? The hospital may have the supplies you need."

Hmm, vinegar, dill, garlic, salt, maybe an onion.

"Just some experiments on burns. I was thinking of maybe using a pasta roller to make a sort of graft, but I need to go before the shop closes."

"Brilliant! So, you would replace the burned skin with a thinned-out sheet of donor skin, that would then attach and grow into healthy unscarred flesh? Flannigan! I'm fascinated. Do call me when you've started. I'd love to observe."

"Of course."

He wouldn't. He had no interest in anything he was saying; it was just a bunch of jibber-jabber rolling off the tip of a lying tongue. There were much bigger and more important discoveries to be made. Actual advances in the treatment of addiction—medical miracles to attach his name to.

His zeal translated into a dozen glass crocks, gallons of vinegar and large canisters of spices. Once he had the pickling liquid distributed evenly, he filled the first with his surgical haul.

The problem was flesh supplies. He certainly couldn't harvest as much as he'd need from living donors. Clearly, he was being closely monitored as it was. He should have taken more from the poor fellow with the big hernia. Had Flannigan known the man was going to have a fatal heart attack coming out of anesthesia, he would have taken more.

"Hell, I could have taken the whole damn body." *Yes. Yes. He could have. He still could, in fact.

He checked his wristwatch. There was little time before the pathologist finished his dinner and arrived to examine the corpse. The grouchy old coot would be none too pleased to find to find the body—by some clerical error, no doubt—had already been released to the family. How he'd grumble about coming all this way for nothing. And that would be the end of it.

"At least you'll have your dinner by then while I'll just be starting to prepare mine." He giggled at the thought. No. Now he couldn't start thinking of any of it as food. It was a cure, a process to withdraw from the beast of addiction. A homeopathic cure. Not food. Not cannibalism. A distraction and nothing more.

How far he'd come from the sniveling alcoholic, begging the very man he'd saved in the war for a job. And in such a short time.

Imagining the reception he'd receive if he prepared a paper on The Flannigan Cure for Alcoholism and other Addictions, he put his hands in his pockets and whistled a tune as he meandered through the hospital and down to the morgue.

No one looked twice at a surgeon wheeling the corpse through the hallways. It was so much easier than he'd anticipated. On the way to his lab, he contemplated his research. Where would a supply of human flesh come from to treat all the addicts out there? Perhaps the government, in its prohibitory zeal, would offer up prisoners? Imagine that! A lifer committed for a third offense of drinking alcohol being euthanized to help treat those who wanted to save themselves the same fate. *It could work! It really could work that way! And all thanks to Joseph Flannigan, M.D., former alcoholic.*

The fame and accolades alone would make him immortal. The cure itself would make him rich. He'd never tell that his pickling formula contained just enough alcohol (the newest ones would be a purer medical grade rather than the old specimen preservative that had been equally disbursed for his own personal use.)

Flannigan had never actually broken down an animal (or a human, for that matter) from whole to consumable parts. His surgical instruments were far too delicate for the task. The corpse sat skinned and trimmed as best he could with what he had, but ultimately, it would need to be cut into smaller parts to be disposed of.

Eddie. Eddie could help him. He would have no choice. If Flannigan went away for destruction of a corpse, Eddie would lose his "on-call" surgeon.

He made the call—Eddie and a few select friends were on the way. While he waited, he disbursed what he had collected into the jars that he'd lined up on the counter and then continued his work by cutting organs into bite-size pieces for easy chewing.

Flannigan never heard the click of the lock giving way on the lab door. He'd just popped a piece of spleen into his mouth, testing the flavor of untreated flesh, when the clash of breaking glass and the high-pitched scream brought him out of his single-minded reverie. He looked up to see his nurse Anna's horrified expression before she took off for the door.

"Anna! Stop!" He ran past the broken bottle of gin she'd dropped in surprise.

The scene he encountered on the street outside robbed Flannigan of all rational reasoning. Police just getting out of their car, parked behind a non-descript black Cadillac. Although no one had yet stepped out of it, he recognized it as one of Eddie's many daily drivers.

"Is this him, ma'am?" the officer asked the still sobbing and hysterical Anna.

"Yes, he…he, well he's been drinking, and I went in the lab to check on him, and…"

"You said he attacked you?"

Flannigan watched the volley of questions and answers in a state of confusion. She had already called them *before* she saw what he was doing? Was she setting him up?

"I haven't been drinking. This must be a misunderstanding, officer."

"I don't want to hear a word from you, Dr. Flannigan. The lady's clearly hysterical. Besides, we know all about your drinking habits."

"You should go in there. Go see his lab! The bottle of gin it fell to the floor and broke, but it's there and he was—"

"I was doing an autopsy on an unfortunate patient who passed away during surgery. I assure you, there is nothing illegal going on here," Flannigan said.

"Put him in the back of the car, Henderson," the officer ordered another. "Then come on in with me. We better have a look."

From the back of the police car, Flannigan watched in disbelief as Eddie exited the Cadillac and grabbed Anna in his arms. He watched her sob against him and tried to read her lips. At one point, Eddie pushed her out and held her at arm's length. He looked angry and said something to upset her further. She pushed away from him and stomped over to the car where Flannigan was now imprisoned.

"You killed my boy, Doctor. Eddie should have shot you dead then and there, but he let his job cloud his thinking. Mothers don't work that way; we have nothing else. Now? You don't either. I almost felt bad for setting you up, but whatever it is you were doing in there—it wasn't an autopsy. You're a monster, Flannigan. Rot in hell."

Realization dawned far too late. She'd snuck in the lab with a bottle of gin, intending to have him arrested for his third offense, sending him to jail for life. But he'd cured himself. He was working on a cure! There never would have been a third offense.

He watched helpless as Anna climbed into the Cadillac and it drove away.

Henderson returned and got into the front passenger seat. He turned to Flannigan.

"Dr. Joseph Flannigan, have you heard of Michigan's 'Life for a Pint' Law?"

EV Knight is the author of the Bram Stoker Award winning debut novel *The Fourth Whore.* She released her sophomore novel *Children of Demeter* in August 2021 and is the author of three novellas including her recently released autofiction, *Three Days in the Pink Tower.* She has also written several poems and short stories published in various anthologies. EV lives in one of America's most haunted cities—Savannah, GA. She is a huge fan of the Savannah Bananas and the beauty of Bonaventure Cemetery. When not out and about searching for the ghosts of the past, EV can be found at home with her husband Matt, her beloved Chinese Crested Gozer Augustus, and their three naughty sphynx cats—Feenix, Bizzabout Fitchett, and Ozymandias Fuzzfoot the First.

PAPA'S NIGHT
(OR THE SHORT, HAPPY LIFE
OF ELENA DE HOYOS)
BY DOUGLAS FORD

". . . I continued to give the body nourishment as long as possible."

-from *The Lost Diary of Count Von Cosel*, entry dated 1933

Maybe it was Vincente who first asked about the bull's ear. Papa couldn't remember, the evening having gone hazy, not just because of the drinks, but also because of the fist that landed on the side of his head. Damn stupid of him for not protecting his left flank. Now his skull rang, and he needed to keep blinking his left eye to keep things in focus. On top of that, they wanted to hear the story again about how the Spanish matador killed the bull and presented Hadley, Papa's first wife, with the bull's ear, pestering him about whether that made him jealous.

Some stories you get sick of telling.

"But did she eat it?" Vincente wanted to know. "Do tell us if she ate that ear in front of you."

"Shut up, Vincente," Papa said, and everyone at the table laughed.

They'd all enjoyed a good day of boxing in the courtyard of Papa's house on Whitehead Street, and now, while cooling off with drinks in Joe Russell's bar, they wanted a good story. But Papa still couldn't see straight. Did Vincente hit him, or one of the others? He couldn't remember.

Papa looked for something further away to focus his eyes upon, and he saw the little German seated at the other end of the room, gazing upon their group through thick spectacles.

"Go on, tell us," said Vincente.

Papa slammed his glass on the table. "No, she ate the goddamn book I wrote instead. Remember, I gave her all the royalties."

They all laughed uproariously at this, but Papa didn't join them. Instead, he began to feel uneasy under the German's gaze. The man looked damned peculiar, his bald head mottled with age spots and a chin sporting a pointed white beard, but his most telling feature were his eyes, magnified by the round glasses, fixed squarely in Papa's direction. He looked like an undertaker, even wearing a black suit with a matching bow tie, a fashion not at all conducive with the heat on the southernmost tip of the United States. A small island at that, where many knew the German as an employee at the Marine Hospital. He called himself Count something or other, though Papa figured that name was bullshit. He also heard the man had fallen in love with some Cuban girl who came to the hospital years ago, though the details proved cloudy after the boxing and drinking.

And with Vincente refusing to let such an old, tired story go, now Miguel offered quips about the girth of Hadley's throat. Vincente pounded the table with laughter, and once more Papa's head throbbed with the memory of the fist striking his head. These men had wives and ex-wives of their own, except for Pelayo, who had a prostitute who visited him regularly. Still Pelayo referred to her as his "wife," but only Papa found this amusing, the others willing to grant the fisherman his illusion. Papa tried to bait them into some good-natured needling, but they wouldn't bite. For some reason they found Pelayo's feelings sacred, but a decade-old story about Papa's being cuckolded with a bull's ear made them burst into riotous laugher.

Now he watched Pelayo saying something to the bartender, his face animated with frustration. The bartender cut the air with his hand, as if to end the argument.

"What's that conversation about?" Papa asked Miguel.

"Pelayo's wife didn't show up last night. Pelayo's worried she found a new man."

"You mean a new customer," Papa said.

No surprise that no one laughed. Everyone loved Pelayo and became piqued whenever Papa tried to shatter his precious illusion. "No one has seen her for days," said Miguel.

Now they watched as Pelayo grabbed the bartender's arm. The bartender responded by slapping Pelayo across the face.

"Hey now," Papa said. Papa staggered his feet. Nobody manhandled his friends, even Pelayo. Miguel followed his lead. Vincente shouted at the bartender, demanding him to go gentle on Pelayo since the poor man suffered from a broken heart. They all rushed forward to defend Pelayo, except for Papa, who had to steady himself against the table, his head still buzzing. He wanted to follow them, prepared to tell the bartender that any new mark on Pelayo's face would only make him uglier, but he slumped back into his chair. Vaguely, he became aware of the chaotic throng moving outside, leaving Papa by himself.

Except for the little German, still staring at him through those thick lenses. The man stood and walked over to where Papa slouched. He spoke in halting English.

"Sir, if you could forgive the intrusion, I wish to introduce myself. Count Von Cosel at your service." He clicked his heels and bowed.

Through squinting eyes, Papa considered the little man's formality. Vaguely, he recalled someone telling him the German's real name. Carl, or something like that.

When Papa offered no reply, the count continued: "No need to introduce yourself to me, of course. Everyone knows you as the famous writer. The greatest in the world. I've hoped to meet you one of these evenings. I have a wonderous story to share with you. A story about the love of a beautiful woman. When you hear it, you will want to write it down. I wish to grant you this amazing story. Will you come meet her?"

Papa found a glass still containing some liquid. He drained it quickly and looked around the room. Where had the others gone? Spilled out onto the street apparently. The funny little German awaited his answer.

"Meet who?" Papa asked.

The count smiled, revealing a mouth full of tiny teeth. Papa didn't trust men with tiny teeth. "A beautiful woman. The most beautiful woman on the whole island. Nay, in the whole country. Nay again: in the whole world! I wish to introduce her to you. Her name is Elena de Hoyos."

Papa searched his memory. The name rang a bell. He looked around the room.

"I see no one here but me and a German with an assumed name," Papa said.

As impossible as it seemed, the man's smile widened and revealed more teeth. "She's at my home. Will you come meet her? Tonight will mark a glorious occasion. Trust me, you will want to tell this story."

Papa looked for signs of his comrades. It seemed almost as if someone had closed the bar for business and left him here alone with the German. Fuck them, Papa decided. They crushed his skull with their fists and now they had abandoned him. He thought about it. He could in fact use a new story to tell.

It took him several tries to get to his feet, and he needed to lean on the German to walk. Despite's the man's stature, he proved sturdy enough to keep Papa from falling over. "So be it. Take me to this beautiful woman of yours. What did you say her name was?"

"Elena de Hoyos," said the count, joy reverberating through his voice.

Count Von Cosel continued to support Papa's weight as they walked through the darkened streets of Key West. The count talked non-stop the whole time, describing his job at the Marine Hospital and how he worked behind the scenes to find cures for ailments, both common and uncommon.

"And that's how I met Elena de Hoyos," he said.

"The beautiful woman," said Papa.

"You'll see that I'm right." He went on to explain how Elena came to the hospital in a terrible state, suffering from the ravages of tuberculosis, and how the count recognized her as someone he'd seen in his dreams and visions. "Before I saw her in the flesh, I dreamed of her walking with me on these streets as I do now with you. She would sing to me the most beautiful songs in Spanish, and I would sing back to her."

The count demonstrated a few bars, but that only made Papa's head hurt worse. The street before them loomed dark. Had power gone out on the island somehow?

"No more singing," Papa said. He stumbled, but the German somehow kept him from falling on his ass.

"She likes my singing."

"I do not."

So the count went on to describe how things looked very grim for Elena, necessitating some novel strategies to ensure her survival.

"What did you say you were a doctor of?" Papa asked.

"I am a radiologist. I have access to sophisticated machines. When the hospital tried to limit my resources, I brought my equipment to her home. I used X-rays and electronical currents. Oh, her family thanked me effusively for my efforts. Her mother brought me teas as I worked, and when Elena grew tired, I sang her lullabies. I dressed her in colorful clothing and adorned her in fine jewelry. Later, her family gave me permission to build her the finest mausoleum on the island. Ah, here we are. This is my home."

Papa tried to process what he just heard about the mausoleum as he took in the bungalow. Not much more than a shack by the looks of it. It sat nearly hidden in the darkness underneath the branches of an impressive banyan tree, a short walkway leading to the door.

The count proceeded up the walkway, pulling Papa behind him. The night air did help rejuvenate Papa a bit, so he didn't need to lean on the count nearly as much.

"Did you say *mausoleum*?" asked Papa.

The count fumbled with the key, apparently not hearing him. He seemed to remember something about Elena de Hoyos now. The information might have come from Vincente, who considered himself an expert on beautiful women. Papa told him that he found that no surprise since Vincente was practically a woman himself. Vincente just laughed and told Papa that a woman who broke his heart with her beauty had sadly died, and that some poor sap built her a mausoleum with one odd feature: a telephone. It all started to come together.

The count disengaged the door bolt and looked at Papa through his thick lenses, his face serious. "I funded it myself. The finest on the island. Only the finest would suffice for her. Come inside."

A growing sense of unease settling over him, Papa hesitated. He couldn't see the little German any longer thanks to the bungalow's lack of lighting. But he also couldn't resist. Didn't the man promise him a story? And besides, Papa had survived battlefields, wars, untold violence. A little bungalow on this sleepy island should not fill him with such trepidation. He crossed the threshold just as the count lit a candle, its flame causing the lenses of his glasses to appear opaque.

"The power is out," said the count, "and I've retired my generator: perhaps an unwise decision given how many storms strike the island. But Elena no longer requires electricity nor ultraviolet rays. I have another, more simple means of rejuvenation, one that should prove more lasting. I'm delighted for you to bear witness."

"So I can tell the story."

"Indeed."

Following the little German, Papa began to berate himself for becoming involved in something so strange. The candle flame guided them past what looked like an old church organ and toward a bedroom at the back of the bungalow, where Papa anticipated seeing something truly awful. Hadn't that fop from Mississippi written a story about a woman who kept her dead lover in a bedroom for years? Certainly Papa could write about this experience, and not only write a finer story but do it in fewer words.

But when he stepped into the doorway, he saw no desiccated corpse lying in a state of putrefaction. No, in fact, the candle lit the face of a woman who did possess a peculiar beauty, her face far from skeletal but full-fleshed, her hair flaxen and spread across her shoulders. Dressed in a wedding gown, she sat positioned upright on the bed, her unblinking eyes already turned toward the men who appeared at the threshold of her chamber. She seemed almost expectant. A floral scent permeated the whole room.

Holding the candle, the count introduced Papa, who established his position in the doorway. The count, meanwhile, took the seat next to the bed and rested the candle on a nearby table. In the dim lighting, Papa also saw an expensive-looking radio-phonograph. Near that sat several bottles of perfume, the source of the room's thick scent.

"Here is the writer I told you about," the count said to the figure on the bed.

"How do you do?" said Papa.

The woman neither spoke nor moved. In fact, Papa didn't see so much as a blink, her eyes remaining fixed and almost comically wide. The count lifted her hand and pressed it to his lips as he gazed with love upon her strange face. Such an uncanny sight reminded Papa of when he and Pauline, his current wife, bought the house on Whitehead Street, a scene of dilapidation at the time. Pauline took one look at the crumbling walls of the house and deemed it haunted. What would she think of the scene before him then? Papa felt that he'd found something truly uncanny in this woman who didn't move or talk.

Then it hit him. He said, "You've taken me here to see some sort of doll."

The count's bespectacled eyes turned to regard him. "Oh, she's no doll. She's real. Isn't she beautiful?"

Papa smirked, but he crossed the threshold to see more. The hair seemed real enough. A wig, perhaps? The skin looked made of putty, as if he could press his finger against the cheek and have it sink all the way to the knuckle. Clearly, the count was barking mad, but Papa found himself growing amused. Maybe he did find something he could write about.

"Forgive me," said Papa, "I obviously don't know a real woman when I see one."

"She's very real. Aren't you Elena? She even sings to me. Ah, that reminds me." He reached for the radio-phonograph, and Papa watched as the man turned several dials, but of course, with the power outage, he could find nothing. What a daft man, thought Papa. The count continued: "She dances, too. Just the other night, she got out of the bed and danced with me around the living room. I even let her lead."

"You don't say."

"Oh, yes, but such animated moments don't last long. Tonight, however, I shall try something new. Something different from electricity or X-rays. Tonight, I try a special diet. To see if she likes it and see if it gives her more lasting energy. Will you keep her company while I prepare it?"

The German stood and left the room before he received an answer. Papa considered his options before finally settling himself in the vacated seat.

The voice of Count Von Cosel came from outside the room, startling him momentarily. "Hold her hand, would you please? She doesn't like to be alone. And to feel the hand of a great author? I know she would love that."

Papa grimaced, but curiosity compelled him to do as instructed. He touched the hand, cautiously at first. The texture of the skin repelled him initially. It reminded him of molds applied to the damaged flesh of men mutilated during the Great War, those missing eyes and noses, even whole sides of their faces. Papa realized that he felt more clear-headed than he'd felt for much of the evening, and his sobriety allowed him to overcome his revulsion, so he lifted the hand. It fit pliantly into the form of his own, almost like a real hand. Such a small, delicate hand, and such a convincing likeness that he could imagine that he felt muscle and cartilage. But in the candlelight, he saw no evidence of such things, not even the ridges of blood vessels. If forced to identify its texture, he would say some kind of oiled silk. Maybe beeswax.

In the count's absence, he studied the face, too. The fixed staring eyes shone like glass, the orbs too wide to appear natural. They were obviously painted to look like the real thing. Leaning in, he realized that the face did not possess eyelids.

In time, he detected the aroma of something cooking. It cut deliciously through the thick smell of perfume in the room, and Papa's stomach growled. When had he last eaten? He couldn't remember.

He might have relaxed in anticipation of a meal, if not for the sound that startled him. Static. The radio, he realized.

Good. They finally restored power to the island. He expected music, but what he heard sounded like muffled conversation, the soft murmurings of a female voice. Then the singing began, as if the talking served as the preamble to a song. A lonely one, too, in Spanish. Papa guessed the broadcast came from Cuba, just ninety miles to the south.

He found himself listening, enjoying the respite from the quiet.

"Lovely voice," he said out loud, though he knew this strange doll, this effigy to a woman named Elena, could not hear it. "I suppose you want to get up and dance."

He felt pressure applied to his hand, as if the doll replied with a gentle squeeze.

Startled for a second time, Papa dropped the hand and stood, staring at the strange, fixed face.

But he must have imagined it.

In that moment, the music stopped, the radio going dead. Did the power go off again?

"Getting to know one another?" asked the count, who appeared in the doorway, holding a plate of food.

"What game are you playing?" Papa said. He remained on his feet as Count Von Cosel sat. The count set the plate on the nearby table and began cutting with a knife.

"No game, I assure you," he said, holding up a fork, its tip spearing a hunk of what looked like cooked liver, the source of the smell that made Papa so hungry. "Do you have ideas for your story yet?"

"I have ideas," Papa managed to say, still recovering from the shock of feeling his hand squeezed. But he obviously imagined it.

"Very good, very good," the count said. "Now, for what I wanted you to witness. I've tried using food before, but I realized she might require a special diet. Let's see if it has the effect I'm hoping for." Papa watched as the count placed the fork near the doll's prone lips. Of course, the mouth did not open.

"Strange," said the count. "She refuses. I thought for certain she would like this dish." He pressed the meat against her mouth, as if that would make a difference. "Perhaps she needs some assistance." Using his finger, he gently pried her lips apart.

The inconstant light cast by the candle made it difficult to say for sure, but Papa thought he saw the form of brownish teeth when the lips parted. More of his mind playing tricks.

The count made a frustrated noise. "She will not eat."

"Perhaps she isn't hungry."

"Oh, she is."

Once more, Papa heard a woman's voice, but it did not come from the radio this time. Instead, it seemed to come from outside the room--outside the bungalow, in fact.

"Tanzler!" the voice said. "I know you're in there! Show yourself!"

But the count just sat there, the fork still poised in the air. Papa now recalled that as the count's real name--*Tanzler*—and it seemed as if the sound of it had left the man frozen.

"Come out and face me." The voice sounded slurred. "You have my sister. I know it!"

His curiosity aroused even further, Papa watched the count to see what he might do. The fork still upraised, the count swore. He looked at Papa through his thick lenses. "I apologize for this interruption."

"Who is that?"

"Elena's sister. She does not share the gracious, benevolent heart of her family. Would you?" He held out the fork and the plate.

Papa saw the food and heard his own stomach growl.

Perhaps the count heard it as well.

"See if she will eat, I mean. I'll take care of this…interruption."

Papa shrugged, accepting the fork and the plate. Though impatient for the evening to end, a mischievous idea came to him. "Don't be long," he said.

The count smiled and promised he would return without delay. He left Papa with the food. Papa knew he shouldn't drink on an empty stomach. He considered the expressionless face on the lifeless effigy before him as he sniffed the meat still impaled on the end of the fork. "This will be our secret," he said out loud. Then he ate it.

And it was delicious.

He recognized the recipe from his travels—*saure leber*, from the southern region of Germany. Though Papa would have chosen a better wine, he had to hand it to the little man. He'd proven his German credentials with his culinary skills.

Papa used the knife to cut a second bite, then a third, savoring the texture of the liver. He would have to ask the count where he came by his meat. He'd nearly finished the whole thing when he heard more of the conversation outside.

"I'll call the authorities," said the drunk woman. "Everyone knows that the mausoleum sits empty."

The sound of a slamming door followed, then the patter of feet. The count appeared in the doorway, looking flustered. But his face immediately brightened when he saw how little of the meal remained. "Oh, you've had luck! I knew she would respond to you. May I?"

Feeling slightly guilty and more than a bit perplexed by the words of the visitor, Papa nodded. He relinquished his seat to the German and handed him the plate.

"I knew she would be hungry," said the count as he carved off one of the remaining bits and held it to the doll's lips. "She'll need more. This will be a glorious night indeed. Would you?"

"Would I what?"

"Go into the kitchen. Bring back another plate."

Papa nodded, his appetite growing. He wondered what the count might have in the way of drink. His eyes now accustomed to the dark, he found his way to the kitchen, where he found the stove, along with a frying pan with meat still simmering in sauce. Papa stood over the stove, using his fingers to help himself to more. It really was delicious.

Still chewing, he saw the ice box. He opened it, hoping to find a bottle of beer that had not gone warm yet.

But he saw nothing of the kind.

Instead, he found the source of the liver.

Bits of it, at least.

At first, he stared without comprehension, not sure what to make of the pale skin. Had the count bought a whole pig? He regarded the rough signs of butchery, the jagged cuts in the flesh suggesting haste. The animal had a tiny head, too, with one large eye that seemed to consider Papa imploringly.

He leaned in for a closer look.

When he recognized what he saw, he nearly toppled over in panic and confusion.

Not an eye at all. Not a head. A woman's breast, the areola of her nipple.

Perversely, he remembered Pelayo's "wife," the prostitute who had gone missing.

He suddenly knew why, just as he knew the source of the liver still simmering on the stove.

Papa vomited on the floor.

Once he emptied his stomach, he steadied himself and made his way back to the bedroom, where he planned to murder the German. He heard the little man's voice before he arrived.

"She's doing it," said the count. "She is eating. She really is!"

Papa stopped in the doorway. He stared at the scene before him.

The thing on the bed, the doll, was in fact leaning forward and eating from the fork held in the count's hand. Papa blinked, trying to make the image go away, but it would not. The thing's mouth chewed, and once more Papa saw brown teeth, clinging with bits of a dead prostitute's flesh.

The count looked over his shoulder at Papa and smiled. "She loves it. She'll truly dance now."

Papa stumbled away, his hands fumbling for purchase on the walls as he rushed toward the front door of the bungalow. He didn't know what he'd just witnessed. He just knew he needed to get away. The count's voice called after him as he practically fell into the street outside. There was still no power, so everything lay in darkness. He looked about, hoping he would see the sister of that thing in the bed. He thought of what she said. *Everyone knows that the mausoleum sits empty.* Not a doll, but a corpse, its putrefaction disguised by layers of cloth and perfumes.

But Papa found himself alone, no sign of the sister. He paused to establish his bearings and began walking the darkened avenue in the direction of home. His stomach roiled, still holding remnants of his meal. He resisted the urge to stop and vomit again, wanting only to see the lighthouse that stood on the opposite side of his house on Whitehead Street. Surely, he reassured himself, it would come into view soon.

Not only had he eaten the flesh, but he'd seen that madman feeding it to the corpse, its jaws moving. If only he could say that the darkness played tricks on his eyes. What would Vincente say to that? If he liked the story of the bull's ear, he would go on and on about this one.

Papa thought about what he hadn't told Vincente—how he offered to fry up that bull's ear for Hadley, teasing her that if she ate it, it would make her a better lover. Give her more energy, as the Spanish said the flesh of a bull would.

What then would eating the butchered flesh of Pelayo's "wife" do for that corpse covered in cheesecloth and beeswax? As he walked, the night air did little to help him contain his revulsion.

In fact, the wind seemed to carry a voice. At one point, he slowed his steps, hoping he would find the sister behind him. She could talk sanity to him.

But the voice sounded familiar in a different way. It sang the notes of a love song popular in Cuba a few years ago. Papa didn't know all the words, but he recognized the song as the one heard playing on the madman's radio earlier, even without electricity. Something about passion in the breeze, a love that would not die. Then the smell of that perfume, a scent he would never forget. The sound of steps, too, feet moving in rhythm with the song. Dancing. Waiting for a partner to join in. One who would not feel opposed to letting her lead because she felt so fresh and alive tonight.

Papa did not turn to look. Even though the voice and steps and that awful scent followed him all the way home.

According to Stoker Award-winning author Tim Waggoner, **Douglas Ford** "wields language like a sinister surgeon with a night-black scalpel." Ford's short fiction has appeared in magazines and anthologies like *Generation X-ed*, *Tales to Terrify*, and *Dark Moon Digest*. His collection of weird fiction, *Ape in the Ring and Other Tales of the Macabre and Uncanny*, was published by Madness Heart Press in 2020, earning praise from Owl Goingback, who called it "a must have collection for every horror library." Ford followed this collection with *The Beasts of Vissaria County*, a novel released by D&T Publishing in 2021. His novella, *The Reattachment*, appeared in 2019 courtesy of Madness Heart Press, and that same press released *Little Lugosi (A Love Story)* in 2022.

THE HUNGRY WIVES OF BLEAK STREET
BY GWENDOLYN KISTE

Your family likes the taste of you. They always have.

"You should consider it a compliment," your mother and father used to say back when you were only fourteen, your body barely in puberty, everything about you so gangly and new that it hardly even felt like your skin belonged to you.

And as it turned out, your skin didn't belong to you. It belonged to them. First to your parents with their tight smiles and so-called good intentions, and now to your husband with his broad shoulders and Alan Ladd good looks. When the two of you got hitched in a white Methodist church with a rose garden and a trellis, you promised to love and obey, and that night, you did exactly that. In the honeymoon suite at a little pink motel, you sliced off a bit of your thigh, and your groom devoured you raw.

"You're perfect," he whispered, and back then, you wanted to believe him.

Now it's five years later, and the two of you have crisscrossed the country, ending up on the West Coast with the promise of California sunshine and a California future.

Except these days, it doesn't feel like you have much of a future at all. Like you've got no right to even dream of one. You and your husband settle in a quiet village with its quiet streets, the kind with clever names. A block away, there's the intersection of Nice and Easy Street. Down the road, there's Peaceful Parkway and Sweetheart Alley.

But that's not where you are. You bought a prefab house with red shutters located smack dab in the middle of Bleak Street.

"It's just a joke, honey," your husband said when you objected to having such an address, and before you could say another word, he put his signature on the mortgage note.

That's because he liked this place, liked the look of the people and the look of the skyline. All suburban homes and suburban possibilities, a smiling community in the foreground, a plain gray power plant in the background, tufts of white smoke billowing from the nuclear stacks like spun sugar. Everyone said this was the way of the future: industry as far as the eye could see.

Everything in this community is the same as far as the eye can see, too. Each day, all the husbands on Bleak Street go to work at the power plant, and each night, all the families enjoy the flavor of their wives. That's the way things are done here. That's the way things are done everywhere.

It's another dubious Friday night, which means another dubious dinner party. You and the other wives are gathered in the kitchen, each of you arrayed in your New Look dresses and pale petticoats.

Your hands shaking, you pass a butcher knife around, each of you slicing off a piece of yourself and daintily placing it in a blender with a block of cream cheese. Together, you'll make a most delightful chip and dip.

"This isn't so bad," says Mrs. Locke, the oldest of the group, and the rest of the women titter in reply, gossiping about their husbands and the teachers at their children's school.

Only not everyone is gossiping. Across the room, backed into the corner, you see her there. Your next-door neighbor Theresa. She's about your age, and she's the only one who isn't married. She lives with an ailing mother, her withered skin scarred and pink, her mind adrift in a colorless sea.

"At least she can't remember anymore what these people did to her,"

Theresa told you once, the two of you standing on either side of a white picket fence that separates your backyards. Even now, you remember the sound of Theresa's voice, how her sharp, mournful tone made your flesh prickle.

Tonight, she makes up an excuse about why she can't participate.

"I think I'm coming down with a head cold," Theresa says, and passes the knife on, her skin gleaming and unblemished.

"It's not right," your best friend Millie whispers to you, but neither of you argue with Theresa, even though you envy her a little. The way she says no without ever having to speak the word.

Meanwhile, the knife keeps coming on down the line until it gets to you. You breathe deep, thinking how you have to be careful. You have to choose the right spot on your body. Not too deep, or you'll end up needing stitches. Not too thin, or you won't look like you're trying hard enough.

As the clock ticks by, all the women's heavy gazes set on you, you pick the underside of your left arm, the soft skin still raw from last month's dinner party. That must be the perfect spot, though, because the appetizers have barely been served before your husband beams at you.

"I can taste a bit of you in there, darling," he says, giving you a big toothy grin. You fold your hands in your lap and force a smile. For as long as you can remember, everyone's always told you that your flavor is a true delight. Sweet as candy, but a little smoky, too: like a bonfire sparking beneath the autumn moon.

Nearby, Mrs. Locke stands back from the others, staring down at the decorative rug. Nobody ever likes to speak it aloud, not when she can hear them, but the whole street knows the truth: that her flesh tastes like ash and rancid garlic.

"I'm doing my best to fix it," she murmurs to whomever will listen, her beehive hairdo wilting a little to one side. You sit back on the Simmons-brand sofa, almost feeling bad for her. She's tried all the latest fads—supplements and bile beans and the cabbage soup diet. But no matter what she does, nothing ever seems to make a difference. She always tastes the same.

"Come on," her husband says, putting a gruff hand on her back, as he escorts her to the door, the two of them vanishing into the swelter of the July evening.

The party breaks up soon after, as though the flavor of Mrs. Locke can ruin any good time.

The moon settles behind the factory as you and your husband make your way down the driveway in the dark.

"It must be nice for her," you say.

"Why's that?" your husband asks, one eyebrow raised.

"Because nobody ever wants too much from her." You purse your lips, defiance simmering in you. "Nobody ever expects her to cut too deep."

Your husband turns sharply toward you. "Is that what you want? Not to cut too deep? Not to be like the others?"

There's a razor's edge in his voice, and you already know you shouldn't have said it aloud. This one rule that you've nearly broken.

"I'm sorry," you whisper, even though you both know you're not.

You drive home together in silence, the gentle whir of your Studebaker the only melody in the whole world. Your arm aches quietly, but you pretend not to notice.

For years, you promised yourself that things would get better. Your husband would tire of whittling away at your body. The community would tire of these insipid parties. But each season, it feels like Bleak Street only figures out new ways to live up to its name.

Summer's over now, and you're heading out to the Harvest Ball. You're wearing your favorite satin dress, the one with a small snag on the front. During the campaign of '56, your husband made you wear an *I Like Ike* pin, and he didn't even care when you begged him not to ruin the fabric.

"We've all got to make sacrifices," he told you, but you wondered even then exactly what kind of sacrifice he was making in all of this.

Outside, Theresa's raking leaves in her front yard. "Off to the country club?" she asks, a devious smile on her face. Theresa and her mother aren't members of the club. Not that it bothers her. Theresa wears her exile like a badge of honor.

You watch her, envying her again, the way her skin hasn't been cut to ribbons. It happens so slowly at first that you barely notice it. A nibble of a finger here, a slice of thigh there. Unlike Theresa, you and the other wives are always more than happy to give yourselves to the community. That's what you do.

It's what any good mother would do.

Except you're not like the others. You aren't a mother, not yet. It's a conspicuous crater in the middle of your life, one that everybody reminds you about.

"Why won't you give him a child?" the others ask, as though it's as simple as proffering a stranger bus fare.

"I'm not sure why it hasn't happened yet," you say, but you know that's a lie. You'd do anything in the world to keep your body as your own, your insides cavernous and empty. There's hardly room in your life for you. Why would you ever want to make room for someone else?

Besides, what kind of monster would want to bring another person onto this street? Even you don't want to live here.

"Misery loves company," the smiling wives say, but you don't see how anybody could love anything about this place.

It's nearly dinner time at the country club, and you and the others sneak off to the kitchen. This is what's expected of you. To give just a little of yourself, even on special occasions like this. *Especially* on special occasions like this.

You learned at a young age not to cut too much flesh at one time. Otherwise, it won't grow back. Instead, you take only thin ribbons of skin like you're slicing up prosciutto.

"It's not fair," Millie tells you the next day when you're both at the park, watching her two daughters whirl around and around on the merry-go-round. "We should at least get a reprieve when we're dining out."

She rubs her shoulder. The skin is raw and red and angry. You can tell without asking that there's a pot roast waiting in the oven at home. She always takes a trim of meat off her shoulder for pot roast night.

"Maybe we could just skip it sometimes," you say. "Maybe they won't even notice."

"I've tried that," Millie whispers, fear flashing on her face. "My husband always knows. Then he accuses me of lying. Of being the kind of woman who would try to trick him."

At this, you say nothing, because you know exactly what she means.

That night, as your husband snores in bed next to you, you stare up at the shapes in the drywall and try to remember who you were before this place gobbled you up. It seems like such a pointless diversion now, trying to remember. After all, what difference does it make if you could have had a different future? All that matters is the future you got.

But if you close your eyes, you can almost see it. There was a whole world you invented for yourself. A place where you could take refuge. A place that wouldn't want to unravel you, one piece of flesh at a time.

"You should do your best to make your husband happy," your mother told you then, and you nodded, because what else could you do? A girl is supposed to trust her mother, isn't she?

It's nearly Thanksgiving when Millie cuts herself so deep she needs six stitches. You drive her to the emergency room and sit with her for three hours while you wait for the plastic-faced doctor to sew her up like a useless ragdoll.

"It happens to every wife," he says with a chuckle, as though he understands it all too well. As though you're all a bunch of delightful little fools.

"Maybe it does happen to every wife," you say, your jaw clenched, "but then why doesn't it happen to every husband?"

At this, Millie chokes up a breath, as the doctor stares back at you, confusion surging through him. "Please excuse me," he says and disappears without another word.

"You can't say things like that," Millie whispers to you as you drive her home. "People will talk."

"Let them talk," you say, your hands tightening on the wheel. "It's better than always staying quiet."

But even when Millie returns home, her wound fresh and puckering, her family still isn't satisfied. Not with the dinners that are always set on the table on time and not with the sacrifice she's making to put them there.

"You've got to keep trying," her husband says, eyeing her up as though she doesn't care at all. As though she wants their daughters to stay wan and weak and lagging behind the other kids.

The next week, with her stitches still oozing beneath her double-breasted coat, you and Millie shop for Christmas gifts at the Sears and Roebucks downtown. There's garland on all the doorways. Theresa works at the perfume counter, spritzing little old ladies with the mist of Chanel No. 5 and Elizabeth Arden, and you and Millie linger near her, pretending you're interested in the latest brands when really you're only interested in talking where no one can hear you.

"There ought to be another way to live," Millie whispers, and Theresa leans in closer.

"There is another way," she says, a glint in her eye, steel in her voice. "We've just got to be brave enough to do it."

But all the bravery inside you isn't enough to fix the mess this world has made of you. After bidding goodbye to Millie and Theresa, you drive home in your Studebaker, taking inventory of every house on Bleak Street. They all look the same. Flat roofs, glass walls, stairwells with no handrails, nothing to guide you at all. You all live in impractical houses in impractical places.

An open plan, the realtor called it. Not that anything felt open in this place. The moment you moved in, you felt the whole world closed in on you.

That night as you're making dinner, you grip the knife the same way you always do, the blade ready to pierce your skin. But then something shifts in you, and at the last moment, you put it away in the nearest drawer. With your head down, you caramelize a bit of sugar in a pan, making something sweet, something smoky. Something that tastes like you.

Then with a bright smile on your face, you serve it to your husband.

"It tastes different," he says, doubt churning in his eyes, but you just keep on grinning.

"It's the same as always," you say, and the lie tastes sweeter than anything you've ever served him.

Another evening at the country club, your life dissolving around you like a cup of borrowed sugar in a boiling pot. At the bar, the men are in their smoking jackets, guffawing at jokes no one else finds funny, and at every table, the wives are tugging at the hems of their dresses, always making sure you can't see their scars.

Theresa's here, a guest of Mrs. Locke. The community keeps hoping to marry her off, the last loose end of the street. But she pays them no mind. As the orchestra plays Glenn Miller, Theresa dances alone, gleeful as a demon, and the others just shake their heads as if to say she's a lost cause.

You only wish they saw you as a lost cause, too. But even though you're screaming in silence every moment, you do what's expected of you. Sit up straight, shoulders back, chin up. You're doing a good job—just be sure to keep it up. You wouldn't want the masquerade to slip. You wouldn't want them to see you as you really are, the rage rising up in you, your hand quivering on the steak knife on your placemat. You wonder for the first time what your husband tastes like. You already know you aren't supposed to think those things, but why not? Why are you the only one making sacrifices?

Across the table, Millie hunches over. Her eyes have gone sallow, her skin rawer than before. She only wears long sleeves now, anything to conceal what she's doing to herself. What these people expect her to do. Nearby, her husband looks brighter than usual, the inverse of what his wife's become. It must be so easy to devour the world without even thinking about it.

Before Millie leaves for the evening, her steps as slow as a shambling corpse, you catch her arm, a delicate hand against her skin.

"Be careful," you whisper to her, and she glances up at you, desperation settling in her pallid face. For a moment, she parts her lips to say something, but when she tries to speak, no sound comes out.

It's a week before Christmas when Theresa's mother dies. She does it quietly in the middle of the night, the ambulance arriving at daybreak to take away what's left of her.

You stand with Theresa, the two of you still on either side of the white picket fence. Then you do something you've never done before. You open the gate that separates you, and you cross into her yard, the frozen grass crunching beneath your feet.

"I'm sorry," you say and take her hand, both of you so cold in the morning light, the sun barely making an appearance this time of year.

"Thank you," she says, not looking at you.

Already, you can guess what she's thinking. There's nothing to tether her here now.

With your breath fogging around you in the winter chill, Theresa leans closer. "We could run," she says, but that doesn't mean much to you. After all, running is an action—it's not a destination. And it's certainly not a solution, not in this world, where women are dissected slowly, one aching day at a time.

You shake your head. "I'm sorry," you say again, but this time, you think how you aren't apologizing to her. You're apologizing to yourself.

Only Theresa isn't so eager to give up on you.

"If you change your mind," she says, and slips something into your hand. You put it into your purse without looking at it. Later, when you're back home and your husband's fallen asleep again in front of the rabbit-eared television, you glance at what she gave you. It's a colorful postcard from somewhere you've never heard of. A mid-sized town in the heart of the

Midwest. A nice little place in the middle of nowhere where it's easy to disappear.

The next day, Theresa's gone, and the whole street's tittering about it.

"How dare she just up and vanish like that?"

"She was never a very good neighbor."

"Good riddance to that strange young woman," Mrs. Locke says, and that seems to be the final word on the matter, even though you can see it in their eyes. The glint of jealousy. The longing to do exactly what Theresa's done.

You don't mention the postcard. You just keep it in the bottom of your purse where no one will find it. Where you can hold onto it like a talisman.

Like a silent promise.

You're at the country club on New Year's Eve when you learn about Millie.

"She was so young," Mrs. Locke says, melancholy tinging her voice.

"What happened?" you ask, as you and the other wives gather around the table, but no one knows for sure. It's easy enough to guess, though. A cut too deep. Maybe even a cut on purpose.

As the men carouse at the bar, you sit back in your seat, everything in you turning numb. The minutes creep by, but none of you move. You just stare down at your placemats, the silverware positioned in a neat little row, the metal glinting up at you.

It's almost dinnertime, and the husbands are watching all of you from the other side of the room, waiting for you to sneak back into the kitchen. To do what's expected of you.

When you don't move, they start coming closer, one after another, your husband at the forefront.

"Darling," he says, his hand on your back, "what are you doing?"

"Nothing at all," you whisper, and you wish with everything in you that he'll leave you alone. That they'll leave all of you alone.

You don't get that wish.

It happens in a flash. His grasp, gruff and cruel, yanking you to your feet. You with your fingers already wrapped around the steak knife on the table. A quick cut, right across his throat, the piece of skin as thin as lace.

He gapes at you, stunned for the first time in his life, as you beam back at him. With a flourish, you swallow his flesh raw.

For a moment, nobody in the room moves, the air rancid with blood and regret. Then all at once, a dozen manicured hands twitch toward the steak knives on their placemats, and everything in the room goes red.

Your families have always liked the taste of you. But now you realize you like the taste of them even better.

It goes on for a long time, the hours ticking by, the New Year coming and going, the wait staff running for every exit. You only stand back and smile. The other women are still dining on the men, their hands stained and slick, their mouths smeared with gore, but you leave the husk of your husband's flesh on the dancefloor and drift toward the door.

That postcard is still in the bottom of your purse. The world might catch up with you before you reach the California border. Or maybe it won't. Maybe you'll vanish into thin air, becoming just another forgettable woman, as invisible as a ghost.

You can only hope.

With the Studebaker whirring like a dream, the highway unfolds before you as you head into a new year, a new you. You say goodbye to Bleak Street, your gaze set ahead of you, and what's left of your heart is fluttering with promise.

Gwendolyn Kiste is the three-time Bram Stoker Award-winning author of *The Rust Maidens, Reluctant Immortals, Boneset & Feathers, And Her Smile Will Untether the Universe, Pretty Marys All in a Row*, and *The Invention of Ghosts*. Her short fiction and nonfiction have appeared in *Nightmare Magazine, Best American Science Fiction and Fantasy, Vastarien*, Tor's *Nightfire, Black Static, The Dark, Daily Science Fiction, Interzone*, and *LampLight*, among others. Originally from Ohio, she now resides on an abandoned horse farm outside of Pittsburgh with her husband, two cats, and not nearly enough ghosts. Find her online at gwendolynkiste.com.

TEXAS IS THE REASON
BY BRIAN ASMAN

In the fall of 1962, I was a twenty-four-year-old patrolman in Dallas PD, driven and anxious to make my mark. I liked patrol: plenty of paperwork, but plenty of action, too. I was low man on the totem pole, so they had me working down in Frogtown with all the pimps and whores. Real eye-opener, coming from Connecticut. Dad moved us down here in '44. Guess he watched too many cowboy movies, got a bug up his ass to become a Texas Ranger. Ended up getting killed by one instead.

It's why I became a cop.

On November 4th, I was sour because I wanted to work the Texans/Oilers game but didn't have seniority. Got the callout to this shit motel, the Apollo Inn, a two-story motor court. We knew it well. I pulled up in the cruiser with my partner, Lyons, who had maybe ten years on me. We never did get around to trading ages, both of us being quiet types. I knew he was a bachelor, a decorated Marine Corps sergeant and sniper who notched seven kills on the barrel of his M1C, and a pretty decent training officer—that was about it.

An old Mexican stood outside Room 6, yellowed white shirt tucked into his jeans, face a paler shade. Manager, I guessed.

"*Allá!*" he yelled, pointing.

"Yeah, put a sock in it," Lyons said.

The old Mexican retreated to his office.

"Ready?" Lyons asked, hand on his gun. He always had a hand on his gun.

I nodded. Seemed bad, but I'd seen some OD's in my two years, traffic accidents. And Ramón Cuaron, shot in the head with a .22. The damage was mostly inside Ramón's skull, leaving him a relatively tidy corpse.

That would not be the case tonight.

Inside, it smelled wrong, like a diner, burnt bacon under all the blood and mildew. Churned my stomach, but I didn't puke.

When I saw the girl on the bed, sliced open from neck to loins, ripped skin pulled back and ribcage cracked open, a ghastly amount of blood seeping through the cum-stained sheets? Sure, I felt sick. Real sick.

But I didn't puke.

Not even when we found the BBQ grill in the bathroom, underneath the window, a fan angled up so nobody would die other than the girl. Bizarre geometric symbols drawn all over the walls in what looked like grease.

Lyons flipped open his penknife and ran it along the grill slats. "This what I think it is?"

I looked at the crispy, blackened—god, I don't want to say *flesh* but that's what it was—and felt the ham and cheese I'd had for lunch rocketing up my throat.

And swallowed.

"Yeah," I muttered, fist to my mouth. "Think so."

After the detectives arrived, Lyons and I got put on crowd control. The parking lot was clogged with pimps, prostitutes, assorted lowlifes, and one reporter.

One of the suits caught him before I could, gave him a talking-to. The reporter, a burly man with coffee stains on his shirt, got back in his Buick and took off.

"What's that about?" I asked Lyons.

"Nothing. Keep your voice down."

End of shift, we were driving back to the station. The thing with the reporter bugged me—I was wet behind the ears, but it sure looked like somebody was trying to keep the story out of the papers.

Said so to Lyons, who told me to shut the fuck up.

"Dave, throw me a bone here. Whose toes are we stepping on?"

Lyons looked at me, and no matter how many times we wrestled perps or got shot at, I'd never seen him like that.

"It's the Spellmans. But you didn't hear it from me."

I wanted to ask how these Spellmans had so much juice they could do something so awful and nobody said boo. But the way Lyons was looking at me?

You wouldn't have asked, either.

Lyons pulled into a package store and I threw in for a bottle of Early Times, even though I wasn't much for drinking. We drove out to the trainyard and sat on the hood, watching the rising sun glint off the cattle cars, passing that bottle back and forth.

"Yeah," Lyons said, once, then drained a quarter of the bottle.

So you can't say we didn't talk about it.

Not my first murder, but my second-most fucked up. Woke up covered in sweat most nights. Girl I was seeing then, LuAnn, worked as a secretary for some finance company downtown, said I moaned in my sleep, thrashed around.

One dream I do remember, all these years gone by. A different motel room, one I stayed in as a child when we stopped in Texarkana. I remember because Mama took a picture of me gaping at the pool.

I'd never seen one before.

In the dream, Dad's nowhere to be found, my mother's in the bathroom. The tub's going, steam's seeping through the crack under the door. She's singing softly, a radio jingle that maybe existed and maybe didn't, and this is the part I always think I'm getting wrong, because I wouldn't have heard that name until '62.

But she's singing: "What a treat, they can't be beat, nothin' tastes better than Spellman Meats!"

And then that steam from the bathroom? It turns black, stinking-sweet like burnt pork, and my mother's sobbing but she's still singing.

"What a treat…they can't be beat…"

And then smoke fills the whole room and I'm choking, choking—

Fall gave way to winter, spring, summer—1963, now. I slept like shit, LuAnn met some banker whose dreams were presumably less disturbing than mine. Kept an ear to the ground for scuttlebutt about the Apollo Inn murder, never heard anything, which seemed to confirm my suspicions. Granted, it was one of a hundred-and-three homicides committed in '62, but a scene like that should've made the tabloids.

Even if nobody else cared, I couldn't get it out of my head. Snuck into the file room after roll call one night—told Lyons I was taking a shit—and pulled the report. Turns out our girl wasn't one of those hundred and three homicides, because per the report, cause of death?

Heart attack.

That sweet, sickly pork smell from the motel room came rushing back and I almost vomited right in the file cabinet. Somehow, I held it down and worked my shift.

"You okay?" Lyons asked after we rousted some dealers who were getting too cozy on their corner.

"Yeah."

"You look pale. You should get some sun."

I did, waiting outside the library for two hours after shift. Then it was back into the dark, hunched over a Recordak, one name ringing in my head.

Spellman.

I never made it out of patrol, but I had decent street cop instincts. Or maybe decent librarian instincts. Took me months—autumn again, now—eyeballing old newsprint on that Recordak, but damned if I didn't put together one hell of a story.

Spellmans were older'n Texas. An ancestor, Reginald, fought at the Alamo, while a scion—Samuel—currently played tight end for the Oilers. In between, they ranched and banked and bought and sold all over the state before finally settling outside Waco.

Spellmans weren't just older than Texas, they *were* Texas.

Much of what I found was sanitized, made 'em out to be heroes, that mythical Sam Houston bullshit Texans wolf down like chili. But the cracks were there—DUIs, drugs, illegitimate children.

And murder.

Nothing like the motel scene, but there was the trial of one Erath Spellman in the '20s, whose brother Sheldon sired that tight end. Too big to keep out of the papers, money and influence be damned, because Erath shot the mayor of Waco to death over a spilled drink.

Got strange—three men tried to steal the mayor's body from the morgue, were chased off by a particularly salty mortician with a shotgun.

Their father, Garrison, was running for state senator at the time, and even all their wealth couldn't save his campaign—or Erath, who got the chair. Any political aspirations the Spellman clan had seemed dead.

Still rich, though, and able to do as they pleased. But this wasn't like Bad Back Jack's affairs getting hushed up, this was some truly depraved and godless shit.

I kept going. All the way back to 1827, the February 15th edition of the *Arkansas Gazette.* A wagon train captained by a German, Gerhold Spielman, got stranded in the Ozarks and had their own little Donner party—seven settlers, butchered and eaten. Gerhold hanged for his part in it, but his teenage son Reinhold survived, resurfacing years later in Texas as Reginald Spellman.

He of Alamo fame.

I wasn't letting it go, no matter what Lyons said.

Don't get me wrong. I didn't think I was Phil Marlowe. More like a dog chasing cars. You know the old joke. What's he gonna do if he gets one?

I didn't think.

I just ran.

First thing that tumbled for me was the game happening the night of the Apollo Inn—our Texans versus the visiting Oilers. Paper at the library told me #81, Samuel Spellman, recorded two catches for thirteen yards.

No picture of him, but I found his '61 rookie card at some sports memorabilia store out in the suburbs.

Still had another two nights left on shift. Worked with a flutter in my chest and that football card on my dresser. Lyons kept asking why I was so jumpy.

"Maybe you should switch to decaf," Lyons muttered. Then a call came in about a supposed liquor store hold-up—a prank, presumably orchestrated by the guys holding up a different liquor store eight blocks away—and Lyons shut the fuck up about coffee.

Driving into Frogtown, I felt like an idiot. What was I doing, playing detective? Chasing some obscenely wealthy psycho family? Taking my career in my hands, all because some prostitute came to a bad end?

Was it even *especially* bad? Maybe they smothered her first?
No, they didn't they didn't they wouldn't—

Then my mother's singing that goddamn jingle, black smoke's burning my eyes, scouring my throat—

Pulled into the Apollo a little after seven. A kind of anti-magic hour in Frogtown—the daytime crowd all fucked out, the nightshift putting on lipstick and inspecting their genitals for open sores. Perfect time to ask questions.

The parking lot was empty except for all the broken beer bottles. A light was on inside the office. I rapped on the doorframe.

The old Mexican came out of the back, dabbing the corner of his mouth with a napkin. If he recognized me, he didn't show it.

"Room?"

I flashed my badge. "Questions."

"No ingles."

I sauntered up to the counter, clocked the worn Chandler paperback behind the desk. *Farewell, My Lovely,* not *Adios, Mi Encantadora.* "You just look at the pictures?"

The man shrugged.

"I'm not here to hassle you, mister—" I vaguely motioned at him.

He held my gaze for a few seconds. "Gerardo," he sighed, with only the faintest accent. "They call me Gerry."

"Lyons." Don't know why I said it, just popped out, and I knew immediately it was a mistake.

"What do you want?"

I showed him the football card. "Ever see him around?"

Gerry donned his glasses, a crack spider-webbing across one lens. He smartly gave the card a long glance—he'd done this enough to know a quick *never seen 'im* wouldn't have gotten me out of his office any faster.

"Don't think so," he finally said. "Lot of people come and go. I try not to look at their faces."

Rare candor. I think I liked Gerry.

"Thanks for your time."

I slipped the card in my pocket and left, made a big show of pulling out of the lot, then drove around the block. Parked across the street, next to the burned-out husk of an even worse motel. Binocs in the glove box gave me a bird's-eye view of the office.

Gerry on the phone, talking animatedly.

I checked the load in my throw-down, a five-shot revolver, running a finger over every cartridge like I was blessing them, even though I wasn't a priest, or a believer, maybe not much of anything.

Possible Gerry was telling the truth and arguing with his wife or something.

More likely I was chasing something I didn't understand.

Thirty minutes later, an Oldsmobile pulled up to the office, and a stout, widow's-peaked man in a tan suit got out, followed by two bruisers who looked like they worked the door at a strip club.

Turns out, they did.

Couple things happened, real fast, and I wasn't ready for any of them.

The two apes flanked the door like they were Secret Service. The man in tan entered the office. Quick convo with Gerry, and Gerry pointed to the lot.

At the spot where I parked.

The man in tan asked another question.

Gerry shrugged.

The man in tan pulled a .38 Colt Cobra revolver and shot Gerry in the face.

Total lights out—Gerry folded, dropping out of sight behind the counter.

The man in tan stowed his piece and raided the cash register, shoving a wad of bills in his pocket—making it look like a robbery.

I'm old now, don't have a stitch of pride left, so I'm not ashamed to say I clammed up and watched a man be murdered because it was three against one and I wasn't supposed to be there anyway.

The man in tan walked outside. Everybody got back in the Oldsmobile and took off.

I thawed out.

Gave it two seconds thought.

I could call it in, face a barrage of questions about what I was doing there, plus the shame of watching a murder and not even trying to intervene.

Or I could follow them.

The Oldsmobile stopped at a downtown titty bar. The Carousel Club, second floor above the Real Pit Barbeque—the name of the place made my stomach churn. Club was hopping, parking lot jammed with cars. The man in tan parked in a reserved spot and went inside with his buddies.

I waited. Ten minutes, twenty, thirty. More. Eventually, the man came out, got back in the Olds.

Solo, this time. I liked that quite a bit.

The man in tan hopped on I-35. An easy tail: there was enough traffic to confuse things. We crossed the Trinity and he got off on Colorado, pulled into a gas station and hit the payphones. I stopped to buy a pack of smokes just to eavesdrop for a second on my way in.

"—and now I got my hands full with this guy asking questions. What? Yeah, we're on his house. Going over there right now to check in. Don't—"

Whose house?

Then I was through the door. The clerk sold me the only pack of cigarettes I'd ever buy—couldn't abide the smell because of my father—and I watched the man in tan through the window, getting back in his Olds.

First time I was close enough to see he had a dachshund on his lap, yipping up a storm. The man tickled the dog under the chin, coochie-coochie-cooed. I crossed the parking lot, head down.

The Oldsmobile pulled out—west on Colorado. I threw the Lucky Strikes on the seat and followed.

He pulled onto North Beckley—residential, nowhere to hide—but I followed anyway. The Olds stopped in front of a single-story ranch house. I kept going to the end of the block, feeling the man's eyes on me, and pulled around the corner. Popped out, binocs in hand, took cover under a shrub.

The man in tan was out of the car, dachshund under his arm, rapping with another guy who'd come out of nowhere—a shadow from this distance. The guy pointed at a house across the street and gave a thumb's up. This seemed to satisfy the man in tan, who climbed back into his Oldsmobile.

I hauled ass to my own car, jumped in, and almost shit myself when I saw the man with the gun in the passenger seat.

"Easy now," he said, pointing an S&W Model 49 Bodyguard at my ribs. His pinstripe suit and high-and-tight haircut screamed fed.

He confirmed. "Davis Ward, FBI."

My heart slowed just a hair. "I'm a cop. My badge is—"

"I know, we ran your plate. If I put my piece away, you're not going to get all squirrelly, are you?"

"Nope."

"Smart boy. Mind if I smoke?" He held up my Lucky Strikes.

I nodded and he lit one. I rolled down my window and tried not to breathe.

The Oldsmobile pulled out, cruising past, headlights pinning me to the seat.

And then off into the night.

"Why're you following Jack Ruby?" Ward asked.

I assumed he meant the man in tan, whose name I didn't know. Feds aren't as smart as they think they are.

"Who says I'm following anybody?"

Ward half-smiled—bright white veneers. "This how you want to play it?" He leaned in so close I could smell the Burma Shave. "What's your sergeant going to say, he hears you witnessed a murder and didn't call it in?"

"Did you?"

"Not your concern, but it's being handled, yes. What's in your shirt pocket?"

"You want a toothpick?"

Ward brought his hand to his ear, thumb and finger splayed out, pantomiming a phone call.

"Fine." I slipped the football card over to him.

"Dome light?"

I flicked it on. Ward looked older than I thought, late fifties. He peered down at the card.

"Figured you for a Texans fan," Ward said.

"More of a baseball guy myself."

"So what's with the pigskin card?"

I flipped the light back off. "I'm thinking you already know the answer."

Ward laughed. "Fair. But I want to hear it from you."

I didn't reply.

"Look, I can't say whether we want the same thing," Ward said, slowly, his smoky breath hot on my ear, "but good enough for government work? Surely."

Maybe it was because Lyons didn't want to hear it, but I started talking. Didn't stop for what felt like an hour. I told Ward everything, except the dreams, the smoke, my mother singing that jingle. The last didn't matter much for his purposes.

Even though it was everything to me.

Ward said little the whole time. When I mentioned the grill, he muttered, "Seems unwieldy."

End of the story, he tapped his fingers on the dash, then got out of the car. Before he shut the door, he leaned back in. "You're a good street cop. Stay out of trouble, yeah?"

Wasn't until I was halfway home that I realized he kept Samuel Spellman's rookie card.

Finally crawled into bed, trying to put everything out of my mind. Maybe there was some sense to make of it all, but I'd do it tomorrow.

Or today, rather—between the murder, rolling stakeouts, and a half-ass attempt at brushing my teeth, the clock struck midnight.

It was November 21ˢᵗ, 1963.

Sleep came hard, and when it did, the dreams came too—Gerry dressed up like a mariachi, yodeling that goddamn Spellman Meats jingle, black smoke spewing from his mouth. Behind him, a line of barbecue grills stretched to the horizon, charring hands and feet slowing turning on the red-hot surfaces.

My mother, wearing a grease-spattered leather apron, dropped to her knees, unbuttoned Gerry's trousers.

Woke myself up, thankfully.

Sun streamed through the blinds. I checked the clock. Afternoon.

I got up, washed my face, gargled Scope. Usually I'd make coffee, but I didn't want to smell anything roasting after that dream. Plus, I was so wired, all I could do was wander around my apartment, drink a glass of water, take another piss, and wonder how the hell I'd gotten to sleep. Guilt seeped in—had I gotten that old Mexican killed? Or had he done that himself: phoned his executioner? Didn't he?

And what the hell was going on with the Spellmans, the FBI, the house on North Beckley, this Jack Ruby character?

'Lot of moving parts. I should've gone bowling.

Instead, I drove over to Lyons' house.

He wasn't the most forthcoming guy, but I didn't have anyone else to talk to. Never mind he warned me off, he was my partner, and that meant something.

Lyons lived in a post-war bungalow on the other side of town. His red 1950 Chevy Skyline—immaculately kept—sat in the driveway. I hadn't been to his house but the once for a BBQ, just me and a couple other patrolmen drinking Lone Stars and trampling the crackly brown grass in his backyard. Lyons didn't have a wife and kids. Maybe they were somewhere else, but I got the feeling it'd always been that way, and always would be. He never struck me as the marrying kind.

I parked behind the Skyline and knocked on the front door. Lyons didn't answer.

But the door swung inward.

The smell hit me first—blood and charred flesh—followed by buzzing flies. I gagged. My hand went to the throwdown in my waistband, but I knew there was only one person in Lyons' house.

Or what was left of him.

"Police!" I called out, less a warning than an invocation, like maybe the shield I'd left on my dresser could protect me.

I should've left. Called it in.

Gun leading, pulling my shirt up over my mouth and nose, I entered the living room.

There'd been a struggle—the TV was tipped over, rabbit ears pointed right at me. Bloodstains on the sofa, toppled bookcase, broken picture frames, glass ground into the carpet.

I found Lyons in the kitchen, tied to a chair, torso cracked open and vomiting viscera like the girl at the motel.

Sticky blood congealed on the linoleum, and I stepped in it without thinking. "Shit."

I set my gun down and cleaned my sole off as best I could with a paper towel. Went to toss the paper towel in the trash under the sink—

Then some cowardly son of a bitch clobbered me over the back of the head.

No dreams—concussed hallucinations. The same shit: my mom and Gerry the troubadour and all that stinking black smoke—except this time, my dear old dad drunk-drove a train into the pool, a flask in one hand, and then the pool itself turned into an inferno, hell-hot, raging, and it's sucking us all in like a whirlpool, and Dad's shoveling coal into the deep end like there's no tomorrow, and my mom's singing that damned jingle and so's Gerry and then my dad pitches in—basso profundo, so deep it hurts my ears, reverberates down my jaw—and I'm hopping around in the burning pool, scorching my feet, and Dad leans over me and he's got a carton's worth of smoldering cigarettes stuffed into his eye sockets, choking me with black smoke, and it's always been his, his—

And then Mama picks me up, throws me headlong through a glass pane and I'm sailing off into the night sky, and far, far below gunshots ring out—

The bucket of water woke me up.

Rudely.

I gasped for air, dirty water running into my mouth. I spat it out, blinking.

"Good, you're awake."

I was taped to a wooden chair, shirtless, in a dingy storage room with one buzzing yellow bulb dangling above. The man in front of me looked like a priest, draped in jet-black vestments covered in arcane gold symbols—like the ones from the motel bathroom. A hood over his head. Big, broad-shouldered, blue eyes.

Figured he was probably the same guy from that '61 rookie card.

"Where am I?" I mumbled.

"I'll ask the questions." He had a bit of a drawl, slight, but his words were measured, his diction precise.

Money.

Samuel Spellman crossed his arms over his chest. "Here's an easy one. Who are you?"

I looked around, trying to get my bearings. The room was filled with shelves, boxes, a couple of wooden chairs stacked one on top of the other. Nothing obvious that could help me, and my hands were tightly bound to the arms of the chair with electrical tape.

"That's okay, I didn't expect you to cooperate."

He lashed out with a vicious punch that whipsawed my head. My neck burned.

"I'll start." He pulled my wallet from a robe pocket, inspected my license. "Shawn Flynn. If that's even your real name." He giggled, high-pitched, and ambled over to a shelf, opened a metal tacklebox. Held up a screwdriver.

My eyes went wide—not at the screwdriver, but the object next to the tacklebox.

My throwdown.

I strained against the tape binding my hands. Gave myself a decent friction burn.

"Why were you following Jacky?"

Everybody loved saying the guy's name. They were making that part of the job easy, at least.

"Fuck you."

"Have it your way—" he stepped towards me, brandishing the screwdriver.

Somebody pounded on the door.

"God damn it." Spellman opened the door a crack.

"They're almost ready," somebody said.

"I'm coming." Spellman shut the door. "Where was I? Oh yes." He jabbed the screwdriver into my chest. Blood drizzled down my pec.

Not too proud to say I screamed. Loudly.

Spellman stepped back, stuck the screwdriver's tip under his hood. Made some slurping sounds I'd rather forget.

"Sweet." Then he plunged the screwdriver into the meat of my thigh.

It took a full second before the pain hit me, and I screamed again, my ragged voice echoing in that tiny room.

"You're undercover, aren't you?"

I shook my head reflexively—between the concussion and the screwdriver in my leg, I couldn't think. The pain was immense. At least it took my mind off the chest wound.

Spellman rolled the screwdriver around in my leg, like he was stirring a pot filled with muscle and nerve endings.

Christ, the pain.

"Look," he said, tone softening, "we saw you at Oswald's with Agent Ward. He's your boss, yes?"

Holy shit, this asshole thinks I'm FBI.

Through all that pain, what passed for a genius idea hit me.

I nodded.

Spellman clapped his hands. "Ha! Ellis owes me a hundred bucks. Look at you, must be right out of Quantico."

Somebody banged on the door again.

"I'm coming!" Spellman shouted over his shoulder.

The person on the other side of the door yelled back, nothing I could hear.

"Oh—hold on." Spellman yanked the door open and slipped out. "You can't start without me, I'm the Exalted Scion—"

The door shut.

I didn't have much time. Feds weren't hookers or even city cops like Lyons, and my supposed station had to give Spellman pause. Probably why his face was covered: plausible deniability. Maybe they'd knock me out again, dump me on the side of the road with a headful of suspicions but no real evidence.

But I wasn't taking that chance.

I let out a breath, bent at the waist, and yanked the screwdriver out of my leg with my teeth. Tried not to look at the blood spurting from the wound. My saliva slicked the handle. It nearly slipped out of my mouth, but I managed to twist around and jam the screwdriver into the tape wrapping my right wrist. Too hard—the tip pierced the tape *and* my flesh, almost made me scream, but I kept biting down, working the screwdriver back and forth, slicing through the tape.

When it felt loose enough, I yanked my hand away.

I went to work on my left wrist—a whole lot easier with a hand. A few seconds later, I was free.

Just when the door opened.

I howled and threw myself across the room.

Spellman didn't even have time to get his hands up.

I stabbed him in the face, the screwdriver's tip grinding against bone. I yanked down, cutting a jagged slash in his hood. We both tumbled into the hallway. He hit the opposite wall, breath knocked out with a *whoosh*.

I stabbed him in the chest, and the screwdriver must've caught in his robe because it tumbled from my grasp, clattering on the stone floor.

Spellman took a swing at me—blind, rage-fueled—but I ducked and rabbit-punched him in the side a few times. He groaned, slid down the wall.

I reared back and kicked him in the face, putting every ounce of anger I had into the blow.

For me.

For Lyons.

For that poor girl in the motel, and god knows how many others. Maybe even for the dreams I'd been having since the Apollo.

Spellman's head cracked against the wall, and he crumpled into a pile of silk and lay still.

I stood over him, chest heaving. I spun around, ignoring the blood running down my leg, and grabbed my throwdown from the storage room. Put it to his head.

Didn't know whether I'd make it out of this hellhole. But Spellman wouldn't.

I pulled the trigger.
Click.

Opened the chamber—empty.

"Damn."

I kicked Spellman in the head until I figured he wouldn't be getting back up any time soon.

Even with the screwdriver slash in the mask, Spellman's clothes were a better ticket out of there than my own filthy pants. I bound my leg with electrical tape—the rest of the roll was in that tackle box—and slipped the robe on, the useless gun clutched at my side.

Maybe everybody didn't know it was empty.

I moved quickly, dragging Spellman inside the storage room. Part of me wanted to finish him off, but without a gun, all I had was the screwdriver to work with. Maybe some people can do that, but not me.

So I left.

Hardest thing was acting like I owned the place, instead of like a scared jerkoff limping around in somebody else's clothes. I tried to keep my back up, walk with purpose. No idea where I was going, so I just picked a direction, hoping no one would talk to me. The walls were rough-hewn stone, lit by wrought-iron sconces. Few doors, none looked like exits.

I turned a corner and up ahead was a set of stairs—stone, too, maybe eight feet wide. If they had a staircase this grand in the basement, I could only imagine what the rest of the joint looked like.

Taking the stairs two at a time, I paused at the top. I was in a hallway, well-appointed with oil paintings of Texans doing Texan shit. To my right was the kitchen, where a few servants were bustling around, stirring pots on the stove.

Didn't want to think about what they contained.

"There you are!" someone called.

My heart thudded. I slowly turned, clutching the useless gun underneath my robe, finding myself facing another guy wearing the same damn outfit with slightly different gold symbols stitched across the breast.

The robed figure cocked its head. "What happened to your kapuze?"

I shrugged, tried to ape Spellman—high-pitched giggle, then, "Oh, you know."

"Everybody's ready, come on."

I considered fight or flight, but we were in full view of the entire kitchen staff. They'd catch me in a second, and then they'd find Samuel Spellman—god, why hadn't I just killed him?

Who was I kidding? I was going to follow him. It's what I'd been doing since we found that body in the motel.

The figure headed off down the hall.

I hurried after. Near the end of the hall, murmuring came from one of the rooms, dozens of voices all talking at once. We entered a grand hall with a stage on one end, a dozen round tables scattered throughout. There must've been forty people dressed in robes like mine, everybody out of their seats. The women wore red, cloth cut tighter about their bodies, and their hoods were different, veiled with string. Everybody was laughing and having a good old time. Waiters in white jackets circulated with silver trays, people picking at hors d'oeuvres and slipping them under their masks. My heart beat faster and faster.

But then Sheldon Spellman stepped onstage, robed but maskless—I knew him well from the microfiche—and everybody shut the fuck up.

The lights dimmed, people sat down. I did the same. I was near the back, maybe I could slip out.

"Family," Sheldon began, lights dimming further. Torches flared to life onstage. "Family is everything. We've done well these last few centuries. Texas has been good to us. The *meat* has been good to us."

A cheer went up through the crowd.

"But," Sheldon continued, expression becoming grave, "there's one thing we've been denied. And as our family motto says—"

Here the whole crowd joined in, shouting, *"Die ohne alles haben nichts!"*

I looked it up later. *Those without everything have nothing.*

"Tonight, that changes. Some of you, even our own Exalted Scion—" he pointed off into the darkness, at me I guess, but luckily, the house lights didn't come up, "—question my decision to grant an outsider the sacrament Herzfresser, but soon you'll see. Bring him!"

Two men came in from offstage, one helping the other walk. I knew the helper.

Jack Ruby.

The other was about my age, dark and wiry and clearly drugged, eyes glassy, head lolling back. Unlike the rest of the crowd, he wore a white t-shirt and black pants.

The next day, his visage would be plastered on every TV from coast to coast.

On Sunday, he'd be shot to death in the basement of Dallas Police Headquarters.

Ruby brought him center stage, helped him stand. A waiter in a white jacket brought a covered dish onstage, and then Sheldon Spellman led his fucked-up congregation in some kind of German hymn, but I swear it sounded just like that fucking jingle in my dream.

And then the silver lid was lifted, revealing a blackened, steaming hunk of muscle.

Took me a second to realize it must be Lyons' heart, and I almost vomited right there, but if I did, I'd be dead. I just swallowed and watched.

Watched Lee Harvey Oswald eat my partner's goddamn heart.

Every. Last. Bite.

The second it was over I got up. The guy sitting next to me—maybe that was Ellis—said something. I whispered, "Gotta piss," and he nodded, seemed to buy it.

The hall was empty. I hurried back the way we came, found the grandest damn door of them all, and let myself out into the night. Some valet was smoking outside. I showed him my throwdown, he gave me the keys to a navy-blue Corvette, and then I was racing into the night, tossing that screwdriver-slashed mask out the window, and I couldn't tell whether I wanted to laugh or cry so I did both.

All the way home.

I packed a bag and cut south, jawing with Lyons' ghost the whole way. Wasn't till I hit Matamoros, heard about the shots from the book depository, when the whole thing tumbled into place.

JFK. Dead.

My jaw hit the floor when I saw the coverage. The man I'd seen onstage, eating my partner's heart? The assassin. Jack Ruby waxed him in the bowels of DPD. Insane. The Spellmans must've had something on Ruby, because that was a damned suicide run.

Dallas County medical examiner Dr. Earl Rose was not permitted to perform an autopsy on the president. The autopsy was allegedly performed later, at Bethesda National Naval Medical Center.

Whether JFK's heart was missing, I do not know.

But I suspect.

Guess all their bullshit worked, because in 1968, Sheldon Spellman ran for governor and won by a landslide. Served two terms before a heart attack gave the job to his lieutenant governor.

And of course, you already know what happened to Samuel Spellman. Missed the December 1st game against the Chargers with an undisclosed illness, but otherwise things turned out all right.

Amongst other things, he's got an airport named after him.

Never did find out what Agent Ward's part in it was, whether he was helping it along or working against it. Maybe he wonders the same thing about me.

Or like me, wonders about himself.

Mexico seemed too close, so I kept on going all the way to Peru. Worked a fishing boat. Went home with my back aching, palms rubbed raw from pulling lines hand-over-hand. But alive.

Plenty of nights went bad, so bad I wished for the old dreams, my mother and the black smoke. The new dreams were Lyons and those I don't have much to say about. There were times I didn't think I could take them, and that throwdown called to me.

But, honestly?

Maybe Lyons died bad, and maybe he would've lived a long, long life if I hadn't dropped his name in a panic. But who's to say he wouldn't have butted up against the grinding machinery of the Spellman family and all their goddamn enablers anyway? That's who was really at fault.

Putting a bullet in my head wouldn't make a single fucking thing right.

There's a video where you can see it. Still floating around on the net, went wide before they could suppress it.

You know the shot—Samuel Spellman, now in his sixties, reading a book about a billy goat to some elementary schoolers. An aide walks in, whispers what Al-Qaeda just did to the NYC skyline in his air.

And, after a long moment where he sits, shell-shocked, staring off into space, wondering why the grand puppeteer chose *him* for this godforsaken moment?

The tears come.

You're wondering how a guy like that could cry, after everything I've told you? See, monsters like him, it's not that they don't care. They care about the wrong things. Maybe he's not crying for the lives lost, the country shattered, the children at his feet who will always remember where they were when the World Trade Center fell.

He's crying because he got what he wanted but it's not perfect.

Anyway.

When he cries, the makeup on his cheeks runs. And there, at 8:46, before he has the presence of mind to cover his face with a handkerchief, you can see it.

A pale, jagged screwdriver scar running from his right cheekbone to his upper lip.

My mark on history.

Brian Asman is a writer, actor, and producer from San Diego, CA. He's the author of the hit indie novella *Man, Fuck this House* (recently optioned by a major streaming service). His other books include *I'm Not Even Supposed to Be Here Today* from Eraserhead Press and *Return of the Living Elves, Nunchuck City* and *Jailbroke* from Mutated Media. He's recently published short stories in *Pulp Modern, Kelp, Welcome to the Splatter Club* and *Lost Films*, and comics in *Tales of Horrorgasm.* An anthology he co-edited with Danger Slater, *Boinking Bizarro*, was released by Death's Head Press. A film he co-wrote and produced, *A Haunting in Ravenwood*, is available now on DVD and VOD from Breaking Glass. His short "Reel Trouble" premiered at GenCon 2022 and is currently touring festivals. Brian holds an MFA from UCR-Palm Desert. He's represented by Dunham Literary, Inc. Max Booth III is his hype man.

TENDER FARM
BY C.V. HUNT

"You should've been there, man." Harry took a bite of his alfalfa sprout sandwich, chewed, and spoke around the masticated food. "I'm telling you…it was mesmerizing."

"I wish I would've lived here then," John said. He pushed the vegetable soup around with his spoon.

It had been Harry's idea to check out the newest and hottest restaurant in town, The Source. It was said that John Lennon and Marlon Brando had eaten at The Source. John scanned the establishment, hoping to spot someone famous or cool. His gaze locked with a brunette girl sitting at a table with a blonde girl. The brunette smiled broadly at him before leaning toward the other girl and whispering something. The blonde looked at him and giggled before both girls leaned toward one another and began talking.

Harry swallowed his food. "It was amazing. The whole place went dead quiet, man. Even the waitresses stopped serving drinks. Everyone was just vibing with whatever Morrison was doing. I'd heard them play 'The End' before…but not like this. It was poetic and hypnotic. But then he started saying—" he dropped the volume of his voice so no one seated around them could hear "—'fuck the mother, kill the father'. Anyway, The Doors never played another song at Whisky a Go Go." Harry took another bite of his sandwich and stared off into space. "Best concert I've ever been to. You had to be there."

John took an unenthusiastic bite of his soup. It felt like everyone in L.A. was vegetarian and it was all they could talk about. John grew up in Texas on a cattle farm. There wasn't a meal to be had that didn't have some form of meat included back home. But The Source was on the lips of every vegetarian. The only thing that really hit the spot for John was eating at Original Tommy's World Famous Hamburgers. He was dreaming of a hamburger when a waitress in a white flowing skirt and top approached their table.

"How's your soup?" the waitress asked. She gave John a huge smile he thought seemed forced.

John lied. "It's great. Thank you." He swallowed a spoonful and smiled at her to emphasize the lie.

"Good." She slid the bill onto the table, face down, before she turned to Harry. "I overheard you talking about The Doors. Sounds like you're into some groovy music. How would you like to see some live music tonight?"

"That would be groovy," Harry said eagerly.

"Father Yod is playing this evening—"

"Father Yod?" John interrupted the waitress.

She turned back to John with that forced smile and he detected a bit of annoyance in her tone. "Yes. Ya Ho Wha 13."

"Ya Ho Wha what?" Harry said and laughed.

She turned back to Harry and giggled. "Ya Ho Wha 13." She reached into a hidden pocket in her skirt and retrieved a folded piece of paper. "Here." She handed the paper to Harry. "The show starts at nine. Tell them Moon Flower sent you." She left the table to tend to another table.

Harry unfolded the paper.

"What is it?" John said.

Harry flipped the paper around so John could read the feminine handwriting. He wagged his eyebrows. "An address."

"You're not going, are you?"

"Why not?"

"I don't know. Something…Call it a gut feeling."

Harry laughed. "A girl gave me an address. Of course I'm going. This isn't Texas, man. Don't be a downer. There's plenty of love to go around."

John spotted the brunette staring at him again. She lifted her hand and wiggled her index finger in a come-hither motion. John looked over his shoulder to see who she was inviting to her table but the other people in the restaurant were involved in their own conversations and no one was paying attention to her. He looked back at the girl, pointed to himself, and mouthed the word *me*. She responded with an enthusiastic nod.

Harry turned his head to see who John was silently conversing with. He said, "Looks like you have an admirer yourself."

"No way." John's inclination was to always deny any acknowledgment of the opposite sex. He didn't think he was hideous but he also didn't have women beating down his door. Especially one as attractive as the girl beckoning him to join her. And where he was from, it was rare for a girl to approach a guy.

Harry leaned toward John. "Go over there."

"Are you sure?"

"Go. I gotta take off myself." He waved the paper with the address on it. "Gotta meet Moon Flower about a yada yada something or another." He smiled, slid the paper into the pocket of his bell bottoms, stuffed the last bite of his sandwich into his mouth, and stood.

John flipped the bill over, retrieved some cash from his pocket, and tossed the money beside his nearly uneaten soup. It felt like such a waste of money. John made up his mind as the cash hit the table that the next time he and Harry met to eat, he would choose the restaurant. Harry left in a hurry and John turned his attention to the brunette who'd summoned him to her table.

The girl smiled as he approached and whispered something to her friend.

"Hello," John said. "You invited me to come over?"

The women gave each other a coy smile.

The brunette waved her hand at an empty chair at their table. "Have a seat."

John noticed that neither of them had food in front of them, only glasses of water. "I don't want to interrupt your meal."

The blonde laughed and said, "We're not eating."

John wondered if the two of them were high. They both seemed giggly and a tad *too* happy, as if there were some joke between the two he wasn't privy to.

"And by the looks of it," the brunette said, "neither are you."

John glanced back at his former table. A bus boy was clearing away his untouched soup.

"Yeah, uh, um," he sputtered. "I don't think vegetarianism is for me."

"It's okay," the brunette said. "We're not much into vegetarianism ourselves."

The blonde stifled a laugh.

He was about to ask why they were at The Source then, but the brunette spoke.

"Sit," the brunette commanded. "We'd love to have the company of such an attractive guy."

John didn't know how to take the compliment and decided to ignore it even though he could feel heat in his cheeks. He took a seat and extended his hand to the brunette. "My name's John."

She took his hand, flipped his palm skyward and examined its surface briefly. She ran the tip of her finger along a crease in the skin. Her touch stirred John sexually. She lifted her eyes to meet his and released his hand.

"My name's Ara," the brunette said. She waved her hand at the blonde. "And this is Carina."

"It's nice to meet you both," he said.

"You're probably wondering why I wanted you to join us."

John didn't want to say why he thought she wanted him to join them but he had a pretty good idea why. Ara emanated a sexual vibe that was hard to miss. He noticed a few other men in the restaurant having a hard time not gawking at her. Everything about Ara, the way she moved, the softness of her voice, the tenderness of her touch to his palm, felt sensual to John and his attraction to her was growing by the second.

John shook his head, indicating he didn't know why she'd beckoned him.

Carina placed an elbow on the table and rested her chin in her upturned palm. "It didn't look like you were having a groovy time."

"With your soup," Ara added.

"Uh, no, I'm not used to this type of food." He hesitated before lowering his voice and adding, "I grew up on a cattle farm."

Ara said, "That's great!"

"It is?" John replied, confused.

Carina scooted closer to him and touched his arm. "We're wondering if you'd like to join us for dinner?"

"Tonight?" John asked.

"Right now," Ara said.

"Now?" John said.

Carina said, "Do you have other plans?"

Ara placed her hand on John's thigh and he felt himself stir.

"No," John replied a tad too loud. Ara's touch had excited him and he didn't realize he'd nearly shouted until he noticed a few people at the tables near them staring at him. "No," he replied at normal volume. "I don't have anything to do until tomorrow."

"Good," Ara said. "Then you can come eat with us at Tender Farm."

Carina drove the worn Volkswagen bus. They left the city and were making their way through a heavily wooded area.

John was in the back with Ara. The back seats of the bus had been removed and the empty area was home to a mattress. He didn't pay much attention to where they were headed. He told Ara about Texas and the cattle farm. She told him all about Tender Farm and emphasized how it was self-sustaining, which intrigued John. Ara asked him tons of questions about his living situation (alone), his family (back in Texas), and friends (he'd only managed to make a single friend since moving to Los Angles—Harry). As soon as he started to ask Ara questions to get to know her, she began caressing his thigh.

After they made it to the edge of town, Ara's hand traveled to his groin. They dove deep into a heavy petting session and he lost track of where they were heading and it didn't seem all that important anyway.

He felt embarrassed about their overtly affectionate display in front of Carina and told Ara as much. But Ara had assured him it was fine and he shouldn't let the puritanical views of the world strangle his sexuality. Carina backed Ara on this and encouraged them to do what their bodies desired. Who was he to argue with them?

Ara had just unfastened his pants and slipped her hand into his underwear when Carina interrupted them.

"We're here!" She slowed the bus and turned the steering wheel.

John groaned and quickly refastened his pants. He rose to his knees to peek out the front window. They were driving on a dirt path surrounded closely by trees. The branches scraped the sides of the bus as Carina drove the vehicle toward what John thought was an open field.

"Wow," John said, "this place is really hidden."

Ara hugged him from behind and placed her chin on his shoulder. Her breath tickled his ear and made him shiver. She said, "It's an Eden away from prying eyes. We could live here forever and never leave."

Once they'd made it to the clearing, John understood her reference to Eden. There were several men and women milling about. A large group of them toiled away in a large vegetable garden. Some worked together to build a small log structure. A few animals milled about freely. And most of the people were completely naked. A few wore pants or shoes but for the most part, there wasn't much clothing to be seen.

Ara pulled away from him and pulled off her top before she shimmied out of her skirt. She was completely naked before Carina had parked the bus beside one of several yurts scattered throughout the open field.

Carina killed the engine and immediately began disrobing. John was having a hard time keeping his eyes off Carina as every inch of her was exposed. He'd heard rumors of communes like these but had never experienced one.

Ara laughed, "You seem shocked."

"I…uh, I'm not used to…I mean…"

"Oh, don't be a prude," Carina said. She gathered up her clothes and tossed them in John's face.

Ara grabbed the edge of his shirt and began to pull it up over his head. John grabbed her hand to insinuate she should stop.

"I don't feel comfortable…" John dropped his eyes to his crotch.

"Oh jeez," Ara said. She let out a little laugh. "It's human nature. No one is going to judge you here. We live how humans should, as part of nature and on instinct. Like the animals we are. Humans are meant to get aroused. We're meant to procreate and eat and live. Just like the animals. Just let your freak flag fly."

John hesitated and the girls watched him expectantly. He finally let go of Ara's hand and she helped him disrobe. His nervousness killed his erection and made him feel slightly less anxious. Carina climbed into the back of the bus with them and Ara threw open the bus door. The trio exited the bus and John was introduced to the plants, the animals, the people, and everything that made up Tender Farm.

As the sun sat that evening, everyone gathered around a large fire. A large cast iron cauldron sat in the glowing coals at the edge of the fire, its contents simmering. Several wooden bowls sat further from the fire. The bowls were filled with fruits, vegetables, and salads. A spit was spun slowly by a woman who appeared exhausted. The bright stretch marks and loose skin of her lower stomach, along with her almost painfully distended nipples, made John think she'd possibly given birth recently. The meat on the spit appeared to be some type of roast wrapped and tied in string. The air was filled with the scent of pork and John's stomach grumbled.

A couple of men with long beards and long hair took up some bongos and began to play. Almost all of the people started to dance around the fire, hopping from one foot to the other and waving their hands as if they were trees blown by the wind.

Ara tugged on John's arm. "Come on! Let's give thanks for the food Mother Earth has provided."

John was reluctant to join the group. Everyone had been nice to him up to this point, but he wasn't really part of their group and didn't want to impose. It felt like joining in a religious ceremony where he wasn't part of the religion. He didn't feel comfortable.

Carina approached the couple with a wooden cup and extended it toward John. "Here."

John took the cup. "What is it?"

"Tea," Ara said. "We pick the ingredients from the woods."

John looked down at the grayish liquid and its floating debris. "What's it made of?"

Carina laughed. "Mushrooms." She took the cup back from John and drank some of the tea before handing it to Ara.

Ara said, "Magic mushrooms," and drank from the cup. Once she was done, she handed the cup back to John.

"Let's take a trip!" Carina said.

John stared at the tea reluctantly. He scanned the group of naked people as they danced and laughed. A group of three women passed a cup, similar to the one he was holding, amongst themselves, taking large swallows as they sensually embraced each other. A man and woman made love on the ground nearby, the woman appearing to be in the later stages of pregnancy. It dawned on him there were quite a few pregnant women at the farm. It seemed like there were more women pregnant than not.

He turned his attention back to Ara and Carina as they watched him expectantly.

A man wearing only boots—Orion, if John remembered his name correctly—approached them. He held both hands together over John's cup and squeezed them together. A liquid poured from his hand and into the tea.

The man slapped John on the shoulder with a wet hand. "Lemon makes it taste better and work faster."

Ara stroked his arm. "It works as an aphrodisiac too."

John didn't hesitate. He drank the tea.

Orion said, "Far out, man. Let's get trippy."

John lost track of time as the dinner gathering morphed into euphoria. Every sense became heightened as Ara and Carina caressed and stimulated him. The dancers became a blur of flesh and color. The beat of the drums became his heartbeat for everyone to hear. And the air smelled of the most delicious foods he could ever ask for.

The world came alive and his stomach revolted. One of the girls held his hair as he vomited into the grass. Each blade of grass screamed as he emptied his stomach of what little it held.

"I'm sorry," John said to the grass.

"It's okay," the grass replied with Ara's voice, "your body is preparing for the feast Mother Earth has provided."

The people around him fell into an orgy. It didn't take much convincing for John to follow Ara and Carina's lead. Every touch from the girls was electrified, and he felt every hair on his body tingle as they engaged in an animalistic frenzy of sex. He came with Ara first and didn't think he'd be able to go again, but they must've been right about the mushrooms being an aphrodisiac. The women became a blur of enveloping comfort. A velvety warmth of sex. He heard them purr and growl like the animals they were.

John found himself having sex with the woman who he'd seen turning the spit. Her face and body were replaced by another and another. He didn't know when the orgy had stopped but, at some point, the group began to eat the food. There was another short ceremony he didn't understand. He saw animals flooding out of the woods and encircling them but he didn't think they were animals he'd ever seen before. Someone handed him a small chunk of roasted meat.

He wasn't sure if the meat was tender and delicious and like nothing he'd ever eaten before because of the mushrooms or because of how it was prepared. He dropped down on all fours, set the meat on the ground, and devoured it like a ravenous animal. Everyone appeared to be pleased as he consumed the meal, laughing and encouraging him to eat more. Once the food was gone, the orgy continued until most of the group passed out under the stars.

The sound of birdsong and someone in distress lured John from sleep. The sky was the color of civil twilight. Light wisps of smoke danced above the nearly dead bonfire. Some of the group were waking too, others were already starting their day, but a lot of people still lay sleeping around him. He didn't see Ara or Carina anywhere. He wasn't sure if they'd slept beside him or not. The previous night's activities were a blur.

A woman's cry sounded from within one of the yurts closest to him and he realized it was what had woken him. A man a few feet from him groaned at the sound and rolled over.

John wasn't sure where to find Ara and Carina but he needed to get home soon. He was scheduled to work later that day and since he'd only had the job a few months, he didn't want to give his boss a reason to fire him. Although an alternative like living at Tender Farm was an option if he had no income, he didn't think it was the life for him.

John got to his feet and his back felt as stiff as he imagined it would for sleeping on the ground all night. Someone growled from within the yurt but no one awake seemed to be bothered by the noise. John made up his mind that starting at the yurt to look for Ara or Carina was just as good as searching anywhere else on the farm. He didn't want to seem nosy, but the door flaps to the structure were open. He didn't think the place was off limits or someone would've shut them. A flickering light danced inside, and as he got closer, he realized the source was a few gas lamps used to illuminate it.

He spotted a small group of people inside. The furniture was sparse. He scanned the whole scene as he entered, stopping dead in his tracks once he realized what he'd walked in on.

Ara and Carina, along with a long-haired man, stood at a long butcher's block with slabs of meat. The three of them were naked, as usual, and covered in blood up to their elbows. Blood was also smeared on their torsos. They appeared to be slathering the meat with some type of herb mixture and laying the cuts in a row, overlapping each edge, and rolling the pieces to form a roast before wrapping string around it and tying it to keep its form.

A table was positioned beside the butcher's block. The table held a woman in the process of delivering a child. The woman writhed in pain, panting and groaning. Two other women tended to her. One stood at the head of the mother-to-be with a rag and a bowl of water, repeatedly wiping her forehead with a damp cloth and rewetting it in the bowl. The other woman stayed positioned between the mother's legs, giving instructions, and eagerly waiting to catch the infant. The inside of the yurt smelled of blood and feces and something John had never encountered before. He could only think to associate it with afterbirth or something to do with the birthing process. It made him want to gag.

John wasn't sure if he should leave or not. He'd never experienced a birth before. Back home, he'd seen plenty of calves born but had never been privy to a human birth. He was certain the drugs he'd taken the previous night were still lingering in his body as he felt a little spacy and mesmerized by what was happening. Ara looked up and noticed him, only acknowledging him with a smile before returning to her task. No one seemed to be bothered by his presence, so he continued to watch as the woman coaching the delivery demanded the mother give her one more push, promising it would be the last one. He found himself mindlessly walking closer to the group to get a better look, even though he felt as if he should ask for permission, but his muddied mind didn't want to connect with his voice.

The woman in labor lifted her upper body and placed her elbows on the table. The woman who'd been in charge of wiping her forehead helped to support her as she bore down and growled one final time to finally expel the child.

The birthing coach caught the child, and in one quick movement, snatched up a meat cleaver from the prep table where Ara and Carina were working and brought it down on the umbilical cord. She quickly tossed the infant—along with the cleaver—onto the prep table as if it were insignificant and turned her attention back to caring for the exhausted mother.

John struggled to process what he was seeing. His feet took him closer toward the prep table. Ara grabbed the meat cleaver, raised it high above her head, and brought it down on the infant's neck, severing its tiny head. The sudden shock of seeing the infanticide made John gasp and his body spasmed as he tried to fill his already full lungs.

The three at the butcher's block let out a sigh of ecstasy.

John struggled to breathe. His body instinctively wanted to gasp again but there was no more room in his lungs.

Carina began to flay and skin the infant.

Ara said, "Thank you, Mother Earth, for this blessed meat. We thank you for your gift of substance."

A tingling sensation flooded John's body as he gulped for air. Something like a squeak came from his mouth.

The man beside Carina began to prepare more herbs.

Carina looked up from her work and said, "Nothing goes to waste at Tender Farm, John."

"Even animals eat their young," Ara said.

The air stuck in John's lungs came rushing out, and he wasn't sure if he'd ever be able to stop screaming.

C.V. Hunt has authored over twenty books, including *Ritualistic Human Sacrifice* and *Halloween Fiend*. They are the owner and head editor of Grindhouse Press. In their spare time, they enjoy watching shot-on-video and low-budget horror movies. C.V. Hunt lives in Ohio with their partner and pet snake.

WHEN A STRANGER BITES
BY L. STEPHENSON

"Oh gross! Get it all out!" 17-year-old Jo squealed in the back seat as her best friend, Lilah, plucked pieces of popcorn out of her auburn beehive.

"You should feel lucky," Lilah said glumly as each piece was sucked out of the car window. "This means that Tommy likes you."

"I don't feel lucky." Jo frowned. "I just feel…sticky."

Both girls burst out laughing. Lilah threw out the last piece of popcorn before she started to close the window.

"Lilah May, you know better than to roll up a window on a July evening!" Angie scolded her daughter from the driver's seat. "Wind that thing down!"

"Yes, Mom." Lilah rolled her eyes as she did as she was told.

"My gosh, look at that sky," Angie remarked. "I'm afraid it's going to be dark by the time we get you home, Jo."

"That's okay, Aunt Angie." Jo smiled.

"I was hoping to get you back before…" Angie said, suddenly lost in thought.

"Is something wrong, Mom?" Lilah leaned forward and put a hand on her mother's seat.

"Someone in the neighborhood was attacked earlier this evening," Angie told them.

"No!"

"Mrs. Wilson," Angie nodded. "She got bitten."

"Was it a stray dog or—"

"Oh, this was no animal," her mother cut her off. "This was a person.

Maniac bit right into her. Word is that he smiled at her while he chewed the bite he took out of her."

"Oh my god: that's horrifying!"

"It's this damn moon landing business. It's got to be." Angie shook her head. "It's got all the crazies coming out of hiding."

"Do they know who did it?" Jo asked her auntie.

"I think it's one of those goddamn hippies," she replied heatedly. "This is exactly the kind of trouble I've come to expect from them."

"Mom, you blame everything on the hippies." Lilah giggled dismissively. "Ha! The hippies and their 'witchy' lifestyle."

"*In other news, an update on this week's grisly discovery, the human remains of an as-of-yet unidentified adult female were found in the early hours of the morning. At first thought to be the result of an unfortunate animal attack, the victim's injuries suggest a much more sinister explanation for the condition of the body. An expert in the occult brought in to consult with law enforcement has concluded that the strange markings that were left on the body were, in fact, ancient moon symbols, and even went as far to say that what they were dealing with was the result of some form of human sacrifice—*"

"Oh! That's enough of that!" Fiona shivered as she snapped off her radio.

How did the time get away from her? she wondered at the sudden realization that it was already dark outside.

"I'm on my way home from the movies now," her daughter Jo had said on the phone earlier.

"Well, you hurry straight home, or you're going to make us both late for the Stetsons' moon landing watch party," Fiona had reminded her. But that must have been an hour ago.

Grabbing the clothes basket from the kitchen counter, she could just make out the white of her bedsheets as they hung there in the yard, watching her move through the house like lonely ghosts.

Making her way to the back door, she flipped the switch for the patio lights to turn on but stopped when nothing happened.

She tried the switch again.

Still nothing.

And again.

Still no light. Only darkness.

Dropping the empty basket to the floor, Fiona unlocked the back door and slowly pushed it ajar as she leaned her head out to take a look. But she could barely make out the light fixture as it sat twelve feet above the yard at the far corner of the house.

Pulling the back door shut, she retrieved a flashlight from the nearest drawer and fumbled at the finger-worn buttons until the beam blinked on.

Outside, the yard was darker than she realized. She could feel it cover her with its heavy curtain. Raising the flashlight, she followed the stone garden path to the corner.

Fiona glanced around the side of the house to the street.

All seemed to be well.

She squinted up at the patio light socket in confusion, taking a step closer to be certain of what she was seeing.

The bulb was missing.

Maybe it fell out?

Moving the beam back and forth like a spotlight, she searched the path for its shattered remains only to find no traces of broken glass.

Someone must have removed it.

Fiona turned as she caught a glimpse of something moving past the front of the house. Probably just a neighbor walking their dog. Dismissing what she had seen, she returned to the kitchen and snatched a set of keys from the wall. Patience dwindling, she wrestled the padlock to the garden shed open and marched inside.

The wall rack was a shrine of long forgotten holiday memories, from ice-skates to rollerblades, from bicycles to paddling oars. Fiona gritted her teeth as she tried not to think about the tiny creatures crawling across the ceiling, falling into her hair and running up and down her clothes. She eventually happened upon the drawer of replacement bulbs. But after she fought it open, she found only empty boxes.

"Of course," she sighed.

Composing herself, she locked up the shed, left the flashlight on the kitchen table, and stepped back out into the yard with the basket underarm.

Placing the washing at her feet, she set about unpegging the first of the sheets. As she reached blindly, she knocked the peg bag from its hook. She heard it land upon the grass somewhere to the side of her. Scolding herself, she crouched down and searched the ground with her fingers, collecting peg after peg as she went.

Rising to her feet with as many as she could find, she fitted the peg bag back onto the line when she heard the sound. Something was softly scraping the stone of the garden path. The noise was so slight that she ignored it at first. But as she heard it again and again, she finally turned to take a look.

Fiona choked back a gasp as she found someone standing by the side of the house.

Clasping a hand over her own mouth, she backed away into the clothesline, allowing the sheets to fall over and around her, hiding her from sight.

She tried not to move.

She tried not to breathe.

Trapped between the narrow textile walls of that cold, dark prison cell, all she could do was listen to the creeping footsteps of the intruder as they moved slowly along the garden path. Keeping her hands up and away from touching the sheets that hung in front of her, she sidestepped as quietly as she could until she felt the night air on her skin.

Holding her breath, she looked towards the house.

What she saw was not a man, but the absence of light in the shape of one. She watched him as he lurked in the window of the back door, peering into her kitchen, long fingers caressing the glass as he searched for her.

She felt a sudden chill as she heard him turning the door handle.

Panting heavily, she backed away into her hiding place and closed her eyes tightly as she could not bring herself to watch him enter her home. Swallowing tears, she covered her ears when she heard the low creak of the back door as he pulled it open. But then she surrendered to the need to listen to the dull squeal of metal as he released his grip on the handle.

And then nothing?

No more sounds?

Why couldn't she hear anything?

Gathering herself, Fiona gave in to her curiosity and chanced another look out from inside the clothesline.

The man was nowhere to be seen.

But the back door was hanging wide open.

All she had to do was sneak a few yards to the side of the house and escape to safety.

Fiona closed her eyes and whispered a prayer as she prepared herself to go, but before she could finish—

Her daughter Jo's voice called out from inside the house. "Hi, Mom! I'm home!"

"Jo, no!"

Fiona tore the sheets aside and made a run for the back door, stopping in her tracks when she realized the radio had been moved to the kitchen table. Suddenly, a hand grabbed her by the soft flesh of her throat and ripped her flailing body back into the clothesline.

Jo's attention was fixed firmly on the movie flyer between her hands as she entered the kitchen. She leaned against the doorframe as the radio blared away.

"For those of you just tuning in, the show's hot topic is the moon landing. And our next guest joins us tonight by telephone, professor and teacher, Dr. Patrick O'Brian."

"Good evening, Tom. Thanks for having me."

"You're welcome! Now, Dr. O'Brian, in the spirit of the main event, can you give our listeners any strange facts about the moon that they may not know?"

"Well, I hate to disappoint any of you out there, but unfortunately, the moon is actually not made out of cheese."

"Oh, gosh darn it! Do ya hear that folks? Looks like we'll have to have our brie imported from elsewhere!"

Unimpressed, the teenager snapped off their ridiculous chatter.

"Mom?" she looked up.

Jo paused when she found the door to the backyard lying wide open.

She approached slowly, trying the patio light switch. It didn't work.

"I know you're out there, so if you're trying to scare me, it's not gonna work." She tried the light again, but it was no use. "You forgot to hide the basket, Mom. Game over."

No stephonse.

Rolling her eyes, Jo tossed the flyer onto the empty table and glanced down the length of the kitchen, her eyes searching for food. But a creak from the clothesline snapped her gaze back to the yard.

With the sound of a *CLICK!* a bright light appeared, illuminating the bedsheet before her like a shadow puppet show. The shape of her mother's figure stood there, unmoving.

"Okay… I see you now…" Jo leaned her head through the back door. "So just quit it, okay, Mom?"

But her mother gave no reply as she stood behind the sheet, perfectly still, arms dangling limp on either side.

"Mom?" Jo uttered again. "Answer me, or I'm gonna lock you out."

"Don't do that, Joanna," a man's voice whispered.

The shadow of a third arm emerged from her mother's side as a hand reached for the edge of the sheet.

"I've been waiting for you all night," the voice told her as long fingers curled around into view.

"Mom…"

A blood-curdling scream pierced the dark as something burst from the clothesline and bounded towards the house. Jo slammed the back door and locked it. Huge palms smashed against the glass, startling her backward.

She bolted in the other direction, knocking aside everything in her path as she went. Fighting the porch lock open, she leapt out onto the front stoop.

There was a tall man waiting for her at the corner of the house, leering at her with wild eyes. Jo spied the blood first, still spreading down his shirt. Then she saw the smile: those big, dripping red teeth glistening in the shadows.

He charged.

She lunged back the way she came, slamming the front door so hard that it bounced off the frame before Jo could lock it up tight. As she backed away into the house, it dawned on her how ordinary the man on the other side of the door appeared to her. In his plain shirt and trouser pants, he could be a schoolteacher, or someone's father returning home late from work for the hundredth time. He could be anyone. He looked so normal.

A face that you could easily lose in a crowd.

Except for that look in his eyes.

And the blood…

Her mother's?

The very thought stalled her heart.

She cried out as the mail slot choked open.

"Have you seen the moon tonight, Joanna?" the voice from the clothesline said to her. "It's really pretty."

"What did you do with my mom?" she demanded with trembling words.

She saw the outline of the man pressed up against the front door as he pushed a fingertip against the glass and slowly dragged it down the surface, leaving a bloody mark in the shape of the moon in waxing crescent phase. She winced at the squeal of his milky flesh on the window.

"What did you do to her?" she yelled out to him.

"Let me in…and I'll show you…"

Jo screamed as a skewer half the length of a man's arm punched its way through the mail slot. Its razor tip stabbed the empty air as it twisted left and right, searching for innocent skin.

"Go away," the girl whimpered.

"Oh, Joanna, Joanna, Joanna," the voice sighed. "I'm not going anywhere."

"Why not?"

"Silly girl," the man laughed. "I've already been inside your house once tonight. That's how I know your name."

The warmth drained from Jo's face.

"Can you guess if I also found out where you keep the keys?"

Suddenly, the skewer retracted, slamming the letterbox shut. A thick drop of blood was left in its place as it slid down the door.

The lock below the handle made a few clicks, then started to turn.

Gasping, Jo headed for the stairs and raced up to the landing. Hearing the front door open below, she held her breath as she followed the wall into the nearest bedroom. Her mother's room.

Grabbing the rotary phone from the bedside cabinet, she frantically dialed for help.

She checked the bedroom door.

Someone answered.

"I need the police," she whispered desperately into the mouthpiece. "Please hurry."

She checked the door again.

"My mother and I are being attacked," Jo continued when the dispatch officer came on the line. She struggled to keep her voice down. "Please send someone to 116 Delgaty Road right away. And please hurry. He's going to kill me—"

The phone hit the floor as long fingers wrapped around her throat. Snatching her off her feet, the tall man forced Jo around until they were face to face. She screamed in pain as the skewer scored across her left cheek to her right brow, just missing her eye.

They toppled onto the bed where he pinned Jo down, dragging the tip of the skewer in a zig-zag over her forehead. She shrieked through gritted teeth as her face ran thick with blood. The tall man chuckled madly with excitement, bucking and bouncing atop her as he lapped at her wound with his huge, pointed tongue.

Groaning with disgust, she clenched her fists as he licked her nostrils, her eyelids, and earholes. Just then, out of the corner of her eye, she caught the gleam of the skewer in his hand as the tall man set his sights on her jugular. With a roar, her hand broke free and punched the weapon out of his grip. She heard it hit the bedroom wall with a *CLANG!*

"You delicious little girls," the man rasped. "The moon belongs to me. Do you hear me? The moon is mine, and you can't have it! But don't worry your pretty head. I'll let you have one last look at it before I consume you."

The tall man's jaws latched onto Jo's cheek. She howled in agony as she helplessly beat at his arms and chest. She screamed louder as his teeth dug deeper. Finally, he released her face as he let out a yelp of his own.

Her attacker tumbled to the floor with the skewer lodged in his back.

Fiona appeared by the bed, her face streaked with the blood and one of the paddling oars she'd brought with her from the garden shed waiting for her by the wall.

"Don't worry, baby, I'm here now," she said soothingly as she caressed her daughter's head.

Taking hold of the paddle, she whacked the tall man across the face as he crouched on the carpet like a spider, trying to remove the skewer.

"Now, *you!*" she growled as she kicked him towards the door. "Get the *hell* out of my house! Or I swear to God *I will kill you!*"

Shaking and sobbing, Jo lifted herself off the bed, making it to the landing just in time to watch her mother send the tall man rolling down the stairs with a hard blow to the chin.

At the bottom, he ripped the skewer out of his back and aimed its razor tip at her, smiling as he began to climb back up the steps towards her.

"The moon is *mine...*" he hissed.

But then, the sound of sirens.

The tall man's smile disappeared. He turned and headed for the kitchen, making his escape through the back door.

Mother and daughter held each other as they sat at the top of the stairs, waiting for help to arrive.

In the early hours of the morning, Fiona carried a mug of hot chocolate into her daughter's room where Jo was already sitting up in bed waiting, bandaged and exhausted.

"How are you feeling, baby?" her mother asked her as she handed her the mug.

"I don't know…" Jo shrugged. "I'm not sure what I feel. Sore. Mostly."

"The drugs the nurse gave you should kick in any minute now." Fiona wandered over to the window and stood there silently gazing up into the sky.

"Sorry you didn't get to watch the moon landing," said Jo. After a long, calming sip, a look of concern stung her aching face as her mother failed to respond. "Mom? Are you okay?"

"It's just crazy to think that this happened to us all because of that tiny little thing in the sky," her mother said as she pointed up at the moon.

Fiona put an arm around Jo's shoulder as her daughter came to join her at the window.

"This wasn't exactly the watch party we had in mind, was it?" Fiona sighed.

Jo laughed as her vision wandered along the backyards of their neighbors until her eyes halted at one in particular. "Mom…?" she could barely speak.

"What is it, baby?"

"Aunt Angie's back door is open," her daughter replied, her stomach sinking.

Within the hour, police were entering the residence, guns at the ready. In the house's kitchen, a huge stockpot sat on the stove, its contents furiously bubbling over as it filled the room with thick clouds of steam.

"Turn that thing off!" the first officer ordered his subordinate.

"Yes, sir!" The second officer holstered his weapon and approached the burner. He twisted the cooking dial and then peered into the open pot.

"Holy Christ!" he cried out in shock. "Sir, I think there's someone's leg in here!"

They found the tall man in the living room, sitting on the sofa, the distorted image of a spaceman walking slowly across a desolate moonscape on the bulbous television screen in front of him.

"Put your hands in the air!" the first officer bellowed.

The tall man raised a finger to his lips and hushed him. "Show some respect," he said as he sat between what remained of Angie and her daughter Lilah May. He grinned, flashing the policemen his big, white teeth flecked with bone and sinew. "We're watching history in the making here."

A child of shameless slasher sequels and Richard Laymon novels, **L. Stephenson** is a queer horror cheese maniac. Since graduating university with a degree in Film & TV Screenwriting, L's work has been published in a handful of anthologies and a couple of magazines, the highlights of which you can find in the mini-collection *Candles, Bullets, & Dead Skin*. In 2021, he published his first novella, *The Goners*, and this year, he releases his debut slasher novel, *The Boatmore Butcher*.

ALL EARS
BY CLAY MCLEOD CHAPMAN

Dad didn't come home an addict. He just came home *hungry*. You'd think he hadn't eaten through his whole tour, a living skeleton decorated in medals, all gaunt and haunted. The veins lacing his bones looked like baker's twine bound around a box of butter cookies. His eyes sunk back into the foxholes of their sockets. When he looked at you—looked at me, his own flesh and blood—his eyes never seemed to settle, focusing instead on some far-off spot that felt inside and outside of space all at once, there but not there, somewhere in between.

That wasn't my father. He was still over there—parts of him, at least.

I wanted all of my dad back.

None of the other kids in the building had an enlisted father. I used to recite his tour of duty to just about everybody on our floor—*My dad is fighting for our country, Private 1ˢᵗ Class Marshal Dennison, 2ⁿᵈ Squadron, 9th Cavalry Regiment, 3ʳᵈ Infantry Division, Pleiku, Ban Me Thout, Kontum, Republic of South Vietnam*—all of it spilling out from me in one overflowing run-on sentence, never breathing between words. I'd be lightheaded once I finished this giddy litany, downright dizzy with pride, gasping for air only after I had reached the end.

Daddy's little soldier, the blue-haired biddies all called me, ruffling my hair with their hands and slipping me a butterscotch wrapped in cellophane. *Your father must be so proud…*

Sure, I wanted to serve my country, but most of all, I just wanted to serve my dad. Damn right I'd been ready to enlist right alongside him, following in my father's footsteps with my plastic rifle pressed firmly against my chest. All the way to Quang Ngai. All six years of myself.

He was gone for thirteen months. When he left in May of '68, he was only twenty-nine, but when he came back in the summer of '69, he looked like he'd just turned eighty. His old job at the Domino Sugar Factory was waiting for him when he returned home, just over the East River in Williamsburg, but he lost his spot on the processing line within the first month, simply staring off at nothing all day. That same empty space only he could see inside. Wherever it was.

Turns out he wasn't looking into space.

He was *listening* to it.

I can understand why Mom would believe he was hooked. It was everywhere. On our own street corner. I grew up in the Lower East Side. The real lower east. There's the lower east and then there's the lower-*lower* east. I'm not talking south of Houston Street here, I'm talking all the way below Delancey, where the Williamsburg Bridge barricades us in just next to the East River. The tenth circle of Hell. Nobody goes down this far unless they're looking to score.

This was my home.

My family lived within the Amalgamated. Our apartment building was one of four beehives on the north side of Grand Street. Over 237 units all told. Built back in 1929, these pre-war projects were supposedly inspired by the architecture from Vienna. Crumbling art deco, that's all. The fountain in the center of the courtyard garden hadn't spat fresh water in years. Not since I was born, at least. Nothing but sludge comes chugging out of the spigot anymore, spackled in pigeon shit. Chinatown and Little Italy were just a stone's throw away, but our building was Little Everything. There were a whole lot of Hispanics. Lot of Blacks. Lot of Polacks. Some Hasidic. South Asian. All kinds called the Amalgamated home. I remember I could hear all the different languages from around the world seeping out from each apartment. Walking through the halls was like drifting over the globe, passing through each country at every door.

All those voices. Just drifting. Imagine hearing them all at once in your head, what that might feel like. The absolute cacophony of it all, worse than the 5 Train during rush hour.

Mom put together a shindig to welcome Dad home, even though he'd been back for a month. A real bash. He didn't want it, I could just tell, but it gave Mom something to focus her nervous energy on. Distract herself. She decorated our cramped apartment, turning it into a whole ballroom with crepe paper streamers hanging off the walls. A brick of frozen fruit punch sat in a glass bowl Mom only brought out on holidays. The punch had chunks of pineapple and cherries embedded within it, melting into this alcoholic soup. She invited all our friends. Some neighbors. The ones who spoke English, at least. Practically the whole apartment building came to pay their respects to my dad, tell him thanks for his service. Felt like a funeral to me.

Voices filled up our living room. It was hard to pick up their conversations. Adult talk. Stuff like the garbage strike. *That asshole John Lindsay.* I couldn't see anybody's face, there were so many folks crammed into our apartment, all these people milling about, shoulder-to-shoulder, creating this dense brush of bamboo slacks that I could maneuver through on the floor, crawling across our shag carpet on my elbows. I had my plastic rifle with me. Locked and loaded. I was behind enemy lines on a rescue mission to find my father. Bring him home.

I found him sitting in the corner of the room. He had an empty glass in his hand. Staring at the wall. At the streamers. There was a window open, so the humid wind sent those strips of crepe paper billowing in the breeze. I crept up to him, keeping my head low. When Dad spotted me at his feet, there was a flicker of a grin. His thin lips peeled back. All those teeth. Landmines.

Whatcha up to, soldier?

I'm not sure why, but I brought my rifle up to him and fired, making shooting noises with my mouth—*kapow, kapow*. Dad clutched his chest. *Bullseye.* He brought his fingers up and fashioned them into a pistol, firing right back. Then his focus drifted back to the crepe paper.

All those intestines, he said. I think he said. *How'd they get in the trees?*

Honorable discharge got knocked around a lot, even though I didn't know what the heck that meant. When I heard he came home with a purple heart, I didn't understand that either. What's with everyone going on about the color of my father's ticker? Folks kept asking to see it and all I could imagine was him digging his fingers into his chest and with both hands cracking his own ribcage back, until everybody could finally see that purple muscle pounding away.

Dad kept his medals in a velvet-trimmed box that remained on the mantle. He'd pop it open only if Mom insisted he show it to our guests— *Show them your purple heart, hon*—and there it would be, this medallion Dad never seemed to want to touch, like it burned his skin.

Blessed, the old biddies from the building always said. *We're blessed to have him back.*

Alive and in once piece.

But Dad rattled around inside. Everyone sensed it, even if they never talked in the open about it. Nobody ever mentioned this sort of stuff. Not around me. I'd hear Mom whisper to her friends on the telephone. Distant voices that silenced themselves the second I stepped into the kitchen. She'd cut herself off mid-sentence, the conversation halting as if the line went dead. She'd have the telephone cord coiled around her fingers, twining her fist in the curled cable so tightly, her knuckles looked like they were about to pop. All I saw was barb wire.

Have you seen Daddy taking any medicine when Mommy's not around? Mom asked. She told me what to keep an eye out for. The pin pricks scabbing between his toe joints. The beads of blood. She wanted me to spy on my own father, but I was no narc. Even at seven I knew that *snitches get stitches*. That's what the older kids from the building always said whenever I stumbled upon them spray-painting the fountain. That's just the law here in the Amalgamated.

I wasn't about to rat out my father.

Dad didn't talk like he used to, didn't look at me the way he used to, before he left. Always before. That phrase got thrown around a lot now. *Always before* this, *always before* that. I had a hazy memory of this giant before Dad went to war. I was only four, but I swear I held on to this vision of him. Green fatigues. A square jaw. Dimpled chin. An honest-to-god G.I. Joe doll. Mom used to tease me by telling her friends I believed my father was an action figure.

He was. My father was a hero. Why was everyone pretending like he was okay?

Couldn't they see he was hurting?

I'd seen his shakes. The tremble in his wrist at the dinner table. Whenever he'd pick up his glass, the water sloshed. His meal went uneaten. I never saw him pick up his silverware.

Look for his works, Mom whispered. *We're missing too many spoons.* She thought he had a heroin habit. Most soldiers dealt with addiction coming back. She didn't know any better.

None of us did. Not yet.

During the summer, when all the kids played in the center courtyard, you could hear different voices rebounding out from the open windows surrounding us. Different music. I remember hearing Otis Redding. Aretha Franklin. Creedence. But then you'd get these other songs from countries playing along as well, ballads from across the ocean. Music that made no sense to me—my ears, at least—but it added to this pleasant morass in the center courtyard.

Only our apartment kept quiet. Before he left, always before, Dad used to love playing The Ronettes on the Hi-Fi. He'd grab Mom as she'd wandered by, reel her in like the two of them were a pair of ballroom dancers, cutting a rug in our living room. He'd serenade her with the song and she'd tolerate it all, smiling as he dipped her, her head nearly touching the floor.

Not anymore. Whenever Mom reached for the stereo now, Dad simply hissed at her to shut it off, rubbing at his temples like he was kneading a migraine out from his skull. His skin was too tight. It was bound to split at any moment.

Whenever I came back from the courtyard, Mom would ask me to keep it down. For Dad. *Your father's just resting right now, hon,* she'd say. *Why don't you go back out and play?*

That meant back to the courtyard. We were lucky, I guess, living in the Amalgamated. Those four buildings created a barricade for us kids to run around. Reminded me of one of those old Jamestown forts we learned about in history. Each apartment complex served as its own watchtower. None of us kids spoke the same language but that was okay. We didn't have to talk. All we wanted to do was kick around a soccer ball or try to scare off the pigeons from the fountain. We never had to leave our own private enshrinement, fortified behind these projects. It was the piss-ridden city outside you had to worry over. We were safe inside here.

Then kids started to go missing.

There had been a garbage strike all summer long. This pile of trash bags had been gradually growing outside our building for over a couple of months by then, swallowing the block. I overheard the older kids all calling it *Mount Shitpile*, which I repeated at the dinner table one night and got a smack across the back of my head from my mother. The trash was drawing in the rats like you wouldn't believe. You could hear the garbage bags shift and skitter and you just knew they were in there, those rodents squirming around inside, chewing their way through their own gnawed tunnels. If you poked a garbage bag with your heel, you'd send a whole swarm of rats scattering across your feet. Us kids loved to do that. Talk about a gas.

The heat elevated the stink. I could smell it all the way up on the sixth floor, baking the garbage right on the sidewalk. A concrete skillet frying up the melon rinds and dirty diapers.

They found a boy's body buried within a mound of black garbage bags. His corpse was somewhere in the center of the heap, like a preserved caveman—cave boy?—this prehistoric child from apartment 4B preserved in the permafrost, only starting to thaw out and decay in the sweltering August heat. Mom wouldn't let me go anywhere near those bags after that. She didn't want to fill my head with all this nightmare talk, so she'd shush down whenever I entered the kitchen. The only juicy bit of gossip I picked up when Mom wrapped herself up in the barb wire of our telephone was that the boy had been missing his ears. Both of them. Sliced right off.

Dad didn't say much of anything. He just kept quiet.

One night I woke up and swore I felt a rat crawl over my leg under my blanket. They were gathering outside in Mount Shitpile, ready to lay siege on our building.

Dad was standing before my bed. *They're feeding on you too,* he said.

He leaned forward, staring me down, until I felt the weight of his eyes pressing against me. *You know what they like to eat the most? The soft spots. The cartilage. The ears. They always start on the ears…*

Then he turned back around and left.

You couldn't pry a word out of him. Whatever happened over there was locked in his mind, inside a steel box packed far away from polite conversation. He never talked about it. He'd simply sit by the window, staring out at the courtyard below. To the kids kicking around down there. Listening to them laugh as they circled the fountain, scaring the pigeons away.

Before he left, always before, Dad read to me. I'd nestle against his chest, the picture book shielding our faces, his breath caught between the pages. He smelled of coffee then. Now that he was back, he'd tried putting me to bed a few times, reading to me, but he just couldn't focus on the words anymore. *The sentences don't make sense*, he said. He'd stare at the page, drifting off to some spot beyond the paper, almost as if he were traveling through the pulp itself.

Never sleep, he said so suddenly, I didn't realize at first that he was speaking to me. *Always got to keep one eye open. If you don't, you'll wake up to the rats gnawing on your ears.*

He was shivering, even though we were lost in the dog days of summer. The rest of us sweated away on the sixth floor, suffocating up top, with nothing but open windows and piddly electric fans to cool us down, but here's Dad, loose teeth chattering like it's the dead of winter.

Can you keep a secret?

How could I say no?

I want to show you something, but you can't tell your mother. You can't tell anyone. Promise?

I promise, I said, so proud that I was suddenly being brought into the fold.

He pulled out a tin box from his jeans. Its hinge was rusted. The lid was embossed in blue: *Edgeworth. Extra high grade sliced pipe tobacco. Larus & Bros. Co. Richmond, VA. U.S.A.*

This is it, I thought. This is what my mother was telling me to keep an eye on. I was supposed to be on the lookout for hypodermic needles. Rubber tubes. Pills or wisps of powder.

But this was none of that. This was different.

This was worse.

First, there were coins. Foreign. None of them look familiar to me. He tilted the tin to one side so the coins slid directly into his palm. They even sounded differently than nickels. They didn't clink like American coins. The metal was somehow softer in my mind.

Dad was talking while he emptied the tin, one artifact at a time. *We were told to shoot at anything that moved. Didn't matter who. Soldiers. Civilians. Nobody could tell the difference.*

He pulled out these slips of paper. Currency left over from overseas. They had pictures of people I don't know. Presidents, maybe? It was hard to tell.

We wiped out entire villages, he kept going, talking to me but not talking to me. *We were so jacked up, it just didn't matter anymore. Hearing their voices. Begging. Screaming.*

Then I saw the cotton. I spotted a wad of gauze, folded neatly together. Dad carefully unfolded it, layer by layer. By the third layer, I started to see a brown rust seep through. Flakes.

You never stop hearing them, he said. *They're always in my head.*

It was an ear.

A human ear. The skin had gone all grey, a crust of dried blood still caked to it. I swear I saw the ridges and curls of the lobe start to spiral, as if the flesh had melted into taffy and was now coiling down the drain of the ear's own canal, twisting off into darkness.

He told me he used to have more before. A lot more. A whole necklace's worth.

He showed me a picture. It was folded in half at the very bottom of the tin. He carefully opened the black and white photograph of himself and his squadron, as if it were a Christmas card. I had to squint to make out their beaming faces and figure out which one was my father.

He'd earned those ears, he said.

Those were confirmed kills, son. Every last one… It was a tally. To keep your numbers straight. He couldn't bring them all back home. He could only save one—*My first,* he said—wrapped in gauze, tucked into his tin and stowed away where no one would be able to find it.

You ever eat a candy necklace before? That's all it was.

Yeah, I had a candy necklace once. For Halloween, we all trick-or-treated within the Amalgamated. We didn't even need to leave the building. I got one of those candy necklaces from the old lady in 3G. She had primo treats. The elastic band stretched as I slipped the necklace over my head, its strap snapping around my throat. The beads pressed so tightly against my neck, they left indentations in my skin, these spoke-like impressions, a grin of gritted teeth. I'd tug on the band and bring a bead up to my mouth, slip it past my lips and crunch. Tasted like Smarties, maybe a little less powdery, but still the same texture, same flavor.

Look at your old man, he said, eyes on the photo. *Just look at them all. I had the most.*

I didn't understand. I didn't know if I wanted to understand, but I knew my father was trying to explain something important to me. Something he'd been bottling up ever since he'd come home. This may have been the first time he was opening up to anyone about any of this. I wanted to do right by him—help him—so I listened, straining my ears as hard as I could to try and decipher the words and what they meant to the best of my seven-year-old knowledge.

He brought the ear up. Blew into it, as if blowing off some dust. Testing it like a microphone to see if it still worked. Then he lifted the ear up to his own, straining to hear.

I swear, from the way his expression shifted, it looked as if he heard something.

Wanna listen?

I nodded, afraid to say no. This was the most he'd said to me in days. Weeks. There was a yearning in his eyes, a clarity that hadn't been there before. He needed this. Needed me.

He brought the ear up to my own. I don't think I touched it, but the proximity to the shriveled husk of skin sent a dull current of electricity through the rest of my body. A pulse.

You hear that? Can you? What's it sound like?

The ocean, I said. Swallowed. *I can hear the waves.*

Dad shook his head. *No,* he said, deflated. *That's not right... That's not it at all.*

I had let him down. Failed him.

All because I couldn't hear.

You gotta be all ears, boy, he eventually said. *So that you'll hear.*

When word got out about another missing kid from the building, apartment 2F, I knew who'd done it. The police were going floor-to-floor, knocking door-to-door, interviewing tenants. They scribbled apartment numbers down in their notepads for those folks who didn't answer their door, which were usually the families who didn't speak English, who didn't want nothing to do with the police, so I knew it was best to just get it over with and play along.

I'd seen that boy in the courtyard. He was Polish. We'd play every now and then, even if there wasn't a word we could share between us. Mostly we'd just toss a ball. Do dumb stuff like try to lure a rat out of the sewer grate and see if we could trap it. Last time I saw him was two days before he disappeared. I remember because it was laundry day for most of the building. There was a web of clotheslines suspended over the courtyard. I'd feel this drip of water on the back of my neck, like it was beginning to drizzle, from the wet clothes hanging over our heads.

We had a washer-no-dryer in the basement. That's what we called it—*washer-no-dryer*—as if that's the full name. Kids were told not to go down in the basement, but we did.

Dad shook me awake in the middle of the night, dragging me out from my sleep. For a split second there, I swear his fingers felt like rats nibbling their way into my shoulders.

Wake up, son. I'd never seen him in such a panic before. *Please, I need you—*

Dad asked if I could help him. He was in a real bad way by then. He couldn't do this on his own anymore. He needed a steady hand, he said. I needed to do the slicing for him. His wrists just weren't steady enough. His hand kept shaking whenever he picked up the knife.

I waited too long, he minced his words, jaw-joint clicking, wrists trembling so much. *Too many voices in my head…*

I'm not proud to admit it, but I found myself getting jealous, just thinking of my dad asking that Polack to play, the envy of his attention rising up within me.

I just wanted my dad back. Whatever could return the rest of him home was worth it, I figured. If this was the help my father needed, and I was the only one he trusted to do it, then I'd do it. For my father, I'd do it. I'd do anything.

All I had to do was cut off his ears. Dad would handle the rest.

He came home with his K-bar knife, serrated teeth running down the back of the blade. He taught me how to slice, talking me through every step. Where to pinch the lobe. How to saw down, curving the serrated edge inward by just a fraction so the blade didn't slip and slice out. He told me he imagined a Thanksgiving turkey the first time he did this and suggested I should do the same, but the way he said it made me wonder what he thought he was trimming now.

I've never seen my father happier than the moment after he swallowed. The absolute bliss of it all. He was at peace. He was whole. I could see the muscles in his throat take the plunge, working the mouthful down, delivering their payload and from there…he simply drifted. My father was someplace else now. Somewhere warm. Where he could be all ears.

Thank you, son. He clumsily ran his hand across my right cheek, fingers like sandpaper scraping my skin. His eyelids were at half mast, this fish-lipped grin on his face. *Thank you…*

He started talking, but it felt like he wasn't speaking to me, even if I was the only one there. The words oozed out from his mouth, a thin trickle of his voice dribbling down his lips.

Most soldiers only sliced off one, he said, *which is bullshit if you ask me. You need both. One to eat, the other to keep. Keeps the line of communication open. You listen with one, talk through the other. Ever play telephone with a tin can? Same thing. Same basic principle. Send and receive. Transmit, pick up. In order to do that, you got to be all ears. You hear me, son?*

Laundry day was unofficially, not really but still kinda designated by what country you came from. The Asians did theirs on Tuesday. Poles on Wednesday. That sort of thing.

The baby was in the basement. So was his mother. She was doing her laundry while the baby was in one of those—I don't know what they're called—plastic rolly-chairs. It had a saddle in the center, like a diaper wrapped in a plastic donut. There were wheels at the feet, so the toddler stayed perched upright on their own tippy-toes. Helps teach them how to walk, I guess.

The baby was just rolling all on his own.

I could hear his mother humming some song as she was filling up the washer-no-dryer. She was so focused on stuffing the machine full of their linens, she wasn't paying attention to her child rolling away. I held up my shoe and the roller stopped when it hit my toe. I could hear his mother humming from further off, her song filling up the whole basement, even as I ran.

All Dad ate were their ears.

I thought the police might take it easier on him if they knew that. You know, be more lenient or whatever. It wasn't like he ate all of them. It was just this one part. Just the ears.

So he could hear.

They found the baby's body a lot faster than the last boy. Apartment 5K. The police just had to follow the rats. Wherever the rodents were at their worst, a knot of tails, the garbage bags boiling over with frantic activity, well…that's where they knew to look.

Dad woke me up that night. He waited until Mom was asleep. I could tell something was wrong—or more wrong. Even wronger. He sat at the edge of my bed, covered in sweat. When I sat up, he brought his arms around me and squeezed. Squeezed so hard I couldn't breathe.

You can always talk to me. Just call. I'll be here whenever you need me, I promise.

It wasn't sweat. It was blood.

They found him in the basement, leaning against the washer-no-dryer.

K-Bar in one hand, a note in the other. Two slopes of flesh at either side of his skull, shirt soaked through.

We were now living in the Van Gogh Apartments, all on account of the missing ears. They finally cleared out all the garbage bags from our block, cleaning up the streets before October. Now the jump-ropers on the sidewalk skipped to the beat of their own song:

Don't go go go inside the Van Gogh-go-go
You never know-know-know
Where you'll go-go-go…

Good luck moving out of this place. Who could afford to leave? We couldn't. Where could we go? Mom and I were stuck, trapped in the Amalgamated. Our front door was always branded with some sort of graffiti. Spray-painted all over the walls. We stopped bothering to paint over it. The words just kept coming back, like weeds growing over our home. Like ivy.

SICKO. PSYCHO. CANNIBAL.

He was my father. I loved him, even when he came home hungry.

He just needed somebody to listen to him.

To understand.

I kept his tin. Tossed out the old ear and wrapped dad's in the gauze. His left one. Some nights, when I get lonely, I pull it out. Unravel dad's ear. I bring it up to my lips and blow, *testing, testing, one two three.* Like Dad said, you need both. One to eat, the other to keep.

You got to be all ears. So that you can hear.
Dad? Are you there? Can you hear me?

Clay McLeod Chapman writes books, comic books, children's books, and for film/TV. His most recent horror novels include *Ghost Eaters, Whisper Down the Lane,* and *The Remaking.* Please visit him at www.claymcleodchapman.com.

SEASONS OUT OF TIME
BY JEFFREY FORD

When he finally got arrested in 1979, Victor Giden was found in a room with a smoldering hibachi and three bodies in various stages of consumption—one, a young woman, Margery Sample, who was a neighbor on Victor's street. She was still alive when the police broke through the door. There were teeth marks in her flesh and long bloody slices taken off like strips of bacon. His condiments were garlic powder and rosemary flakes. He grilled while drinking a beer and paging through the latest issue of *People Magazine* with a bare-chested Telly Savalas on the cover. The "dinner guests" were tied to chairs with socks stuffed in their mouths. As they jerked and writhed in silence, the knife cutting into them, Victor was reminded of an ad for the recent film *Alien*, "In space, no one can hear you scream." It was his favorite movie that year, barely beating out his old beloved *Texas Chainsaw Massacre*. It was the god-like nature of the sleek Xenomorph that won the day.

Victor's face had no angles, pale and rubbery with jiggling jowls and a perpetually panicked look in the eyes. He always wore a smile—not a smart smile, nor a cynical one, forget friendly: a smile devoid of joy. Those who saw it wanted desperately to believe it was a *good* smile and went out of their way to delude themselves that there was simple kindness there. His receding dark hair was pitch black and, what was left of it, long and stringy. He carried a comb in his shirt pocket protector along with a red pen he used for writing in his journals. He stood 5.8 and slouch shouldered. He wore the waist of his seersucker pants pulled high up his pudgy body, fastening the belt only inches below his chest. His favorite shirt was a mint green Banlon number with three buttons at the top and a collar. He was a quiet person in public places, padding cautiously by in his black sneakers, head down, carrying his Evel Knievel lunch box containing two joints, a lighter, and a Payday candy bar.

Victor's murderous cuisine most likely would have been discovered sooner if he'd had to work. His father, Victor senior, now deceased, along with his wife, Joan, had left their only son a small fortune. The old man had all the contracts across the country, in nearly every hotel, for the printing of those paper banners that went around toilet seats and announced, **Sanitized for Your Protection**. His money would have run out soon enough if he'd not been arrested for the triple homicide (his neighbor, Margery Sample succumbed to her wounds—a lack of throat tissue). Those toilet banners, as they were called in the industry, didn't make it out of the 80s. There are almost no hotels or motels left that use them. So, his future business interests were less than auspicious, but at the time, still steady and fruitful enough for him to survive in his parents' old house on Argyle Lake in Babylon, New York and have enough money to sustain himself and his desires.

A lot of people who encountered Victor thought he was just a low wattage individual, but there was a shrewd brain working behind his pudgy exterior. Later, when he was serving multiple life sentences in Attica, he was given a battery of psychological tests, and although all the results were above average, he tested off the chart for organization and strategy. He was like a vicious fox hiding in the body of the Pillsbury Dough Boy. In his own testimony he acknowledged, "Upon the instant I was aware of wanting to eat human flesh, I began planning how I could make it happen." He admitted to being stuck in his scheming until the gas crisis hit in the latter months of '73. That afforded him an opportunity, seeing that some people were desperate to the point of delusion.

Victor confessed that, although his entire life to that point had surreptitiously been building toward it, he'd inevitably come to cannibalism one day at the Babylon 5 & 10. That morning, he'd smoked one of his three weekly Angel Dust-dipped joints. He'd been a pot smoker since his early teens when he'd discovered his mother's stash. Afterward, he'd contacted a local dealer and purchased it regularly through the years. It took the edge off his loneliness. He had no friends and few acquaintances. In '72, his dealer, one of the only people he conversed with on a regular basis, suggested he purchase a few "dippers." Jonah Banko, the dealer, cautioned him to only use the dust a couple times a week. "More than that and it'll turn you into more of a numb nut than you already are."

It was as the angels were returning Victor to earth after a dipper session that he went into town, looking for a candy bar, and entered the 5 & 10. On the checkout counter there was a display of mood rings stacked seven high in rows of six on a cardboard display the background of which was a dark blue sky full of stars. At that moment, all the rings were pink. And although it wasn't, he imagined it to be the same pink as the flesh of the young woman behind the counter. He told the psychs at Attica, "Creamy to eat, like eating a pudding with the outer casing of a hot dog so that it had just the subtlest snap to it." Stuttering slightly, he complimented the young saleswoman on a tattoo of a sea monster poking its head up out of her halter top and then fled, the candy bar left on the counter, all the mood rings gone black.

In the notebooks found after his arrest, he mulled the fact that he needed to get his victim into his house. Killing someone would not be easy, and he imagined what a racket one could make on the street if one's life were in mortal danger. A gun was out of the question. Everybody within a half mile would hear it and someone would send the cops. He knew he wasn't going to be able to lure them with his charm. Even people on the street who might say hello in passing never let the greeting fall into a conversation. Victor knew he had to find something that people wanted, needed, and were willing to drop their guard in the pursuit of. Something valuable. And then in the latter months of 1973, the U.S. supported the Israelis in the Yom Kippur War. The Arab backlash was an oil embargo against the West.

Over a period of weeks in the late autumn and early winter of '73, the papers and TV news were full of crazy stories about the lust for gas. Station attendants had taken to carrying guns. A few places had a security guard with a shotgun, sitting at the pumps all day and night. The number one fantasy people had at the time was a chance to kill a driver who'd cut ahead of them on a gas line, strangle them with bare hands. Fistfights broke out every morning at rush hour along the lines. There had been cases of prostitution, the participants trading in gallons instead of dollars. The gas crisis continued into '74, and the price rose from 35 cents a gallon in 1973 to a walloping 57 cents.

The old Giden place was situated on the Northwestern edge of Argyle Lake, at the junction of Trolley Line Road and Argyle Avenue. It was a hulking, brown Queen Anne, built in the early 1920s. There was a wrap-around porch, a turret room and a widow's walk. The oak shingles were splintering, falling off, and the roof was leaking in various places. Its interior elegance lay beneath two inches of dust and the rooms were crammed with all manner of junk Victor picked up off the street in his daily wanderings. The only neat space amid the maze of rooms in the old behemoth was the room on the second floor Victor had decked out as his Flesh Kitchen. Gleaming sets of butchering knives, bone scrapers, and cleavers, the hibachi of course, and a small set of speakers. Before ever luring his first victim, he knew the song he'd play when tasting flesh for the first time would have to be "Seasons in the Sun" by Terry Jacks. The 45 was cued up on a victrola Victor had gotten as a gift from his parents when he was ten.

Just a short walk down Trolley Line brought you to a gas station that was in operation until the early 80s. Victor often walked down there at night and watched the antics, studying with his fox mind what might be a good time to strike. Every night at 8 p.m., there was a near-brawl at the pumps as the attendants closed with at least a car or two not getting filled. Sometimes these people would have waited on the line since 6 o'clock and they were pissed. One night, he almost crossed Trolley Line to get closer to a young fellow who was left alone, his car out of gas, the station lights turned out. As Victor was stepping off the curb, a thought crossed his mind and he retreated.

The next day, he went to the dog pound and adopted an old black lab that was due to be euthanized. He brought it home and called it Jester. He took good care of it, and every night at 5 to 8, they walked down Trolley Line. It was his hope that the ease with which the old dog moved through the world would mask his own anxiety. To do what he needed to do, he would have to talk to people, and in some way, convince them he wasn't dangerous. So, they walked every night, sometimes even crossing the road and passing within mere feet of the last, shut out, drivers as they mumbled curses and yelled at the poor passengers in their cars. One night, a riled customer attacked one of the attendants, wrestled him to the ground and was choking him. The other attendant hit the assailant on the head with a squeegee, ripping his ear partially off and leaving a huge gash in his cheek. The sight of it made Victor hungry, but he knew the police would be there soon and so trundled away at top speed, having to nearly drag Jester.

Through the weeks of late summer, he surveilled the gas station and practiced different imagined dialogues with men and women desperate for gas. At the end of September, the final piece of the plan arrived in the mail, a new 12-volt, Hot Shot, Cattle Prod. It took weeks to arrive, and he laughed out loud when unwrapping it in the Flesh Kitchen. It was a ten-inch-long silver tube with a wooden handle and a pair of electrodes at the end. Along the side there was a yellow decal with the word *Hot Shot* in black letters that looked like they were speeding past. It came with eight batteries. He opened the prod and slid them in. Then he called to Jester, who was sleeping in the hall outside the Kitchen. "Tonight, we hunt," he said as the dog entered the room. It took one look at Victor's expression and fled back into the remote hallways of the house. "Coward," he called after and turned the Hot Shot on himself. The pain was a blast of hell. He fell out of his chair onto the floor, but after the pain subsided, Victor had tears in his eyes. He'd found the experience to be an emotional one.

In addition to his scrupulous planning and the cover of darkness, there was so much murder afoot in the country no one would blink at another missing unfortunate. By 1974, murders had doubled from previous years. Prostitutes were going missing off the streets in the city. And all around, as the passage of time revealed, it was the year of the serial killer. Ted Bundy, the BTK Killer, John Wayne Gacy, Coral Eugene Watts, and Paul John Knowles launched their grim careers. What with all the frustration and anger, the boiling violence at the pumps, you might expect a murder or two in the neighborhood. In fact, that autumn, Babylon saw a horrific murder, still unsolved. A dead man on the tracks just outside Babylon station. The body had been mauled by some animal, most likely a stray dog, which made it hard to gather forensic evidence.

That evening, having skipped dinner with the hope of a divine repast to come, Victor hooked Jester to the leash, and they went out into the light drizzle. They took their usual route up Trolley Line Road toward the gas station. Victor wore his regular getup (BanLon and chest in pants) but had thrown on a drab green raincoat and carried an umbrella. He topped off the outfit with a tattered Mets baseball hat he'd found cast away on top of one of the piles of junk in the room that used to be his parents'. He thought that final touch would make him seem a "regular guy." He'd considered bringing his father's pistol, but more than anything, he wanted his flesh to come from the living. "I'm not a vulture," he said proudly. There were few streetlights along that road, and this allowed him to relax somewhat. Any car that passed at a normal speed would never get a good look at his face.

As he and Jester approached the gas station, he could see there was a car parked at the pump and a woman with long blonde hair speaking to one of the attendants. This time, he didn't hesitate to cross the street. He loosened his grip on Jester's leash and let another yard or two play out. Instead of stopping, he strolled past the two at the pump, who seemed to be bickering. The attendant, Victor knew by sight: crew cut, big ears, a little dopey. The young woman, no more than twenty, dressed in a black mini-skirt, Ugg boots, and a zipped up, hip-length, rabbit fur jacket. The fact that she was wearing the fur of a dead creature gave him an adrenalin rush that swamped his fear. According to the missing person's report that appeared in the local paper a few days later, her car was a turquoise blue 1968 Chevy Impala. Victor noticed from the condition of the car that it was no doubt a hand-me-down from her father. From that small detail, he surmised she had been given everything her entire life. The thought made him smile.

"If I give you even a gallon of gas, I would be fired," said the attendant.

"Who would know?"

"Look, your plates are even numbered. Come back tomorrow and I can give you gas."

"I need it tonight," she said.

"Can't do it…" the attendant's voice melted behind Victor as he walked on two blocks toward the spot where the road went over one of the streams that fed Argyle Lake. There, he counted to a hundred, all the time worried he'd not make it back before the young woman took off in frustration. In his planning, he'd warned himself not to rush, not to arrive as the savior until things seemed at their bleakest for his victim. He breathed deeply, pirouetted, and started slowly back. When the gas station attendant passed him on the sidewalk riding a bike, Victor threw caution to the wind and broke into a medium trot. He drew even with the station and immediately spotted the young woman in the phone booth near the office. As quickly, he slowed his pace. He knew if she stayed on the phone, he would have to let her go and come back the next night. That was how things looked like they were going to turn out, until, with a sudden whoosh, the phone booth door opened, and she headed for her car.

He couldn't have planned the logistics more precisely; he was closest to her just as she reached her car door. He cleared his throat and said, "Forgive me, Miss, but I heard you arguing with the attendant a moment ago when I passed." She stopped while opening the door and turned. She nodded. "Yeah, that jackass wouldn't sell me four gallons of gas."

Victor shook his head and winced at the injustice of it all. "It's unAmerican," he said.

She laughed. "Well, not exactly treason, but it's up there."

Victor said, "Have a good night."

She waved to him and continued to get into her car, but before she could shut the door, he said, "I just thought of something. I have some extra gas in a can back at my place, just around the corner up here." He pointed behind him. "I live right down there. You can see the light on in the turret of my house."

The door didn't shut. "How many gallons would you say it is?"

"It's a five gallon can and it's full."

"Would you sell it to me?" she asked.

"Sure, but I'm going to charge you a little more than what these guys would have."

"No problem."

With that, Victor just stood there, not knowing what to do.

"Well," she said, "Do you want to get in and I'll drive us there?"

Without realizing what he was going to say, he opened his mouth, and the words came out of their own volition. "My dog's afraid of driving in cars. He'll claw up your upholstery and go nuts. We can walk there in two minutes. You can see the light in the turret room from here." He pointed down the street. She got out of the car and locked it. As she walked toward him, flipping her keys back and forth, she asked, "What's your dog's name?" She leaned over and petted the lab. Jester gave a low growl and Victor gave a tug on the leash.

"Jester," he said.

"What's your name?" she asked Victor.

"Anthony Blake."

"OK, Anthony, I don't have to worry about you, do I?" She stopped walking, waiting on his answer. He noticed her irises were a golden color. Light. Light hazel maybe?

"If I was in a book, they'd describe me as *avuncular*."

"What does that mean?"

"Like an uncle."

"Uncle Tony," she said and nodded. She proceeded forward and he was startled by the suddenness of her decision to trust him. He scrabbled out of his daze that had been brought on by the fact that his plan was happening.

"What's your name?" he asked.

"Michelle Ivy."

"And where do you need to get to tonight, if you don't mind my asking?"

"Oh, I have a half a tank now, but I need a little more to get to the city and back. I'm meeting my boyfriend to see a new band at CBGB's."

"No doubt music I've not heard of," said Victor and laughed.

"Punk rock," she said.

"Are you a punk?" he asked, amazed at his new courage to make conversation.

She smiled, "No, but my boyfriend is."

They came to the corner of Argyle Avenue. "Just over here," said Victor, pointing across the large, wooded lot. He looked around to see if anyone was watching them. Once off Trolley Line, there were no more streetlights, and it was true night under the towering pines that ran the perimeter of his property.

"That's some place," said Michelle. She swung her head to the left so the long hair that had fallen in her face whipped over her shoulder. How much will I owe you?" she said, digging in her jacket pocket.

"At 57 cents for five gallons, that comes to 2.85. Let's make it an even 4 and I'll let you keep the can."

"Deal."

They walked along the sidewalk past the wrought iron fence and turned into the drive that led to a garage. Victor pulled his hand out of his coat pocket, holding a remote. He pressed a button, and the door lifted into an open position, no light, like the maw of Leviathan. "Come, just in the garage," he told her and then crouched down to unhook Jester from the leash. He and the dog stepped into the dark. She followed to the edge where the drive entered the garage and stopped. Uncle Tony disappeared up past the deepening shadows around an antique-looking car.

"Come on in," his voice called from absolute night. "I just have to get to the light switch." His words were followed by silence, and then there was the sound of a door opening and quickly closing.

A few minutes passed and she said, "Hey, did you find the light switch?" She leaned forward to peer into the garage, and said, "Isn't Anthony Blake the character Bill Bixby plays in that TV show *The Magician?*" There came the sound of footsteps in the gravel of the drive behind her. Before she could turn, something poked into her bare thigh, and agony like a lightning bolt shot through her. Without so much as a moan, she fell to the ground a helpless puddle of blonde and rabbit fur. Victor stepped past her with the Hot Shot, heading into the garage to get the sock for her mouth and the clothesline he'd cut into two-foot lengths. He'd laid everything out carefully before leaving and had practiced finding it in the dark, just as he'd planned how best to pass through the house and sneak up on his prey if they refused to enter the darkened garage.

He returned to bind and mute her, pushing out of his mind images of the smoking hibachi in the Flesh Kitchen sizzling with her fat. "One thing at a time," he admonished himself. "Slow and steady wins the race." And then he came to the spot where she had fallen, and she was gone. He grunted and turned quickly to look up the drive but saw nothing moving in the shadows toward the road. "Shit," he whispered, realizing that the prod wasn't powerful enough to knock her completely out. He hadn't been knocked out by it when he'd used it on himself. What made him think it would put her down? Self-admonitions leaped in his head like steel crickets. Turning in a circle, he scanned the ground to see if she'd crawled off a few yards. Then he heard Jester bark, but not in the garage, in the house. He realized she must have passed down the opposite side of the antique car and then slipped through the same door he had when he went through the house to sneak up on her.

The thought of her roaming through his space, among his things, made him bolt into the garage and close the electric door. Flipping on the lights, he grabbed the cattle prod off his work bench and shoved the cut clothesline into his pants pocket. Jester barked again, this time more distant, and Victor entered the house, quietly shutting the door behind him. He stood in the hallway that led to the living room and listened intently for the sound of footsteps or creaking boards. He inched forward, silently.

The room was lit only by a weak bulb in a lamp whose base was a fisherman in a yellow slicker. His mother was obsessed with nautically themed accessories to all the rooms. She'd been unfathomable. The dust ridden furniture—a couch on three legs and a recliner with a gash in the back from when Victor was practicing his knife work—were adrift on a sea of green shag carpet. Right in the middle of the floor was the rabbit fur coat. He walked over to it and stared down. Eventually he kicked it with his toe, afraid to lift it. This was a confusing move on her part, no doubt an attempt to put him off kilter. There were two exits from the living room, a stair that led up and a hallway that led into the larger part of the house. He checked the coat closet by whipping open the door and shoving the prod in between the hanging jackets.

In a bedroom down the hall, he found the black miniskirt, a pink top, pink socks, and the pair of Ugg boots. Again, he stood over her things and now realized he was frightened. It came to him that she might be taking her clothes off in a playful manner, as if inviting him to have sex if he could find her. The idea of it made him nauseous. In the next room, he discovered her long blonde hair. He crouched down next to it and reached out his hand as if the wig was a fire, warming him. The door of the room he was in flew open, and he turned. A black blur rushed at him out of the dimness of the hallway. Jester knocked him over onto the wig. As he scrambled to his feet, Victor lashed out with a kick. The dog dodged it and went to stand in the open doorway.

"Show me where she is," he said, and Jester led the way. They headed for the very back of the house where there was a tight hallway with two guest rooms, the doors facing each other across the hall. Jester settled in front of one of them and clawed at the closed door. Victor tightened his grip on the prod and then grabbed the knob and turned. Even though the knob didn't budge, obviously locked, he still heard a door squeal open. Before he realized what was happening, she'd lunged out of the room across the hall and slammed into him headfirst into the locked door. He turned to face her and jabbed with the prod, bringing his free arm up to cover his face. She lunged and snapped at him with teeth that had at some point become fangs. Instead of the soft meat of his cheek, her jaws closed on his forearm, and she ripped a chunk of flesh out of him. He heard her swallow as he drove the prod home into her naked stomach, and she fell backward into the wall and slipped down with a cat-like cry. Victor wasn't waiting to see what would happen next. He fled the hallway.

In the adjoining bathroom of his parent's room, he shut the door. With his free hand he found an ancient bottle of mercurochrome and twisted the top off with his thumb. Positioning his forearm over the sink, he poured a half bottle of the reddish-brown mess onto the open wound awash with blood and cried out. He took a few moments to catch his breath, and then tied a hand towel around his arm to stop the bleeding. He knew right then, he would have to kill her, and he wasn't so sure he wanted to eat her flesh if she was a were-cat, a creature he'd read about on a trip last year to the library. "How can that be?" he kept repeating to himself. All the while, her bald head was an image he couldn't shake. Eventually, he grabbed the prod, went into his parents' bedroom, where Jester waited for him, and found his old man's pistol in the top drawer of the broken-down dresser. He whimpered from the pain of his wound as he checked to see if the chambers were loaded. Snapping the cylinder shut, he whispered for the dog to follow, and they left the room. "If I try really hard, maybe I can wake up," he thought, but the bite argued that things couldn't be realer.

Three steps out of the bedroom, and he realized there was music coming from upstairs. His heart dropped when he made out that it was "Seasons in the Sun." She was in the Flesh Kitchen. He tried to take the stairs as quietly as he could, but the neglected house complained with creaks and groans throughout his ascent. He hoped the volume at which she was playing the record would cover his approach. As they neared the door of the Flesh Kitchen, Jester hung back and let Victor take the lead. And then the music suddenly stopped. He listened into the silence, but the sound of his own heartbeat and labored breathing was all he could hear.

He opened the door and pushed it in. The room was dark. As he stepped forward and felt around for the light switch, the music started up again with a great bang and a scratch, the needle dropped in the middle. Finding the switch, he flipped it up and the clean brightness of the overhead fluorescent lamps he'd installed revealed an empty room. The song played at top volume. He lunged toward where the victrola sat on a small end table, now afraid the racket of it might be heard by neighbors.

She pounced from behind the door, landing on his back, her arms around his shoulders. Her teeth gnawed at the back of his neck, trying to catch a fold of skin they could rip off. He tottered and turned, nearly falling, but righted himself and ran backwards into the wall, denting the sheetrock with her body. With that, he flung her off. Instead of merely falling, she crouched into a roll and came to her feet. As she rushed him again, he saw her now as if for the first time—bald head gleaming in the overhead light, the golden eyes glowing, the incredible incisors, and a two-foot tail he couldn't believe he hadn't noticed earlier beneath the miniskirt. There was no time to even wonder what she was: she barreled into his gut headfirst at top speed. The gun and the prod went flying and he doubled over and went down on the floor. She stood above him and hissed an animal sound of dominance before she dropped onto his body. He used his arms to try to ward her off his throat, which seemed to be her target. The towel on Victor's arm was immediately ripped away.

She scratched both his cheeks. He hadn't noticed how sharp her pink fingernails were earlier. Her strength was far greater than his. While he wrestled, doing his best to prevent the fangs from digging in, the thought surfaced that here would be his end, eaten in his own Flesh Kitchen. "Somehow it all seemed foreshadowed," he later wrote in his journal. She managed to get one of his arms under her knee and immobilize it. Then straddling him, she worked to gain control of his other arm and it was a certainty it would eventually happen. Victor begged for his life, sniveling, wishing he'd at some point in his life learned to cry, but it wasn't clear if he was dealing with a human being anymore. That's when he felt something heavy drop into his trapped hand. Out of the corner of his eye, he caught a glimpse of Jester, who'd brought the gun to him.

With a last great effort to save his life, he kicked his legs and bucked his hips and managed to throw her partially off him. In that moment, his arm came free. He shoved the gun into her ribs right below the left breast and pulled the trigger. The shot blew her off him and onto the floor. As he was finally rid of her, he kicked her in the head and shot her again in the right leg. There was no sign of consciousness, but he could tell from her pulse that she was still alive. He noticed that in the struggle, one of the golden irises had wound up on her chin. Victor picked it off her. It was a colored contact lens like they might use in Hollywood. He reached down, opened her mouth, and pulled out the prosthetic fangs. When he rolled her over, he saw the stitch marks and knew then she was not a monster, but simply someone like him, "born different into a dull world." That was how he put it when he recounted the previous events both to his handlers at Attica and in his own journal.

Yes, he got the hibachi going, cut a few strips from her thighs, which he admitted to hungering for the moment he laid eyes on them, applied his seasonings, and ate his fill. Jester, that remarkable beast, was given some lightly grilled cheek meat as his reward. Victor said of the dog, "It was as if he'd done all of it before." Michelle the cat lady died at dawn, and late the following night, he weighed her partially devoured corpse down with rocks and rope and slipped her into Argyle Lake from his dock. What was left of the body surfaced a few years later, out in the middle of the water, and was spotted by skaters, who saw her peering up through the ice with one golden eye in a rotted face. It was that discovery that started the investigation that finally, six years later, ended Victor's career as cannibal.

He wrote, "Flesh was not the mood ring pink custard I'd dreamed of. Instead, it was like shish-kabob steak, chewy with an almost citrus tang of civilization. The best part was that since she had eaten a piece of me, the realization that my first divine meal was made not only of her but myself as well sustained me, driving me to hunt again."

Jeffrey Ford is the author of the novels *The Physiognomy, Memoranda, The Beyond, The Portrait of Mrs. Charbuque, The Girl in the Glass, The Cosmology of the Wider World, The Shadow Year, The Twilight Pariah, Ahab's Return, and Out of Body.* His short story collections are *The Fantasy Writer's Assistant, The Empire of Ice Cream, The Drowned Life, Crackpot Palace, A Natural History of Hell, The Best of Jeffrey Ford,* and *Big Dark Hole.* Ford's fiction has appeared in numerous magazines and anthologies from *Tor.com* to *Magazine of Fantasy and Science Fiction* to *The Oxford Book of American Short Stories* and been widely translated. It has garnered World Fantasy, Edgar Allan Poe, Shirley Jackson, Nebula Awards and a *New York Times* Notable Book of the Year. He lives in Ohio's farm country in a 120-year-old house and teaches part-time at Ohio Wesleyan University.

LET'S HEAR IT FOR THE BOY
BY BRIDGETT NELSON

October 1981

Their bodies slapped violently together. Sweat glistened on their skin. Their moans grew louder, more guttural.

They climaxed. Troy rolled off, onto the mattress, mimicking the sprawled position of da Vinci's *Vitruvian Man*. He stared at the shadowed ceiling in sated satisfaction as Rob snuggled against him. A ceiling fan spun lazily above them, cooling their damp bodies. Once he'd caught his breath, he rolled over and kissed Rob's shoulder.

"I love you."

"Yeah, yeah. You just want me for this fine bod."

Troy gazed at Rob's smooth ebony skin and taut muscles. He sure as hell couldn't deny Rob's physical beauty.

"No," he replied. "I love you for your smart-ass mouth."

Rob chuckled as Troy massaged his thigh. The radio on their alarm clock played "Endless Love," Rob's current favorite song. "I do have a pretty bitchy mouth, don't I?"

Troy let out an amused snort. Rob was definitely not the quiet type. He tensed as his fingers grazed over a spongy lump on Rob's leg. Concerned, he sat up and turned on the bedside lamp for a better look.

"What's this, babe?"

Rob, who had been gazing dreamily out the window and humming along to the music, mumbled, "Wha…?"

"There's something on your thigh. Don't you feel it? It's pretty big."

He shrugged. "It's probably an infected hair. I get those sometimes."

"Definitely not an infected hair. Come over into the light so I can get a better look," Troy requested.

Rob scooted to the edge of the bed and gasped when he saw the quarter-sized, bluish, bruise-like mass, stark against his dark skin. "What the hell is that?"

Troy continued to inspect the tissue. "It looks like a bruise. Does it hurt when I push on it?"

"Nah. I don't feel a thing," Rob replied.

"Okay, not a bruise. The skin is raised."

Rob had already lost interest. "Eh. I'm sure it's nothing. Probably be gone in the morning."

Troy wasn't so sure. The growth didn't look like 'nothing' to him. It looked serious. He didn't want to worry Rob, though, so he said, "Yeah, probably nothing. But hey, keep an eye on it, okay? Better safe than sorry."

"Yeah, I will." Rob's voice was untroubled, carefree. "Join me in bed?"

Admiring his long, lean form—and feeling the familiar stirring between his legs—Troy put the bewildering lesion out of his mind.

April 1983

"I'm really sorry about Rob, man," Joey said.

Troy was damn sorry too. Even though he'd stayed and watched the crewmen lower the casket into that dark, gaping void, and then fill the gravesite with sandy soil, he still couldn't comprehend that Rob—his always happy, bursting-with-life lover— was buried in the dirt. With worms.

He gave Joey a brief nod of acknowledgment but kept his eyes fixated on his drink. He knew if he looked into his friends' sorrowful faces, he'd lose whatever control he had over his emotions.

Coming here after the funeral had been a bad idea.

When Joey first suggested they all go to Rob's favorite club to celebrate his life, Troy had thought it a fine proposition. Rob would have loved his friends coming together, sharing amusing anecdotes, and toasting the man he'd been.

But now that he was here, the music was too loud, the lights far too bright. He stared at the scantily-clad dancer on the elevated stage, who was wearing nothing but a neon-pink Speedo and plentiful body oil. He looked healthy. No atrophied muscles. No withered appendages. But then, Troy noticed a dime-sized, dark-red lesion where the dancer's neck met his shoulder. His heart sank in his chest as he downed a large gulp of his drink.

The virus spared no one.

President Finch, the CDC…none of them seemed to be taking it seriously, despite the fact it had killed over four thousand gay men so far, including Rob. Troy still remembered the homicidal rage he'd felt upon hearing Finch's press secretary joking with reporters about the "gay plague."

It was clear no help was coming from the top.

"Is there anything we can do?" Sam asked Troy, genuine concern in his stormy-gray eyes.

"Nah," Troy responded, overcome. "I lost my job because my boss was scared of me. Rob's gone. My family no longer claims me. All I have to look forward to is taking my final breath. Then all the pious assholes can cheer that another dead fag is in the ground."

Joey and Sam exchanged glances. Joey gave Sam a brief nod, and then faced Troy. "Listen, Troy," he began, "we weren't going to mention this tonight, but I think maybe you need to hear it. Word on the street is that the CDC has a facility here in the Bay Area. They're running medication trials, but only accepting those in the end stages." He paused. "Like you."

"Not interested," Troy said.

"Well, you should be," Sam replied. "You're only twenty-four. You have a lot of life left to live. Come on, save yourself, man! You know that's what Rob would have wanted."

"Do you really think so? Do you think Rob would be thrilled to have died days before these so-called miracle drugs appeared? Because I think he'd be *pissed.*" Troy pushed his drink away and stood up, intending to leave.

Just then, the latest Irene Cara song began to play—the theme song from the movie *Flashdance.* Troy's eyes watered, thinking of how he had propped Rob up in his wheelchair and taken him to the movie theater on the film's opening night. How his partner's face had lit up as he watched the movie just one week before his death. How they'd both chosen to ignore the people who'd fearfully left after seeing Rob's moribund condition.

His angry indignation depleted, Troy plopped bonelessly back into his seat, put his head into his hands, and cried. For the first time since Rob's death, he let himself feel the tremendous loss. Sam and Joey gathered around him, two mother hens soothing and protecting.

"I…I…can't believe he's…he's…gone." Troy gasped for air as his grief overwhelmed him. "He suffered so goddamned much! And why? He was kind and cheerful and never met a person he didn't adore. He was so fucking young, but did anyone care? Nope. Because he was just another queer motherfucker who got what was coming to him!"

A couple in the next booth glared at him, but Troy was beyond caring.

"Can't you see, Troy?" Sam pleaded. "We don't want to be sitting here six months from now saying the same things about you. Please consider checking out the CDC facility. Please?"

"Even if it doesn't work, isn't it worth a shot?" Joey asked. "It could extend your lifespan. I kid you not, Troy, I heard the results are really promising. Don't just give up on us, dude."

As Toto Coelo's "I Eat Cannibals" blared through the speakers, Troy pondered whether or not he even wanted to live. Unlike Rob and his other friends, he still looked relatively healthy, aside from some moderate weight loss.

So far, all his lesions were internal, stealthily lining his digestive track. Everything he ingested caused him pain—an intense burning that often forced him to lie curled in the fetal position. Even the ginger ale he'd just consumed made him uncomfortable.

Did he want to live like that for the rest of his life? Even if this facility offered some sort of wonder drug, Troy was under no illusion that it would be a lasting cure. This disease, one way or another, was going to end his life.

But still…

"Yeah, okay," he said. "I'll give it a shot."

Troy knocked on the door. "Ma, you home?"

He heard her footsteps echoing down the hallway. When she saw him, she smiled, but it didn't reach her eyes.

"Troy. What can I do for you?" Her demeanor was heartbreakingly stiff.

"Is Mike around?" he asked.

"No, your brother's at school."

Troy could have sworn he heard her whisper, "Thank God" under her breath.

"Oh, yeah. Of course." He shook his head. "Anyway, Mom, I just wanted to stop by and get your opinion about something. Maybe enjoy some of your delicious peppermint tea?"

His mother's reluctance was obvious, but she responded, "Of course."

The kitchen, which doubled as the dining room, was small, dominated by a large wooden table. Troy had to squeeze past his mother to get to his chair. She flinched, let out a yelp, and rushed to the sink to scrub her hands—the vigorousness with which she scoured her skin reminiscent of a surgeon heading to the operating room.

Troy's head dropped in embarrassment.

And profound sadness.

When the tea had finished steeping, his mother poured two cups, sat opposite him, and placed one cup in the middle of the table so he was forced to reach for it. They sipped hot tea in tense silence, neither looking at the other.

Finally, his mother asked, "Why are you here, Troy?"

He paused, let out a quivering breath, and said, "Rob passed away last week."

"I'm sorry to hear that," she responded stoically.

"Yeah, it's been tough. It made me realize just how short life is and how we shouldn't take those we love for granted. I...I miss you, Mom."

"That's nice of you to say."

An awkward moment passed. "So, uh, yeah...okay," Troy said, hurt and sad and disappointed but somehow not surprised. "I also wanted to discuss my future."

Her tone turned acidic. "I already told you I'm not paying for your funer—"

"Not that, Mom!" he cut in. "Listen, the CDC is actually trying to help us, though they're keeping it on the down-low. They have a facility set up here in San Francisco, and they're looking for volunteers for a clinical trial."

"What's the point?" she asked bitterly. "Even if they find a cure, it's not like you're going to change your...your *ways*." She gave a disgusted shiver.

He sighed. "It's who I am, Mom, and I refuse to apologize for that. But I…I don't want to die."

"Maybe you should have thought of that before you started…having *relations* with other men!"

"Mom…" he began.

"No. I don't want to hear about your perversions! If your father were still alive…" She drew a deep breath. "You do what you think is best. Nothing I say will change your mind."

"Mom, can't we just—" he tried again.

"Michael will be home soon, and I'd rather he not see you looking so…frail," she said. "I think it's best you leave."

Troy got up and walked out without another word, pretending not to notice the way his *mother* threw the teacup he'd used into the garbage, and then resolutely sprayed the room with Lysol.

"Are you sure you know where you're going?" Sam asked Joey, peering at an unfolded city map.

"Sure I do!" Joey said "Potrero Hill…Utah Street, I think. Not far from where I grew up." He made a left, easing into a parking spot outside a large, three-story building.

Troy, in the back seat, looked it over. The red brick exterior had long-since faded to a vintage orangey-hue. Seven small, arched windows graced each of the top two floors. At ground level, there appeared to be a sturdy-looking steel door and nothing else. The neighborhood seemed oddly uninhabited. The few houses he could see were at the far end of the street—solid working-class homes, small but well-kept.

Pulling his black, polyester duffel bag with him, he climbed out of the car. He studied the run-down building's façade more closely, feeling a keen sense of disappointment. This wasn't a place where miracles happened. He'd envisioned a clean, modern clinic—definitely not this sad, crumbling structure.

He had no idea how long the medicinal protocol would take…or how he'd feel during the process. Or if he'd even come out alive.

Doing his best to hide his dismay, he hugged Joey and Sam, secretly wishing his mom and brother had come along to see him off. While he'd been waiting to hear if he'd been accepted into the clinical trial, he'd written to Mike, but he'd never gotten a reply. He suspected their mother had burned the 'contaminated' mail before Mike even saw it.

Unsure of when, or if, he'd see his friends again, Troy stood on the sidewalk, waving until Joey's car was completely out of sight.

They were the only family he had left.

He reluctantly turned and walked toward the door, which looked and felt more like a barrier.

But was it meant to keep people out? Or in?

Forcing a chuckle at his paranoia, he gave three firm knocks. The door was immediately opened, and, though Troy knew he was being silly, the relief he felt upon seeing a tiny, elderly lady in a blue-print floral dress was overwhelming. He gave her a warm smile as she motioned him inside. Introducing herself as Elsie—"It means, 'pledged to God'"—she led him to a small desk in the back corner of a reception area.

Drawers opened and closed as a small pile of paperwork began accumulating on a clipboard. She then handed it to Troy, along with a blue ball-point pen.

This was not how he imagined a national public health agency would run things, but again, what did he actually know about the CDC? Not a damn thing.

After filling out the stack of paperwork, which not only delved into his medical history, but also his daily habits and hobbies, he was taken to the third floor.

Troy, who stood over six feet tall, weighed a healthy two hundred and fifteen pounds before he got sick. He was now down to a hundred and sixty pounds. His once glossy blonde hair was dull and limp, his tanned skin gone pallid. Yet he looked full of vigor compared to his roommate, who was so emaciated, Troy wondered how all his organs were still functioning. Skeletal, he did not move from his bed but accepted Troy's handshake. In a gravelly whisper, he introduced himself as Ozzy.

"Well, I'll leave you two to get and know each other," Elsie said. "Your nutritional requirements will be given to our dietary team, and appropriate meals will be made for each of you. Dinner is served every evening from 6:30 to 7:30 in the dining room downstairs. If you feel unable to make it to the dining room, please let one of our team members know, and room service can be arranged. Wheelchairs have been provided in each of your closets. Feel free to explore, but please be considerate. If a door is locked, there is a reason." With that, she turned and walked out of their room.

"That Elsie sure is a ray of sunshine," Ozzy said, grinning at Troy.

"So bright and warm! I'm glad she didn't offer to shake our hands… probably would have burned us. Not ideal with our less-than-optimal immune systems."

They both laughed at the joke, which was lame, but enough to seal their friendship. Over the next hour, they discussed their CD4 lymphocyte count, how much they hated the night sweats and daily fevers, and which foods they missed the most. Ozzy shared how he'd acquired cytomegalovirus, which had caused inflammation of the retinas in his eyes. He explained that it was a "herpes-like" virus, and that he was still dealing with the blurred vision and light sensitivity it had caused. Predictably, both also suffered from "gay cancer," as the media had dubbed it, though Troy knew it was actually Kaposi's sarcoma—the cause of the bruise-like lesions that had become so prevalent in their community.

Deciding to check out the facility, Troy helped Ozzy into a wheelchair, and they began exploring. There were fourteen identical rooms on each of the top two floors. It seemed the facility could hold fifty-six patients at a time. From what Troy could tell, they were at full capacity. He was fortunate to have claimed a bed when he did.

The first floor contained Elsie's lobby, several medical exam rooms, a small pharmacy, an exercise/physical therapy room, the dining room/kitchen, a couple of doctor's offices, and a huge gathering space full of couches, recliners, a television, shelves full of books and board games, and even a pool table. There also appeared to be access to a basement, but that door was locked. Satisfied with what they'd seen and exhausted from their exertions, Troy and Ozzy decided to head back to their room and nap before the evening meal.

Dinner was a quiet affair. The staff, which included Elsie, two CDC physicians, two nurses, and three assistants, had a table to themselves. The dietary crew was nowhere to be seen. Troy and his fellow patients shared four picnic-style tables. Troy was shocked by the toddler-sized portions. Though it was tasty, the amount of food wouldn't satisfy a small dog. Beside each plate was a medicine cup filled with all colors and sizes of pills. Each patient's appeared the same, although, as Troy understood it, half of the men received placebos. Only the pharmacist knew which patients were getting the actual medication. Clinical trials worked that way—it prevented research bias, and any differences in the outcomes could be attributed to the active treatment.

After the meal, in the elevator, Troy found he could hardly keep his eyes open. Ozzy was already slumped over in his chair, snoring.

Had they been given a sedative? He realized sleep was an important component to good health, but he felt as though he'd been dosed with enough to sedate an elephant.

Too tired to contemplate the issue further, Troy pushed Ozzy's chair down the hallway and into their room, shook him awake and told him to get into bed, and then fell face-first onto his own twin-sized mattress. Within seconds, he was asleep.

Lights.
Echoes.
Movement.
Voices.
Troy felt the dampness of his clothes against his skin, aware in some vague part of his brain, it was from his persistent night sweats.

Was that…Elsie talking?

Whatever his body was reclined on came to an abrupt stop. After some rough jostling, he was moved to a firmer surface. A bright light blazed over him. He shut his eyes and felt something hard cover his lower face. An unpleasant chemical smell infiltrated his senses, and he knew nothing more.

Bright sunlight pierced through the shadows as Troy opened his eyes.

His alarm clock read 11:14.

Ozzy was still sound asleep in the other bed, his breaths deep and regular. His face looked flushed with fever, but he seemed comfortable.

Troy sat up, stood, and staggered, nearly falling to the laminated floor. What in the hell was the medical team doing? He was pretty sure his head would hurt far less if some crazy dude was stabbing it with an ice pick.

Stumbling into their tiny, attached bathroom, he looked at himself in the mirror, and saw a trickle of dark red blood coming from his left nostril. Knowing his bodily fluids were a huge source of fear, he grabbed some toilet paper and quickly wiped off the blood, flushing the contaminated wad down the toilet.

He wasn't sure what, if anything, had happened to him last night, but he found himself wondering if the initial paranoia he'd felt upon entering the building yesterday might have been legitimate.

Troy and Ozzy sat quietly in the dining room, attempting to eat their lunches despite the pain they were both experiencing. Ozzy had awoken with symptoms identical to Troy's, which had both men bewildered.

Once again, their food portions were ridiculously small, but Troy's appetite was nonexistent. After a few bites, he pushed his plate away. The pain was making him sick to his stomach. Ozzy fared a little better, finishing half of his lunch.

Just before Troy wheeled him out of the dining room, a doctor in a long white coat caught up to them.

"Good afternoon, gentlemen!" Her smile was radiant. "I'm Dr. Clark, and I have you both scheduled for your first intravenous infusions this afternoon. If you'd be so kind as to meet me in medical room number three in an hour, we'll get you set up."

"No problem," Troy replied, despite his qualms of unease.

Ozzy nodded his agreement.

"Great, see you then!"

The doctor hurried away, and Troy pushed Ozzy to the large gathering room. They attempted to watch television with some of the other patients, but neither was interested in talk shows.

"Do you remember if anything weird happened last night?" Ozzy asked.

"I remember telling you to get into bed, but everything after that is a black void."

"I don't even remember getting into bed."

Troy glanced around and then leaned closer. "Do you think they drugged us?"

"Must have. With the fevers and night sweats, I haven't had a full night's sleep in the past year. That was so far out of my normal pattern, it had to be drugs." Ozzy's voice seemed more gravelly than usual.

"But why?"

"No clue."

Troy stared at the ceiling. Hours had passed since he'd gone to bed, but this time, he couldn't sleep.

He was wired—had been since his infusion that afternoon. He tried not to let himself get too excited by the results, but there was nothing subtle about the way he'd felt afterward.

Alert. Powerful. Energetic.

He still felt that way. Did it mean he was being given the actual medication and not a placebo? And even more importantly, was it working?

His stomach rumbled. For the first time in months, his appetite was back. He was ravenous. Slipping on his robe, Troy quietly left the room he shared with Ozzy and ran down the two flights of stairs—no elevator needed tonight! He headed into the dimly-lit kitchen. Surely the team wouldn't care if he made himself a sandwich.

Yet all the cabinets, pantries, and refrigerator doors were locked. The canisters on the countertop held nothing.

"This is some bullshit right here," Troy grumbled. His stomach continued its unhappy growling, but there was nothing he could do.

As he began the climb back up the stairs, he heard a commotion in the lobby. He hid in a shadowed corner and watched as a large group of people descended into the basement, through the usually-locked door. Their excitement was palpable.

At three o'clock in the morning.

He could think of no logical reason a random group of people would be coming into the building in the middle of the night, let alone going to the basement. A flare of apprehension wasn't enough to stifle his curiosity as he tiptoed to the door and tried the handle.

Unlocked.

Checking behind him to make sure he was alone, he crept slowly down the wooden stairs, sticking to the outer edge to avoid creaks. From below, he could hear the animated voices of the crowd.

Reaching the bottom step, he peeked around the corner.

Approximately fifty people filled tiered lecture-hall style rows of seating overlooking a large, sunken chamber through a sturdy glass wall. He studied them as well as he could in the dim lighting—more men than women, a wide range of ages and ethnicities; overall, an average-looking bunch.

Unable to fathom what was going on, but compelled to learn more, he ducked into a dark corner that concealed him while affording a 180-degree view. He realized he was humming "Maniac" from the *Flashdance* soundtrack under his breath and had to cover his mouth to stifle both the humming and a nervous titter of laughter.

Troy didn't know whether to be impressed or horrified by the set-up.

The audience suddenly silenced their chatter, facing forward, attentive and expectant. A man—the male doctor, with whom Troy had, thus far, had no interaction—stepped before the crowd and smiled benevolently, looking more like a pastor than a physician.

"Hello and welcome!" he said. "I know this is the first time many of you have been able to join us, so please allow me to introduce myself. My name is Doctor Dasan Miles. I'm a neurobiologist and also a deacon of Christ's Divine Cavalry church."

He paused, as though waiting for applause, an aura of arrogance surrounding him that Troy found immensely unappealing. And...a deacon? Church? What did that have to do with anything?

Dr. Miles went on. "As you all know, thousands of homosexual men have brought hellfire down on our great city, in the form of a plague."

Ah, now it made sense. Troy's body stiffened in surprise and anger.

"The great book," Dr. Miles said, holding up the King James version of the Bible, "says in Leviticus 20:13 that '*If a man lies with a male as with a woman, both of them have committed an abomination; they shall be put to death; their blood is upon them.*'"

The audience nodded and murmured their approval. Troy could not believe what he was hearing. He twitched with pent-up fury.

"Those of us at Christ's Divine Cavalry church, or..." He smirked. "...the *CDC*, take these passages to heart. Men who lay with men are an abomination in the eyes of God! They must be destroyed before they spread their sickness…their disease…their pestilence! …unto the righteous men and women who make up God's Cavalry." He stomped his foot like a petulant child, giving this performance everything he had. The crowd, sheep that they were, responded enthusiastically. "Our government certainly doesn't care about these perverts. President Finch, bless his heart, has no interest in offering them aid. He knows about this project of ours…and approves. In fact, he secured this building and had this amazing theater constructed just for us."

This earned a standing ovation, while Troy's hands squeezed so tightly, his nails dug into his palms. He could feel the slick warmth of his blood dripping onto his pajama pants. "Jesus fucking Christ, the *president*?" he whispered.

"Dr. Gabriella Clark and I," said Miles, "long contemplated how we could use our vast medical knowledge and skills to take out these ghastly abominations without the public ever knowing…and without tarnishing our unblemished souls in the process." A sardonic grin stretched across his face. "What we came up with, my friends, was—well—it was brilliant. Using nothing more than word of mouth, referrals, and an incentive program, we lured these sinners to our domain, and, under the guise of research and clinical trials, implemented our plan."

Troy could have choked, could have screamed! He felt tricked, betrayed, and horrified all at once.

"*Step one*: Starvation. Well, *deprivation*. Don't get me wrong. We're not barbarians." He laughed. "Three very low-calorie meals each day, so that even with their decreased appetites and weakened conditions, they go to bed every night with empty stomachs. Most of the pills we give them are simple placebos—no nutritional or medicinal value at all. But we do give them a potent appetite stimulant."

With all that was happening, Troy had almost forgotten the hunger that had brought him downstairs in the first place, but his stomach growled again—so loud he clapped his hands over his midsection.

"*Step two*: Sedation. During their first night here, each patient is fully anesthetized and brought to a surgical suite here in the basement. Using the endonasal method, a noninvasive procedure that allows us to manipulate specific parts of the brain by threading a small endoscopic tube through a nostril, we implant chips into each man's hypothalamus and amygdala."

Hearing this, Troy remembered the sensations of light and motion, the voices, the feeling of something covering his face, the strange chemical smell. It hadn't been a dream. It hadn't been a dream at all.

That sure explains the nosebleed, he thought, *not to mention the rip-roaring headache.*

Meanwhile, Dr. Miles went on. "Both areas help regulate hunger, thirst, and satiety, but the amygdala is the part of the brain where our emotions about food are formed. It's where our fear of starving originates. It creates that angry feeling we get when we're really hungry but unable to eat. And speaking of anger…"

The audience hung on his every word, leaning forward avidly in their seats. So did Troy, though his was less from anticipation than dread.

"*Step three*: Infusion. Our patients receive an intravenous combination dose of cocaine and a steroid. It gives them energy they haven't had—in some cases, for years, makes them believe they're part of the 'active' trial and that it's actually working. It provides *hope*. Fruitless, of course. It also helps us influence the irrational, hyper-aggressive anger needed for this program to succeed."

Hope…just like the hope he'd experienced following his infusion. Another damn lie.

Dr. Clark joined Dr. Miles at the front of the room, carrying what appeared to be two remote controls. She handed one to him.

"And so," declared Miles, "without further ado, we present...Shane and Arthur!"

A door opened in the room below and two nude men were ushered through: men Troy recognized, fellow patients, clearly puzzled and uneasy. Their confusion grew as they surveyed their surroundings—bare walls, a tile floor with a drain in the center—and when they noticed the glass-walled gallery full of eager onlookers, they nervously tried to cover their nakedness.

Their bodies were gaunt, abdomens so concave that their jutting hip bones appeared deformed. Lesions and sores covered their skin. Sunken cheeks and hollowed eye sockets sculpted once youthful faces. None of the patients at the facility were older than forty—Troy had garnered that information during his intake process—yet their crepey, wrinkled skin made Shane and Arthur look twice their age. They were skittish and shaky, their eyes psychotically bright.

"Shane and Arthur have been with us at the CDC for eight weeks," Dr. Miles said. "Their bodies have been starved, their brains hijacked, and their dependence on cocaine is absolute. In fact, they were given their final infusion just before they entered the theater. Tonight, they shall fulfill their destiny."

The doctors pushed buttons on their individual remotes, and both men in the chamber clawed at their stomachs in agony.

"Jesus, man! We're starving! Give us some goddamn food!" screamed Shane.

"The intraneural chips, as you can see, have now been activated." Miles spoke over Shane's shouting and swearing. "Heightening their irrationality, hyper-aggression, and anger."

Arthur shrieked and threw himself at the closed door, then began punching the walls with his bare fists. Crimson blood dribbled down the uneven gray surface.

"Gentlemen, gentlemen," Miles chided. "Look around you. Food is plentiful." As they wildly searched the room, desperate to eat, the doctors pressed more buttons on the remote controls. The results were instantaneous— strings of viscous drool hung from Shane's parched lips and Arthur growled like a beast. They circled the room, eyeing each other hungrily—two starving predators intent on making the kill.

Arthur struck first, darting toward the wall, running up it and pushing off into a back flip—a weird, naked ninja. He landed on Shane, causing both men to fall heavily to the ground.

"Get off me, asshole!" Shane yelled.

Arthur savagely bit into Shane's chest, ripping off a wet, bloody chunk. From Troy's vantage point, it looked as though Arthur was munching on a mouthful of nipple, purple lesions, and large, oozing pustules. Troy gagged.

Shane, seeming more enraged than in pain, shoved Arthur away and then sprang on him, clawing his skin with ragged, grimy nails. He lapped blood from the scratches before digging into the muscle with his teeth. Arthur thrashed and rolled, frenzied and fighting back.

Troy gagged again, feeling the meager contents of *his* stomach rush up his esophagus. He tamped it down but still felt sick. *What the fuck?*

As the battle continued, each man became less concerned with the trauma to his own body and more interested in the damage—and devouring the results of the damage—he inflicted on the other. Arthur finally got to his feet and punched Shane in the face, hard enough to knock him to the floor, unconscious. A half-chewed gobbet of meat, part of Arthur's shoulder, still hung from Shane's slack mouth. Arthur seized it for himself and wolfed it down.

This grotesque act of auto-cannibalism quelled some of the excited clamor from the audience. A few of them looked as stunned and shocked as Troy felt, but most had a vicious gleam of satisfaction in their eyes.

His empty stomach finally quieted, Arthur stared at Shane's naked, vulnerable body...and began stroking himself.

The onlookers groaned in revolted protest, but Dr. Miles gestured for their attention.

"The hypothalamus not only stimulates hunger, it can also stimulate sexual arousal," he said. "We knew this was a possibility, but had yet to see it happen. What you're witnessing is history in the making!"

History in the making, indeed, as a fully-erect Arthur knelt over Shane's prone body, thrust his penis into a convenient hole, and started eating Shane's face.

"Holy shit!" Dr. Clark hissed, her mouth hanging open in a parody of exhilaration and disgust.

Shane revived enough to try and scream, but couldn't. Arthur bit through his tongue, still pumping wildly. He went for Shane's nose next, but quickly spit it out.

"Probably too much gristle," suggested the corner of Troy's brain still capable of thought. The rest of him was numb, staring helplessly at the degradation and cruelty.

An eyeball went next, the brown-irised orb crushed between Arthur's teeth like a grape. As its gelatinous juices sprayed from his lips and dribbled down his chin, he grunted and bucked in climax, ejaculating violently.

Arthur rolled off Shane. He was breathing hard, but his body was relaxed. Sated. The spectators shuffled uncomfortably in their seats. Dr. Miles cleared his throat, preparing to speak, but just then Arthur's head snapped around, cocked alertly like a threatened animal's. He stared at the bloody mess that was Shane...a bloody mess which was, somehow, still breathing. Arthur let out a deep roar and bit savagely into Shane's neck, sending a geyser of blood straight into the air as the carotid artery relinquished its life-sustaining, ruby fluid.

Witnessing that finale, Troy finally lost his battle against the nausea.

Although his stomach was next to empty, he dry-heaved, loudly, body wracked with convulsions for what seemed like forever. When his guts finally stopped rebelling, he looked up, dolefully unsurprised to see everyone in the gallery looking at him.

Troy stepped out from the corner, arms raised, his pajamas covered in stinking gastric juices. He tried for the 'good ol' boy' approach, manufacturing a broad, sheepish smile.

"Hey, everyone! Sorry I ended the party on such a sour note...I'll just head back to my room and get a much-needed shower. I reek."

Nobody made a move or said a word, so Troy took that as a good sign and sidled toward the stairwell, only to find his way blocked by two burly medical assistants.

"Come on, fellas, I couldn't see anything, it was dark. The virus just makes me really sick to my stomach, and I puke a lot. No big deal." Seeing they weren't falling for it, he made to bolt past them, but they caught him by the arms and dragged him over to Drs. Miles and Clark. After a brief heads-together consultation, Dr. Clark turned to the audience.

"It looks like you're in for quite the show tonight," she announced.

A few of them laughed. Most of them didn't. Troy certainly didn't, as Dr. Miles instructed the assistants to take him below.

"Let Arthur have a bit more fun," he said.

"No!" Troy cried. "I didn't do anything! This isn't fair! This isn't right!

And you people call yourselves a church?"

He kept on shouting as they lugged him downstairs. Thankfully, they didn't make him disrobe, but a third assistant yelled, "Hey! Time for dessert!" before he flung open the door and forced Troy through.

His heart sank as the door slammed shut behind him. Although he felt more energetic than he had in months, he'd had the infusion well over twelve hours prior. There was no way he stood a chance against Arthur: the same Arthur who was currently grinning at him, looking like a blood-drenched *Carrie* on prom-night, his gut bulging from gorging on Shane.

Maybe he's full? Troy thought, with last-ditch optimism. *Maybe he's not hungry anymore?*

It didn't matter. Through the glass, he saw Dr. Miles raise the remote control and push a button.

Arthur, snarling ravenously, lunged and tackled Troy to the floor. Within seconds, he was helplessly pinned, trying to fend off Arthur's gnashing teeth. Not wanting his final image to be some deranged, diseased stranger, Troy's eyes searched the upper gallery. He scanned the spectators' faces, hoping to find one with some humanity, some sympathy and kindness.

Instead, he found a familiar pair of eyes looking soberly back at him, and the shock jolted him to the core.

"Sorry, dude," Joey said with a guilty shrug. "You know I need the money."

Arthur bit.

Once an operating room registered nurse, **Bridgett Nelson** so enjoyed playing with human organs, she decided to turn her macabre interest into a horror writing career. She was a 2022 nominee of the Michael Knost "Wings" Award and won second-place in the KillerCon '22 Gross-Out contest in Austin, Texas. Bridgett has contributed to multiple anthologies, including *Counting Bodies Like Sheep*, edited by K Trap Jones. Her debut collection, *A Bouquet of Viscera*, is now available in all formats. Visit her website at www.bridgettnelson.com.

GO AT THROTTLE UP
BY RONALD MALFI

Tuesday, January 28, 1986

Laurel Coombs was a nervous wreck. She'd been anxious all week, her skin breaking out, her stomach slowly twisting into a knot, her breath souring because she kept forgetting to eat. It wasn't as though *she* were being launched into space, although maybe that was the reason—an opportunity missed. Some other schoolteacher was going to flee this pale blue dot (if just for a time), while Laurel—dowdy, anxious, pimply Laurel Coombs— remained here with her feet rooted firmly to the ground.

As she pulled into the parking lot of the Shadwell Day School (*Shadwell Students are loyal and true*, proclaimed the school motto), she twisted the car's radio dial one last time, hunting for some last-minute snippet, some morsel, about the launch. She ultimately snagged a signal at the far end of the dial that crackled with static: "...after three delays is finally scheduled for launch this morning from Florida's Cape Canaveral. The mission, designated STS-51-L by NASA, will be the tenth flight for the *Challenger* orbiter and the twenty-fifth flight of the shuttle fleet. The countdown is scheduled to begin today at—"

The blast of a car horn nearly shot Laurel out of her seat. She looked up at the rearview mirror and saw a pea-green Pinto idling behind her, its tailpipe belching out clouds of black exhaust as the driver waited to park. It was Mr. Damask, the Phys Ed teacher, agitating behind the Pinto's wheel; when he realized she was staring at him, he urged her to get out of his way with one hand.

She pulled into a parking space at the far side of the lot, intent on listening to the rest of the broadcast before going into the school. But the broadcast about the shuttle launch had ended, the disc jockey having transitioned to sports, and once again Laurel felt as if she'd missed some grand opportunity.

Before climbing out of the car, she glanced at her reflection in the rearview mirror, saw that the rouge she'd applied that morning was doing its best to hide the greenish bruise along her left cheekbone, and then she glanced down at the gold bracelet that dangled loosely from one red-freckled wrist. Larry's latest apology. When she thought of Larry lately, it was not his fists that immediately came to mind, but his derisive laughter, the way he'd called her stupid, the way he'd forced her to tear up her application last year. Laurel had come to realize that those things—the laughter, the derision—were worse than taking the occasional uppercut to the belly or an open-handed crack across the jowls. Physical pain faded over time; that other shit left scars.

The buses were arriving, a cheddar-yellow convoy creeping along Capshaw Street in front of the school, which meant Laurel was already late. She leapt out of her car and hurried halfway across the parking lot before remembering her brown-bag lunch on the passenger seat. Not that she was all that hungry—she hadn't been hungry for days, it seemed, her anxiety was so great—but she returned to the car, grabbed her lunch, then hustled into the school just as the pneumatic doors of the school buses hissed open and the students began tumbling out.

Principal Akers stood on the other side of the doors, just as he did every morning, not so much to greet the students as to observe, like some predatory bird perched on a high branch. Akers was a morose, gloomy-eyed academic, and it was well-known throughout the pistachio-colored hallways of Shadwell that he was a man of routine—he even wore the same tweed sports coat with the suede elbow patches every day. Laurel knew it had caused Principal Akers some minor consternation to allow for that morning's assembly, where the first-, second-, and third-grade students would gather in the library to watch the *Challenger* launch live on television. It had been Mrs. Howell who had harangued Akers into submission—it was an event not to be missed, Mrs. Howell had argued a week prior while deliberately interrupting Akers' lunch hour; history in the making, and with a *schoolteacher* on board, no less! For the children to miss it would be downright criminal. How could Akers say no?

Laurel was secretly pleased. She hadn't wanted to miss the launch, of course, but unless Akers acquiesced to the assembly, she'd be stuck listening to it on the small transistor radio she kept in her classroom. That Mrs. Howell had been ballsy enough to make such a demand...well, Laurel admired the older woman all the more for it.

"Good morning, Ms. Coombs," Principal Akers said, nodding perfunctorily in Laurel's direction. Laurel smiled, averted her eyes, then scurried past him down the hall.

The classroom was an eruption of primary colors and students' artwork. Despite this visual overstimulation, the room was also quiet for the time being, and Laurel luxuriated in it, knowing her students would be charging down the hall and spilling into their seats at any moment. She turned on the radio beside her desk and rolled through the dial, hunting for another snippet of that morning's launch. But there was nothing but rock music and commercials on the air now.

And then they came, a tidal wave of screeching rubber soles, piercing voices, and all manner of indistinct animal sounds that signaled, as always, the beginning of the school day here at Shadwell. Chair legs scraped along the scuffed linoleum floor; the bell shrilled. A collection of eyes gradually migrated in Laurel Coombs' direction.

The morning was mostly uneventful. She had them work on art projects—construction paper, tubes of paste, safety scissors, *make your own rocket!*—while she kept returning her attention to the radio beside her desk. She had the volume so low that the kids couldn't hear it. *She* could barely hear it herself, but it made her feel like she was part of something—part of the launch—to have it on.

Twenty minutes into the morning, Michael Tremens came into the classroom. He was often late, so Laurel knew better than to ask him for a note; she just watched him slip through the door, slink along the wall, his enormous backpack too heavy for his slender, eight-year-old frame. Strange little Michael Tremens, with his book of animal facts tucked under one arm, chunky eyeglasses pinching the bridge of his nose, and a bruise on his right cheek that served as an eerie companion to Laurel's own. Most of the other students paid him no attention; Eli Wentmoore, however, looked up from his messy art project—he'd been gluing pieces of construction paper to his desk—and zeroed in on the smaller boy. Laurel watched as Eli's piggish gray eyes narrowed and one corner of his lipless mouth hooked upward in a spiteful grin. That look made her think of Larry, and how he'd looked very much like that on the day he found her application hidden in her underwear drawer. How he'd smirked and laughed at her. Called her stupid.

Eli muttered some comment that elicited laughter from a few of the students. Michael Tremens ignored him and sat quietly in his seat at the back of the classroom. Laurel, who had been surfing the stations on her radio until now, got up and brought some art supplies to Michael's desk. The kid looked up at her, his large brown eyes swimming behind the lenses of his glasses. She felt a pang of sadness at the sight of that bruise.

"Fact," Michael Tremens said. "A chameleon's tongue is as long as its body."

Eli Wentmoore pointed and laughed at him. This enticed some of the other students to laugh, too.

"Settle down, now," Laurel said. She set the basket of art supplies on the corner of Michael's desk then crept back to her desk, her radio.

Then—and she must have zoned out, because it was as if no time at all had passed—Principal Akers' voice came crackling through the intercom system, inviting the lower grades, first, second, and third, to the library. A ripple of excitement rolled through Laurel's classroom. Laurel, too, was excited, so much so that her stomach was tied all in knots again and her hands were beginning to tremble.

She collected her students in a single-file line at the door, then led them out into the hallway. Other classes were already trickling down the hall toward the library, Mrs. Howell at the front of one line, her sharp, no-nonsense face as looming and prominent as one of the statues on Easter Island. Mrs. Howell held her clacker above her head—a small device that made a loud *clack-clack* sound—and sent those loud little reports echoing down the corridor. The children covered their ears but stayed in line.

Laurel, too, fell in line. She and her students followed Mrs. Howell to the library. They entered to find a boxy television set had been wheeled into the library on a cart. Obedient little cherubs, the students all hunkered down on the fire-retardant carpet in tidy rows, cross-legged, a vein of itchy excitement pulsing collectively through them. Their chatter simmered to a hushed, breathy sizzle as Akers stood before them, also appearing itchy, nervously twitchy, clearing his throat over and over like a scratched record while one of the school custodians got the TV to work.

Laurel watched as Mrs. Howell and some of the other teachers relocated to the wall of windows. Mrs. Howell cranked open one large window, and soon they were all smoking, their heads, like those of cattle in a pen, crooked out the open window where they expelled plumes of cigarette smoke into the air. Up until a year ago, Laurel had smoked, too. But she'd quit once she decided to fill out the application. She'd started running, too, and shed pounds quickly. She was healthier now, one year later, even though Larry had made her tear up that application. Even though he'd called her fat and stupid.

Across the library, the children cheered when the flight crew appeared on the television screen. All seven of them in their matching blue flight suits, smiling for the cameras, so ready to leave planet Earth that Laurel could taste their anticipation, a sour giddiness, at the back of her own throat. The footage was prerecorded, Laurel realized, when the camera cut to a shot of the shuttle on the launch pad. The children cheered again.

The countdown began, and a nervous energy once more started to permeate the entire room—from the children to the duo of custodians, the librarian (a surly old cuss who'd been there for half a century), the other teachers, and even Laurel herself as she exhaled nervous, jittery breaths while her hands wrestled with each other. The bracelet Larry had given her as an apology for the bruise caught a beam of sunlight and sparkled like cold fire. It hurt Laurel's eyes.

What if I was the schoolteacher launched into orbit, watching the world shrink and shrink and shrink as I left it all behind?

That space shuttle on the screen, facing skyward. An unseen male voice saying, "T-minus fifteen seconds," and that knot in Laurel's belly, pulling tighter. A shot of the engines igniting, spitting orange fire that burned to invisibility, and the unseen man that said, "T-minus ten, nine, eight," and that knot turned to a fist, "seven, six," and Mrs. Howell spat smoke out into the atmosphere, "five, four, and we have main engines start," tighter and tighter, burning brighter, "three, two, one, and liftoff, liftoff, of the twenty-fifth space shuttle mission, and it has cleared the tower..."

The shuttle went up, went up, went up. Laurel watched, her body perspiring despite the January chill coming in from the open window. Up and up, and then—

What if that was me—

—an explosion of white smoke, bisecting like a tuning fork, tendrils soaring silently through a bright blue sky, was suddenly all she could see on the screen.

(what if)

She just stared at the image, unable to comprehend what she was seeing. A man's voice issued from the TV, eerily calm, repeating, "It seems...it seems..." White streamers of smoke arced down, great spidery tendrils, and there was nothing left, nothing.

Oh, Laurel thought.

The camera cut away, to the crowd gathered below now, and there were the schoolteacher's parents, gazing heavenward, desperate to make sense of what they were seeing, confused, much like Laurel herself had been only moments ago, still somehow grinning at the inferno thousands of feet above their heads in the blue, cloudless sky.

Principal Akers, trembling and green, the wide expanse of his forehead glistening with a constellation of sweat, stood in front of the TV. He fumbled with the buttons until he managed to switch the set off. Then he ran a hand across his receding hairline, revealing a dark, damp stain in the armpit of his tweed sports coat. Even from across the room, Laurel thought she could sense the panic trembling up the long, rigid stalk of his body.

"Out," he bellowed, thrusting an index finger toward the open doors and at the hallway beyond. "Get them all *out.*"

Mrs. Howell flicked her half-smoked Marlboro out the window. The clacker was back in her hand now, firing its sharp little barks into the room, *clack! clack! clack!* The students jolted to their feet and formed a single line at the library door.

"Out," Akers repeated, his voice reedy and hoarse. "Out *now.*"

"Wake up," Mrs. Howell said very close to Laurel's face as she waved her students out of the library and into the hallway.

Laurel blinked. Took a breath. Felt that knot in her belly tighten even more. Then she rounded up her brood, assigned Becky as the line leader, and had Becky marshal them all out into the hallway.

"Send them outside," Mrs. Howell was telling the other teachers. No one would argue with that pinched, angular face.

Laurel led them down the hall to their lockers, where they gathered their coats and hats, and then she ushered them out onto the playground. In somewhat of a daze, she watched them descend upon the swings, seesaws, jungle gyms, and ball fields, their aggression merciless as an assault. It was as if nothing had ever happened. It was as if the world kept on turning and these children were none the wiser.

"Ms. Coombs?"

She looked down and saw Michael Tremens standing there. Meek, bullied, quiet Michael Tremens. His clothes outdated, his hair never combed, a pair of big bright eyes like searchlights behind those too-big glasses of his. He had both hands pressed to his belly.

"What is it, Michael?"

"Fact," he announced. "I feel yucky."

She closed her eyes. Her head was spinning. "Go play, Michael."

But when she opened her eyes, he was still standing there. That greenish-purple bruise shone on his cheek. She'd pulled an older kid off him last week, on this very playground. Kids could be vicious little shits. Although, now that she thought of it, he'd brought that bruise with him from home.

We're quite the pair, she thought.

"What?" she barked at him, then immediately regretted it.

Something trembled behind his eyes. It looked as if he were going to say something more—another ludicrous fact, perhaps—but in the end, he whirled around and bolted across the blacktop toward the field.

Mrs. Howell was suddenly standing beside her. "Let them run around and work off some energy. Then we'll send them to lunch."

Laurel closed her eyes. She kept seeing that forked tongue of smoke wherever she looked—in the bisecting branches of a tree, as a crack in the pavement, in the tuning-fork shape of the veins along the back of her left hand. Larry's bracelet—

(I'm sorry, okay, for doing what I did, Laur, so hey, here, I got you this, just, you know, to show just how sorry I am, because, well...I mean, I love you, Laur, but still...)

—flashed along her wrist. So bright, it hurt her eyes.

"Laurel? Are you okay? What's wrong with you?"

"I think I might pass out," Laurel said.

"Yes. You look terrible. Go to the nurse's office and lie down."

Laurel nodded, but didn't move. The children's shrill cries on the playground sounded almost birdlike to her ears.

"Go before you take a spill and hit your head," Mrs. Howell instructed.

Laurel managed to suck in a breath. She looked out across the playground—those crisscrossing jungle gym bars echoing the shape of that shuttle explosion, and Christ, had that really just *happened?*—then she retreated back inside the school.

The hallway was silent. The older kids had watched the launch from their classrooms, and those classroom doors were shut now. Laurel hurried past, glancing into one of the rooms as she went, right through the wire-mesh strip of glass beside the door and at the stone-white faces of the students inside, the teacher, Ted Clammock, speaking animatedly with his hands. The sight of him as she fled down the corridor caused something to flutter at the back of Laurel's throat.

The school nurse was a meticulous, middle-aged woman with a bosom like the prow of a frigate. Everyone at Shadwell Day School called her Nurse Nylons. That wasn't her real name, of course, but a nickname bestowed upon her (by the faculty, not the students) because of the way her heavy thighs rubbed together whenever she shuffled through the halls, making her hose go *shish-shish*.

Nurse Nylons was straddling a stool, reading a paperback romance novel when Laurel blustered through the door.

"You're as green as pea soup," Nurse Nylons said, levitating off the stool. "You eat the tapioca pudding again?"

"That space shuttle blew up," Laurel said. She felt hot, sticky.

"What's that?"

"The, uh, the *Challenger*? The space shuttle with that, um, that teacher on it?"

"Here, sit down." Nurse Nylons patted the padded table with its sheet of butcher's paper stretched across it.

Laurel sat on the edge of the table, the butcher's paper crinkling as she shifted her weight. She looked around the room, at the eye chart on the wall, the canister of tongue depressors, a blood pressure cuff hanging from a stainless-steel hook. There used to be Sesame Street posters in here, and one of Clifford the Big Red Dog, but Nurse Nylons wasn't keen on Muppets or oversized cartoon dogs; the only posters on the walls now were landscapes captioned with inspirational phrases. The pièce de résistance was a one-off of Jesus Christ with his benevolent arms outstretched, backlit by some weird volcanic—

(explosion)

—light.

"Here." Nurse Nylons thrust a small paper cup filled with water in front of her. "Drink this down. You'll feel better."

Laurel sucked the water down her constricted throat, and when she was done, Nurse Nylons took the paper cup from her, crumpled it up, and dumped it in the wastebasket beside her desk.

"You didn't watch the shuttle launch?" Laurel asked.

Nurse Nylons clamped a sweaty palm to Laurel's forehead. She ignored Laurel's question. "You don't feel feverish. What exactly is the problem?"

"I guess I just got dizzy for a minute."

"You need a little more skin on them bones, you ask me."

"I'll be okay. Just need to catch my breath."

"And what happened here?" Nurse Nylons' hand went up to touch the bruise on the side of Laurel's face. Laurel jerked backward, knocking the side of her head against a gooseneck lamp protruding from the wall. "Oh, honey..."

"Can't...breathe..." Laurel rasped.

Nurse Nylons pivoted to her desk, dumped food from a brown paper bag, then handed the bag to Laurel. "Deep breaths, dear. Deep. You'll be okay."

Laurel expelled stale air into the bag. Her whole body was trembling.

"There you go. See? Better? Now what was it you said happened?" Nurse Nylons asked.

Laurel lowered the bag. Took in a lungful of clean air. "That space shuttle. It...it exploded..."

"Oh." Nurse Nylons' eyes went large, and she covered her mouth with one short-fingered hand. There was a radio on the corner of her desk; she went to it now, switched it on. Static at first, but then she found a station where a man was saying, "...here, now, this national tragedy, the *Challenger* has exploded seventy-three seconds into its flight, with all seven crewmembers aboard, including schoolteacher and payload specialist Christa McAuliffe..."

"Please," Laurel said, clamping both hands to her ears.

Nurse Nylons switched the radio off. The silence that followed was deafening. She must have recognized the anguish in Laurel, because she came over and put a tender hand on her back.

"That could've been me," Laurel said, her voice barely above a whisper.

"What are you talking about, dear?"

"I never told anybody. I never even told Larry, although he found out when he discovered the application for the Teachers in Space Program. I lost weight, I stopped smoking. I wanted to *go*."

"Go where, dear?"

Away, she thought, but couldn't bring herself to say. *Away from here, far away, from this school and from Larry and from the terrible bullies, young and old, and all manner of mankind. Away, away...*

"Let me get you some more water," Nurse Nylons said.

Just then, a door slammed somewhere out in the hallway. It was as loud as a gunshot, and both Laurel and Nurse Nylons jerked their heads toward the closed door. Heavy footsteps resounded down the hall, growing louder with each approaching detonation. Another sound, too—a high-pitched keening, intermittent, like some mechanical whine. Nurse Nylons hurried to the door, *shish-shish,* and threw it open.

The heavy footfalls belonged to Mrs. Howell. She appeared in the doorway, her face stricken white. Her mouth was set so firmly, she was nearly lipless. She was accompanied by Eli Wentmoore, who was sobbing to beat the band: great jellyfish tears rolled down his beet-red cheeks. He was clutching an arm to his chest. Laurel could see blood seeping through the clasp of his fingers.

"What happened?" Laurel asked, but she spoke in a tone just hardly above a whisper, and anyway, no one was paying her any attention at the moment.

"This!" Mrs. Howell shouted. "Look here! Look what happened!" And then she practically shoved little Eli Wentmoore against Nurse Nylons' formidable bosom. "His arm. Will you look?"

Eli Wentmoore howled as Nurse Nylons pulled his injured arm away from his chest.

"It's beastly," said Mrs. Howell. Then she glanced at Laurel, a strange fire in her eyes. For a split second, Laurel felt as though Mrs. Howell's stare was accusing her of some indecency.

"Oh," said Nurse Nylons, rather softly, as she observed Eli's arm.

From where she sat, Laurel could see the jagged wound oozing blood, a pocket of flesh scooped out from the boy's forearm.

Nurse Nylons said, "How'd—"

"He was *bitten*," said Mrs. Howell. "That's a *bite* on his arm, for Christ's sake."

"My Jesus," said Nurse Nylons, and then she genuflected. "What in the world bit him?"

Eli Wentmoore screeched and tugged his injured arm back against his chest.

"*What?*" Mrs. Howell said, her eyes going even wider now with apparent incredulity. To Laurel's astonishment, something akin to a laugh juddered up the woman's throat. *"What?"*

"What bit him?" Nurse Nylons repeated.

Under her breath, as though she were relaying a terrible secret, Mrs. Howell muttered, *"Who,* you mean. That little weirdo. The Tremens boy." She said this through clenched teeth.

Laurel said, *"Michael?"*

"It's his home-life," Mrs. Howell said, clearly exasperated now. She kept glancing at the bloody gash on Eli Wentmoore's arm. "There are problems in that house, you know. Those people! He's always bruised up. And now he's acting out, taking it out on other children—"

"No, no, he's bruised because a fifth grader was beating him up on the playground the other—" But then she remembered, no, that wasn't where he'd gotten the bruise; he'd gotten it at home.

"There are problems and then there are *problems,*" Mrs. Howell practically hissed. Laurel had no idea what the woman was talking about. "There are issues, and then there are *issues.*"

"We need to call this boy's mother," Nurse Nylons was saying. "That's a serious bite. I've never seen a bite like that. The human mouth is filled with all sorts of bacteria. He may need a shot. He may be infected. And he definitely needs stitches."

This caused Eli Wentmoore to cry louder.

"Where's Michael now?" Laurel asked. She could feel reality clawing its way back inside her.

"I had Leo Damask take the nasty little biter to Akers' office," Mrs. Howell said.

Laurel slid down off the padded bench, the butcher's paper crackling and sliding halfway down with her.

"Someone should call his *mother*," Nurse Nylon repeated. She was opening a bottle of peroxide, though she looked skeptical about using it on such a fierce wound.

Laurel didn't wait around to see what the nurse would do; she went quickly to the door.

"Where are you going?" There was something like indignation in Mrs. Howell's voice now.

Laurel said nothing and instead fled the room and hurried across the hall toward the front office. A bank of windows, behind which sat Steffie Proust, Principal Akers' secretary, loomed before her. Steffie was ordinarily a cheery, good-natured woman, but she'd gone marble-cold in the presence of little Michael Tremens, it seemed, seated across from her now in a chair that looked about ready to swallow him up. He was so small, his feet dangled three inches off the floor. He had his hands planted on his knees and looked like a kid in a movie theater waiting patiently for the feature to start.

There was blood smeared across Michael's mouth, and some on his shirt. Eli's blood.

Mr. Damask stood beside the boy's chair, his arms folded across his chest. He wore a horror-struck expression that belied any authority he was trying to project.

Laurel said, "Michael?"

Michael stared up at her. That swipe of ruby-red blood across the boy's lips caused that knot in Laurel's belly to roll over, a lead weight now. She plucked some Kleenex from the box on Steffie's desk, bent down, and rubbed at the blood on Michael's lips. He let her do it.

"What happened, Michael?"

"Kid went nuts," Mr. Damask said. "He attacked that Wentmoore boy on the playground. Bit him like a rabid dog."

She held Michael's gaze with her own. Squeezed his shoulder gently with one hand. "Why, Michael?" she asked him. "Why'd you bite him?"

Something behind the boy's eyes went foggy. Laurel drew back, the wad of bloody Kleenex clenched in one white-knuckled fist.

The door to Akers' office opened, and the principal shuffled out. He looked pale, shaken, confused. He'd taken off his tweed coat and had the sleeves of his button-down shirt cuffed to the elbows.

"I just got off the phone with Eli Wentmoore's father," Akers announced. "He's...he's going to press charges. He said to keep young Michael here with us until the police can—"

"The *police?*" Laurel said, standing. "Is that really necessary?"

"It's an assault. An...an attack..."

"Eli has been bullying Michael all year. I'm sure he was just defending himself."

Akers rubbed a set of overlong fingers across the ridge of his brow. He looked instantly exhausted. "Ms. Coombs, that isn't for you or me to decide. Mr. Wentmoore was quite upset. And the school, as you know, has a strict zero tolerance policy on—"

"Oh, that's ridiculous! His son is a bully!"

"Ms. Coombs, *please...*"

"Well, then you need to call Michael's parents, too."

Akers shifted his tired gaze to his secretary.

"I've been trying but no one answers," Steffie said.

"Keep trying, I guess," Akers suggested.

Steffie nodded, picked up the phone, and began to dial.

Laurel looked back at Michael. Eli's blood had stained his lips, making him look hideously clown-like. Those foggy, distant eyes kept swimming behind the thick lenses of his glasses.

"At least let me take him to the bathroom to clean him up," she said.

"Uh," Akers said, and shot a glance at Mr. Damask.

"I'll take him," Mr. Damask said. He reached down, groping for Michael's arm.

Michael pulled away from him, curling up in a ball in one corner of the chair.

"*I'll* take him," Laurel said. She extended a hand to the boy, Larry's gold apology bracelet glittering on her thin, freckled wrist. "Come on, Michael. Come with me."

The boy hesitated. But then he reached out, took her hand, and climbed up off the chair. She led him out of the office and down the hall. The door of the nurse's office was still open and she could hear Eli Wentmoore wailing in there, could see shadows moving along one wall. This prompted her to pick up the pace.

The classroom was empty, the children still out on the playground. She released Michael's hand and hurried over to her desk, snatching her purse off her chair. Then she urged him back out into the hall.

"Hurry, hurry," she told him.

"Where are we going?"

"To my car."

She winced against the daylight as they fled from the building, car keys already jangling in her hand. It took her three times to jab the key in the door, but she finally got it.

"Get in," she shouted.

Michael opened the passenger door and climbed inside the car.

She jumped behind the wheel, cranked the ignition. Her mind whirling, she heard the static-laden crackle of a man's voice, saying, *and liftoff, liftoff, of the twenty-fifth space shuttle mission, and it has cleared the tower...*

She reversed out of the parking space too quickly, and felt the car jolt as it struck another vehicle. She glanced around and saw she had knocked a headlight out of Leo Damask's ugly green Pinto. She switched the car into Drive then gunned it out of the parking lot.

Michael didn't speak until they were halfway across town. "Fact," he said. "The cheetah is the fastest land mammal, reaching speeds of nearly seventy miles per hour." He looked up at her, those brown eyes exaggerated behind his too-big glasses. "Where are we going, Ms. Coombs?"

"I'm taking you home, Michael." She knew Michael Tremen's address by heart, since she'd written so many letters to the boy's parents—all unanswered—in the past. She'd pawed through his file, too, from time to time, and had even considered contacting Social Services after the kid had come to school with suspicious marks on his arms and face. Poor kid, with his recitation of strange facts and his body blackened with bruises. "They're gonna call the cops on you, but that's bullshit, Michael. That Eli Wentmoore, he's a bully. He's trouble. Not you." And then she looked at him. "Why'd you bite him? What'd he do to you?"

Michael shook his head, shrugged his shoulders. "Nothing," he said.

"Nothing? He didn't hit you? He didn't shove you down?"

"No."

"Then why'd you bite him?"

"Fact," Michael said, his voice a thin rasp. "Cannibalism is common among animals. Typically, it is the strong who eat the weak." Then he smiled, his lips stained red with Eli Wentmoore's blood. His teeth, too. "But not today, Ms. Coombs. Not today."

The radio, she realized, was on. A voice rushed out at her: "...and when I saw the fireball in the sky, I knew...no one could describe...I just knew..."

She switched it off.

They drove the rest of the way in silence until she asked him which house was his.

"There," Michael said. He pointed at the small blue house nestled among a wedge of trees at the end of the street. A rundown, ramshackle, single-story house, with the shades drawn over all the windows. There was a chain-link fence around the property and a sign that read BEWARE OF DOG.

Beware of Michael, she thought, a finger of giddy laughter rising up inside her.

She pulled up to the curb and switched the car to Park. The place looked strangely deserted, although there was a vehicle in the driveway.

"Hey," she said. "Are your parents home?"

He hesitated, then said, "Yes."

"Should I speak with them? Tell them what happened?"

He seemed to consider this. In the end, he said, quite simply, "No."

"How come they don't answer the phone?" *Or any of the letters I've sent from the school,* she thought, but did not add.

Michael just stared at her. Said nothing.

She glanced at the house again. The trashcans on the side of the house were overflowing. A notion—such a bizarre notion—crossed her mind. But it was there and then gone, quick as a flash of firelight in the sky.

"Okay," she said, and gave him a smile. "Off with you."

"Goodbye, Ms. Coombs." He popped open the passenger door and dropped out onto the sidewalk. After he slammed the door, she watched him wend his way through an opening in the fence, across the overgrown yard, up the crumbling walkway. He paused before entering the house to peer back at her from over one narrow shoulder. Something in those eyes again, though she couldn't quite decipher exactly what it was. Anyway, she wasn't sure she wanted to.

And then he was gone, swallowed up by the house. It was as if she'd dreamt the entire escape from the school, the drive out here, the strange discussion of cannibalism in the car. All of it—just a dream.

She thought, *Shadwell students are loyal and true.*

Life was funny like that. For example, how funny was it that Larry had inadvertently saved her life by making her tear up that Teachers in Space application? That could've been her on that space shuttle this morning. Here one second, gone the next, in a burst of fire and a puff of white smoke.

She switched the radio back on. The station was replaying the shuttle commander's final words to ground control. *"Roger, go at throttle up."*

And then: silence.

(could've)

She looked down at the bracelet, sparkling there on her wrist. He'd saved her life, and wasn't that funny? Maybe she'd been too hard on him. He loved her, after all.

Laurel Coombs pulled out into the street and shuttled toward home.

Ronald Malfi is an award-winning author of many novels and novellas in the horror, mystery, and thriller genres. In 2011, his novel *Floating Staircase* was nominated for a Bram Stoker Award for best novel by the Horror Writers Association and also won a gold IPPY award. In 2021, *Come with Me*, about a man who learns a dark secret about his wife after she's killed, became a bestseller and has received stellar reviews, including a starred review from *BookPage* and *Publishers Weekly*, who stated, "Malfi impresses in this taut, supernaturally tinged mystery... and sticks the landing with a powerful denouement. There's plenty here to enjoy." His most recent novel is *Black Mouth*, published by Titan Books. He currently lives along the Chesapeake Bay with his wife and kids. When he's not writing, he's performing with his rock band, VEER.

TIKI BAR AT THE EDGE OF FOREVER
BY DANIEL BRAUM

Long Island, New York. 1987

The Tiki Hut's pink neon sign is a beacon in the night to the Friday night grown-ups coming from their breathless, non-illuminated lives. From our vantage in the Dairy Barn parking lot, we've got the perfect view. June's first fireflies hover at the edge of the streetlight out in front of Tom's Hardware and Richie's Stationary, The Deli, and the soda shop on the corner where we gather to get our smokes for fourth period. They're closed and dark except for the ever-present glow of the Galaga console leaking through The Deli's window. How can it be that there are only two days of our routine left?

A couple my parents' age, laughing and almost giddy—on shore leave from suburban existence, open the Tiki Hut's black front door. It's made of the same opaque glass as the window. I catch a blast of something obscenely bouncy before it closes behind them and they are gone.

The echo of firecrackers going off on a nearby cul-de-sac reaches us.

"Hey, Ihaka, put a tape in to kill the quiet," Sarah says from the back.

Despite the linebacker's frame and rock-star black hair he's grown into, I'll always see him as the kind boy next door. His glazed-over stare disturbs me.

"These are all the ways America eats itself, right," I say, hoping for a reaction.

It's the sort of thing that usually gets him going. But he remains a ghost in the front passenger seat.

Dairy Barn's lights go off. David's spindly frame appears a minute later, Ihaka's lei still around his neck. With his almost-moustache, shock of curly hair, and old Hawaiian shirt, he looks a lot like the manager he likes to complain about, mostly for the offense of not letting him play Rush tapes during his shifts.

The fresh lei was a graduation gift from Ihaka's grandma, who's been sending them for as long as I can remember. Those leis were the one thing generous Ihaka would never take off, yet he gave this one to David yesterday just like that.

"Hi Wendy, I'm home," David says in his best Jack Nicholson impersonation.

A hint of gunpowder and the sea is in the humid night air. Along with the reek of Dairy Barn's dumpster. David hops in the back seat with Sarah and proceeds to go through my tape case.

"Tangerine Dream, more Tangerine Dream…I can barely read your writing, Melissa; you *are* going to be a doctor."

The Tangerine Dream tapes were gifted to me while sleeping out for Jones Beach tickets last year. A woman old enough to be my mom and high as could be gave them to me and told me to put them on when in bed with a boy. I dig the band, though her very-stoned burst of generosity I remember with a strange sadness because it's as close to any big sister advice anyone's ever given me.

"…Kitaro, The Police, The Cars…Melissa, really? Gag. Okay, *Master of Puppets*—"

"Give it here," I say and put it in.

Usually Ihaka has to wait his turn for it. Kirk Hammett is the only Hawaiian rock star I know of.

"Turn it up, Mel," David says. "Hey, Ihaka. Flask, please."

Ihaka mechanically hands him the flask. It's full of his notorious green mixture of Midori liquor.

"Drink up," David says. "I'll drive tonight."

"Poison to me."

"It's the last week of school, come on."

"Sugar is death. At least for me. And everything becomes sugar. Speaking of which, I totally forgot to take my shot."

I ask Ihaka to hand me my bag at his feet. As I take my insulin kit out of my bag, red and blue cop lights flash on in the dark corner of the lot. I stress but see it's Mr. Millman, our neighbor from the block. He walks over with his flashlight trained on me.

"Melissa. Ihaka, kids," he says. "Anything going on here that's not supposed to be?"

"Nope. Just picking up David, Mister M. Realized I forgot to do my shot."

I can feel David and Sarah squirming. Our pot is safely hidden in the glove box, in the first aid kit.

Mister M shines the light around. He's worried about us. Once upon a time, it was only the City that ate you alive. He knows we go to the beach. Everyone's heard about the bodies found out east. It's all over the evening news.

"Two more days and you are high school graduates," he says.

It's his way of saying *be careful*. After he departs, Ihaka abruptly gets out of the car.

"Hey? What's up with you?" I say.

"I don't feel like going to the beach."

Lauren, the new girl at school, has stepped out of the Tiki Bar and is standing outside having a smoke. She's the daughter of the new owners.

Ihaka crosses the street and goes to her.

"What's with him?" David says. "He's known 'friends come first' since like sixth grade."

"I don't think it's that," I say.

I start the car, pull around, and double park in front of the Tiki Bar. Ihaka's nervous. Finally, a reaction.

"Hey, guys, this is Lauren. Lauren, these are my pals."

"Hey," I say. "We're gonna cruise the causeway and pull over at one of our spots, Ihaka, so you know where we're gonna be. You both can come with, though."

Lauren is ordinary. She's dressed in busboy's blacks and smokes with the intensity of a grown-up. This is the closest I've ever been to her. Despite her looks, I can tell there is nothing ordinary about her. Nothing I can articulate. Maybe she spends too much time around grown-ups.

"I gotta get back to work, thanks," Lauren says. "You want to come in sometime? I'll ask my folks."

She flicks her smoke and opens the door.

There's a blast of air-conditioning and shitty music again and then everything goes black, all-encompassing black. An after image of fireworks only in a thousand shades of darkness swallows me.

Then I'm behind the wheel. Ihaka is getting back in the car and something about the way he moves tells me he's shrugged off his pensiveness. I've missed something. Missed a few seconds.

"Gang's all here again. Woo-hoo! Let's go," David says.

"Okay, let's go," I say slowly, trying to shake off my disorientation. "Just gotta take my shot first."

David takes a swig from the flask and passes it to Sarah.

I listen to them cheer each other on as I ready my injection.

You are what you put inside you. They just don't grasp it yet. Ihaka cranks the stereo. The thrashing rhythms wash over us.

I come home high. I pass Mom's best friend in the driveway who does a sloppy cheerleading thing when she notices me. They, of course, have had too much wine.

I head for the kitchen and hunt the fridge for a snack.

"Sweetie," Mom says. "You're excited for the prom."

It's a statement not a question and I'm betting it's to try and mask that she's lit. I can smell the cigarettes she "doesn't smoke" on her from across the room.

"I couldn't care less, Mom. Ihaka and the gang want to, so you know, to the prom it is."

This sends her into quiet contemplation so I speak before she can launch into some lame Hallmark philosophy.

"Mom, hey, how long has that Tiki Bar place been there up by the soda shop?"

"Oh, dear, well, let's see, we moved here in '72. It was there back then."

"You and Dad ever go?"

"No," she says. "Things were tight. We had work. And we had you. There wasn't much else…"

A stray thought about Ihaka's "Hawaiian" grandma jumps to mind. I remember Ihaka saying she's from New Zealand originally.

"…but when I was a girl, your age, back when I lived in Brooklyn, I went to the Mai-Kai a few times."

"The what?"

"It was the big deal place in the City. The well-to-do kids had their sweet sixteens there. It cost eleven dollars. That got you got a fancy drink, dinner, and the tropical show. Ooh, it had sexy head-hunter-guys dancing. Sort of like…Chippendales—"

"Mom! That's awful. I'm going to pretend I never heard that."

I know Hawaii only from Brady Bunch reruns. Curses and idols. Luaus and palm trees. Hula girls. One of Dad's friends went there on a trip he won for being salesman of the year once. I always knew Ihaka's feelings about Hawaii were something…intense. Something in the depths of his personal world unknown to me. As Mom rattles on about Don Ho, I wonder what it must really be like to be different like him. Being in Hebrew school was sort of like that, but I had Ronnie Greenbaum and the Seigels on my side when people called me a dumb blonde or a stupid JAP. Does Ihaka have anyone that understands him or even sees him at all?

After school, I give David a lift to Dairy Barn. His manager isn't there so he pops a tape in and the steady, low, opening notes of Rush's "Subdivisions" I've heard a billion times starts in.

"Enjoy yourself, Bozo," I say.

"You'll be back," he says in his best Schwarzenegger voice. "No, seriously, I'm off at eight. Come get me on the way to the beach."

Instead of going home, I drive across the road and park in the lot behind the Tiki Bar.

I put my face down on the steering wheel and allow myself to cry because here, with no one around, I can.

The Tiki Bar's back door opens. Lauren exits, hauling a black trash bag in each hand. After she throws them in the dumpster, she sees I'm here.

She motions for me to roll the window down and comes over.

"How can *you* be fucking sad," she says. "You're like miss number one cheerleader, everything's perfect."

"It's not—"

"Sorry, that was obnoxious," she says. "I didn't mean it that way. I know there are a million reasons to cry. You know this is my parents' place. Want to come inside and get wasted?"

"I don't drink."

"We have awesome coconut ice cream. It's for this new frozen drink. Wanna raid it with me?"

"I really shouldn't, but yeah, just this once, okay."

Without the cloak of night and artificial light, the bar's back hallway looks like someone's basement. Old wood paneling. Old everything and a sense of being stuck in time. The passage opens into the dark main area where the smells of dry beer and lemon floor cleaner hit me. It's even more humid than outside with ghosts of cigar smoke and cigarettes everywhere. A five-sectioned mural adorns the wall above the shelf of liquor behind the bar. The center section is a portrait of a Hawaiian Queen in formal attire, hair up and regal, sitting on a throne. The panel to her left is of a tall ship anchored off a beach full of idols and tikis. The panel to her right has a bunch of Hawaiian guys in grass skirts, holding knives and spears to the neck of an old-fashioned, fancy-looking white guy. The two outer sections are of local people in Hawaiian shirts, each of them holding up a tropical drink.

So this is the place? The location of so many stories of debauchery from my friend's older siblings? It's a freaking dump. Being an adult must suck.

Lauren disappears into the dark.

"This is my first time inside a bar," I say.

I hear her flip a switch. Strings of Christmas lights crisscrossing the ceiling wink to life, illuminating a wall adorned with license plates and a patchwork of photographs. Layers of faded polaroids overlap crisp glossy prints. All are shots of people in the Tiki Bar. The wall across from me is done up with paper Halloween skeletons draped in plastic flowers. A lone structural column is covered with plastic skulls and the husks of dried-up real flowers.

Lauren goes behind the bar and serves up two highball glasses full of ice cream.

"I mean, I can make you a fancy float if you want," she says. "I like it like this."

I plant myself on a bar stool, take a small amount onto my spoon and I put it in my mouth. The painting behind Lauren is staring down at me.

"That's Queen Lili'uokalani," Lauren says. "And that guy's Captain Cook."

"Who?"

"Captain Cook was the explorer dude that pretty much bullied Hawaii around. They eventually sent him back to his ship in pieces though. Queen Lili, she was the ruler of the Kingdom of Hawaii before it was overthrown."

"Who are all those bozos?

"Probably our neighbors, right? You know it's Senior Prom for Eisenhower High, tonight, right? Want to work a shift?"

"It is? Are a ton of kids coming?

"No. Their parents will though, Dad says. They come here until it's time for their kids to come home or pick them up from wherever."

"I can't. We're going to the beach."

"Didn't you go last night?

"Yeah. It's what we do. Where else is there? You can come."

"I gotta work."

I take another mouthful of ice-cream. The Christmas lights blur. Blackness gathers in the corners of my vision. I hear the mumble of a crowd. One of the bony hands of a skeleton on the wall moves.

"Okay, I've had enough."

"You barely touched it."

"I just had more sugar than I eat in a month. I'm diabetic."

"Oh, shit. I didn't know—"

A door on the wall of photos swings open. A man in jeans and t-shirt tromps across the floor.

"Dad, you're early. This is—"

"She the new busboy?"

"No she's my friend—"

"Mai-Tai," he mutters.

Lauren grabs bottles from the shelf behind her and beneath the bar and begins fixing a drink. He's bombed. She's scared of him. The situation is…revolting.

"Um, I'm gonna go. Thanks, Lauren."

Why would adults want to come here when they could do anything in the world at all? The bottles are pretty and the drink Lauren is making is colorful and bright, but it's all poison, pretty-looking poisons. I never want to come to a bar again.

We're given the cold-shoulder and are run off of our first choice of beach spots by a bunch of rich, NorthShore, surf-shop kids. I take us to our next choice, one of our plan B spots. A bunch of the ever-present little straw-brown bunnies flee my headlights as I pull over on the shoulder. I gun it in reverse into a little gap nestled in the dunes, perfectly out of view of both sides of the road and nosy cop-eyes; the state troopers are not as kindly as Mister M.

It's Sarah's turn for a tape and she's got some live Doors on the boom box.

I hear David and Ihaka talking as they start the fire.

"…after I graduate? I'll probably be in Hawaii by the fall."

"That's far. You've never been there."

"Hawaii never gave up its independence. It was forced into becoming a state. The Kingdom is still a real thing. You don't have to be part of the U.S. There is a choice…"

There's a huge splash in the waves. Then another and another. Dolphins are jumping just off shore, heading West parallel to the coast. Sarah and Ihaka clink paper cups at the sight of them.

"Here's to all the fools," Sarah says. "All the fools who are so close and don't even know dolphins are here and that you can do this."

"And hey, to our last night," David says. "Our last night before the last day of school! We should sleep here, on the beach."

"We have to make it to the bleachers by midnight," Sarah says.

It's a tradition for seniors to "sleep out" on the bleachers on the last night. Mostly, it's become an annoying game of cat and mouse with the teachers and the cops though.

David takes out our pot, shields a joint from the wind to light it, and takes a deep pull.

"There could be anything out there," David says, looking out to the ocean.

"And there probably is," I say. "Like sharks or a monster."

"Dude, your dad is from Scotland, right?" David says to Ihaka. "Didn't you tell me he saw the Loch Ness Monster once?"

Ihaka sprays green alcohol from his mouth with his laugh.

"He totally did," Ihaka manages to say while cracking up.

After he collects himself, he passes the joint.

"Dad is being totally cool," he says. "We're all set for the prom. He totally hooked me up with a bunch of bottles from his store."

I'm happy to see him acting like himself again. Sarah's house party and the prom is going to be a shit show but all things pass. I head into the dunes to pee.

Something moves in the beach grass. I expect to see a bunny fleeing at the sight of me but a child steps from the growth into a patch of moonlight-illuminated sand.

"Oh, hello," I say. "Are you lost?"

The little boy does not have a shirt on. He can't be more than two or three. He's calm. Too calm for a kid alone in the dark in the middle of nowhere.

"Are you okay?"

Looking past him, I see the silhouette of someone on the dune about a dozen yards away, just standing there, motionless. The breeze blows the grass, framing the person's shape. I squint and all the colors of the night-time sea appear in the blackness: an infinite amount of grays all muted in shadow.

There's another splash. The dolphins are throwing a fit of clicks and whistles.

The kid takes a wobbly step forward and falls on his face. His back is red and raw. There is a steak shape of missing flesh carved out of him. He has to be on drugs to not be screaming in pain. The cut is too clean and precise to be anything but intentional.

The figure on the dune shifts its weight, a barely perceptible movement, and the moonlight catches on the long knife I realize it is holding. Blackness creeps into the periphery of my vision, threatening to take me. My ears rumble. My throat goes dry. I fight to keep conscious and try to sneak a glance at the figure's face. I see…Lauren? No, she's not that tall. Is it the face of her drunk and sloppy Dad?

He raises his hand with the knife, and then he's someone else, someone more familiar, holding my insulin kit out to me. I think I'm going to scream, only, I'm looking at myself. It's me. *I'm* holding the carved cutout of the little boy's flesh. My teeth are sharp: triangular shark teeth too big for my mouth. I bite into the raw, steak-shaped flesh. A car crash fills my mind's eye. A body flying through a car windshield, impaled by thick chunks of glass. All goes black.

"Mel? Mel, snap out of it!"

I've fallen in the sand. David, Sarah, and Ihaka are helping me to my feet.

"I…saw the killer."

"What?"

"I saw him."

"No, you didn't," David says.

"Wait, how do you know what she saw?" Ihaka says.

"If she saw the killer, we'd all be dead."

"Did you forget your shot again, Mel?" Sarah asks.

"I did have too much sugar today, but I swear."

"Let's look around," Ihaka says.

They scour the area and look through the grass. They find nothing.

"There are no footprints here," Sarah says. "Nothing at all."

"I know I saw something."

"I'm on your side," Ihaka says. "I'm on *your* side. And I'm on *your* side," he says to David and Sarah. "It's the four of us back to back. Forever. No matter what happens. Okay, that's what I know. That's what it's all about.

That's what I wanted to tell everybody tonight."

"I'm spooked, man," David says. "Is she okay?"

"Mel, you okay?" Ihaka asks.

"I…guess so."

"She's okay, so here's what we're gonna do. We're gonna get high. We're gonna put on some Tangerine Dream for Mel. And we're gonna listen to the waves for a bit to mellow out, then head over to the bleachers for the last night of high school, okay?"

"Okay," David and Sarah answer in unison.

I say okay too, though I'm not okay. The body I saw go through the window was Ihaka. I think about going home and telling Mister M about the kid and everything, but we're so high and what good at all could come of it now?

Ihaka and I sit in his car with the windows rolled up, our place for important conversations. In the rearview, I see neighborhood kids run past, playing in the afternoon sun.

"What do you mean you're not going?" Ihaka says. "This is totally last minute, Mel. Why? Because you saw something—no you *think* you saw something—last night?"

"Just trust me. I saw you…getting hurt. Why is it so important? Please don't go."

"I need to belong somewhere."

"The prom is going to make you belong?"

"No, but you're pretty and can fit in anywhere."

"Fitting in is just an illusion. All that shit's just skin deep."

"Even if it's all fake you can still have it if you want. I'm going tonight to feel that, just for once. Please don't tell me you think there's anything wrong with that."

Through my front screen-door I watch Ihaka carry the alcohol his pop gave him from his house into his car. The kids have stopped their game and are staring at him in his tux, like I'm doing. They resume their play as he drives away.

"What's wrong?" Mom asks.

"I'm afraid I'm never going to see him again."

"College doesn't start until August. You have all summer, and then there's always Homecoming and Thanksgiving…"

She's right. It's just the stupid prom and we'll be back on the beach tomorrow.

"… your father's been working hard. We're going to be able to get you one of those new insulin pumps."

"Um, right. Thanks. Bye, Mom. Be back later."

I cruise over to the Tiki Bar and try the back door. Lauren's there, in the hallway carrying a tray of washed glasses.

"Hey, you came!"

"I did."

"Oh my god, do you want a cocktail? Let me make you one."

I follow her in and she sits me down at the bar. The place is full. In the night, with the lights and people, the "shithole" feels different.

"People will tell you otherwise but three ingredient cocktails are the way to go," Lauren says.

She pours pineapple juice into a metal shaker.

"Pineapple juice, with lime juice and rum is the best. The secret is fresh ingredients but the real secret is aeration."

"Besides tasting the green stuff from Ihaka's flask, this is the first I've ever had."

"You like it?"

"I don't taste any alcohol."

"Good!"

I hear the sizzle of a grill and the smell of something cooking reaches me. In the corner of my eye I spy a drink on the bar next to me, the unmistakable bright green of the Midori Ihaka uses. I turn and see it's Ihaka there, right there sitting next to me. Long red welts run down his face and neck; the angry wounds disappearing beneath his shirt. I realize the place is full. A crowd is pushing against us. Hands grab Ihaka. Fingers dig into his cuts and pull. His flesh peels away and I realize what is sizzling.

"Mel, you look pale," Lauren says. "Hey, are you are okay?"

"I don't think I should have had this drink," I say and fall forward into black.

I wake to the sounds of electric hums and beeping. The room is stark white. I'm in the hospital. I don't know what time it is. Mom is sitting in the chair next to my bed.

"Oh dear, you're awake. I was so worried about you," she says. "What were you thinking? You know you can't drink alcohol."

"Where is everybody? Is the prom over?"

I don't like the look on her face. A flash of the bar patrons with their hands coated in Ihaka's blood races through my mind.

"There was an accident," Mom says. "David is here. He's in stable condition. Ihaka…oh, honey." She pauses. "He didn't make it."

One year later

There's a fresh lei on Ihaka's grave.

It's late in the day. I didn't expect to run into anyone but Sarah is here. I haven't seen her in forever and we talk.

"I never see David, either," she says. "I heard he's living in the city or something. Oh, Mel, it's so sad. Ihaka never got to go to Hawaii."

"Hawaii wasn't just a place to visit for him," I say.

"Well, yeah. You know what I mean."

She points to the pump strapped to my waist.

"Oh, you've got that now. Good, you don't have to worry so much about the sugar."

The darkness isn't from sugar. It comes all the time now. She won't understand.

"Um, did I tell you, I got in to SUNY Binghamton?" she says to put something in the awkward quiet. "I'm transferring in the fall. We're totally going to stay in touch."

"Totally. We totally are."

The lie comes easy. She leans in and we embrace. I move my hand to her lower back and rest it there, above where her kidney is.

We're not slipping away slowly, painlessly, the way people do. We're already gone. Some things, like Ihaka, are just gone and there is only before and after. We're in the after, only she doesn't know it.

I'm in busboy blacks. Lauren's getting the bar top polished and ready for happy hour. WLIR is on the radio. Lauren's dad will put it back to dinosaur rock when it's time to open.

"Hey, Laur, I haven't been to the beach in so long. We should totally go."

"You know I've been living here, how long, over a year, and I've never been. I don't even know what to do?"

"I'll show you."

"Okay."

"Promise?"

"I promise. Not tonight though, but I promise. Hey, can you get the clean glasses from the kitchen hung up and ready?"

"Got it."

The DJ gives the traffic and weather and an update on the latest bodies that were found. Then it's opening time and the whirl of night begins.

After our shift, Lauren and I go outside and have a smoke. I ask her to change her mind and come to the beach tonight. She refuses.

"How about coming to Hawaii then," I say. "You ever been?

"What? Hawaii? No, that's a million miles away. Why?

"I don't know. I want to go. You know, for Ihaka."

"Really? What difference is it gonna make to him now?"

"I don't know. I just know it does."

"You should do it then. Go get a plane ticket."

"Now?"

"Yeah, now, before you change your mind."

"You're right. I'm gonna go to Kennedy and get a ticket."

"Whoa, you're serious? Am I gonna see you tomorrow for opening?"

"Yeah, of course. Unless I run away to Hawaii."

The neon sign in my rearview is a beacon in the night. A lure calling to the breathless. An irresistible, invisible hook to snare the empty-hearted. Ihaka knew it's what you put inside you that counts. Sadly, he wasted his time with that green booze he put in his flask. That was the way he liked it, with no pretty illusions or props.

I'm not going to get a plane ticket. I know what's really calling to me. I stop at home and nab a shovel from the tool shed. I drive to one of our old back-up spots off the causeway, pull over and reverse it into the dunes.

No tapes tonight. No campfire. I know Lauren's going to love it here, though.

In the sand, under the moonlight, I dig.

Daniel Braum writes "strange tales" in the tradition of Robert Aickman. His stories, set in locations around the globe, explore the tension between the psychological and supernatural.

His latest collection *Underworld Dreams* contains the story "How to Stay Afloat When Drowning," which also appears in the *Best Horror of the Year Volume 12* edited by Ellen Datlow.

His first collection *The Night Marchers and Other Strange Tales* and his first novella *The Serpent's Shadow* are being reissued as trade paperbacks by Cemetery Dance Publications in 2023. His first novel *Servant of the Eighth Wind* is forthcoming from Lethe Press.

He is also the author of *The Wish Mechanics: Stories of the Strange and Fantastic* (Independent Legions 2017) and the chapbook *Yeti Tiger Dragon* (Dim Shores 2016). His work has appeared in publications ranging from *Lady Churchill's Rosebud Wristlet* to the *Shivers 8* Cemetery Dance anthology alongside Stephen King.

Braum is the editor of the *Spirits Unwrapped* anthology and the host of the Night Time Logic series and the annual New York Ghost Story Festival. Find him on his You Tube channel DanielBraum, on social media, and at https://bloodandstardust.wordpress.com.

FLESH COMMUNION
BY HOLLY RAE GARCIA

"I've said all this a hundred times. Can't you just read a report or somethin'?"

"I'm sorry, but we need to go through it one more time." A middle-aged man in a cheap suit sat at a wide metal table across from the woman. He leaned toward the dented tape recorder on the table between them and pressed a button. "Please state your name and address for the record."

"My name is Claire Brody. I don't have an address anymore. Y'all kept me locked up for the past six months."

"Mrs. Brody, were you a member of the Branch Davidian Cult living at Mount Carmel in Waco, Texas?"

The woman sighed. "It wasn't a cult, and it was *just outside* Waco, but fine…yes. I was."

"Can you tell me about the events of February 28th, 1993?"

"You should know everything. Y'all were there."

The man reached out and paused the recording. "Mrs. Brody, I need you to cooperate here. For the record." He leaned in closer. "Cooperate, and you'll get to see Jenna."

Claire's eyes narrowed, and she held her breath.

"I'm serious."

"And then we can leave?"

The man tilted his head like he was listening to someone in his ear. He nodded before answering, "Yes, then you can both leave. Go wherever you want. Go back, if that's what you want. I hear some of the crazies are rebuilding."

She wiped the back of her hand across the fresh tears on her cheek and nodded. Once the man hit RECORD again, she straightened up in her chair and spoke. "The morning of February 28th, I was in chapel with some of the other women. We were halfway through our lessons when it sounded like a car backfired over by the road. Then the window shattered, hurling a hundred pieces of glass into my right arm and shoulder."

The woman grazed her fingers across burn marks on her arm. Somewhere below the angry ridges lay a splatter of glass-shaped scars. Her hand stayed there while her eyes fixed on the two-way mirror at the center of the wall. The twin cassette wheels turned, humming in the silence.

She cleared her throat, turned to face the man, and continued: "I stood by the window, staring at the blood on my arm. It seemed to bubble up in slow-motion. All around me, women were running, falling, screaming… but I couldn't hear them. They were just a blur at the side of my vision. Like the swimmy things in the corner of your eyes that disappear when you try to look directly at them. But I didn't look at the people around me. I just stood there, staring at my arm. Enid screamed, so I finally turned around. She was crying and shaking her son Elijah. I'll never forget the way his head just bobbed there against her chest. Limp, like a doll. It was weird, you know? Like everything was happening on the other side of a long tunnel until it all rushed in, pounding me in the chest so I couldn't breathe. It was all so *loud*. I'd never heard such a noise before. The chapel guard shoved me down and took my place near the window, crouching beneath the hole. I jumped up and ran for the door. All I could think about was Brian."

The man glanced at a stack of papers in his hand before asking, "And, for the record, who is Brian?"

"Brian was *everything*."

The man raised his eyebrows and waited for her to continue.

"Do you have kids?" Claire asked him.

He shook his head. "We aren't here to talk about me."

"Of course, you don't. If you did, you'd understand why I did what I did. But you don't, so you won't." She took a sip of water from the small Styrofoam cup on the table in front of her. "Brian is…*was* my son. He was two-years-old and the most beautiful little boy you ever saw in your life. Looked just like his daddy. That day, he was three doors down from the chapel with a few of the other kids. The Prophet liked to keep families apart as much as possible, said it 'strengthened our reliance on God' or something. I was having my doubts about that long before a bullet came flying through the window. When the Prophet took Jenna—" She stopped, leaned in toward the recorder and stared at the man as she continued, "my *fourteen-year-old daughter*, as one of His wives, it bothered me. By that time, I'd been one of His wives for about three years. It's not like He'd always kept to His own age. He took brides as young as sixteen before, but never as young as Jenna."

The air-conditioner kicked on with a thump and a rattle above them. The stained ceiling squares shuddered, then settled back down.

"We'll get to that. For now, let's focus on what happened February 28th."

"Yes, yes. Everyone wants to know what happened. I needed to find Brian. I ran down the hallway, and the windows ahead spit out more bullets and glass, but I finally made it to Brian's door.

"The classroom didn't have windows. The Prophet though it would be too distracting for their young minds to see the world outside when they were supposed to be focusing on His teachings. Young minds wander more since they don't always have the self-control of the older ones. You'd know about that if you had kids. Anyway, they were huddled in a corner of the room without a single adult in sight. Marcia and Penelope were gone, probably off looking for their own kids. I didn't really blame them. Isn't that what I was doing? Though I hadn't abandoned six toddlers to do it. Brian ran up and grabbed my leg with a fierceness I'd never seen from him before. I crouched down to hug him and told him I was there for him, always. That I'd always find him. Then more gunshots rang out. I asked if he could be a big boy for me, then asked him and the other five kids to hold hands and follow me out of the room. They were all quiet. That's weird, for them. I mean it *should* be weird. A child's response to chaos isn't normally quiet obedience."

"This is when you took the kids to the kitchen?" the man asked.

"Yes. I'm getting there. We stayed low against the counters. We heard more gunshots, and then a heavy thumping flew over the building, fading off into the distance. It was a *helicopter.* A helicopter was flying over Mount Carmel. We were under attack, just as the Prophet had predicted."

"What happened next?"

"I could still hear Enid crying from the chapel, and I pulled Brian into my lap and kept my arms around him. That could have been *us,* you know. Anyway, heavy footsteps thundered down the hall and I held a finger to my lips and made eye contact with the two kids on my left, and the three on my right. The steps moved on into the cafeteria and I quietly thanked God for His protection over us. I learned later there wasn't anything to fear. It was just William and Paul, checking on everyone."

"Did you see the Prophet?"

"No. I did wonder where He was at that moment, if He held my Jenna safely in His arms or had left her alone and scared like those women left the little kids. I didn't see Him until later."

"They were checking on everyone…so it was over?"

"They said it was. But it was far from over. You know that. I don't really remember how we got to the common room, but we all stayed there the rest of the night. The whole place was as quiet as the dead. Everyone was too scared to talk. I think we were all in shock. I mean, yeah, we expected to be attacked. We trained for it. But it's different when it's actually happening, you know? No, you wouldn't, would you? Mind if I smoke?" She pulled a pack of cigarettes from a bag at her feet and lit one without waiting for an answer.

Claire exhaled a puff of smoke, then lowered the cigarette. "Oh, I know, I know we're supposed to be *healthy*. Bodies are temples and all that. The whole time I was at Mount Carmel, I never once smoked. Gave it up cold turkey. The Prophet wanted us *pure,* and we always did whatever He wanted. We didn't smoke or drink, and we ate right."

"Weren't you vegetarians?"

"Sure. Well, mostly. Anyway, back to the thing. The shooting stopped. Though that's never been the issue, has it?"

"I'm sorry?"

"It's never been a matter of when the shooting *stopped,* but who *started* it to begin with, right?"

"Who do *you* think started it?"

"Honestly? I don't know for sure. These guys were waitin' for a fight. Both sides. But if I had to put my money on it, I'd say y'all started it, not us. That shot in the window was the first sound I heard, and it came from the outside in. 'Last I checked, we weren't shooting *ourselves.* Didn't really matter, though. It was gonna happen eventually." Claire tapped ashes into the empty cup in front of her.

"Because the Prophet said so?"

"Well, yeah."

"What else did He predict?"

"He knew there would be sacrifices. People were gonna die. And they sure did, didn't they?"

"What happened next?"

"We went on with normal life. Breakfast, teachings. Lunch, teachings. Dinner, teachings. Sleep, repeat. All the time with the teachings. We didn't always eat between them: sometimes he made us fast. But that was just before the special services."

"What happened during the special services?"

"Ohhh, I get it now. That's why I'm here? Y'all want to know more about *that*? I'll tell you anything you wanna know; 'don't really care anymore. I'm a changed woman…just wanna see Jenna and get out of here." Claire finished her cigarette and tossed the butt into the cup with the ashes.

"So, the *special* services…us women would go down to the basement with the Prophet. The other men were in charge of the kids. Most of 'em, anyway. That was probably the most time they ever spent alone with 'em."

"But in the basement…" he prodded.

"Yeah." Claire paused and looked at the two-way mirror set into the wall.

"There's no judgment here. I'm just trying to get all the facts. What happened in that basement?"

Claire turned back to the table and leaned forward on her elbows. One leg was wobbly, and the table shifted with her weight. "*Flesh Communion,*" she whispered.

"Please speak up," the man said as he gestured toward the recorder.

Claire leaned against the back of her seat and took her arms off the table. It tilted back into place. She glanced at the mirror again, took a deep breath, and said, "Flesh Communion. That's what He called it. 'You familiar with communion?"

"Yeah, I used to be Catholic."

Claire nodded her head and said, "So, you know."

"Well, we didn't exactly…"

"Oh, of course you didn't. No one did. But the Prophet explained it all to us. It was the only way."

"The way to what?"

"To getting closer to the twenty-four. He said if the women took part in the Flesh Communion, God would bless our wombs and we would produce the twenty-four that would rule after the return of Christ."

The man stared at her.

"It's in Revelations. Look it up."

"But the children He used…"

"Were His? Yeah. You think it don't make sense, right? Why take His own kids if the purpose is to have more?"

"Well…*yeah*."

"We didn't do it all the time. Just every nine months. And He took the weak, the disobedient. Sometimes He'd take them to get back at their mothers for some perceived slight. The Prophet was good at that, finding faults in people. I can see that now. I can see a lot of things now."

The man tilted his head again and stared ahead, unfocused, as he touched his earpiece. He nodded before saying, "Ok, let's stay in order here."

"The suits in your ear want the whole story, then?"

"Let's go back to February 28th. You said you went on with your normal routines?"

"As normal as we could, anyway. The women and kids were told to keep to the schedules. The men didn't."

"What did the men do?"

"Mostly? Talked, argued, tried to figure out what to do about y'all in the front yard."

The man flipped through the notepad in front of him, then said, "A few of the women and children evacuated. Why didn't you leave with your kids then?"

"I could have. *Should* have. Maybe everything would have turned out different." She looked down at her hands clenched tightly in her lap. "The Prophet didn't want any of His kids to leave. And, you know Brian was His child, so he had to stay. Since Jenna was His wife, He wasn't letting her leave either. I *did* try, you know? To get out. I begged Jenna to go with me and Brian. We were gonna climb out the broken chapel windows when no one was looking. But she was too scared. I could have left without her. Could have gotten Brian out. But I thought I could convince her, thought it would be okay until then. I chose to stay there with her, even though we weren't even allowed to see each other. What kind of mother does that? Chooses one child over the other? *Sophie's Choice* is what that is. And it's *my* fault he's dead."

Claire kept staring at her hands in her lap. She twisted at her fingers until the burn scars turned white. "But, uh," she said as she cleared her throat and looked back up. "We didn't get to leave."

"Did you ever hear the Prophet talking about His plans?"

"Oh no. They wouldn't let us near all that. Beatrice said they were making some kinda deal, but I guess she was wrong 'cause that's not how things ended." Claire lit another cigarette, took a long drag, and watched the smoke curl upward toward the ceiling.

"Y'all wouldn't let us sleep. Do you know what that does to someone's mind? Of course, you don't. Every night it was noise. Chants, music, animals being slaughtered. Who does that? Was it you? Did you decide what to play all night to keep us awake?"

"No."

"That song, 'These Boots Are Made for Walkin', over and over." Claire scratched her ear. "It's permanently crocheted into my ears now. Leaks into my brain at night. You should find out who played that stuff. Maybe give him a head check himself. Keep *him* in a room for six months."

The man sighed and shifted in his chair.

"I heard later it was fifty-one days. You know, during, it felt like ten years and ten seconds all at the same time."

"Did you ever go into the basement again?"

She exhaled, seeming to shrink into her chair before answering, "Yeah, several times. He didn't want to wait nine months in-between anymore. Like I said, sleep deprivation makes you act different. He was also shot, but y'all know that already. He got shot that first day. Probably woulda healed fine, if He'd gone to a hospital or somethin'. But it was smelling real bad by the end. Maybe that's why He did it…"

"Tell me about the first time you went there, after the shooting happened."

"It was, I don't know, maybe a couple of days after that first shooting. We thought maybe it was gonna happen because we didn't have breakfast. But with everything going on, we weren't sure. We were gettin' kinda low on food by then. I thought maybe they were just rationing. By lunchtime, when there still wasn't food, I knew what was going on."

"Did it usually happen around lunchtime? This 'Flesh Communion'?"

"Oh no. It was always at 3:00 am."

"Why?"

Claire shrugged. "The Prophet said so. He said Jesus died at 3:00 pm, up there on the cross. I mean, we all know that, but He said the Flesh Communion should happen in the mirror time of that. To be closer to

God or something. We weren't allowed to question Him."

"Okay, it's 3:00 am. What happens next?"

"Well, about 2:30 am, the guards started waking up all the women. We went down into the basement while the other men and kids slept. Two guards stayed in the kitchen to make sure nobody interrupted."

"And the child that was picked?"

"Oh, we never knew that until afterward, when we went back to our rooms to check on our own kids. You'd always know who it was by who didn't show up for breakfast the next day. The Prophet allowed for a day of mourning for the mother, but no more than that. Anything more, and you were just being dramatic, you know?"

"So, you're going down into the basement with the other women…"

"There was a long table down there, probably could have seated the whole commune. We'd sit down in front of empty white plates. There wasn't any order to the seats or anything. And then we'd wait for the Prophet to enter." Claire leaned back in her seat and looked across the room at the blank wall behind the man. The end of her cigarette turned to ash and hung, waiting.

"He'd come down wearing these white robes. Then, He'd take his seat at the head of the table, and one of the guards would uncover another, smaller table at the back of the room. In the middle of that was a Dutch Oven. Do you know what those are?"

"Yeah."

"Oh. Some men don't. Guess you've done a little cookin'. Anyway, it was an old one, covered in chipped blue paint with white spackled all over it. They would set the whole thing in front of the Prophet."

"He'd eat, too?"

"Are you gonna let me tell this? I'm only doing it once. It's…too much."

"Sorry. Please go on."

"The woman to his right always went first, whoever that was. That first time after the shooting, the time we're talkin' about, it was Margaret. I only know because I was on *her* right. Margaret stood up, picked up her plate, and moved closer to the Prophet. That's when He opened the Dutch Oven. The smell…that's what I remember most. Smelled like my mom's Sunday pot roast. Oh, I see your face. I know that's horrible, but that's the only way I know to describe it. It would be hot, still steaming. For a second, all that steam would hide the Prophet's face. Then it would clear, and He'd smile at us."

She tipped the ashes into the cup.

"Margaret held out her plate, and He sliced off a thin sliver of the meat and placed it there. Then she sat back down, and I was next. This was repeated until every woman had meat on the plate in front of them. Then, He'd place the lid back on and the guard would pick it up and put it on the table in the corner. I never knew what they did with the leftovers. Maybe they fed it to the dogs? They hardly ever got meat. We're vegetarians, you know."

"Yes, you said that. You said you were 'mostly' vegetarians."

"Well, this is the 'mostly' I'm talkin' about now, isn't it?"

"What happened next?"

"He'd read from the bible."

"You remember the verse?" Before Claire could respond, the man held up his hand, popped the cassette player open, and flipped the tape to the other side. Claire drummed her fingers on the table as she watched him. He shut the recorder with a loud snap and pushed the RECORD button.

"Of course, I do. John 6:53-58. *Jesus said to them, Truly, truly, I say to you, unless you eat the flesh of the Son of Man and drink his blood, you have no life in you. Whoever feeds on my flesh and drinks my blood has eternal life, and I will raise him up on the last day. For my flesh is true food, and my blood is true drink. Whoever feeds on my flesh and drinks my blood abides in me, and I in him. As the living Father sent me, and I live because of the Father, so whoever feeds on me, he also will live because of me."*

"Then?"

"What do you think? We ate."

The man shook his head in disgust, opened his mouth, glanced at the recorder on the table, then closed his mouth again.

"Yeah, I know what you're thinking. But you weren't there, were you? Not inside, anyway. Plenty of you were outside, driving tanks around tryin' to scare us."

"What happened next?"

"We went back upstairs and found out which kid was missing."

"You said it usually happened every nine months, but more during the fifty-one days?"

"Yes."

"How many more times before April 19th?"

"Five. Five more times. We had to use candles later, once y'all cut our power off. But at least it was cooler down there than in the house."

"Do you remember what happened on April 19th?"

"Yes. But the most important thing happened the night before."

"What was that?"

"Our final Flesh Communion." Claire took a deep breath and continued. "Happened just like all the others. Until we went back to our rooms…"

The man watched her.

"… and Brian was missing," Claire choked as tears flowed down her face. "I had eaten…" She sobbed, put her arms on the table, and laid her head in them, burying the rest of the words.

The man stared, then looked toward the window. He couldn't see the men on the other side watching, but they spoke to him again through his earpiece. He cleared his throat.

"Do you know why? Why Brian was chosen?"

She picked her head up and whispered, "Oh yes. I know why." Claire wiped her eyes and stared at the man. "I tried to leave again. *Begged* Jenna to come with us. She said no, that what I was saying was blasphemous and against the will of the Prophet. Then she went back to His room."

"The Prophet's room?"

"Yeah. She told Him. I don't know why. Surely she wouldn't have, if she had known… He turned her against us. It wasn't her, it was always Him. She was just a child herself. He was a very charming man. You've seen his videos?"

The man ignored her question as he asked, "And this was the night before?"

"Yeah. The next morning, since I was allowed to stay in my room for my day of mourning, they left me alone. That's where I was when there were great big rumbling noises, and the whole building shook. Gunfire rang out again, just like that first day."

"You were in your room the whole time?"

"Oh, no. I got Him back."

"Excuse me?"

"I shot Him."

"You shot who?"

"Him. The Prophet. It was loud and everyone was running around. I thought I was gonna die, but I didn't care about that. In the hallway, someone lay face-down under a window. The back of their head was missing, and their gun was on the floor next to them. So, I picked it up."

"You just picked it up? What about the tear gas?"

"Oh yeah, it was bad. I almost didn't make it to Him. But luck was on my side. Who's God watching over *now*, huh? The Prophet was leaning against a wall by the kitchen, mostly dead from his infected wound. But I shot him in the head, anyway."

"You… *what?*"

"Shot him. In the head. But you can't blame me. I was under *extreme emotional distress*, you know. And sleep deprived. But I'd do it again right now if I could. I'd shoot him a dozen times if I had the chance. He deserved it."

"And where was Jenna during all this?"

Claire looked down at the table and picked up the Styrofoam cup, now filled with ashes and cigarette butts. She turned it around in her hand as she answered, "They told me she got out, and that's when I started the fire."

"*You* started the fire?"

"I did. I wanted Him to burn for what He'd done. And I was okay to burn with Him, just to make sure it was done. Didn't have nothin' to live for anymore. Jenna was safe. Brian was gone…"

"But you got out."

"I'm here, ain't I?" Claire rubbed the burn scars on her arm. "You know, I'll never forget that smell."

"What smell?"

"People burnin'. Smelled just like that Sunday pot roast."

The man leaned forward, eyes narrowed. "There's been zero evidence of this 'Flesh Communion' happening."

"Well, there wouldn't be, would there? The basement collapsed in the fire. We were Branch Davidians, not engineers or carpenters. You ever wonder why there aren't many basements in Texas?"

The man sighed and leaned back in his chair. "No, never thought about it."

"I looked it up one day, after. Not like there was anything else to do while y'all had me locked up. There's loads of reasons. Water tables are too close to the surface, marshy soil is too unstable, and you wouldn't want 'em below sea level down by the coast. And too much flooding with all our rivers and bayous."

"There isn't evidence of this because of water tables?"

"You combine shiftin' ground, unstable basements, and piss-poor structural support and what do you get? An accident waiting to happen. I just helped it along, is all."

"We'd still find bones, though."

"He buried 'em. Never let nobody help. We never knew where they were."

"We're supposed to just take your word for it, is that right? How do I know you're telling me the truth?"

"It happened. I swear on it. You're just gonna have to believe me."

"Why would I believe you?"

"Because I'm a *victim*. I didn't deserve any of this. You think I enjoyed killing Him? Enjoyed *eating my child*?" Claire pulled on her hands harder.

"Yeah, I do, actually. I think you were so deep in that cult, you'd have done anything He asked you too, even putting Him out of His misery there at the end."

Her hands became still as she looked up at him. "Doesn't really matter what you think, now, does it?" Claire studied his face for a moment, then leaned forward, lowering her voice to a whisper. "Only matters what you can prove, darlin'."

Holly Rae Garcia is the author of *Parachute*, *The Easton Falls Massacre: Bigfoot's Revenge*, and *Come Join the Murder*. Her short fiction has appeared in numerous places online and in print, including the recent anthologies *Slash-Her* (Kandisha Press), *Generation X-ed* (Dark Ink), and *Dancing in the Shadows: A Tribute to Anne Rice* (Yuriko Publishing). More information can be found at www.HollyRaeGarcia.com.

Y2K FEAST
BY JEFF STRAND

December 31ˢᵗ, 1999, 11:37 p.m. EST

"It's almost here," said Grant, lovingly stroking the shotgun on his lap. "We're totally prepared for this, and there's no reason to fear it. The end of the world is going to be bad for most people, but it's going to be perfectly fine for us. Maybe it'll be...utopia."

"Probably won't be utopia," said his oldest son, Kirk.

"You need to quit your damn pouting. Your reliance on technology made you soft and squishy. At midnight tonight, it's all going to stop working, and humanity won't be able to handle it. There'll be panic. Riots. Terror from coast to coast. But when the world is cast into darkness, we'll have all the candles we need. And I mean that literally and metaphorically."

Grant looked at each of his family members. His beautiful wife, Megan, gave him a solemn nod. His youngest son, Bryan, was desperately getting in some final moments with his handheld video game. His daughter, Elise, was on the phone with her boyfriend, crying.

Grant didn't care if his family was miserable. For him, hearing that shortsighted computer programmers had overlooked the bug that would throw everything into disarray when 1999 became 2000 made him positively giddy. He wasn't one to giggle maniacally, but he was giggling maniacally on the inside.

"Do any of you have anything to say before this glorious new existence begins?" he asked.

Megan shook her head. Everybody else ignored him.

"We have plenty of food," he said. "But the food won't last forever. I need to know that each of you is prepared to eat human flesh if it comes to that."

Bryan lowered his video game. "I'm sorry, what?"

"We may have to eat our own kind to stay alive."

"Are you trying to make sure we were paying attention?"

"No," said Grant. "To survive, we may have to do things we previously thought unthinkable. And one of those things may be to cook and eat humans."

"You said we might have to *kill* somebody," said Bryan. "You never said anything about eating them!"

"I'm saying it now."

"You can't just drop that on us twenty minutes before the apocalypse! You should've led with that!"

"And what would you have done?" asked Grant. "Learned those outdated programming languages so that you could fix the Y2K bug on your own?"

"I'm not sure what I would've done," said Bryan. "But I would've figured out a way to not be turning into a cannibal!"

"Will you guys keep it down?" asked Elise. "I'm trying to talk to Chad!"

"Dad said we're going to become a family of cannibals."

"What?"

"I said no such thing," said Grant. "I said that we might have to be prepared to eat human flesh."

"Right! That's what 'become a family of cannibals' means!"

"No, you're acting like we'd go feral and hunt human prey. We'd only kill and eat people if the opportunity presented itself."

"Screw that," said Elise. "I'm not eating anybody."

"Again, I'm not talking about *The Texas Chainsaw Massacre* or *The Hills*

Have Eyes. We're not going to lay a trap across the road, converge upon their vehicle, and rip hunks of flesh off their bodies with our teeth. That's not *at all* the scenario I'm describing."

"So closer to a Hannibal Lecter thing?" asked Kirk.

"Well, no," said Grant. "We're not going to be pretentious about it. And Lecter eats human flesh because he likes it—we'd choke it down just to survive."

"I still want to know why we're only now hearing about this," said Bryan. "We've been prepping for two years, and this is the first we've heard about having to eat people."

"I was waiting until you were ready to handle it."

"I don't *want* to be ready to handle it! I don't want to look in the mirror and think, 'Yep, I'm cool with eating a person.' What's next, having sex with each other to repopulate the earth?"

"Ew," said Elise. "Mom, make him stop."

Megan frowned at Bryan.

"Enough," said Grant. "I'm not asking you to 'be cool' with it. I'm asking if you're prepared to do it as a matter of survival. Yes, we'll have nightmares afterward. We may even experience some self-loathing. We may feel like we've lost a piece of ourselves that we can never get back. But at least we won't starve to death."

"I won't do it," said Elise.

"Oh, you won't? When you can see your ribs through your chest, and you're so hungry that every waking moment is pure misery, and you're minutes away from dying, and I hold a piece of well-cooked succulent human flesh up to your mouth, you're saying that you won't eat it?"

"Why did we bother stockpiling so much canned food in the basement if we're going to just eat people?" asked Kirk.

"We're not going to turn into cannibals at 12:01 tonight!" said Grant. "You aren't paying attention to what I'm saying. Here's the deal: Because the computer nerds were trying to save precious memory in the olden days, they only used the last two digits for years. So if it was 1985, the computer would think of it as 85. Are you all with me so far?"

"That's not the part we're questioning," said Bryan.

"Are you all with me so far?"

"Yes, Dad."

"Everything was fine until the nerds went, 'Oopsie, what's going to happen in 2000?' And they realized that these computers and DVD players and traffic lights were headed toward extinction. Instead of accepting the inevitable and making the transition into an old-fashioned way of life, they kept on using their electronics. At midnight tonight, they'll pay the price. At first it'll be 'Waaahhh! My Walkman doesn't work!' But soon it'll be 'Heavenly Jesus, please protect me from these looters.' The weak will fall quickly. Others will cope with the loss of everything they once knew, and some of them will make it for a good long while, but the post-Y2K world is only for the strongest of the strong. Eventually, the supplies in our basement will dwindle. We'll go out on foraging expeditions, but the stores will have been ransacked. Though we'll have retained our sanity as a family, others won't have been so lucky, and we'll be attacked by ravagers. We'll defeat them. We'll kill them. And then, with food lying dead on the ground before us, we'll need to gaze within ourselves and decide if we have the courage to do what must be done. That's all I'm saying."

"Why can't we just hunt deer?" asked Bryan.

"It may not be an option."

"Why? We'll use a bow and arrow. How come you're asking us about eating human flesh but haven't trained us to hunt deer? What about rabbits?

The rabbit population isn't going to disappear. How about a garden? Why aren't we growing bell peppers in our backyard? Why are we talking about eating human meat instead of shoving seeds in dirt?"

"Don't talk back to your father," said Megan.

"I don't understand why this is so difficult for you to understand," said Grant. "Of course we'd try to eat bunnies first. I thought that was so obvious it didn't need to be said out loud. But, failing to hunt fauna, and failing to grow flora, and forced to kill somebody in self-defense, I just want to know that we aren't going to let perfectly good protein rot in our driveway."

"Do you even know how to prepare a human carcass for consumption?" asked Kirk.

"I've read a little about it, yes."

"Here's the thing, Dad. We all know that, pushed to our limits, we'd do things we would never consider in a civilized world. That's a given. It might involve eating rats, it might involve sawing off our own hand, and it might involve drinking our own urine. But you don't explore a cave and ask if everybody is prepared to cut off their own hand if it gets crushed in a cave-in. You worry about that when the need arises. All we're saying is that your timing is weird."

"Fine," said Grant. "I was trying to make sure everybody was prepared, but I should never have brought it up."

"Right," said Bryan. "You made me waste time I should've been spending playing this game for the very last time."

Elise returned to the call with her boyfriend.

Grant sighed and took Megan's hand. "Better times are coming. They'll see."

At 11:58, they turned on the television to watch the ball drop in Times Square. Grant wouldn't have wanted to be anywhere near there when the lights went out and the mass panic ensued, but he supposed he couldn't begrudge the populace one final New Year's Eve celebration.

At 11:59 and 50 seconds, the countdown began. Grant, Megan, Kirk, Bryan, and Elise counted down with the people in New York City.

"Three...two...one!"

And then it was the year 2000. The television stayed on, showing images of hugging and cheering people.

"Hmmm," said Grant.

"Why haven't we been cast into eternal darkness?" asked Kirk.

"Well, I never thought it was going to happen at exactly midnight," Grant lied. "Give it a few minutes."

They gave it a few minutes.

"Hmmm," said Grant.

"Here's my theory," said Bryan. "All of the money, resources, and countless hours of work that have gone into trying to solve this problem for the past few years actually succeeded."

"Don't be ridiculous," said Grant. "It's a time zone thing. It's the year 2000 in the Eastern time zone, but there are still parts of the world that have yet to transition. Maybe the whole world needs to be in the new millennium before everything crashes and burns."

"Technically," said Bryan, "2000 is the last year of the old millennium. The new millennium begins on January 1st, 2001."

Grant was briefly tempted to point the shotgun at his son but controlled the impulse.

"It'll be fine when the whole world is in 2000," he said, more to himself than his family. "This wasn't all for nothing."

"If it helps, I heard that some digital calendars did say the year was 19100," said Megan, a few hours later, after everybody else had gone to bed. "That's pretty silly, don't you think?"

Grant said nothing.

"This is a good thing, isn't it?" she asked, putting her hand on his shoulder.

"We were lied to."

"Maybe Bryan is right. Maybe the fact that people all around the world have been tirelessly working to solve this problem is why civilization didn't collapse."

"Go to bed, Megan."

"We could still have a nuclear war."

"Go to bed, Megan."

Megan nodded, gave him a kiss on the cheek, and headed off to their bedroom. Grant sat there for a few more hours, lost in thought.

He'd really been looking for an excuse to try human flesh.

He'd purposely understocked the canned food in the basement in anticipation of running out and having "no other choice" but to feast upon his fellow man. He'd been thinking about this ever since seeing a segment on the news about the Y2K bug. It didn't consume his every waking thought—that would be a sign of criminal insanity—but he figured he thought about it maybe a dozen or so times a day. More as the big day approached.

And yet here he was, sitting in his home on January 1, 2000, with no expectation that anybody would break in and need to be killed.

"Dammit," he muttered.

Human flesh. What did it taste like? What did it smell like as it cooked over the campfire? Was it filling? Was it better in sandwich form or right off the skewer? Would he fondly think about the look of fear on his victim's face before his grisly demise?

He couldn't tell his wife and children about this. They'd think he was crazy.

Was an urge to practice cannibalism so very strange?

Yeah, probably.

But at least it wasn't as strange as entertaining thoughts about murdering his family and devouring their bodies to make up for the post-Y2K disappointment.

Now *that* would be nutty.

Or would it?

No, it definitely would.

He didn't even need to ask for outside feedback on that matter. Thinking about murdering his wife, daughter, and two sons just to cook them up and eat them was objectively nutty.

But the thoughts were already in his mind. It was too late to dispel them. What was he supposed to do, turn back time? Oh, that would be a nice trick, wouldn't it? Invent a time machine so that he could take back the cannibalism-related thoughts. The idea was completely absurd, even in this shitty world that still had all of its technology.

What if he only killed one of them?

No parent could choose their favorite child, but he could easily choose his least favorite one: Bryan. That little creep thought he was so smart, with his knowledge and logic. How much would they truly miss him if he were gone?

Grant knew that if you spent too much time agonizing over decisions, you'd never get anything done, so he decided to kill Bryan and eat him before he changed his mind.

The shotgun would be the most efficient method, but it was pretty noisy. Instead, he went into the kitchen, opened a drawer, and took out their biggest knife.

"What are you doing?" asked Megan, standing in the doorway.

"This is none of your concern," he told her.

"I feel like I should be worried that you're holding that great big knife."

"I was going to slice some bread."

"All of the bread in the house is pre-sliced," said Megan. "And that's a butcher knife. And the way you're holding it is really threatening."

Grant cursed. He didn't want to kill Megan, but now she was suspicious, and if Bryan turned up dead later this morning, she'd know it was him.

He let out a battle cry and rushed across the kitchen toward her.

Megan had always been rather meek, so it surprised him when she nimbly stepped out of the way, yanked the knife out of his hand, then twisted his arm behind his back.

"Ow, ow, ow, ow, ow, ow, ow!" he said.

"Why did you have to do that?" Megan asked. "You know I support you in everything you do."

"Ow, ow, ow, ow, ow, ow, ow!" Grant repeated. "You're hurting my arm!"

"What's going on?" asked Bryan, as their three children stepped into the kitchen. In retrospect, Grant wished he hadn't let out the battle cry.

"Nothing!" Grant insisted. "Go back to whatever you were doing!"

"I think that your father was so consumed by thoughts of post-Y2K cannibalism that he decided to kill and eat one of us," said Megan.

"Dad!" said Elise.

"It's not true!" Grant insisted. "I was just going to cut some bread!"

Megan gave his arm a twist. Grant let out a high-pitched shriek as the bone broke.

"I was worried about raiders, so I took some self-defense classes," said

Megan. "I never imagined that I'd have to use them on you."

"I wasn't going to eat any of you! I swear!"

"He's lying," said Bryan. "All night he was looking at me like I was a turkey leg."

"Maybe we should eat him instead," said Kirk.

Megan, Bryan, and Elise all nodded.

"Oh, wow," said Kirk. "I was totally kidding, but I'm in if you are."

"The Internet still works," said Elise. "I'll go look up some recipes."

Grant begged for mercy. Then he decided that this was all one big prank. When Bryan retrieved a hacksaw from the garage and began to cut away at his shoulder, he decided that it was not, in fact, a prank and went back to begging.

On one hand, he was proud of the way his family worked together. Bryan did all of the sawing. Kirk cauterized the stumps. Elise prepared and seasoned the meat. Megan whispered into his ear that everything was going to be all right. If the apocalypse *had* happened, they would've made a great team.

He passed out from the pain and woke up to the scent of himself cooking in the oven. What a waste. He would've done it over a charcoal grill.

He angrily flopped his torso around until he passed out again.

When he woke up, everybody was seated at the dining room table, including him. They'd spared him the indignity of a booster seat, although he was on top of a few pillows. Kirk was slicing into his cooked arm with an electric carving knife.

"Hey, he's up!" said Bryan. "Just in time."

They passed around the serving plate of arm slices.

"Grant, do you want to say grace?" Megan asked.

Grant nodded. "Dear God, if you're watching right now, please kill them all."

"Very nice," said Megan. "Enjoy, everyone!"

Everybody took a bite. They chewed slowly, thoughtfully.

Kirk swallowed and was the first to speak. "It sucks."

"It really does," said Elise. "Even with all the seasoning, it's disgusting."

"I think I'm gonna throw up," said Bryan.

"Stop it," said Megan. "You'll hurt your father's feelings."

"Well, the leg needed more cooking time. Maybe it'll be better."

Grant passed out from the pain again and awoke to his family eating slices of his leg.

"Nope," said Kirk. "This is terrible."

"It's even worse than the arm," said Bryan, spitting a mouthful back onto his plate.

"Maybe we're simply not cut out to be a cannibal family," said Megan. "But it's better to regret the things you've done than the things you haven't."

Grant began to weep.

"Oh, darling, don't cry," said Megan. "Are you sad because we cut off your arms and legs, or because you didn't get to try a bite?"

"Ew, don't give him a bite," said Elise. "Auto-cannibalism is gross."

"We're not going to feed your father pieces of himself," said Megan. "Depravity has no place in this household. But we should probably put him out of his misery, don't you think?"

Everybody nodded, including Grant.

"Who wants to slash his throat with the carving knife?"

Nobody volunteered, which made Grant happy. At least they weren't excited about killing him. They played rock-paper-scissors, and after a few rounds, Megan was the loser. Taking no joy in the process, she sliced the blade deep across Grant's neck.

"Sorry things worked out this way," said Megan, before Grant bled out. "Happy New Year."

Jeff Strand is the Splatterpunk and Bram Stoker Award-winning author of over 50 books, including *Pressure*, *Clowns vs. Spiders*, and *Autumn Bleeds into Winter*. This is far from his first time writing about cannibalism, but he swears he's never tried human flesh, at least not on purpose. You can visit his gleefully macabre website at www.JeffStrand.com.

ABOUT THE EDITOR

Rebecca Rowland is the dark fiction author of two fiction collections, one novel, a handful of novellas, and too many short stories. This is her seventh horror anthology. Her fiction, critical essays, and book reviews regularly appear in a variety of online and print venues. She has been a vegetarian most of her life and editing American Cannibal only reaffirmed that choice (as well as her fear of ever being trapped for an extended time with any of these authors if food became scarce). To surreptitiously stalk her, visit RowlandBooks.com. To take a peek at what shiny object she's fixating on these days, follow her on Instagram @ Rebecca_Rowland_books.

9 798986 358635